COLONY

Also by Markus Heitz

MARKUS HEITZ

DO?RS

COLONY

Jo Fletcher

BOOKS

First published as *Doors ? Kolonie* by Verlagsgruppe Droemer Knaur, Germany, in 2018
First published in Great Britain in 2021 by

Jo Fletcher Books, an imprint of
Quercus Editions Ltd,
Carmelite House
50 Victoria Embankment
London EC4Y 0DZ

An Hachette UK company

A CIP catalogue record for this book is available
from the British Library

PB ISBN 978 1 52940 234 6
EB ISBN 978 152940 233 9

10 9 8 7 6 5 4 3 2 1

Typeset by CC Book Production
Printed and bound in Great Britain by Clays Ltd, Elcograf S.p.A.

Some say history is made by the victors.
Sometimes it's rewritten by an author.

If you would like to know how Viktor von Troneg and his team of experts came to be tasked with rescuing Anna-Lena van Dam and how they managed to enter the cave system beneath the van Dam estate, read from the beginning.

If you would like to go straight to the door marked with ?, please start with Chapter IV on page 97.

INTRODUCTION

FIRST DEAD END

Trepidation.

Trepidation and a sinking sense of hopelessness were all she could feel in the darkness as she wandered endlessly through the stone labyrinth, refusing to succumb to fear.

The smell was one known only to ancient buildings, of cold stone, damp dust and the millennia of abandonment. The leather soles of her high-heeled shoes scraped over rocky ground and slipped on the loose stones rattling around her, but there was no chance of her giving up.

She knew this place; she had heard plenty about it and now she had to find a way to leave – or remain there for ever. Death was coming for her more quickly than she could have imagined: she understood that now.

She tried to keep her breathing as quiet as possible as the LED light on her mobile phone glimmered into life for a promising second, before immediately switching off again, as if out of spite. It continued to flicker on and off, emanating a frantic, cold glow like a stroboscope.

The young woman swiped and tapped the display with her broken fingers again and again, but to no avail. The indifferent message remained: No Service.

If she had been less afraid, she might have felt the

energy all around her, as pervasive as the air she was breathing. It was not electrical, nuclear or even thermal, but rather the sort of energy that might accumulate at a spiritual site: churches, monasteries and sacred places in the middle of forests were full of this kind of energy.

As her phone continued to flash on and off, the young woman swore quietly to herself. 'Stay on!' she whispered, infuriated.

Then the little light lit up and illuminated her face, tearing it out of the darkness. Her features were striking: pure, bright, freckled skin with a light layer of make-up, her coppery hair artfully arranged in a weather-beaten up-do. She wore a small stud in her left nostril and a pair of expensive diamond earrings that glittered in the light as if she were seeking to impress a congregation of the great and the good.

But there was no one around to be impressed by her distinctive appearance.

Dazzled by the light, the young woman screwed her eyes shut and her phone slipped out of her usually well-manicured fingers: the last few hours had clearly taken their toll.

As the mobile fell to the ground, the beam of light passed down her body, briefly illuminating her dark green silk dress, now torn and flecked with mud. It revealed scratched and filthy forearms, the shattered glass of her eye-wateringly expensive watch, a small handbag clutched under her right arm and, finally, the black evening courts, the soles and uppers now covered with scratches. There was nothing practical about this attire for such an environment: her visit here was entirely unplanned.

The phone skipped across the floor and the cold white LED beam brought the stony, dusty ground out of the darkness and illuminated several empty cartridge cases, for use in a modern military weapon. The sound of the impact echoed around the room, the full size of which was beyond the reach of the small light.

After one final rattle, the phone settled on the ground with its light facing downwards. Blackness descended.

'Kcuf.' The young woman quickly bent down and picked up the device. 'Gnikcuf lleh!'

She was fully aware that words were coming out of her mouth backwards: she'd discovered it was just one of the many idiosyncrasies of this place. At first she had doubted her own sanity, then gradually she'd managed to suppress that fear. There were worse things down here.

She picked up the mobile and flashed the light all around her, illuminating walls made of grey concrete and reddish-brown brick that receded into the distance. Eddies of whirling dust danced their way through the artificial brightness like tiny moths attracted to the glow.

Then the beam passed over a series of doors made of stone and weathered wood. Three of them bore wrought-iron knockers and two were bare. The ring that should have been held in the mouth of the beautifully crafted creature adorning the second door was missing. The doors were embedded in the rocky wall as if their existence in this godforsaken place was entirely natural.

'On erom,' she whispered in frustration. 'Please, no more doors!' Her prayer was purely rhetorical.

She walked forwards slowly and cast her light over the

five doors. She had realised long ago that she was not the first visitor to try to unlock the secrets of this mysterious place. There was more than a kernel of truth to her mother's stories after all.

That knowledge was of no help whatsoever.

Markings both old and new were carved into the stone and wood; some had been scratched in, others added in pen, and they were mostly written in languages the young woman did not understand. Some of the characters might have been decipherable by archaeologists or experts in ancient and pre-history; some might even have been of interest to cryptologists or etymologists or those with knowledge of Eastern studies.

What stood out. however, were the thick red question marks on the first three doors, drawn on in lipstick and clearly new.

'Pull yourself together,' she whispered to herself, wiping a dirty strand of hair from her green eyes. Her forehead glistened with sweat and her deodorant had long since given up on her. It was not at all cold in the maze and running had become increasingly more of an ordeal with each futile escape attempt. She was ravaged by hunger and thirst and she could feel the blisters on her feet rubbing with every step she took, but she dared not walk around barefoot. 'Come on now!'

She tried to slow her breathing as she stepped up once more and withdrew a red lipstick from her handbag.

As she walked off the step, the now familiar feeling of a world being turned upside down grabbed her from behind her navel and flipped her over. The first time it had happened, she'd panicked and injured herself on the wall next to her. The second time the world turned on its axis, she found herself half drifting and had managed to manoeuvre herself so she was half pressed up against the wall in an attempt to offset the worst of the damage when gravity reasserted itself. This time she carefully raised her arms in order to remain upright.

She floated, waiting for her inevitable painful return to the stone floor.

Everything loose on the ground started to rattle and clatter around; fine particles of dust swam through the lamplight, accompanied by pebbles, bones and pieces of metal and fabric that had belonged to previous visitors.

After ten seconds, everything crashed to the ground.

She scrambled to her feet and took a few steps, stopping in front of the furthermost of the five doors: the one made from weathered oak. Instead of a knocker, it had a sliding bolt and a box lock. Her grandmother had once told her a story about this door, but she couldn't remember any of the details. The metal was thin, with inlays of gold, tarnished silver and some sort of copper alloy. Using her mobile light as a guide, she pulled out her lipstick and painted a large exclamation mark on it.

A noise suddenly erupted from the surrounding darkness. All she could hear was the pounding of heavy paws and the grinding of claws. She didn't even notice smearing lipstick on her palm as she instinctively covered the light with her hand. The beam scattered through her fingers, framing her face and eyes as if she were in a silent film.

She didn't dare turn off the light, in case she couldn't make it turn back on again.

Listen. Hold your breath. Just one more time.

She hadn't yet caught sight of her pursuer, but she knew this creature was on her tail. Perhaps it was there to guard this place? Or perhaps it was just a being who had heard her moving around and wanted to put a stop to it.

She inched towards the fourth door, which was made of stone with a knocker in the centre, the only one without a marking, and stood silently with her back against the wall, so as not to be ambushed in the darkness.

The quiet scuttling stopped abruptly.

Almost there, she thought as she placed her hand carefully on the latch and tried to push it down. Nothing happened.

She tried the door again while she carried on looking around her, before stopping to listen once more.

All was quiet.

'Kniht,' she muttered, taking a chance and illuminating the door knocker. 'Emoc on, think!'

A heavy silver ring with a bulge at the bottom could be seen in the elaborately carved ebony wolf's mouth resting imposingly on the metal plate in the centre of the door. The stone was dark grey with black grain, with inlays of white marble and onyx forming incomprehensible symmetrical symbols.

She hesitantly stretched out a hand, grabbed the ring and knocked hard against the stone, leaving behind some of the red lipstick that had stuck to her hand.

The noise was metallic, hollow and far too loud, filling the entire room with a deafening *boom*, as if someone had simultaneously played all the notes on an organ in a cathedral. An iridescent flickering accompanied the eerie yet welcoming clamour above the door. All the worlds and planets and creatures of the known and unknown universe now seemed to gather to witness her arrival.

The flickering light leaped to the other doors, illuminating them briefly, the markings on the walls gleaming as if they'd been written in gold and giving off a warm light that betrayed the presence of a fine vein in the rock. It was visible for no more than the duration of a heartbeat. A crackle and a crunch flew through the room before mutating into a whisper and a rustle.

The young woman suddenly felt as if a giant were pressing down hard on her shoulders, the gravity in the room becoming overwhelming, forcing her to her knees and compressing her vertebrae and joints so hard that she cried out in agony – but it stopped as suddenly as it had started.

The darkness returned; the weight was lifted.

'What on earth . . . ?' she muttered, rising to her feet.

She put her hand gently back on the latch, which this time offered no resistance.

Relieved, she slowly opened the door.

She was met with the presence of a soft, silvery light, accompanied by the sound of owls hooting and foxes barking, intermingled with the peaceful whoosh of falling leaves. A fresh, cleansing wind began to dance through her coppery hair. It felt as if she were being offered the freedom she had been hoping for the whole time she had been wandering through the maze.

She wanted nothing more than to step across the threshold into a world that could soothe her ills – then the growl of a predator cut through the idyll like a knife, stopping her in her tracks. It was followed by the lingering, mournful howling of a wolf: a pack was being summoned for the hunt. She drew her foot back carefully: this was a freedom she would pay for with her life. She knew she wouldn't stand a chance against such skilled hunters.

The silvery light lit up the area behind her, revealing an empty cavernously high room with only one entrance: the one she had come through. As well as the scribbled inscriptions, notes and memos from previous visitors, the brick and concrete walls were also decorated with rusty brown splodges and ancient flecks of spilled blood. Some had used it to write a final message or curse before succumbing to their anonymous deaths.

The broken ring of the destroyed door knocker lay on the ground, alongside all manner of broken grey bones and the scattered remains of skeletons.

The light also revealed something else.

A man – a *dead* man – could be seen just at the edge of the light's reach, through the haze, where silver became ghostly grey, crouching in an unnatural position. He was wearing grey-white camouflage gear with a Kevlar vest over the top; in his right hand he clutched a sub-machine gun. Empty magazines and dozens of bullet casings littered the floor around him. His throat had been slit and the blood that had poured out of it had dried and plastered his body.

Panting, the young woman quickly shut the door and using her phone, once again the only source of light, saw a large red X marked on it. 'Not there,' she whispered. 'I can't . . .'

The sound of heavy paws could be heard again, coming ever closer, accompanied by a scratching noise, as if there were several beasts approaching, all manner of beings who, in her imagination at least, would do all manner of terrible things to her if she ever found herself in their clutches.

'Go away!' The young woman shone the light all around her as if its weak glow suddenly had the lethal cutting power of an industrial laser. 'Evael em enola! I've got a gun!' she lied. 'Stay yawa morf em!'

For an instant, an enormous shadow could be seen in the trembling cone of light – then everything went dark.

'Kcuf! *Fuck!*' She frantically pulled on the door knocker and the gleam of the wood lit up the room. With a cry of anguish, she yanked the door open again.

The silvery light struck her once more as the wind blew through her hair as if to welcome her in.

The young woman hurriedly crossed the threshold and entered a world she knew would not offer her the freedom she desired. Perhaps she had merely exchanged a quick death for a slow one.

Giving up was out of the question, however.

She armed herself with a branch from the ground and ran off into the unknown.

CHAPTER I

Germany, Frankfurt am Main

Viktor headed straight through the 'Nothing to Declare' doors. The white duffle bag slung over his right shoulder and his casual sporty attire rendered him utterly inconspicuous amid the throng in the arrivals hall.

The plane had been stacked for more than an hour as a result of bad weather, turning what ought to have been a forty-minute flight into a two-hour débâcle as they waited for a runway to become available. It had made Viktor's mood somewhat sub-optimal, and it was only exacerbated by the rumblings in his stomach.

He looked at his phone and read the message from his prospective client once more:

DEAR MR VON TRONEG
LOOKING FORWARD TO MEETING YOU AND GLAD TO HEAR YOU'RE
WILLING TO START SOON. MY CHAUFFEUR MATTHIAS WILL PICK YOU
UP FROM ARRIVALS. KEEP AN EYE OUT FOR HIM THERE.
REGARDS
WALTER VAN DAM

Viktor looked around.

There were several people milling around at the exit holding pieces of cardboard, mini whiteboards or tablets bearing the names of the passengers they were waiting for, although his name was nowhere to be seen.

He decided to carry on through the hall to track the man down. His blue eyes were concealed behind a pair of sunglasses and on his head he wore a white baseball cap. He was in his mid-twenties, in excellent shape, and hardly seemed to notice the weight of his waterproof bag; one of the reasons it had taken him very little time since leaving his previous job to become one of the finest potholers in the world.

'Where is this chap?' Viktor muttered, pulling out his phone again to give his client a ring, when he spied a man in a dark blue suit with a cap and black leather gloves. He was holding a printed card that read 'Cave Tours' and carried himself in a manner reminiscent of a gentleman's valet.

Van Dam should have called him Jeeves as his work pseudonym, Viktor thought. He turned around and waded through the crowd towards Matthias; as he did so, he thought about Walter van Dam, about whom there was disconcertingly little information to be found online.

He'd been born in the Netherlands and was the head of a global import/export company founded for overseas trade in the eighteenth century. Very little was known about the man himself; he shied away from the public gaze and for the most part sent proxies to his official engagements. The van Dam family had allegedly branched out further, but Viktor had not been able to find out much beyond that. That was understandable, as there was quite a trade in kidnapping and ransoming the very rich. The less the public knew about you, the better.

It was ultimately irrelevant to Viktor, as long as the Dutchman did not attempt to drag him into any criminal activity. The first payment had already landed in his account and was substantially higher than anything the German state had paid him for far more dangerous jobs.

Next to the chauffeur stood a gaunt man about fifty years old, wearing a bespoke checked suit and highly polished brown shoes that made him look a bit like an Oxford professor. His foot was resting on an expensive-looking aluminium case, as if he were trying to stop it escaping, and he was reading a newspaper. The designer glasses gave him an arrogant demeanour.

'Good afternoon, gentlemen.' Viktor removed his own sunglasses, catching a glimpse of his three-day-old beard in the reflection as he did so. 'Mr van Dam is expecting me. My name is Viktor Troneg.'

'Welcome to Frankfurt.' The chauffeur inclined his head in greeting. 'My name is Matthias. The rest haven't arrived yet.' He gestured towards the other man, who was still absorbed in his reading and did not react. 'May I take this opportunity to introduce you to Professor Friedemann, renowned speleologist and geologist.'

Viktor inclined his head and Friedemann, whose long grey hair was drawn up in a ponytail, nodded in reply without looking up from his newspaper; Viktor thought his angular face had more than a passing resemblance to a skull.

'This is Mr von Troneg, a potholer and free-climber,' Matthias said. 'From what I gather, he's got quite the international reputation.'

'Very good.' Friedemann turned the page and busied himself in the next article.

Viktor already knew which one he liked the least. 'Were we all on the same flight?' he asked.

'You were indeed, Mr von Troneg.'

'No need to keep the *von*. I'm not overly keen on my ancestral name.' Then he broke into a grin. 'Whatever would you have done if it had crashed?' he asked.

'The plane? Highly unlikely,' replied Matthias. 'In any case the clairvoyant wouldn't have boarded.' He laughed drily.

'Clairvoyant? Well, that's something, I suppose.' Viktor lifted up his baseball cap and slicked his long black hair back before replacing it. 'And what if she *had* got on?'

'She'd have suffered a tragic death, and rightly so,' commented Friedemann, without looking up. He carefully adjusted his glasses.

Viktor grinned and was about to respond when he noticed a particular woman out of the corner of his eye – and he clearly wasn't the only one: practically all the passengers appeared to have turned their gaze in her direction.

She was dressed in a tight-fitting, cream-coloured designer dress and pushing a large, outrageously expensive designer suitcase in front her. With a fashionable handbag hanging artfully from her right arm and large sunglasses hiding her eyes, she had the aura of an haute couture model. She held a vanity case in her left hand. Her curly long blonde hair had a theatrically black strand at the front.

Viktor stood there, admiring her. 'Impressive entrance.'

'I hope you're being ironic.' Friedemann finally looked up from his paper and turned his eyes towards her. 'Dreadful person. Sat behind me on the flight and kept ordering champagne. They must have wanted to drown her in it by the end.'

'That is Ms Coco Fendi,' the chauffeur clarified, raising his arm to catch her attention. 'Our clairvoyant, gentlemen.'

'Really? *Coco Fendi?*' Viktor had to laugh. 'Perfect name for a performer.'

'Coco Fendi: a cross between a handbag and a fashion brand. I'm assuming she's really called Sabine Müller or something,' Friedemann added. 'A double fraud, if you ask me. Only frauds need to dress up like that much of a cliché to be able to perform.'

As Ms Fendi was walking through the hall in search of her welcoming party, the lock on her vanity case snapped open, scattering the contents all over the floor. Pendulums, crystals, tarot cards, bone cubes and runestones rattled and rolled around as if a magician's box had exploded. All that appeared to be missing was a white rabbit, a black candle and a painted skull.

'She didn't see that coming.' Friedemann looked back down at his newspaper. 'Not a good sign at all, gents.' The lenses of his glasses flashed in the light, as if to underscore his statement.

Coco Fendi swore so loudly that she could be heard from the other side of the hall: not the sort of attitude her initial appearance suggested. She let go of her suitcase and bent down to pick up her paraphernalia, which was made all the more difficult by her tight dress.

Viktor was about to walk over and help her when a thickset man in a tight jacket, baggy jeans and crumpled shirt approached from the magazine stand. He acknowledged her briefly before putting his own bag down and lowering himself to his knees to assist in the clean-up operation.

'The white knight has come to rescue his fair medium,' observed Friedemann, who had become a rather acerbic commentator.

'By your leave, that's Doctor Ingo Theobald,' explained Matthias. 'He's part of the team as well.'

'Ah, a doctor? Good.' Viktor folded his arms, happy not to intervene now that Fendi and Theobald were doing such a good job of clearing up. 'Still a shame, though. I'd hoped we'd have another young woman in the group.'

'I bet you'd regret that almost immediately,' barked Friedemann with the pomposity of a snobbish fifty-year-old. 'There's not much that can beat the wisdom that comes with age. Knowledge is power and this woman has neither years nor knowledge on her side.'

Viktor wondered how the man was able to see what was going on around him without moving his eyes. *A master of peripheral vision*, he thought.

Coco Fendi was so engrossed in the recovery of her belongings that she only belatedly noticed the helper kneeling beside her.

'Thank you – that's most kind of you.' Her tight dress

was hindering her movements somewhat, but that was the price one paid for beautiful, expensive clothing, which she could well afford. Her bright hair obscured her vision, the curls hanging like a curtain in front of her eyes. 'A true gentleman.'

She positioned her enormous suitcase as a shield, preventing anyone from absconding with her possessions. The small group of people around the chauffeur disappeared behind it.

Coco turned towards her saviour, stroked her hair out of her face and recognised Ingo Theobald, a man in his early forties with greying blond hair falling down to his neck. A pair of youthfully nerdy nickel glasses perched on his unshaven face.

'You?' she laughed, kissing him on the mouth.

Ingo let it happen more out of surprise than anything else. 'What are you doing here?' he asked in astonishment.

'Working,' she responded curtly, bridling at his obvious discomfort at meeting her here. She picked up the tarot cards. 'And you? Investigating a case?'

'Working.' He examined her, then looked over her suitcase at the uniformed chauffeur waving at them. 'Don't tell me . . .'

Coco raised her eyes and understood. 'No! You as well?'

Ingo sighed and took her free hand in his. 'Don't do this, Beate. It's going to be incredibly dangerous!'

'It's well paid,' she retorted. 'And don't call me that. I am Coco Fendi, the acclaimed clairvoyant and medium, known for my work on the radio, television and online. Do you know how many followers I've got?'

She stuffed her scattered belongings back into the case; there would be time to sort everything out later.

Ingo had not expected to see Beate again, and certainly not to learn that they had been commissioned by the same company. He looked at her reproachfully, wanting to say something back – something cruel, like, being a clairvoyant, she must have known they were going to meet again at the airport. Instead, he said, 'That outfit's a bit much, isn't it? You're pretty much confirming every prejudice under the sun about people in your line of work.'

'It's all part of my brand. I'm like Elvira, Mistress of the Dark. Only more stylish.'

'You do realise that Elvira was satirising the whole gothic horror genre?'

'I don't care. I'm giving people what they expect, and that makes them happy – people love clichés. You know I tried doing it differently before and how much of a failure that was. So now they're getting the mother of all extravagant psychics.' Coco kissed him again behind the suitcase and caressed his cheek. 'Play along. Please. Once we're upstairs you can fuck me like it's going out of fashion, I promise.' She looked at him intensely. 'Please, Ingo – it was only your expertise that got me this job.'

'We're not talking about one of your shows where all you've got to do is entertain your followers,' he responded, concerned.

'Just let me do me, okay?' she asked, her voice noticeably cooler. Her kisses had failed to win him around, which annoyed her greatly. She slammed the case closed and snapped the locks shut. 'Just one more time. Then I'll have got enough money together.'

Ingo frowned, remaining silent as they stood up. Thanks to her love of the high life, Beate was always in dire financial straits. She viewed herself as being from the tradition of divas in the Roaring Twenties, although there weren't many men nowadays willing to bankroll a spiritualist. The fact that she looked like a garish walking cliché didn't bother her in the slightest. He found her explanation plausible, but she was giving little away. Beate was old enough to decide how she wanted to come across.

'Wrong bag?' came a stern female voice from behind them.

Ingo and Coco turned around to see a woman in her mid-thirties standing two feet away. She was dressed in city camouflage trousers and a fine rib vest with a brown, scuffed leather jacket over it and holding a steaming coffee cup in her right hand.

The words were not intended for them, but rather for a young man wearing a wide-brimmed fishing hat, who frowned guiltily. She had stopped his bag with her right foot – which was in fact Ingo's bag.

'Hey! That's mine,' protested Ingo.

'It's so easy to pick up the wrong bag at the airport,' said the stranger. With her mid-length blonde hair tied up in a braid, her appearance was the absolute opposite of Coco's: one could win wars, while the other was only good for entertaining the troops.

'Let go of me!' exclaimed the thief as he tried to escape her clutches and make off with his stolen goods. Greed had clearly overridden sanity.

The woman stepped back, then struck him in the

solar plexus. He crumpled to the floor and remained there, panting and clutching his stomach.

She grinned down at him and took a sip of her coffee. Not a single drop had been spilled. 'It's pretty slippery here, so be careful not to lose your footing. Good job you haven't broken anything.' She raised her hand. 'My fist is harder than your sternum. Shall we find out together what that means?'

Two security guards approached with caution. 'Can we help you?' announced one of them, withdrawing his radio to call the security post.

The unknown woman turned to face Ingo with a wicked grin on her face. 'This is a security announcement. Please do not leave your luggage unattended.'

He smiled and extended his hand. 'Thank you! I'd have been lost without you.'

'Lucky you were here.' Coco explained what had happened to the security officers, while they picked up the thief and secured his hands with cable ties.

'Ah, it would appear everyone from the Cave Tours group has managed to find one another,' said the chauffeur, who had appeared alongside the two guards without either of them noticing him. 'My name is Matthias. Mr van Dam has sent me to pick you all up.' He gestured around him and started to introduce everyone. The militant coffee drinker was apparently one of them.

'And this most attentive lady here is Dana Rentski, a renowned free-climber,' Matthias said, concluding the introductions. A flurry of handshakes followed.

'But we're not at full capacity yet,' he continued. 'There's still one missing. Then we can make a move. Mr van Dam will explain the rest to you.' Matthias turned to the two airport officials and handed them a business card, in case there were any further questions that weren't covered by their statements and the security cameras, then the men took the captured thief away.

'Quite the show,' said Viktor to Dana. He couldn't help but notice both her firm handshake and athletic physique.

'Thank you.' She drained the last of her coffee and tossed the cup confidently into the nearby paper recycling bin. 'I like to be of use when I can.'

A silence fell upon the disparate group; apparently nobody wanted to be the first to start a conversation. Friedemann returned to his newspaper.

Meanwhile, an overweight man in a pair of bright jersey trousers and a garish shirt hurried across from the check-in desks. He had clearly tried to emulate the beard and haircut of the comic superhero Tony Stark, but the rest of his look and his physical appearance were utterly unsuitable for the role, making him look more like a caricature of Magnum, PI, than Ironman.

Viktor guessed this was the final person hired by van Dam. The man cut rather a ludicrous figure at first glance, even more so than Friedemann.

The fag-packet Magnum caught sight of the group, raised his arm in greeting and clumped his way over to them.

'Watch where you're going,' he snarled at a little boy walking hand-in-hand with his mother, ruthlessly carving his way towards the people awaiting him. 'Sorry. There was some old biddy taking an age to get her bag off the luggage belt.

I had to wait yonks for mine. She didn't want to let go of her Zimmer frame and took for ever to hobble off with the ancient piece of crap that passed for her suitcase.' He nodded to those around him. 'Pleased to meet you. Carsten Spanger's the name, but you can call me Tony.'

'Helping her might have speeded things up,' remarked Dana coolly.

Carsten scratched his head. 'And then who would have helped me?' he added, before laughing to show that he had clearly misunderstood her. 'Well? Am I the last one here?'

'Yes, you're the last,' replied Dana.

'Don't bite my head off,' Spanger retorted. 'Next time I'll be a very good little Boy Scout and help every old lady I come across.'

'Right, that's everyone then.' Matthias took control of the situation before this minor tussle could go any further. 'If you'd all like to follow me?'

They left the hall together and were soon standing in front of a black Mercedes people carrier. They got in, with Viktor and Dana stopping to help the chauffeur load the cases into the storage area.

'Thanks, that's very kind of you. More than can be said for the other lot,' said Matthias, reaching up to shut the boot.

'The other lot?'

Matthias realised that he'd been blabbing. 'The others, Mr Troneg.' He closed the boot, smiled and gestured to him that he should get in as well, before hurrying over to the driver's seat.

'After you, Ms Fendi.' Carsten allowed her to get on

ahead of him and immediately stood to admire her back-side as she bent over, then wiggled his eyebrows like a sleazy ventriloquist's dummy. 'I'm already your biggest fan.'

Viktor ruminated over what Matthias had said. 'The other lot,' he repeated to himself softly. So they weren't the first group van Dam had hired.

Unknown to Viktor and the rest of the so-called Cave Tours group, an inconspicuously dressed man in his mid-forties was sitting on a bench not far from where the incident with the vanity case had taken place. He had a small laptop resting on his knee, but there was nothing to distinguish him from the dozens of other people milling around, apart from the unusually concerned expression on his face – as if he had just learned about an event that would change the course of history for ever.

The man occasionally looked over the screen to check the arrivals board, then turned his piercing gaze to the right again and looked at the people who were introducing themselves to one another. Frown lines began to form on his forehead.

In the open chat window could be seen the message he had written:

ARRIVED WITH TRONEG AT FFM.
HAS BEEN MET AT ARRIVALS.
PART OF A TEAM. WILL SEND PHOTOS OF THE
GROUP SHORTLY.
INSTRUCTIONS?

The man reached for his paper cup and tasted the drink that had ostensibly been sold to him as an espresso. It looked more like a brown slurry that had been forgotten about and simply heated up again because someone had neglected to throw it away.

The answer arrived with a beep:

FOLLOW THEM.
KILL TRONEG IF YOU CAN.
COLLATERAL DAMAGE ACCEPTABLE.

Next to the chat window, the man had opened a photograph showing Viktor in front of a tumbledown shack, holding a fully-equipped G36 rifle. It was not clear where and when it had been taken, but the colour of his camouflage suggested it was in Iraq or Afghanistan, or another desert country. He had been there with a German unit that had no official reason to be there.

But this was not the reason why Viktor von Troneg was on the hit list. German Special Forces were constantly moving through forbidden terrain without governments or any other regulatory bodies being aware of them.

There was a second photograph underneath, far grainier, that had clearly been enlarged, showing an antique-looking stone door with a door-knocker made from black metal, shaped like a lion's mouth and bearing a golden ring between its white teeth. The signs and symbols carved into it were too pixelated for them to be deciphered. The door belonged to the hut Viktor had been kneeling in front of in the first photo, casting his eyes around for enemies without once looking behind him … which might have been a lethal error with a door of this kind.

The man responded in acknowledgement and, as the chauffeur led the sextet across the hall, lifted up his smartphone to take photos of the group and send them off.

Calmly, the middle-aged man stood up and slinging a rucksack over his shoulder and carrying his laptop under his arm, began to follow them, just one of countless anonymous business travellers making their way through the terminal. No one could possibly guess what he was up to or what organisation he worked for.

The man left the building and leaned against a pillar a few yards back from the black Mercedes people carrier, looking around for a taxi. There was only one car in the rank.

The group had finished getting in; the vehicle's indicators blinked and it drove off.

The man strode purposefully towards the last taxi. 'Hello. I'd like to go to—'

'Sorry. I've just had another booking come through on the radio,' replied the driver through the window with a regretful gesture. 'One of my colleagues will be with you shortly.' He turned on the ignition and drove off.

Shortly wasn't soon enough. There were no other taxis as far as the eye could see.

Cursing, he turned around and took out his phone, keeping his eye on the Mercedes as it faded into the distance. 'It's me,' he said to the gruff voice at the other end. 'I need to find the owner of a black Merc people carrier.' He recited the model and registration number.

In a matter of seconds he knew where he had to go to find Viktor von Troneg.

Instead of waiting for the next taxi to come along, the man walked over to the closest car hire kiosk. His orders were clear and had to be carried out to the letter.

SECOND DEAD END

After her courageous step across the threshold, the young woman in the dark green evening dress wandered a few yards forwards before stopping and gazing around at the dark forest; it was disconcertingly peaceful.

She was surrounded by ferns and the ethereal glow of the silvery moonlight dappling through the giant trees. The earthy cry of a screech owl rang in her ears, accompanied by the barking of a fox. The wind coursed playfully through the branches and foliage, creating a rustling sound all around her.

The young woman was not going to be fooled again, not when everything she had read about in the stories had been proved right. She stood still, casting her eyes all around and listening out for signs of danger while clasping the branch ever more tightly in her right hand.

The ominous rumbling of the predators inhabiting this world had died away for now. She hoped that the creatures had found other prey, preferably this invisible creature from the labyrinth.

It was only when she was certain that there was nothing moving near her that she decided to press on slowly. She looked down at her smartphone.

No Signal.

'For fuck's sake,' she muttered, looking back at the door she had just come through.

On this side, the passage belonged to the remains of an old bunker which had become embedded into the landscape and overgrown with greenery. The markings on the door were illegible and the signs themselves gave away no clues as to their meaning. It was clear, however, that this was not a place that had anything to do with the world she knew. There was nothing reminiscent of the cavernous hall with its five enigmatic doors.

She'd known that would be the case, though.

The sound of an electronic beep suddenly rang out and she looked at the display.

The signal bar started to flit rapidly between showing one and two bars.

'Yes! Please!' she cried out in relief. 'That must mean . . .' She stretched her arm upwards in an attempt to find more reception and strode cautiously forwards.

She had been wrong after all. *Thankfully!* This wood was part of good old Planet Earth, with its mobile phone masts and boosters that would help her to escape. Perhaps she had opened a door to a nature reserve or a wolf enclosure. That would explain the howling.

She slipped through a dense field of lush green ferns, constantly looking for an even better signal. She caught her high heels repeatedly on the soft ground and kept having to avoid unhelpfully located boulders, but finally she emerged in a clearing bathed in moonlight. The celestial body looked considerably larger and closer than normal.

She made her way cautiously into the centre of the clearing and held her phone up as high as she could. 'Come on,' she whispered imploringly. 'Take me home.'

A faint crackling could suddenly be heard and the ferns swirled all around her.

The young woman remained stationary but looked around, listening attentively, her branch thrust out in front of her to ward off any potential attack. Her nose-stud and one of her earrings glimmered icily in the starlight. The other one must have fallen off at some point; she certainly wouldn't be going back to look for it.

At that moment, the display on her phone showed a full bar of signal as her reward. 'Yes!' she screamed with joy.

Her scratched fingers flitted over the device to start dialling.

She kept looking around, trying to avoid becoming something's dinner just before being rescued. She looked at the ferns suspiciously as they swayed in the breeze. A distant howling erupted once more, far enough away for her to not have to fear it, but close enough to remind her that the animals had not altogether gone.

She ducked down reflexively so as not to be discovered; she would have preferred to crawl out of the exposed area and head towards a tree in order to wait for the park ranger or official to rescue her from the compound.

As if to punish her, the signal bar went back to how it had been before.

She stood up again and pressed the phone to her cheek. After what felt like an eternity, it started to ring.

Three, four rings.

A click. Someone had answered.

'Papa – can you hear me, Papa?' she exclaimed joyfully. 'Listen to me! I was at Great-grandad's house—'

A distorted, unhuman voice emanated from the speaker, nothing but unintelligible babbling.

She looked at the display. She had definitely dialled the right number. 'What on earth—?'

She hung up and dialled the emergency services.

Her phone tried to get through again.

The howling returned, much closer than it had been a few seconds earlier, while the ferns suddenly moved in the opposite direction to the wind. Something was running directly towards her, protected under the cover of the green canopy.

'Fuck!' The young woman ran back towards the door through which she had just come. Her prospects of survival felt greater on the other side of this forest, even if there was something else waiting for her in the chamber. At least now she was armed with a branch.

The bar had returned to zero. No Service.

The ruined bunker appeared between the tree trunks; the door was now wide open.

Moonlight shone into the room beyond, illuminating the markings on the concrete and brick walls; it was the closest thing to temporary safety she was likely to get. She could see the broken door knocker on the floor, as well as the skeletal remains and the dead man in his camouflage gear. The sub-machine gun in his hand looked tempting, though she had no idea how to use it. It would at least give her something more robust than the branch to defend herself with.

She'd started panting with exertion but still managed to keep her speed up. She stumbled on the steep ground but just about stayed on her feet.

The rumbling approach of the beasts came ever closer.

I'm going to make it, she kept thinking. She wasn't even ten yards away now. *I'm going to make it!*

A man in a pin-striped suit, his white shirt and black tie arranged immaculately, emerged from inside the bunker and stood in the entrance. His abrupt arrival had something of the surreal about it. His face wore a curious expression as he watched the young woman running for her life.

Then he raised his right arm, revealing a ring on his finger that shimmered in the moonlight. He placed his hand on the door and pushed it shut before she was able to make it to the passage.

'No!' exclaimed the young woman angrily, 'No – I've got to get in! Listen to me – I've got to—' She threw herself against the door at full speed and reached it while it was still slightly ajar; in her attempt to jam the stick into the crack to keep the door open, it split in two and the wood shattered in her hand. 'No! No, open the door!' She rammed her shoulder against the door repeatedly, tearing her skin and green dress in the process. 'You prick!' Warm blood began to seep from the fresh cuts and scratches she had just acquired.

A deep laugh erupted from the other side of the door and the unknown man pushed back. He was too strong for her. The door closed. The lock clicked into place and at the same time a terrible whirring sound could be heard.

The young woman kicked it miserably. She knew what that noise meant: there was no way back.

Now it was just her, the forest and the monsters.

CHAPTER II

Germany, Near Frankfurt

The journey was made in silence at first, the Mercedes cruising along the motorway, taking them further and further away from the airport. Matthias was a cautious but skilled driver, nipping from lane to lane to make decent progress.

Coco Fendi rummaged in her box of tricks and began to rearrange the stones, runes and other odds and ends that had fallen out so ignominiously earlier, then she opened the case completely, spreading it out on the seat next to her so that the other passengers all had to shuffle up, but nobody complained.

Viktor examined Dana Rentski's face in the reflection in the tinted window. She looked vaguely familiar, but he couldn't think where from. He had taken part in numerous climbing competitions over the years and it was not at all out of the question that they had come across each other at one time or another. As soon as he tried to talk to her, however, she made it perfectly clear from her body language that she had no interest whatsoever in having a discussion. She was reading a book on her smartphone and did not wish to be disturbed.

If his feeling of having met her before had anything to do with his old job, then it probably was not going to be a happy story. It would mean they were not on the same page whatsoever.

Spanger dozed, snorting and grunting every time they went over a bump.

'Now then.' Friedemann was the first to speak. The man folded up his newspaper and placed it in his lap before allowing his mocking gaze to pass over the group. 'What have we here?' He pointed to his chest. 'Rüdiger Friedemann: geologist and speleologist.' Then he pointed to Dana and Viktor. 'Two free-climbers.' He inclined his finger towards Coco. 'And a medium.' His brown eyes turned to Ingo. 'You are our doctor, and you' – he looked towards Spanger, who had opened his eyes at the sound of his voice – 'are our technical support, if I had to guess.' He looked smugly at the man with his curious beard. 'You're a bit too tubby for caving, though. We can't have you getting stuck down there.'

Spanger rubbed his eyelids and cleared his throat to reply, but before he could muster a response, Ingo said, 'I'm not a medical doctor. I'm a doctor of physics and parapsychology, from the Freiburg Parapsychological Institute.'

Friedemann laughed. 'A ghost-hunter? Sweet Jesus, what a team we've got here!'

'I'm not just a climber,' said Dana. 'I also do a bit of martial arts on the side. Just about enough to give thieves a good hiding. Or arrogant tossers. Age makes no difference to me whatsoever.'

'Touché,' replied Friedemann, amused. 'How refreshing it is to see someone with a bit of courage about them.'

'Don't be a dick, Friedemann. Just because you're a professor, it doesn't mean you have to get off on your title,' replied Spanger sourly. 'You look like you'd fall over if someone blew on you. Or—'

'With all due respect, *this* is the strangest group I've ever had to lead.' Friedemann looked around the interior of the vehicle.

'*You?*' exclaimed Dana with disbelief. The look she gave him made it perfectly clear that she did not believe he would last an hour in a climbing harness. '*You're* going to be leading our team?'

Friedemann smiled. He appeared to be enjoying this. 'That's what it says in my contract.'

The surroundings they were whizzing past had started to change dramatically. The Mercedes was now driving through an affluent suburb of old mansions and enormous gardens.

By now, Viktor was certain that Dana's face was not familiar from any climbing exploits. 'Help me out here,' he said to her. 'We know each other from somewhere. But it's not from anything involving caves or climbing, is it?'

She shrugged and carried on reading.

Viktor could not fathom Dana's behaviour. He continued to rack his brains but the story of where or how they'd met was lost in the fog somewhere. Or had he become a victim of his own imagination because she resembled someone he knew?

'Why don't you ask our clairvoyant, Mr von Troneg?' Friedemann smiled at Coco, who was still engrossed in her triage. The car slowed down and stopped with a gentle sway.

'She'll definitely be able to tell you where you've met before. Or in what life.' He rolled up his newspaper and thumped it down on her open suitcase. 'Ms Fendi, give this gentleman a hand. Spiritually, that is. Impress us.'

'I don't provide those sorts of services for free. Nor good impressions, for that matter,' she said coolly before closing the case. 'We've all got bills to pay.' She snapped the locks back into place with a flourish and tossed her blonde curls with that unusual black streak in a well-rehearsed, suitably melodramatic gesture.

Spanger laughed bitterly. 'There's something to be said for that. By the way, I'm not an IT geek, Professor Friedemann. I'm a bodyguard.'

The old geologist's smile turned into a vicious grin. He could think of a million jokes to make about the man's corpulence, but he chose to keep the ones about being a cushion for bullets to himself for the time being. 'I'm sure you're the very best.'

The team climbed out, Friedemann leading.

The Mercedes had stopped in the drive of an imposing Art Nouveau mansion in the middle of carefully curated parkland. The sun was warm on their backs and shone welcomingly through the trees; it smelled of the last days of summer, though autumn was well underway.

Matthias walked around them and opened the boot. 'Don't worry, I'll take care of your luggage.'

'As you did for the others?' replied Dana. Clearly she had also noticed his slip of the tongue earlier.

'Please make sure nothing falls open,' Coco reminded him. 'And don't scratch them! Bags can feel pain too – especially when they're as expensive as mine are.' Keeping hold of the case containing all her paraphernalia, she pulled a golden pendulum hanging from a silver chain out of her coat and pointed it at the mansion. 'There's sorrow in this house,' she muttered darkly.

Ingo looked at her in warning, but she smiled dismissively. She was perfectly happy being a walking cliché.

'Sorrow, yes. And even more money,' added Spanger. 'Good for us – means we'll definitely get paid.'

'Go on in,' Matthias implored with a friendly smile. 'Mr van Dam is keen to meet you all.'

At that moment, the front door opened. The servant who appeared in the doorway, dressed in a uniform similar to the chauffeur's, invited them inside. 'Follow me, please. Everything's ready for you.'

The group passed through an imposing entrance hall, glimpsing a series of elegantly furnished rooms on the ground floor, before heading up the stairs. Viktor looked around in amazement; he felt as if he were in a museum. He was not particularly well versed in art, but the paintings looked as if they might have been from the eighteenth century and would certainly have been worth a small fortune, just like the rest of the treasures adorning every room they passed.

Spanger was mimicking the brisk pace set by the staff, his substantial posterior wiggling left and right as he moved. Coco was holding her pendulum out the entire time, her face set in a mask of concern. Ingo, meanwhile, was walking with his hands behind his back as if he were a philosopher.

'We're here.' The woman knocked on the door and,

upon hearing a voice from inside, ushered them through the impressive set of double doors into their client's office. 'If any of you have got any dietary requirements or allergies, please let me know. I'm here to serve.' After making sure no one needed anything right then, she gestured inside. 'I'll be back soon, ladies and gentlemen.'

They were hit by a smell of a fresh aftershave that somehow complemented the room perfectly. The dark interior was a daring mixture of old and new, Bauhaus and baroque, combining steel, leather and wood to give the impression of having been put together at the whim of some progressive designer. Thick, dusty tomes and antique-looking folders stood on sober, functional shelves, while one corner was taken up by a large, elaborately crafted wardrobe that looked as if it might lead straight to Narnia.

Walter van Dam was seated behind his desk, hunched over a laptop. He was about Friedemann's age, mid-fifties, with greying hair and similarly coloured moustache and sideburns, and was dressed in an expensive-looking dark brown suit. He glanced up and gestured to the six chairs in front of his desk. 'Welcome, ladies and gentlemen.'

They offered their greetings and sat down. The woman who'd met them at the door returned, pushing a trolley on which an assortment of coffee, tea, mineral water and biscuits was laid out, before retiring again.

'I must apologise in advance for the urgency of this matter. I'm running out of time, you see, so please don't be offended if I come across as rude,' van Dam explained. 'Do I need to introduce you to one another, or did you get that out of the way on the journey here?'

'Already done,' Friedemann announced. 'They all know I'm in charge, at any rate.'

'Then I'm sure you also understand that you're a rather special group,' said van Dam, his tones clipped. 'Including a medium.'

'Indeed.' Viktor cocked his head to one side, looking at Mr van Dam, who seemed to be more of a grounded businessman than a fringe lunatic. 'For which I'm sure there's a reason?'

'Desperation, I imagine,' muttered Spanger.

Van Dam's business-like manner faded and he appeared to sink a little behind his computer. 'You're right, Mr Spanger, I am desperate,' he admitted quietly. 'Beyond desperate.'

The group exchanged glances.

Coco looked as if she wanted to say something and began to point the pendulum at him, but Ingo gently touched her arm to stop her. Now really wasn't the time. She relented.

Van Dam cleared his throat and took a sip of water from the glass next to him. A few droplets got caught on his beard, making his face glimmer for a moment. 'My daughter has been missing for a week.' He turned a picture frame around to show them the face of a freckled, red-haired young woman, no older than twenty, with a cheeky smile playing on her lips. 'I suspect she's in an unexplored cave system. Alone.'

'I'm so sorry,' replied Viktor spontaneously. He knew all too well what it felt like to be worried about a loved one. He just about managed to stop himself from asking where she had gone missing.

'The police and fire service would be your best bet, then,' Spanger said, making no attempt to conceal his disappointment. He had been counting on something exciting. 'The emergency services, at any rate.'

'I've got nothing against the authorities,' van Dam said, having regained his business-like demeanour, 'but there are some matters that do not concern the government. The last thing I want is to have hordes of curious firefighters or police officers swarming all over my property.'

'I'll track down your daughter, no matter where she is,' Coco assured him in a theatrical voice, as if she were trying to entertain an audience. She couldn't turn it off, no matter how hard she tried. 'That I promise you, Mr van Dam.'

'I have every faith in you, Ms Fendi. Given that you have passed Doctor Theobald's parapsychological tests, you are clearly predestined to do so.' He clasped his hands together. 'As I've said, I'm running out of time. My daughter . . .' He paused, taking a deep breath as he struggled to maintain his composure.

'How could she get lost when she was on your property?' ventured Viktor.

'And what's our resident ghostbuster here for?' Dana enquired, her voice sounding matter-of-fact. 'Do you really expect we'll have to contend with ghosts?'

'There's no such thing as ghosts,' added Ingo. 'I should know, after more than two hundred investigations.'

'My reason for inviting Doctor Theobald is because . . . because he *is* scientifically very well versed. I need the six of you to be prepared for *anything* on this expedition, ready to deal with any situation that might arise,' said van

Dam quickly. 'It is your job to find out how precisely she disappeared, Mr von Troneg. You'll have state-of-the-art caving equipment, ample provisions, as well as helmet cameras and signal-boosters to make sure images are fed back up to me. I'm afraid my claustrophobia will prevent me from accompanying you, otherwise I would have gone to rescue my daughter myself. But even if I can't be there in person, I'd like to know what's going on underground.' He hesitated briefly, then added, 'Firearms and light body armour will also be provided.'

Spanger laughed, his mood improving. 'Whoa – because?'

'As you may be aware, I am a wealthy man. My daughter is usually protected by bodyguards from the moment she steps foot outside the house. But this was not the case on her last outing.' He glanced down at his laptop. 'There's a very good chance that criminals took this opportunity and are holding my daughter captive down there. That's why Mr Spanger is with you. As a firearms expert.' He stood up and smoothed out his waistcoat and tie. 'As I said, you must be ready for anything.'

Viktor found his explanation rather odd. 'Has anyone sent a ransom note?'

'No. The kidnapping idea is just a guess.' Van Dam pointed at the door. 'Please excuse my lack of manners. And I beg you not to consider me unprofessional because I didn't brief you in advance, but the nature of this matter required the utmost discretion, not least because of my daughter's profile. Your contracts have all been signed and the first instalments have been paid. Feel free to check your accounts.' He walked around the desk, clearly heading for the door. 'Time is pressing, ladies and gentlemen – time my daughter doesn't have. Everything you need to know about the caves and your fellow teammates can be found in the files Matthias has given you. You are to leave immediately. As the most experienced speleologist and geologist, Professor Friedemann will lead the group, as per his request. If you'd be so kind . . .'

Viktor raised his hand, which van Dam deliberately ignored, but Viktor continued regardless, 'Sorry, just a quick question. Have you already sent another team out?'

'No.'

His reply was firm and abrupt, but after the chauffeur's slip-up earlier, everyone now knew that they were the second group to have been despatched and that the first had not returned. Van Dam's unconvincing denial served only to suppress any further enquiries.

Everyone stood up.

Friedemann was looking closely at the cabinet behind van Dam's desk. 'These carvings are exquisite.' His face had acquired an expression that was typical of an expert spotting an anomaly or making a spectacular discovery. 'I've never seen such a specimen before. It must be price-less.'

'Not this one. I got it from a flea market. It's just my cocktail cabinet.' Van Dam pointed emphatically to the exit once again. 'Bring me back my child – alive – and I'll make you all rich beyond measure. The hundred thousand euros each of you has received is just a fraction of what you'll get if you return my Anna-Lena safely to me.'

*

The team got back into the same black Mercedes that had collected them from the airport. They began to drive through a wilderness of sorts, passing increasingly fewer houses and ever-deeper woodland, until Matthias announced that they would arrive in a few minutes. 'Don't worry about how remote it is,' he added. 'It'll make your task a lot easier.'

The ragtag bunch read their dossiers in silence.

They were all wearing dark military clothing, climbing gear and light Kevlar vests and were armed with pistols, holstered on thighs or underarm. The semi-automatic she'd been issued looked like an alien life form to Coco, but Friedemann had insisted that she take something other than clairvoyant trinkets to protect herself. Two light rucksacks were resting in front of him and Spanger.

Viktor considered it rather a bold move to arm people with weapons when they no experience in handling them, nor any legal authorisation to do so. He also doubted whether a civvy with a gun would actually be able to hold their own against potential kidnappers.

Friedemann put his folder to one side and fumbled around as if looking for something, before pulling out a well-thumbed notebook from his right trouser pocket. It looked old, both in terms of style and wear and tear. Clearly relieved, Friedemann looked at it briefly, then stuffed it under his Kevlar vest, something Viktor didn't fail to notice.

'Not much information in here,' Spanger grumbled. 'Just a load of stuff about van Dam's daughter.'

'What were you expecting?' Dana put a piece of chewing gum in her mouth. 'He said the cave system hadn't been explored before.'

Viktor and Coco both gave a quiet laugh, which somehow reinforced his suspicion that the clairvoyant could do more than just predict the future. He had been trying to talk to her about the official investigation by the Parapsychological Institute, as he had never heard of a real, verified psychic before, but she was having none of it, claiming she needed to concentrate as she shuffled her deck of cards. She said she'd be happy to tell him all about it after their assignment, by way of consolation.

'I'm curious to find out more about these caves,' Ingo said as he put his folder to one side. 'I've never come across someone who considers a cavern to be his own private property.'

'I don't like caves,' came Spanger's irritable reply.

'I'd have put money on that. You look like the sort of chap who needs a lot of room. I can't imagine narrow spaces are your thing.' Friedemann looked around intently. 'I don't believe this young lady has been kidnapped.'

'Neither do I,' agreed Viktor, who already knew the information in the file off by heart. 'Otherwise van Dam would have hired people with experience in hostage negotiation. Anyone else would put his daughter in danger. Though I suppose it could be the case that the first team was just that but they weren't able to manage it.'

'I'm so pleased I've got your approval,' said Friedemann, his voice laced with mockery. 'I don't foresee any problems. We'll follow the safety rope mentioned in the handout. Anna-Lena is almost certainly just lying around somewhere, waiting for help.'

'What's so special about you that he's put a geologist

in charge?' Dana had doubted his leadership credentials from the start. 'Just curious,' she added. She smiled coolly.

Friedemann looked at her calmly. 'I suppose you think you should be leading us, just because you can climb like a mountain goat?' He rubbed his thumbs over the tips of his index and middle fingers. 'I can see where the rock is fragile and where it's dangerous; where there are cracks and what you need to look out for. And what routes we shouldn't take. I've led dozens of expeditions to the furthest reaches of the Earth. And everyone has returned safely.' He returned her cold smile. 'Just for your information.'

Dana's smile faded; she was clearly still not convinced.

'What about the first team?' Spanger interjected. 'What do you think happened to them that van Dam doesn't want us to know?'

Coco finished her shuffling. 'They might have had a fall, or just given up, or . . .' She pulled out the ace of spades. 'Oh.'

'Oh?' echoed Spanger.

'This is the death card,' she breathed, giving the bodyguard a long, meaningful look.

Dana snorted contemptuously and pulled her ponytail tighter. 'Good job it wasn't me who picked it then.' She looked out the window. 'What's that? It doesn't look like a cave.'

The Mercedes was stopping in front of an enormous dilapidated house. There was something classical about the façade, which looked like the end of the nineteenth century in style, complete with resplendent turrets and oriels.

The windows were stained glass and would certainly provide a fascinating mixture of colours inside during the day. Despite its shabby condition, the house looked far too magnificent to be haunted.

The remains of what appeared to be a small factory could be seen next it; what was left of the collapsed building suggested it had fallen victim to fire.

Viktor picked up his file and skimmed it to check he had not missed anything about this place, but there was nothing to be found. It concerned itself only with the unknown Anna-Lena, a girl of barely twenty years. One week was enough for a person to die of thirst; it could take maybe three times that to die of hunger – less for a skinny girl. Van Dam was right: there was no time to lose.

A black Black Badge Wraith was parked at an angle in front of the building; judging by the layers of dust, it had been there for rather a long time. The Rolls-Royce, which, according to their dossiers, belonged to Anna-Lena van Dam, was a clear sign that she had been here.

Viktor quickly checked his phone to see if he could find anything about Friedemann online, as Dana's scepticism was proving contagious. This gaunt professor truly was a luminary, though he looked rather different in the photographs – more like a distant relative. *Mind you, these photos are probably ancient*, thought Viktor.

'We're here,' Matthias announced redundantly, before getting out. He had a tablet clutched in his left hand. 'It's up to you now.'

The team climbed out the car. Viktor and Spanger grabbed the backpacks and strapped them on as Dana said, 'Let's go.' She checked her pistol, took out the magazine and pushed the slide back and forth, then secured the trigger and loaded the semi-automatic.

Coco was watching her closely. 'That looked ... well-practised.'

'Gun club,' replied the woman with a grin.

'I'll accompany you as far as the entrance.' Matthias strode towards the door of the building, pulling out a large bunch of keys.

'So the entrance to the cave is in the basement.' Ingo pointed at the Rolls-Royce. 'Why is that still here?'

'Mr van Dam wanted it left in case his daughter managed to find her way out on her own. That way she could just set off straight away or ring for help. It's equipped with a VPN.' Matthias walked up the steps to the door. 'Oh, and don't forget the rifles. They're in the boot.'

Spanger hurried back to the car, removed the parcel shelf and had a look at the G36 automatic rifles, complete with several spare magazines and retractable shoulder supports. 'That's more like it!' He picked one of them up and loaded two magazines. 'We could put these to good use.' He began fiddling with it, looking for the magazine ejector, then pulled on the breech block to no effect. Nothing about the way in which he was handling the weapon gave the impression that he had a clue what he was doing.

Coco and Ingo caught each other's eye, silently agreeing that they wouldn't be taking one. There was no way they'd be able to handle them.

Viktor and Dana were looking at the automatic weapons as if they were souvenirs in a gift shop.

'These are good if you're dealing with terrorists, but they're not going to be much use in a cave system.' Viktor tapped the pistol resting in his shoulder holster. 'These are perfect at short range, though.'

To his surprise, Dana took one of the G36s out of its case. She examined it briefly, swivelled around and adjusted the sight. Then she loaded a full magazine, attached it and checked the safety was on before slinging the rifle over her shoulder. She put two cartridges into the holders on her vest, then still without a word, she turned around and followed Friedemann, Ingo and Coco.

Spanger and Viktor looked on in amazement.

'You can find all sorts of dangerous animals in caves,' she called back over her shoulder. She was fully aware that the two men were looking at her. 'Cave bears, for example.'

Viktor hesitated. No one truly believed this was a kidnapping; rather, that some sort of accident had befallen Anna-Lena. Despite not wishing to come across as paranoid, he nevertheless decided he too would bring one of the automatic weapons with him. He went through the checking and loading process with the same ease as Dana.

'She's right,' he said out loud, before setting off.

Spanger looked even more confused. then began to run, his gait making him look like a clumsy bear. 'Hey, Rentski! Can you show me how to use one of these guns?'

'You're better off not using it at all,' came her spare reply.

The rest of the group laughed. They put on the radio headsets and fastened their helmets, which were all equipped with cameras in special holders that would transmit pictures back to the surface from the cave using a series of signal-boosters. Their backpacks contained all the necessary electronic equipment to operate such a system.

'Can you tell us what sort of magic is going on here?' Coco asked Matthias. Her pendulum had been swinging incessantly. She kept all the other items she intended using for detection in a pouch on her belt. 'I'm getting some very strange energy. Something terrible has happened here.' She came across as far less artificial than she had at the airport or in van Dam's office.

'We can all see the burnt-down shed next to it as well,' Spanger muttered.

'Yes, but you're only looking. I'm listening to the full story.'

'The fire on the woodwork has been there for ever.' Matthias opened the double doors, which were studded with bronze inlay and set in a heavy frame adorned with intricately carved floral patterns. 'This is a very old property; it has belonged to the van Dam family for years. Once the fire destroyed the factory and Mr van Dam's grandfather retired from the board, there's been no use for it. The surrounding woods have been leased to a hunting club,' he added, pushing open the heavy doors. 'You'll need to turn on your helmet lights. There's no electricity down here.'

Using his tablet to create a small pool of light, the chauffeur led the group through the abandoned house.

White sheets had been laid over the furniture and thick cobwebs had formed in the corners, in one of which could be seen the skeletal remains of a dog.

'Hmm, that's not what I'm getting.' Coco pulled out a bottle of fragrant water, which she began to spray around her. 'It hasn't got anything to do with the fire. It's ... something far worse.'

'Oooooh,' replied Spanger, giggling like a schoolboy.

'Pull yourself together, man,' Friedemann snapped. 'Whatever our talented Ms Fendi is sensing might well be of help to us. It certainly can't hurt to pay attention to the unusual things going on around us.'

The only tracks through the dust and dirt were the lonely footprints made by what Coco identified as a pair of lady's high-heeled shoes, which gave the rest of the group food for thought.

'Tell me, did the first team not come through this house on their way to look for Miss van Dam?' enquired Viktor, ignoring the denial that another group had already been despatched. 'I can't see anything here apart from this pair of size 38 high heels.'

'Forgive me, but that's not something I have any knowledge of,' Matthias responded. He opened another door, revealing a steep stone staircase beyond. 'This is as far as I can go.'

He turned on a monitor, where Messenger was open. Van Dam's moustachioed face appeared on the screen: he looked exhausted but excited at the same time. 'Your mission will begin down there,' came his voice tinnily through the speaker. 'Please get a move on – follow the rope! It's the best way down. And make sure to use the signal-boosters for your helmet cameras so I can see what you see.'

'We will, Mr van Dam. No problem,' Friedemann promised.

Coco took a crystal necklace out of the pouch on her

belt and put it on. 'We'll find Anna-Lena: the cosmic forces are with us.'

'Sure they are. And firepower as well.' Spanger was fiddling in vain with his G36, until Dana snatched it out of his hands and armed it for him.

'For a bodyguard you seem to know very little.' She pointed at the safety catch and raised her index finger to show him he needed to make sure he knew what position it was in.

'I wish you every success. Find my daughter.' Van Dam nodded and the signal switched to stand-by mode.

'Let's be off then.' Friedemann pointed to Spanger, indicating he should start, and he began to move, Dana and Friedemann following, with Viktor and Coco next. Ingo took up the rear.

They made their way down, step after worn step. The beams of light cast by the helmet lamps spun around the room, flitting over old brick walls like the confused rays of tiny lighthouses. It smelled neither musty nor stale, only of cold rock and dust. Carved pillars of the same rock held up the vaulted brick ceiling.

Spanger held his G36 at an angle, his index finger twitching nervously on the trigger as if he were already fearing an attack at this stage of the mission. The light from his helmet fell abruptly on a rust-flecked steel cable stretched horizontally across. 'I've found the rope!'

He looked back along it: the end of the steel cable was wrapped several times around a pillar and held in place by a carabiner that looked disconcertingly old.

Spanger turned his head the other way, the light following.

The finger-thick cable passed horizontally through an inwards-opening door and into the darkness beyond. The beam from his helmet was mostly lost in the darkness, only occasionally illuminating the taut, steel cord in the distance when he twisted his head. There were no walls, no floor and no ceiling to be seen on the other side of the door.

'Holy shit—!' Spanger exclaimed in disbelief. 'Come on – you've got to see this!'

One by one, the others arrived at the bottom. They all looked in astonishment at the open door as they shuffled their way slowly towards it. Coco started to lift up her crystal pendant, but Ingo grabbed her hand and pulled it down.

'Now that's what I call a cave.' Friedemann pressed forward and shone his light into the blackness. Like Spanger's, the beam met no resistance other than the rope. He ran his hand over the door frame and smiled, as if he had found something unspeakably valuable and remarkable.

'I can't hear an echo.' Ingo picked up a stone from the floor and threw it into the void. 'Let's see how deep it is.'

They waited for several seconds, but no sound was forthcoming.

'That's . . . not good,' whispered Coco.

'No it's not,' Viktor agreed. The hairs on the back of his neck were standing to attention. 'I've never seen anything like this before. This cave has got to be . . . enormous.' He looked at Friedemann. 'What do you reckon? Have you ever come across anything like this?'

'No. I fully agree with your assessment.' Friedemann peered uncertainly into the blackness beyond.

Dana took a step past the men, clipped a safety carabiner and a low-friction roller onto the old steel rope and slipped into her harness. 'Van Dam told us to follow the rope.' She took a run-up, leaped through the door and went shooting along the steel cable into the darkness.

'Off you go, Spanger, follow her,' Friedemann ordered.

Spanger swore and hooked himself up to the rope. As Friedemann fiddled laboriously with his own climbing harness, struggling to secure the carabiners to the cable, Spanger too jumped and set off after Dana. Meanwhile, ignoring her complaints, Ingo was helping Coco to lash the last of the straps around her body.

Viktor watched Friedemann's awkward attempts to fasten himself in, which he considered rather peculiar; a speleologist of his renown really ought to be able to do that in his sleep. 'Is this the first time you've used this equipment?' he asked.

'Yes. I haven't needed harnesses on any of my other expeditions,' explained the scrawny geologist between curses. 'Not this sort, anyway. I used to be able to do it, Mr Troneg.'

Viktor bent down to help him. His eyes betrayed his doubts about this statement, but all he said was, 'It could happen to anyone, Professor.'

'Then let's go and save the girl. You bring up the rear.' Friedemann chased after Dana and Spanger, closely followed by the parapsychologist and the clairvoyant.

Viktor could hear the whirring of the rollers through the darkness and caught glimpses of the five lances of light as they flew through the gloom. Instead of setting off straight away, he thought to test the fastening of the rope to the column. Although there were five adults hanging from it, the cable appeared to be completely untroubled by the load.

'There's something very off about this,' he said to himself, screwing up his face. A young woman driving a luxury car to an abandoned house, wandering around with high heels on her feet and sliding down a steel cable? In a cave without a floor or ceiling? Not on your life. A search party who had left no trace of their presence? The dossiers they had been given were useless; there was no map and their client had hidden the fact that he had already sent out a team before them.

But orders were orders – and a hundred thousand euros, increasing to one million if they succeeded, was not something to be scoffed at. He could put that to very good use indeed. He was familiar with the G36, although he had hoped to never have to lay eyes on one again, let alone use one. It appeared he could not shake off his old life that easily.

Viktor examined the carved doorframe in the helmet light. An inlaid stone that reminded him a little of fool's gold reflected the beam.

A door to a cave system, he thought. Who would build such nonsense? He closed the door gently until the edge hit the cable, then spotted a rather puzzling door knocker on the inside: a grotesque face was holding a rusty metal ring between its fangs.

What on earth is this? Viktor touched the skull of this fantastical beast and ran his fingers over its rough teeth. He had seen something like this before, at an old job. Scenes appeared in his mind: the rattle of gunfire, burning wind, blood and screaming.

He quickly started to look for something to focus on to stop him from falling back into the past, back into trauma that could never be defeated. *What would it sound like if I were to use the knocker?* His fingers lifted the ring up carefully.

The hairs on the back of his neck began to stand on end again. Through his gloves he could feel an invisible stream of energy flowing through the metal. *Probably not a good idea.*

'Troneg? Where have you got to?' Friedemann's voice was far away but there was no echo at all. 'Everything all right?'

Viktor slowly lowered the heavy ring, causing it to squeak eerily. He had a bad feeling about what would happen if he brought it down with force – he might not have Coco's abilities, but a quiet little voice at the back of his head was warning him of highly unpredictable consequences if he did so.

'Coming. Just wanted to test the anchoring.' Viktor clicked himself on and took himself as far back as the pillar in order to work up as much of a head of steam as possible. He was breathing very deeply. 'Whatever this is, it's not just a cave,' he muttered, before running forward.

He threw himself onto the rope through the door.

At the same time, Spanger's scream could be heard a long way away. 'Shit, no – *no—!*'

A G36 roared and a bright muzzle flash tore through the darkness.

And the light reflected onto rock.

CHAPTER III

Germany, Near Frankfurt

The man who had secretly followed Viktor von Troneg from the arrivals hall and had photographed the team was sitting in the driver's seat of the BMW X5. He had parked his rental car less than a hundred yards from the dilapidated house, outside which stood the black Mercedes people carrier and the ostentatious Rolls-Royce.

The mini laptop was resting on his lap while he looked over at the estate through his binoculars, which were equipped with night vision. No one from the group had reappeared yet; they were either in the house or in the vault beneath it. Frank Sinatra's 'Strangers in the Night' was coming gently through the car speakers, providing a melancholic accompaniment to the scene playing out before him.

New photographs of the group had come in from headquarters via the car's internal Wi-Fi system. It was impossible these days to keep things secret; nothing was difficult to find if you knew where to look. Thanks to the wonder of the internet and its myriad possibilities, it had been easy enough to track down the sextet and trawl through their backgrounds. And there were several things that did not match what they had told van Dam.

'Those little liars.' His mouth twisting in amusement, he read the most recent report about Coco Fendi, whose real name was Beate Schüpfer. Van Dam had been unimpressed by the tragic past of his psychic, which included a disastrous stage show.

Then he typed into the open chat window:

NEW INSTRUCTIONS?

After a brief delay, the reply appeared:

WAIT.

He gave a short growl of irritation and cast his eyes back onto the estate. It looked as if he would be here for a while.

The beam of his helmet lamp was lost in the darkness. Viktor dragged himself along the rope with his hands, the low-friction roller making it a virtually effortless task. Every now and again he knocked off flakes of rust that were coming loose from the wire.

He could see four beams of light in the distance.

A long muzzle flash emanated from the barrel of one of the G36s as it tapped out a staccato rhythm. Then the shooting ended abruptly.

'Spanger? Spanger, what's happening?' Viktor enquired nervously, preparing himself to intervene if necessary.

'Shit, I'm . . .' came Spanger's incoherent reply.

Viktor slid forwards along the cable towards the group, who had assembled on a plateau several yards wide. Stone walls towered above them all around; there was only rock below.

He landed, scattering the empty ammunition cases at his feet. 'What have I missed?'

Coco held the pendulum in her hand; Dana had her rifle in position, while Ingo was shining his light into the dark corridor opening out next to the ledge.

Friedemann had secured himself to the rope with two carabiners; he and Spanger were standing at the edge, their helmet lamps pointing down into the depths below.

'You won't be getting it back,' said the geologist rather spitefully.

'Shit,' was all Spanger could say in response.

Viktor detached himself and moved over to stand with them. 'What's going on?' he repeated. He stole a glance at the ancient twisted-steel cord that was fastened to a rust-brown bolt that ended at the cliff-face.

Spanger sighed. Staring over the edge, he admitted, 'Utter carelessness.'

'Utter stupidity,' Dana said. 'I told him he should have put the safety on, but he didn't. It's gone – he's dropped it.'

'It happened while we were moving, okay?' Spanger grunted. 'It went *click* and the damned thing moved. My finger slipped on the trigger and—'

Friedemann pulled him back from the edge by his shoulders. 'Now you've just got your pistol to protect us with.'

'We'd better get going,' Ingo shouted, shining his lamp into the passage.

'What's to say that our little van Dam hasn't fallen in?' Dana looked at Viktor. 'We'd never find her body. God knows how long the rope would need to be for us to reach the bottom of this cave.'

Coco held her pendulum out towards the dark passageway and gave a meaningful nod. 'No, she's alive – she's down here!'

'Then let's go and look for her.' Ingo stepped forwards.

'Hey, stop – not without me.' Spanger hurried alongside them as if the incident with the G36 had had nothing to do with him.

Coco followed them.

Meanwhile, Friedemann was struggling with his climbing harness, unable to remove the carabiners from the steel rope.

Viktor walked over to him and released the catch. 'Like this, Professor.'

'I know – I know. I'm just out of practice, Mr Troneg. Too much time sitting at a desk. You get rusty.' Friedemann ignored his suspicious look and followed Ingo. 'Come on, then. If our clairvoyant is saying this young lady is still alive, we need to get her out of danger as quickly as possible.'

'The others are in rather a hurry – and they are surprisingly optimistic. Perhaps Ms Fendi and her superpowers have given them a sense of security.' Dana gestured to Viktor to take the lead, but he refused. 'Fine then.' She took a few steps to the side and shone her light down once more over the sprawling ledge. 'Sure you haven't forgotten anything?'

The beam of her lamp fell upon a black military-style boot poking out from behind a shelf of rock. The foot was trembling slightly.

'What's that . . . ?' As quick as a flash, Dana armed the G36. 'Troneg, can you see that?'

'I can see it. Let's have a proper look.' Viktor moved to join her, his own rifle lowered, the cones of light from their helmet lamps illuminating the ground in front of them.

Someone was lying next to an overhang on a narrow ledge with a vertical drop right alongside. Apart from his boots, he was wearing nothing but a pair of plain grey underpants. He had been shot several times – the state of his chest left little hope for his survival. His body was also covered with scratches and open wounds probably caused by the fall, and there was a hunting knife lodged in his right shoulder. His blood had spread out in a pool all around him, with rivulets running across the stone and dripping over the edge into the black depths.

'Holy shit,' exclaimed Dana.

The mortally wounded man stared blindly into the light, his face etched with pain and horror. He groaned and tried to say something, but all he could manage was to spit out red droplets.

'Van Dam, are you seeing this?' Viktor said over the radio.

'Yeah, I can see it.' The voice through his earpiece sounded agitated.

Dana approached cautiously, knelt beside the dying man and examined his wounds. 'There's nothing we can do for him. It was a nine-millimetre, I reckon. Probably a sub-machine gun.'

The injured man relaxed, as if he were ready to finally move into the light. With a clink, a long tool was released from his slackening right hand, which was lying just outside the illuminated area.

'Do you know him, van Dam?' Viktor asked.

Dana was balancing fearlessly on the ledge. She took off the dead man's boots and searched them, but was unable to find anything inside them that might cast any light on the matter. She walked through his blood and lifted up the object that he had been carrying; the light from her helmet revealed it to be a bolt cutter.

'I've never seen him before in my life,' came their client's curt reply.

Dana and Viktor exchanged glances.

'What was he doing with that?' The blonde woman stood up and examined the steel cable more closely in her lamplight. She ran her fingers along it, then pointed to some furrows she could feel: the spot where the blades of the cutter had been attached. 'Trying to remove all contact from the outside world? Why, though?'

'And an armed stranger prevented him from doing so.' Viktor looked around, wondering if perhaps Dana was wrong in her assessment of it being a nine-millimetre and the man had accidentally been on the wrong end of Spanger's volley. 'Or did he take the bolt cutter off someone to stop them from cutting the rope?' His concern for Anna-Lena grew. 'What's going on here?'

'*Could* it be a kidnapping?' Dana pointed to the coiled

strands. 'Working hypothesis: they follow her for a little while, or even lure her down here under some false pretence or other. Then they bag her up, carry her through another exit and cut the cable – making it impossible for anyone to follow them.'

'But who shot this bloke if we're certain he didn't get in the way of Spanger's salvo? And why?'

Dana put her hand over her microphone and gestured to Viktor to do the same. 'From one of the members of the first team van Dam isn't telling us about,' she said quietly. 'For whatever reason. And it was definitely a nine-millimetre.'

Spanger's head appeared in the passageway, dazzling both of them with his light. 'Where have you two got to, then?'

'We're coming,' called Viktor. 'We were just having a look around.'

'Come on.' Mini van Dam wants to be rescued and I want to be above ground.' Spanger disappeared again.

They both moved off.

'Do you not want to tell Friedemann?' Dana guessed.

'No, only once we've found something that leads to a definitive conclusion.'

'That's a bit risky. We've already got at least one armed stranger on the loose down here.'

'Who could be miles away from here by now. And it's not a good idea to scare the shit out of the others for no reason.' Viktor studied her. 'By the way, you've really got a very good eye for ammunition and bullet holes.'

'I told you all: gun club.' Dana swivelled the muzzle

of her G36 to point at Viktor as if he were her prisoner, gesturing at him to walk ahead of her. 'What do you think of Friedemann?'

'Not all that much. But he's our leader.' Viktor sloped off. The soft click behind him indicated that Dana had carefully switched the gun's safety catch. To *live*.

'That makes two of us.'

It didn't take them long to catch up with the rest of the group and slide into place. Ingo and Spanger were at the front, followed by Coco and Friedemann, then Viktor and finally Dana.

The passage they were hurrying through had been carved out by hand, supported in some places by brick or concrete with rusty iron wires protruding from where the material had been chipped off. The reinforced concrete looked as if the expansion had been undertaken at the end of the nineteenth century – at the earliest.

'This won't have been a mine.' Viktor occasionally stooped to place a signal-booster on the ground, checking each to ensure its diodes were blinking obediently and that he could still hear van Dam. 'Any ideas, Professor?'

'It's not built on any sort of mining structure, not even a mediaeval one. I don't even know what you'd be able to mine here anyway. I'm guessing it used to be some sort of hiding place for smugglers,' Friedemann explained. 'Or perhaps an attempt at a home-made bunker system in the event of Germany being overrun during a war – a precursor to the survivalist movement, if you will.'

Their march was taking them ever deeper into the system. They occasionally came across forks in the tunnel, where they left it up to Coco to decide which path they should take. All the while there were no clear signs or marks on the wall, they were happy to follow the medium's expertise.

'I'm receiving Anna-Lena's signal loud and clear,' she whispered, running forward purposefully, clutching her pendulum in an outstretched hand. 'She's still alive. Yes, I can definitely sense it.'

Ingo threw her the occasional sceptical glance, but she ignored him and he stayed silent. He didn't have the heart to crush her spirits.

Viktor could not help but notice when Friedemann briefly switched off his helmet camera and furtively pulled out his worn notebook from under his Kevlar vest. He was about to start leafing through it when Ingo suddenly stopped in his tracks. Friedemann hastily put it back. 'What is it?'

'Just a sec. I need to get a few things out of my rucksack.' The parapsychologist moved towards Viktor, rummaged around in his backpack and pulled out a tablet and what looked like some gauges. He connected a few wires, then plugged them into the tablet in order. 'This way I can read the results in real time.' With the press of a button he turned on the entire contraption. 'Just in case we need a bit of science.' He studied the display closely.

Spanger watched him, holding his pistol in his right hand. 'What are you measuring?'

'Spanger, keep moving forward,' Dana was hissing when a loud crash erupted, like a heavy door being slammed, or maybe something ramming into a steel bulkhead. The threatening rumble that rolled through the passage and echoed all around them was closely followed by a strong breeze.

Dana immediately dropped to one knee and spun around, ready to fire, while Viktor readied his own G36.

The gauges emitted a series of warning beeps, then fell silent a few seconds later. Ingo stared at the display, babbling something about 'an anomaly' and 'physically impossible', neither of which statements Viktor liked one little bit. It was a fact that 'impossibilities' always spelled trouble. A great deal of trouble.

'A rockslide?' Spanger's face was creased in puzzlement.

'No, it sounded more like . . . a door,' said Friedemann in alarm. 'Or like the sort of large gate you'd find at the entrance to a city. Most unusual.'

'Unusual indeed,' added Ingo distractedly, his gaze still fixed on his readouts.

'There,' whispered Coco. 'Look at that!' She looked at her hand in amazement: the pendulum was floating horizontally in the air, pulling against the chain in an apparent attempt to drag the woman further along the passage.

'How are you doing that?' Ingo lowered his voice so only she could hear him and added, 'Is this some new trick of yours?'

Coco shook her head, her eyes wide with wonder and amazement, as if this were the first time she had truly believed that she actually had clairvoyant abilities.

Friedemann gave a satisfied smile. One hand was resting on the Kevlar vest with his notebook underneath. 'We're spot on,' he whispered delightedly. 'Onwards!'

*

Walter van Dam sat in front of a triptych of monitors, looking over the various helmet-camera feeds. The booming crash that sounded as if someone were banging down the gates of the underworld had made him sit up and take notice.

'Professor Friedemann, what was that?' he asked anxiously. 'What's going on down there?'

'We don't know yet,' he replied, his voice distorted, 'but we've picked up a clear trace of your daughter, thanks to Ms Fendi.'

'If that was a gate or something,' Spanger called out from the background, 'it must be enormous. Why on earth would there be something like that down here?'

'Ingo, have you seen this? The pendulum! It's standing . . . horizontally!' Coco was wittering away, still acting as if this were the first time her gift had ever actually worked.

Van Dam poured himself a drink. 'Well, get on with it then,' he demanded. 'Don't just stand there. Find my daughter.'

'We're going, we're going,' announced Viktor.

'Good – now hurry up.' Van Dam sounded anything but reassured.

Viktor was at the front, his rifle locked and loaded, while Dana stalked along beside him, their helmet lamps lurching from side to side. They could not see anything dangerous in the passageway and the commotion surrounding the loud rumbling had abated.

But they had not forgotten about it.

Ingo, Coco and Friedemann followed, with Spanger

bringing up the rear. The doctor was carrying his gauges, occasionally stealing a quick glance at them. The pace of the group had increased as they trudged along in silence, the only sounds coming from the stamping of their boots and the jingling of Ingo's equipment.

'You're a free-climber then?' Viktor muttered to Dana, who was advancing in the manner of a well-trained soldier. Catching a glimpse of her beside him, he was struck by an image from a very long time ago – and it was at that moment that he remembered where they had met before. 'And a martial arts expert to boot. And a gun-club member. What kind of gun club? It must have been where you—?'

'Not the time,' she growled without looking at him.

'On the contrary.'

She looked at him closely. 'What's with all the questions?'

'As I said, I've seen you before somewhere.' Viktor returned her gaze. 'In Darfur. A report on military reconnaissance that had nothing whatsoever to do with free-climbing. Tell me I'm wrong.'

Dana narrowed her eyes. 'What were you doing in Darfur?'

'I didn't say I was there.'

'But you had access to reports – so you're not just a free-climber either, then, are you?' Dana did not like where this conversation was heading. 'I've got a twin sister who's a mercenary. Not that we get confused for each other much, though.'

Viktor was not prepared to be shaken off that easily. 'I don't know what kind of game you're—'

They both stopped abruptly, their faces wide with amazement at the scene before them.

'What it is?' Friedemann asked from behind them.

'Stop! I'll get some more light.' Viktor removed a flare from his belt, lit it and threw it into the enormous chamber opening out in front of them at the end of the passage. 'I want to have a better look before we go in.'

Dana hurled a second from behind him.

A barren, cavernous room with markings scrawled all over the walls was illuminated in deep red by the hissing, smoking light emanating from the flares. All manner of inscriptions, scribbled notes, arrows, signs and scratched messages could just about be made out, as well as broken pieces of iron and the destroyed remnants of at least one skeleton.

Viktor could see a dead man on the ground. In contrast to the man on the ledge earlier, he was wearing camouflage gear and armour and had a sub-machine gun lying next to him.

Behind him stood five doors embedded into the rock face. They were made of wood and stone, with both old and new markings alike etched onto them. The three doors in the middle had door knockers in the shape of a ring, the second one of which was broken. The two outermost doors were equipped with large box locks. A thickly drawn question mark could be seen on each of the first three doors; the fourth door had an X on it and the last bore an exclamation mark. They were all painted on with red lipstick, and when Viktor touched one of the symbols, he found the lines were fresh and still a little moist.

'What's all *this*?' Spanger exclaimed in disbelief. '*Doors?*'

'Looks like it,' replied Viktor. 'So what's the plan, Professor?'

'We should probably ask our medium.' Friedemann joined them at the front. 'It's beautiful, isn't it? They really are fine specimens.' His gaze drifted to the door in the centre, the one which bore a red question mark. 'That's where the vandals were holing up.' He pointed to the door on the left. 'What a pity the ring has been destroyed – it can't be used any more.'

Dana and Viktor exchanged glances once more. The fact that a geologist was looking at doors as if he had just discovered an extra-terrestrial stalagmite seemed more than a little peculiar to them.

'Doors? In a cave?' Ingo squeezed his way between them into the entrance and was babbling away as if the dead man were not there at all. 'How fantastic! A mystery – I love mysteries. Let's have a closer look.'

'Definitely,' said Coco, exhilaration filling her voice, holding the chain with the energised pendulum firmly between her fingers. 'Anna-Lena is very close by!' She took a step inside the chamber.

Ingo held tightly to her harness.

Only then did Coco spot the dead man with his torn throat. She uttered a low cry. 'By the spirits of the beyond!' She almost let go of the chain. 'Why didn't any of you warn me?' She could not take her eyes off the corpse. Her enthusiasm for their task and this place was fading more and more with every heartbeat. 'I . . . I think I'd rather go back up.'

The flares suddenly rose into the air, along with everything else in the chamber. The sextet looked on in silence: for reasons beyond them all, it looked like gravity had suddenly stopped. Ingo's equipment once again began to emit loud warning sounds.

A young woman entered the foreground, floating up from behind the upside-down armoured corpse; she had apparently been lying against the wall in the man's shadow. Her long red hair enveloped her like a gently blazing flame; her nose piercing and a single earring sparkled in the red glow. She was wearing a badly torn ball gown and high-heeled shoes. Her eyes were closed and her arms and legs were relaxed as if she were underwater.

'There,' Dana shouted, 'that's her – Anna-Lena!'

'Should we go in and get her?' Viktor looked at Friedemann. 'What do you think, Professor?'

The flares, corpse, Anna-Lena and everything else fell back to the ground.

'What ... what was that?' Viktor turned to face the parapsychologist in amazement.

'Not ghosts, that's for sure.' Ingo swiped the display of his tablet. 'That was a—'

Friedemann interrupted him. 'Well, it's stopped now, so we can go and investigate,' he announced, as if this were the sort of thing he encountered all the time on his field trips. 'If your little gadgets pick up anything dangerous again, let us know, Doctor. Let's go and get Miss van Dam out of there.'

The group advanced slowly, plunging into the flickering red light and smoke cast by the flares. Friedemann instructed Viktor and Dana to tend to the young woman lying on the ground next to the dead body; her limbs were somewhat contorted after the fall. 'Doctor, keep an eye on everything else. Make a record of what we've found here. *Everything*. I want to have a look around in peace.'

'Really? Why?' Spanger took a step back towards the passage.

'Because it's all rather exciting.' The professor sidled up next to Dana and Viktor as they were examining Anna-Lena. Looking at Spanger, he muttered, 'You wouldn't understand anyway.'

'Nothing looks to be broken at first glance, nor are there any external injuries,' Dana announced as she lifted the young woman's eyelids and shone a light into her eyes. 'Pulse normal, but no pupil reaction.'

'God, Anna-Lena!' They could hear van Dam's relieved voice. 'Come on, get up – now!'

'Just a moment. We've got to make sure she's physically capable of surviving the journey back,' Dana replied resolutely as she carried on checking the girl over.

Ingo turned off his gauges and pulled out a camera. 'I've never seen anything like this before – not during any of my investigations! Gravity reversal? That's impossible – well, usually.' He began to take endless photographs of the doors, the inscriptions and the symbols. 'You can clearly see magical formulae in the graffiti – some look as if they're hundreds of years old,' he continued enthusiastically. 'Look: there's cuneiform, hieroglyphics, ancient Greek, Persian . . .' He could hardly contain his excitement. 'It's quite possible that our little anomaly had something to do with these.'

Viktor saw Friedemann pulling out his notebook and caught a glimpse of his first entry: *Arc Project // Arkus // Arcus.*

The professor started leafing through it, comparing the markings on the pages with the inscriptions on the doors. Some of them matched.

'I'm here if anyone needs me.' Spanger remained near the entrance, strapped into his harness.

Viktor decided to confront Friedemann about his book later, instead choosing to have a look around. 'Who the hell would build doors in a place like this?'

'What I find far more impressive is their condition and distinctiveness,' Ingo added happily. 'These doors are all from different centuries. The symbols on them . . . are . . . I mean, some of them, well, I don't even know what they're supposed to be. I'm not talking about all the scribbling that's been added later, but what the creators of these doors actually inscribed themselves.'

Spanger had changed his mind. He walked over to the armoured dead man, took his gun from him and began to search his body. 'Sub-machine gun. H&K, MP5, nine millimetre,' he shouted over to the group, adding, 'See? I'm not completely useless.'

'You could learn that just by playing a first-person shooter.' Dana looked at Viktor and raised her eyebrows in triumph. It was this weapon that had most likely done for Underpants Man. The boots belonging to the two dead men were identical in design and tread pattern.

'But he's got nothing on him – no badges or papers or anything. Looks like he could be part of some sort of special unit.' Spanger bent down to examine the wound on the man's neck more carefully. 'Throat slit.' He pointed to the empty sheath. 'And his knife's missing.'

'These your people, van Dam?' radioed Dana after finishing her examination of the unconscious woman.

'I'll tell you again, I haven't sent out another team. Now bring me back my little girl,' he ordered, putting down his glass. 'Tell me, Mr Troneg, have you made sure to put all the boosters down? The picture has suddenly gone all fuzzy and I can barely hear you at all.'

'I have, Mr van Dam,' Viktor replied.

'That sort of thing can be triggered by magnetic fields and radiation,' said Ingo, who was standing next to his equipment and looking at the display on his tablet. 'Oh my God – my devices are going haywire again. I can see . . . measurable differences in the magnetic field and so forth. The gravitational pull is slowly decreasing. A little more and we'll start to feel it.'

'Or it could be a jammer,' said Dana. 'Or someone's found one of our boosters and switched it off. We need to get a move-on. Van Dam, your daughter is in a good enough state for us to bring her out.' She looked at Viktor. 'You can carry her.'

Viktor handed his rucksack to Coco, who in turn handed it to Ingo, and picked up the young woman. He could not believe how light she was – surely no more than seven and a half stone. He laid her gently over his shoulder.

'Pack up your stuff, Doctor,' Friedemann ordered. 'We're leaving.'

Coco looked at her golden pendulum, which was

showing no inclination towards the younger van Dam but was instead pointing at the doors. 'That's ... odd.'

'Your pendulum must be wrong,' said Ingo, giving her a look to suggest the show was over before he turned back to his gauges and stuffed them into his backpack.

'It can't be.' Coco looked at the doors. 'There are more secrets through there.' She looked at the corpse and shuddered. 'Probably for the best that we're not going to be the ones to investigate them.' She put her pendulum away.

'Right, let's go.' Friedemann shooed Spanger forwards with a wave of his hand. 'We've found what we were looking for.' He gave the doors a curious look.

Viktor thought it was almost as if he had really been there for them and not for the young woman.

The group made their way back through the passages by the light of their helmet lamps. The place was silent, making it feel all the more depressing.

Where are you going? said a voice that appeared to be inside Coco's head. *Stay a while longer.*

She slowed down, prompting Ingo to give her a nudge. She began to shiver all over. 'Can you hear that too?'

He can't hear me. I thought I was talking to you. You're rather special, you know, said the sombre voice. *What if I were to kill the others? Would you stay then?*

Coco felt her throat tightening. 'No,' she whispered.

'No?' Ingo looked at her, confused.

We could have ever so much fun, Beate. That is your name, after all. Or would you rather I called you Coco?

She didn't know what she could say that the unknown voice would not consider as a challenge.

Suddenly her mind was flooded with images: a dog-like beast pouncing on and slaughtering the group; an armed unit that wanted to attack and kill them; a monster made of smoke stabbing them with burning blades. A mounted unit riding into a mediaeval battle, followed by drones chasing their group through an unknown city, and finally a man in an American Second World War uniform with his gun raised, aiming the barrel at her face – and pulling the trigger.

Coco's mouth opened into a scream – and everything around her disappeared.

She found herself standing back in front of the five doors.

They were opening and closing, opening and closing, opening and closing, incessantly. They roared and rattled, creating a loud rumble that shook the walls. Scree and stones tumbled down, crashing onto the ground. Blood poured out of the first door, hissing with steam, while liquid fire rushed out of another, with the one next to it producing some sort of acid that mixed with the scattered pieces of bone that came coursing out of the door along-side it; from the final door came piles of putrid entrails. The hellish conglomeration seized Coco and dragged her below the surface.

The decaying corpses of Ingo, Friedemann, Spanger, Viktor and Dana danced around her, their clawed hands striking her. Their shrill, screeching laughter shook her to her core.

'We're dying in this cave,' they sang. 'We're dying! And you didn't warn us – that's why we're going to kill you!

We're going to kill you!' The five of them then threw themselves onto the clairvoyant and opened their jaws as wide as possible.

Coco began to burn, her body dissolved by the acid as she suffocated, while the drifting bones crushed her. As the group feasted upon her flesh and tore her to pieces, she somehow found the strength to utter the loud cry of anguish that had been stuck in her lungs.

The illusion was shattered immediately.

Panting, she stumbled through the passage in front of Ingo, barely able to stay upright on her trembling legs. Fear constricted her heart as the beams from the helmet lights danced in front of her eyes in double vision.

'Everything all right?' Ingo had spotted that something was amiss. 'What's wrong? Pins and needles?'

Coco didn't dare to speak. Horror had paralysed her voice. She was certain that death would fall upon her the moment she made a peep. How was she suddenly able to see these visions? Should she ever manage to escape from this place, she would never step foot in it again.

'Well, that was easy.' Spanger felt heroic when he held the sub-machine gun, just as he had always wanted – maybe not exactly like Tony Stark, but like a man who had done a good deed. It did not concern him in the slightest that their task had been so easy, or that they had found a dead body. If they should happen to stumble upon any enemies, he was ready: ready to pull the trigger and become even more of a hero. 'What was it killed the other bloke?'

'Let's hope we don't have to find out.' Dana was keeping a close eye on their surroundings. The cones of light rendered them easy targets, which was making her rather uneasy. A decent marksman would simply have to aim just beneath the light and it would all be over.

'Oh, I'm sure we can handle it.' Spanger fiddled with the safety catch. 'We're pros.'

'You certainly are,' remarked Friedemann.

'Didn't we say you were going to be a bit nicer to me?'

'Calm down,' Viktor urged them. 'Even if every man and his dog can see us, that doesn't mean we have make a racket the entire way back.'

His reminder had the desired effect: silence descended upon the team.

Ingo kept looking at the recordings from his measurements, trusting that they were all correct. What other experiments could he do in the hall with the doors? Where did the volatile gravity come from? The dead body made him uneasy, but scientific curiosity pushed those doubts to one side. He had already made up his mind that with another, more appropriate team and van Dam's permission, he would return and astonish mankind with what he had discovered.

Ingo didn't know he wasn't the only one with that idea, though.

'Don't dawdle,' Dana hissed at him. 'You can marvel over your findings once we've reached the surface.'

After a short while they arrived back at the platform.

'Good,' came Friedemann's voice. 'We're nearly there – now we just need to cross.'

They secured the helpless Anna-Lena to the rusty cable and began to make their way back through the darkness, moving forwards in silence until they could see the entrance in the glow of their helmet lamps. One after the other, they arrived in the basement.

As easy as their task had been, and as pleased as he was to have found the missing woman so quickly, Viktor thought their mission had been entirely surreal. If you ignored the abnormalities such as the sudden changes of gravity and the two dead bodies, it had been a walk in the park. It wasn't that he had been looking forward to a shoot-out, but he thought it curious that they hadn't encountered a single serious problem. A bunch of Boy Scouts could have saved the young woman, as indeed could the first military unit who had been sent out. Or was this all some kind of a test?

Viktor carried the unconscious woman up the stone steps and onto the ground floor of the villa, where the chauffeur was waiting for them. They assumed van Dam had informed Matthias of their return.

'I've already re-configured the seating in the car,' Matthias explained, adjusting his cap. 'We can get going straight away.' They hurried through the rooms towards the exit. The chauffeur handed Spanger the spare key for the Rolls-Royce. 'I don't suppose you'd be able to take this back?'

'You're kidding!' Spanger grinned. This was the first time he had ever been allowed to drive a luxury car like this.

'Don't you want to call an ambulance?' Dana said over the radio to her employer. 'I don't know whether she's got any internal injuries tha—'

'No publicity,' van Dam interrupted. 'I've arranged for

a team of specialists to come to my house and examine my daughter thoroughly. Then we can decide what to do next.'

When they reached the exit, Coco wanted to weep with happiness. The black Mercedes was parked with its side door open; as Matthias had said, the seats had been joined together to create a large flat surface in the middle.

'Thank you all once again,' said van Dam through their earpieces. 'You will of course each receive your rewards, as promised. Ms Rentski and Mr von Troneg, you'll go with Matthias, while the rest of you can take the Rolls.'

Not a test, then, Viktor thought with a shrug, his mood improving. He laid Anna-Lena onto the seats and shuffled back to allow Matthias to fasten her seatbelt. Relief suddenly washed over him. 'Good job we managed to find her so quickly.' Saving a human life was a wonderful feeling. He could not resist shaking hands with everyone in the group and congratulating them on a job well done. 'I think you'll find we've done rather well here.'

That same joy was clear onto the faces of his comrades too.

'Easy money, that.' Spanger said callously as he fiddled with the key to the Rolls-Royce. 'A million, right? All for just under three hours' work.'

Coco was standing next to Ingo, who was busy checking the measurements on his displays. 'Yes, but what's the explanation for all this?' She felt liberated; the tremor in her hands had abated.

'There isn't one.' Ingo looked excited. 'Mr van Dam, may

I go back down and have a look around? These physical phenomena are crying out for proper, in-depth research.'

'No way. Nothing can make me go back down that hole again,' Coco said quickly, putting down the equipment. 'It's not a good aura at all. Whoever it was who built that place and those doors – they did *not* have good intentions.' She left out telling them about the voice, her vision and her terror.

'I'd like to join Doctor Theobald,' Friedemann interjected. 'These geological structures are quite unique. As my colleague has said, they absolutely *must* be explored further.'

'Unfortunately, I cannot allow that,' replied their client. 'Let's all just be happy that you've returned to the surface unscathed.'

Dana had also detached herself from the harness. She was trying not to catch Viktor's eye, so as not to jog his memory any more. 'We will need to talk to you about a few things once we're back at your house, Mr van Dam,' she said. 'About what we saw down there.'

'That can be dealt with once you're back with me,' he said. 'What goes on in the caves, stays in the caves. That would be my suggestion. Leave everything else to me and don't allow yourselves to be burdened by it.'

Friedemann glanced back through the front door. Who would try to stop him if he went back down? The chauffeur? He could easily bribe the other five to either go with him or leave him alone. With a bit of cunning he was sure he could convince Theobald to make a second descent. By the time van Dam had found another team to get them back out, he could have explored everything he wanted to. He *had* to. He ventured a first, discreet step back towards the verandah.

'What do you mean by that?' Spanger scratched his back. 'What we saw down there? Do you mean the doors?'

'Mr van Dam!' Matthias picked up his tablet nervously. 'I . . . I don't think this is your daughter.'

The group turned to face the chauffeur, who was sitting next to the supine woman.

'What nonsense is this?' snapped the businessman.

'Her eyes, Mr van Dam.' Matthias turned the tablet around and filmed the sleeping woman with its camera. He carefully opened her eyelids with his thumb and forefinger. 'Can you see that?'

The team all huddled around the car.

'I told you so,' muttered Coco. 'The pendulum – it knew we hadn't found Anna-Lena.' The consequences of this realisation made her heart sink like a stone. They would have to go back.

'Ridiculous,' Ingo whispered to her.

'What about her eyes?' Dana enquired.

'They're blue,' replied Matthias, his face growing pale. 'But Miss van Dam's eyes are . . .'

'Green. She's got green eyes.' Van Dam sounded both startled and anxious at the same time. 'Have you checked she's not wearing contacts?'

'Yes. No lenses.' The chauffeur was continuing to film the girl. 'Even if everything else is identical, Mr van Dam – her figure, her hair, even her jewellery – her eyes tell a different story.'

'Is there anything that could have changed her eye colour?' Spanger threw the keys to the Rolls in the air and caught them. 'Bright light or something?'

'Don't talk rubbish,' Friedemann scolded him. 'You can't change eye colour unless you tattoo the vitreous, but in any case, they wouldn't look like this.' He pushed his way forwards and pulled up the sleeping woman's eyelids to double-check. 'See this, Matthias?'

The chauffeur leaned forwards and swore, then checked the other eye himself. 'Green – they're green again! But I swear they were blue before.'

'This is insane.' Dana looked around at her colleagues.

'Beyond insane.' Coco leaned against Ingo, feeling like she needed human warmth and closeness to ease the ominous feeling inside her. Someone she trusted.

'There's only one thing for it.' Van Dam's voice over the radio sounded agitated. 'You'll have to go back down and look for her. Your job is not complete. I need to know for certain.'

'What are we going to do with ... this person?' Dana looked at the sleeping woman. It could still be van Dam's daughter, or someone else altogether.

'Matthias will bring her to me,' the businessman decided. 'I'll have her examined and looked after. In the meantime please find Anna-Lena – *my* Anna-Lena, not this copy or whatever she is.'

'You could always try a DNA test.' Viktor recognised the feeling that had crept up on him. In a matter of seconds his feeling of safety had turned into the very opposite. 'It could still be that this is your daughter,' he pointed out.

'Who knows what happened to her in those caves? There were all sorts of strange things going on down there.'

But Matthias was already reaching out to reclaim the key from Spanger. 'Understood, Mr van Dam. I'll bring the woman to you in the Rolls. The Mercedes will have to stay here because it's got the internet connection.'

'I've got a question.' Spanger handed him the key. 'We will get a million for this one? *Another* million, that is? I mean, technically, we've already got your daughter so—'

'Come on, let's go,' the professor interrupted. 'You're an embarrassment to even ask that.' Friedemann was secretly cheering to himself. He now had a legitimate excuse to descend into the cave again.

'Quite right,' Dana confirmed, putting her own gear back on.

'I don't want to go back down there.' Coco looked at Ingo. 'I'm serious. There's something waiting for us.'

'No, no, it's just a bit of wonky physics.' He patted his instruments. 'And we'll find the real missing girl in no time at all. Just like before. Your pendulum seems to know where she is.'

Coco couldn't detect any mockery in his voice. 'But there's still the small matter of the dead man with his throat torn out. And whoever it was who killed him.' She climbed into her harness as if in slow motion. She still couldn't bring herself to talk about that voice, or her vision. 'It's waiting for us.'

'Nothing's going to happen to us.' Ingo too was looking forward to another opportunity to take some measurements. 'I'm absolutely certain of it. We've just got to be careful, that's all.'

'Departure, take two.' Friedemann sounded like he was in a good mood. 'We've already been successful once. Now let's go and rescue the real Anna-Lena van Dam. Green eyes, everyone: make sure you remember that.'

Viktor and Dana, communicating with their eyes, checked their weapons. They had still not told anyone about the half-naked dying man with the bolt cutter and bullet wounds they had discovered and they wouldn't, not yet, so as not to put a downer on proceedings.

The group set off again immediately, passing through the estate and back into the cellar, readying themselves to slide along the steel cable to the platform once more.

Coco was close to tears.

The unknown man watched the entire scene outside the villa in peace, reporting every detail to headquarters, along with photographs. He had even been able to follow about half of their conversation by lip-reading.

The group surrounding the professor disappeared back into the house; the chauffeur once again opened the side door of the people carrier and lifted the comatose doppel-gänger, carried her over to the Rolls-Royce and laid her down on the back seat.

This time, along with acknowledgement of receipt of his report, he received an order:

IMMEDIATE ELIMINATION OF ALL PARTICIPANTS.
EVEN THE UNCONSCIOUS ONE.

The man closed his laptop and placed it on the passenger seat. He started the BMW and drove along the approach road to the abandoned house, then intentionally stalled. He wanted his arrival noticed.

The chauffeur promptly stepped back from the Rolls and closed the door. He looked at the BMW curiously as it rolled across the fine gravel with a soft crunch.

The unknown man took out a slim boning knife from the glove box. The price tag was still on it – he had bought it after he'd arrived, knowing he would have no chance of getting his own weapons through airport security. With a practised movement he slid it inside his sleeve, then got out of the car and walked towards the dilapidated mansion.

'This is private property,' Matthias called out to him, pointing back down the drive. 'You need to leave immediately.'

'Please excuse me. I've just had a technology omnifuck-up. First my satnav sent me the wrong way and now my rental car has given out on me. It's a good job there's someone here.' The man approached, smiling. 'I don't suppose you could lend me your phone so I can call for breakdown assistance?'

'Ah, understood.' Matthias sighed and briefly looked over at the Rolls to check the woman, but she was still unconscious. Then he removed a packet of cigarettes from his dark blue uniform. 'What's up with your car? Might be quicker if I just help you.' He lit a cigarette and proffered the pack to him. 'I know what I'm doing.'

The man took a step closer. 'I'm afraid with this kind you need a diagnostic computer to make any headway. The curse of the modern world.' He refused the cigarette. 'Bit of an odd set-up for such a deserted place. Nothing illegal, I'm sure?' He grinned to show Matthias he was joking.

'We're in the process of selling the house. Someone's having a viewing.'

'Luckily for me.'

'You could say that.' Matthias felt for his phone inside his pocket. 'Here, go ahead. But I can still try to have a look under the bonnet for you.'

'By all means.' The man's movements suddenly became clumsy as he took the phone. It slipped out of his fingers and landed on the gravel. 'Oh – forgive me! I'm so sorry. I hope your phone's not broken.'

Matthias didn't allow his irritation to show, instead flicking away his half-finished cigarette and bending to pick up the phone.

The man drew the knife out of his sleeve and held it over the chauffeur's exposed neck.

Matthias saw his attacker's shadow with a blade in his hand and quickly turned, his arm raised to defend himself.

Contrary to what Coco had feared, the group travelled the same way through the labyrinth without incident, arriving unmolested at the cavernous chamber with the five doors. Her pulse was racing and she was sweating with fear.

Dana and Viktor once again lit two flares to give them some light, then began to discuss the plan with Friedemann.

'I'm an idiot. I should have brought another G36 with me.' Spanger looked at the sub-machine gun next to the dead man. 'Now I've got to make do with this child's toy.'

Ingo had unpacked his instruments again and was paying close attention to their displays. 'There it is again,' he said with fascination. 'The first tiny deviations.'

Coco walked slowly past the doors, the golden pendulum in her hand. She felt sick. This whole place was dripping with danger. She would not be staying a second longer than necessary, that was for sure. With each passing moment she expected to hear the voice, to see the visions – to be exposed to that same mental torture again.

And that was not forgetting Anna-Lena's doppelgänger with the wrong eyes. Who knew what sort of being they had brought to the surface?

'It's getting stronger,' she announced with simultaneous awe and anxiety. She could hardly stand it; her skin was itchy and prickly. 'You can do the rest yourselves. I've got to get out of this godforsaken hole!'

'Sorry?' Friedemann gave her a look of consternation. 'And how exactly do you propose to do that?' He was holding his notebook in his hand again, consulting it from time to time as he examined the door frames.

'Ms Fendi,' came van Dam's voice in her ear, 'only you can hear me now. I beg you, please stay with the group. I have confidence in your powers. It may well be that the team will find itself in a situation where only your abilities can help them! You saw what happened to the torches before.'

Coco placed her hand over the microphone so that the only sound was the one transmitted through the helmet speakers. 'There's a dead man down here, Mr van Dam. A dead man and something that . . . that wants to kill us. That was not part of the agreement.'

'I'll pay you two hundred thousand euros extra,' he replied. 'The others are watching you, Ms Fendi.'

Coco cleared her throat. 'Mr van Dam, I . . .'

'Nothing's going to happen to you. Think about my daughter, please!'

His heartbroken appeal softened her slightly and she was about to agree when she remembered the cruel voice in the passage. 'You don't understand – you couldn't, not without feeling what I felt.'

'I'm begging you. Without you, my daughter doesn't stand a chance!'

Her sense of duty calmed her fears and drowned out the voices imploring her to turn back. 'All right. I will.' She turned to face the doors so as not to have to look at the man's remains. 'I'll take you at your word, Mr van Dam.'

'Right, we're all here. What are you picking up, Ms Fendi?' Viktor turned to look at the medium. 'Where's our missing girl?'

Coco paused in front of the fourth door, the one bearing the red cross marked in lipstick. The pendulum was standing out from the chain, facing forwards like a pointer. 'Behind this one.' She placed a hand on the enormous handle and tried to pull it, but nothing happened. Shaking didn't help either, nor did leaning on it with all her strength. She took a deep breath. 'By the grandfathers of the four elements . . .' she said, starting an incantation.

'Slow down,' called out Spanger in alarm. 'Who knows what's behind—?'

'*She's*. Behind. It!' Coco's face bore a strange expression.

'By the grandfathers of the four elements . . .' she began again, her voice drifting away into a quiet invocation.

Friedemann put his notebook away, this time stuffing it into a trouser pocket in order to retrieve it more quickly next time. 'No. She's not.' He walked purposefully towards the door on the far left, which also had its knocker intact. 'We'll find her here. There's an arrow on the ground I recognise—'

'Hang on.' Spanger was shining his light at a glimmering spot on the floor that was reflecting the light. 'There: a diamond earring!' The piece of jewellery was lying in front of the furthest door, which had a heavy mediaeval drawbar and a thick box lock. It was this door that had the exclamation mark painted on it. 'Our little van Dam was wearing a pair just like this in the photo in our files.' He looked from Friedemann to Coco and back again. 'What if you're both wrong and she's behind this one?'

Walter van Dam sat enthralled in front of the triptych of monitors, watching what was happening underground with increasing agitation.

Then he noticed that one of the split screens on the right-hand display was black; he frowned with concern. This was not linked to one of the team's helmet cameras, but rather to Matthias' tablet.

He picked up his phone and called his chauffeur, who was supposed to be on his way with Anna-Lena's double.

It rang.

And rang.

And rang.

The fact that Matthias was not answering made him nervous. He poured himself another drink. His nerves shot to pieces by this rollercoaster ride, he had long since replaced water with whisky. Earlier, when they'd announced they'd found Anna-Lena, he had been so happy, but now his anxiety was increasing with every breath. 'Where is my daughter?' he asked again.

'We need to clarify what's going on first, Mr van Dam,' said Viktor. His words were all distorted.

'Unfortunately, there are three possibilities for where your Anna-Lena might be,' radioed Friedemann, who sounded no less distorted than Viktor. The transmission from the cave system must be more or less at its limit. 'Any decision we make could be the wrong one – or the right one.'

'What about the other two?' Van Dam rubbed his moustache frantically.

'We'll check those once we've ruled out the others,' said the professor.

'Show me these doors, Mr von Troneg,' van Dam asked. He would have liked to send Matthias to check the Wi-Fi connection and the Mercedes' built-in modem.

Viktor filmed the doors, which van Dam enlarged on the second screen, and explained the three clues to him. 'Have you seen this before?' he asked. The connection was becoming worse with every word he spoke. 'Anything that could help us?'

Van Dam did not answer but clicked and zoomed in on the feed, took snapshots of all the details and fanned them out on the third monitor to get a better overview.

Then he stared closely at the symbols.

Looking at them caused vivid memories to flood into his mind: memories he would have sooner never returned to. He could still recall his mother's words – and what she had begged of him in her declining years. He had never had the opportunity to carry out her final wishes, and after her death – until this moment – he had all but forgotten about them. He had added Theobald to the group without really believing that his parapsychological knowledge would ever be required – like a parachute you hoped never to have to use. It had come from just a feeling, nothing more, one whose origins lay in the past, indefinable, yet compelling.

'Van Dam?' Viktor's voice was now almost entirely drowned out by a loud humming noise.

Then van Dam heard him say, 'Professor, the signal's gone. He can't hear me any more. What shall we do? Which door do you think we should take?'

Van Dam rose unsteadily and hurried to his shelves. He searched through the books until he finally found the old tome he was looking for, along with the collection of loose papers that had belonged to his grandfather. He removed it and returned to his desk, then put it down and opened it.

Dozens of old drawings of doors were depicted on the fragile, stained pages, and they all had dates and cryptic markings drawn alongside them. He flicked through the sheaf until he found exactly the five doors he had seen on the third screen. The year '1921' was written next to it.

'It cannot be!' he exclaimed.

'Mr van Dam? What did you say?' he could hear Viktor asking. 'If there's anything you know that could help us, please tell us. We need to decide which door to go through first to find your daughter. We can't agree. Do you understand? Any clue you could give us will allow us to find your daughter faster.'

'One moment, Mr von Troneg.' He wanted to make absolutely certain. In a matter of seconds he had compared the symbols on the monitor with the sketches and illustrations in the book and there was little doubt that he was on the right page. Then he noticed a door knocker missing on one of the doors that he had filmed. If his daughter had gone through that one, the consequences would be devastating.

A notification popped up on his computer alerting him to a new email from Professor Friedemann. In the subject line he was asking precisely what time he would be picked up from Frankfurt Airport.

At first van Dam thought it was a delayed message, for the geologist was now roaming around underground looking for Anna-Lena, then he saw the time at which the email had been sent: two minutes ago.

That was surely impossible. But he'd deal with that later; right now he had more urgent matters to attend to.

'Listen to me, Mr von Troneg.' Van Dam propped his head on his hands and fixed his eyes on the descriptions written underneath each door. 'I—'

With a crack the connection died. The monitors went blank and the sound cut out.

'No!' Van Dam stared at the black displays.

Viktor looked at the third, fourth and fifth doors, each representing one of the three most likely possibilities for where to find Anna-Lena, knowing they were running out of time.

Ingo was calibrating his devices in an attempt to update his measurements. He raised his eyebrows as he read the latest results. 'Unbelievable. This . . . this trumps everything else I've seen so far. As we speak, the gravitational values are changing – they're already slightly above the norm. There are enough physical anomalies down here to keep an entire institute busy!'

'We could split up,' Viktor suggested, 'into two teams.'

'No,' said Dana, pointing to the dead man with his slit throat. 'It's far too dangerous for that. We've got to stay together.' She looked at Friedemann. 'You're leading this mission. Make a decision.'

All of Friedemann's earlier certainty suddenly vanished. He stood stock-still in front of the door he had chosen before – the one with the barely visible arrow drawn in the dust – while Spanger bent down to pick up the diamond earring and Coco, muttering incessantly to herself, struggled to control the pendulum tugging on her chain.

'Professor?' Viktor's anxiety was growing. Should they go through the door with the X, or the door with the question mark and the knocker, or the door with the exclamation mark and the antique box lock?

'Tell us where to go, Professor.'

CHAPTER IV

'I'm absolutely certain of my choice, Professor.' Coco looked at the hovering pendulum, which was still tugging at the chain and vibrating softly.

'Just because that's the only door with an X drawn on it? Isn't that a bit too obvious?' Friedemann was standing in front of the middle of the five doors – the one with the red question mark on it – which still had its knocker intact. He pointed at it. 'This is the one.'

The door was made of three different materials; the blackened iron, white wood and copper had been joined together in thin strips to create an interplay of colours. The bronze knocker resembled a grotesque lion's head. Ornaments had been drawn onto the forehead, cheeks and teeth, though the striking plate, made of white metal, was simple and unadorned.

Ingo took Coco's side. 'How have you arrived at that conclusion? And since when have geologists been experts in mysticism?' He had built his instruments into a block that was relatively easy to carry, so as not to have to constantly rebuild it every time they stopped.

Friedemann laughed. 'Oh, you'd be surprised.'

'What do you mean by that?' Coco arched her perfectly plucked eyebrows.

'Surprised at how many places of worship are underground. There are more than just crypts and sepulchres to be found.' Friedemann gestured around the enormous chamber, the reddish light making him look like a self-satisfied demon who had lured them all into his trap. 'What do you think we've got here?' It's certainly not a collection of doors made by an elderly hobbyist looking for an excuse to get away from his wife. Someone knew *exactly* what they were doing.'

Ingo loosened the chin strap of his helmet. 'And this isn't the first time you've seen something like this.'

Friedemann smiled and laid a hand on the broken knocker. 'No, it's not. I once stumbled upon a mysterious door while exploring a cave system.' He pointed to the symbols on the door in the middle. 'It had the same markings.'

Coco stared at the moving gold pendulum, spellbound. 'But ... I can see it reacting to the door with the X – as soon as I think about the missing woman, that is.' She looked uncertainly at Ingo.

'What happened with the door you came across last time?' he asked the professor.

'It brought us back to the surface.'

'What a surprise,' Spanger remarked. He stood in front of the furthermost door, the one with the exclamation mark on it. This was where he had found Anna-Lena's earring: he was convinced the missing girl was behind this one, no matter how clever the professor was or what his game was.

Viktor was following their discussion attentively. He had not expected the geologist to be a connoisseur of these sorts of situations, but it did explain why he had been assigned as their leader.

Dana was divesting herself of any responsibility for the decision. She had positioned herself at the entrance to the hall, ready to face down any surprises that might be lurking in the darkness beyond.

Friedemann gave the lion's mouth on the middle door an almost delicate caress. 'You're quite right it was a surprise. We were about a mile below the surface at the time. And the miracle is repeating itself down here. I'm sure of it.'

'How?' Spanger enquired. 'Was there a lift behind it?'

Friedemann shook his head.

'I've . . . heard of those. Doors that . . . lead to nothing.' Ingo looked at his gauges and their displays. 'But I haven't been able to verify any of these stories to date. Every investigation I've ever undertaken has drawn a blank. Just like with . . . ghosts.' He began to fiddle with the buttons while staring at the displays.

'To nothing. Or to the surface.' Friedemann was convinced he had chosen the correct passage. 'Or wherever else.'

Coco remained stubbornly in front of the door with the X on it. 'I still don't understand, Professor, why you think we'll find the girl through there. My pendulum and the energy it's harnessing are all speaking with one voice.' She pointed to the cross drawn in lipstick. 'The supernatural and the laws of physics are in unison here.'

Friedemann shone his lamp onto the floor. A barely discernible arrow had been drawn in the dust; there was a scrap of dark-green cloth lying next to it. 'That's why. Miss van Dam has left us a clue. I think that trumps your pendulum and the earring Spanger found in front of the last door with the box lock.' He called Dana back to the group and laid a hand on the knocker. 'Get ready. We're going in.'

He jerked the middle door open and it swung outwards.

Behind it was revealed: a wall of rock.

Spanger laughed out loud. 'Oh yes. Much better than a pendulum and an earring. I can see that now!'

Dana dropped to one knee and used the light from her helmet lamp to examine the arrow painted in the dirt. 'This looks a bit older to me. Sure this is from Miss van Dam?'

Ingo kept an eye on the readings from his instruments. 'No change in the base radiation levels around us.'

'Well,' said Coco, giving a meaningful look at her pendulum, which was still pulling on the slender chain like a greyhound on a lead, desperate to pass through the door with the X.

I don't understand!' Friedemann closed the middle door and opened it again, but the result was the same. 'It *has* to work.' His third attempt also revealed nothing more than bare rock. 'It was different before!' He slammed it shut in a rage.

Under the impact on the frame, the ring on the front of the door lifted slightly and struck the plate with a very soft ping.

At that very moment something twitched on Ingo's displays. The devices had recorded something: a jump in resonance for energy, temperature and electromagnetic fields. 'There,' shouted Ingo, 'I saw something!' He looked over at the professor with excitement. 'What did you do differently that time?'

'Hm. More force, I'd say.' Friedemann studied the bronze mouth thoughtfully. 'The ring hit the plate on the door.'

Coco held her pendulum more tightly: it had suddenly changed its mind and now turned towards the door in the centre. 'Surely not!' Had the missing woman moved between rooms behind the doors?

'Looks like your cosmic vibrations are playing silly buggers,' Spanger chuckled.

'Why would the door-knocker be the reason?' Viktor tried to catch Ingo's eye. 'Have you got any explanation for that?'

'These caves are full of puzzles. I barely have an explanation for *anything* down here,' the parapsychologist replied. 'I know this might sound unscientific of me, but I'm finding this whole thing rather exciting.'

'Right. So if it's the ring that's making the difference' – Friedemann gripped it tightly – 'that's what we'll try. Doctor, keep a close eye on the readings.'

He slammed the metal hard down onto the plate.

The impact sounded like a hammer hitting a bell, sending the bright chime ringing loudly through the chamber. The three elements on the door began to shine. The white-gold glow also illuminated the other four passages and from there spread out to the furthest corners of the caves. Every note and every symbol written on the walls and carved into the domed ceiling high above them lit up.

The echo resulting from the impact reverberated around,

creating a cacophony of discordant sounds and producing an acoustic anomaly that did not subside, but instead increased in volume.

'This is amazing,' Ingo exclaimed, clapping his hands with wonder at the auditory phenomena around them. His gauges had gone into complete overdrive, apparently unable to handle the glut of new information. 'I don't know what any of this means, but I don't think anyone has ever recorded these sorts of measurements before.'

Viktor covered his ears. The sounds were making his ears ache; he was feeling dizzy and nauseous. The ever-increasing din was making him lose his sense of balance. 'We're going to go deaf if we stay here for much longer,' he shouted – although he could not even hear his own voice. He pointed at the door with the question mark and gave them the military hand signal to move out quickly.

Most of the team looked at him quizzically, as if he had lost his mind.

Dana was the only one who understood. She armed the G36, hauled open the middle door and jumped into the dark room behind it. Light fell out of it a few seconds later.

Friedemann, Coco, Spanger and Ingo were trying to block their ears with their fingers; their faces were distorted with pain and any sense of fascination they might initially have had for the phenomenon had disappeared. The doctor dropped his measuring block and Coco's legs almost gave way. Viktor, thinking quickly and recognising her predicament, managed to get to her in time to hold her up, stopping her from falling. Their mouths moved, but only a lip reader could have understood what they were shouting.

Viktor pushed the other three through the door before joining the end of their small train, which now found itself in a mediaeval groined vault smelling of homemade sauerkraut and beer, damp stone and salt. A few old light-bulbs with visible tungsten filaments provided a warm, yellowy-gold light, so they could see the floor was made of trodden-down sand.

Only when Viktor shut the door did the booming echoes finally dissipate. The lock clicked shut. The silence that descended upon the vault was made all the more profound by the ringing in their ears.

This side of the door bore no similarity to the ornate portal in the hall through which they had fled. Viktor was overcome by a slight sense of panic when he looked for the knocker and failed to see it.

'Jesus Christ,' moaned Spanger. 'That's worse than any alarm system.'

'You've shut the door, Mr Troneg,' said Ingo, who had just noticed he had left his instruments in the hall and immediately regretted having to forego any further experiments for the time being. 'I can't see a door knocker or anything. Will we be able to go back?'

'I told you, these passages are full of surprises.' Friedemann was far less astonished than the rest of the group were; he had expected there to be a few oddities and he was rather disappointed to find himself in just a cellar.

'Of course we'll make it back. I can find a way.' Coco held up her golden pendulum, looking surprised when the chain lost all tension: after all, her compass had been pointing at this door. She looked around, and spotting something glittering on the staircase, said, 'Down there.'

'But what about your pendulum?' Spanger leaned against the wall, which was covered in saltpetre. He had no intention of moving out of the vault. His opinion had been ignored, so now it was up to them to convince him. 'How come it's not telling us anything now?'

'It doesn't have to. Because there' – Coco pointed to the sand on the staircase – 'is the other diamond earring.'

'Good spot, Madame Fendi,' Dana held the G36 loosely, still alert for any danger. 'These doors are a bit of a lucky dip, aren't they? Now, before we go off exploring, does anyone have any idea as to where we might have ended up?' She glanced at Spanger. 'And don't you dare say "a cellar".'

The sound of men and women laughing could suddenly be heard above them, muffled by a door. Tankards were being slammed down onto tables and somebody was singing a song, which in turn got taken up by several more voices. The cheerful congregation were giving a hearty rendition of 'Ich wollt', ich wär' ein Huhn' – *I wish I was a chicken.*

Viktor observed the stacks of beer barrels on one side and even bigger barrels of wine mounted on the other wall. 'Safe to say we've ended up in an inn.' He pointed to the ceiling and the old lightbulb. 'That's from as early as the last war. Then he gestured towards the rotary switch. 'And that's even older.'

'My grandma's got one of those,' Dana added. 'Dangerous

as all hell, but she won't replace it until the cable gives way altogether.'

Viktor opened the plain wooden door they had just come through. It opened into a larder, from where the smells of sauerkraut and salt were emanating. The sliced white cabbage was fermenting in stone barrels, while meat was being preserved underneath mounds of salt in enormous vats. There were tins of fruit lined up in rows on the shelves, with smoked sausages and ham dangling from hooks behind rabbit wire to protect it from vermin. It all looked extremely rustic.

Viktor inspected the wooden door from the other side. It was much more impressive, nestling in a carved frame that was definitely in keeping with the rest of the aesthetic. He heaved a sigh of relief. 'There's a door knocker here,' he said by way of reassurance to the puzzled faces on the other side. 'It's rusty, but it's there.'

'At least we haven't ended up in the Middle Ages.' Spanger shouldered his sub-machine gun. 'I'd happily give that a miss.' He listened to the song and conducted a few bars of the old classic. 'Carnival association. Who else would still be singing a song like that?'

Friedemann observed his five companions. They looked somewhat out of place in their modern outfits. 'We look very conspicuous like this.' He removed his harness. 'Helmets and armour off, everyone.'

Coco and Ingo followed suit, but after removing their own harnesses, Dana, Viktor and Spanger looked undecided.

'Maybe one of us should have a look at what's up there?' Viktor suggested. The Kevlar vest afforded him a certain degree of protection that he was not about to give up. Their weapons might prove useful as well.

'*Fasching* is great fun: if it is carnival, we won't stand out – we can just tell everyone we've come as a special unit,' agreed Spanger. 'But with real guns.'

'I'll do it.' Dana scurried up the stairs and after pressing her ear briefly to the door, she pushed the latch down and slipped through.

The other four waited in silence.

The song changed. The patrons in the nearby room were now singing along to 'Davon geht die Welt nicht unter' – *And still the world doesn't collapse* – with a soloist whose distinctive voice could easily have been mistaken for Zarah Leander, the Swedish actress who'd made the song so famous during the Nazi regime. Then a rhythm-and-blues band started up, sparking equally frenetic applause from the audience.

Ingo had been trying to get through to their employer over the radio. 'No signal,' he announced. The lights on their helmet cameras were glowing red, meaning they were not transmitting either. 'Our devices clearly can't work at this range.'

'If anyone's hungry, there's ham and sausages next door,' Viktor joked, sniffing the air, although food was the last thing on his mind in a situation like this.

He had underestimated Spanger, though, who immediately stepped into the neighbouring room. His shout of delight made the others break into a grin.

'I know we're all professionals in our field and this is a rescue mission, but I hope I don't have to remind everyone,' said Friedemann, 'that no one is to touch the beer or wine.' Then he made a shooing gesture. 'Apart from that, until our scout returns, I'm all in favour of having a look around to see if we can find any more clues about Miss van Dam.'

They began to investigate the cellar in the warm yellow light of the ancient lightbulbs – all except for Coco. She considered it nonsensical to go trawling through the vault. If the young redhead had been concealed there, she would surely have come out of hiding long ago. Instead, while the men wandered around, shining their torches into every corner of the cellar, Coco stopped at the bottom of the staircase and, keeping her eyes fixed on the passage, she pocketed the earring, which undoubtedly belonged to the missing girl.

'What's that?' Ingo had spotted something on the largest wine barrel, a monstrously large wooden structure with a capacity of several thousand gallons. He stood next to it and opened a small flap. 'The back part's hollow,' he announced.

Viktor laughed. 'Looks like the landlord's keeping secrets from the taxman.'

'An illegal still.' Friedemann looked over the top of his designer glasses. 'Yes, we must be in an incredibly rural area. What's this chap got stored in there, then?'

Ingo reached inside, stretching his arm out as far as it could go, and something rattled around in the wooden interior. He pulled out what he had found. 'I must be going mad—'

He was holding a large flag with a swastika emblazoned

upon it. As he unrolled it, several daggers and metal buckles fell out and landed with a clink on the sandy ground. After a little shaking, a handful of SS badges dropped out as well, followed by a black cap and rank insignia.

'Family heirlooms,' said Friedemann drily. 'Ah, the countryside: always good for upholding our oldest and most noble traditions.'

'I'll put all this shit back.' Ingo picked up the daggers and badges and threw them back inside the compartment along with the flag.

'Is the legendary, long-lost Bernsteinzimmer back there as well, by any chance?' Friedemann put his hands behind his back. 'Although it was supposed to contain more than six tons of amber, wasn't it? God knows how the Nazis ever looted the whole damn Amber Room in the first place! I suppose we'd need a good few more barrels for that.'

Meanwhile, Coco had spotted a loose piece of paper beside the staircase. Upon closer examination it turned out to be a delivery receipt for twenty barrels of Pilsner beer, issued on 21 December 1944 by the Sternburg Brewery at 19 Katharinenstraße in Leipzig. 'Looking at the address, I don't think we're in the countryside after all.' She held out the sheet by way of explanation.

Spanger returned from the larder, chewing his way through a large piece of sausage. 'There are lots of ways that could have ended up in the cellar. Either way, this is super-tasty. Think I'll raid their supplies on the way back as well. We haven't got anything half as good as this shit.'

'Can you hear me?' came Dana's voice over the radio:

at least their communication devices appeared to be working over short distances. In the background they could still hear the rhythm-and-blues band.

'Yes, we can hear you, Ms Rentski,' replied Friedemann. 'What have you got for us?'

'Will we be able to get past all those *Fasching* tossers?' Spanger chuckled and pointed at the wine barrel. 'Though I'd say they're more like Fascist tossers – geddit? *Fasching,* Fascist?' No one shared his cheerfulness. 'It wasn't that bad,' he grumbled, taking a bite from his stolen sausage.

'I'm not entirely sure what's going on here,' said Dana. 'There's a band playing in the main hall, with an audience of normal punters and a load of men in uniform. It looks like a fancy dress party: the soldiers are all wearing British and American Army uniforms from the Second War World, and what the civilians are wearing matches that era perfectly.'

'The music does too,' added Ingo.

Coco looked down at the delivery receipt. 1944. 'What if this is the correct date?' she wondered.

'Ms Rentski, can you see a calendar up there?' Friedemann asked.

'Just a sec.' It was not long before she reported back. 'I'm at the entrance to the kitchen now. Believe it or not, I've got their diary and order book open in front of me and both are saying that today is the thirty-first of December 1944.'

Spanger stopped chewing. 'Well fuck me. We're time travellers now?'

Ingo slapped his hand down on the barrel. 'Looks like someone's de-Nazified themselves – and very quickly indeed.'

'No,' Friedemann furrowed his brow in concentration, 'something's not right with the timeline.'

Viktor silently agreed. The end of the war had been officially declared in May 1945, but it looked like there were Allied troops above their heads, together with citizens of Leipzig, awaiting the turn of the year. 'Does anyone know when Leipzig was liberated?'

'Not until the spring of 1945,' Ingo guessed.

'They're more like Nazis who've got dressed up as the Allies for New Year's Eve,' interjected Coco.

'Ms Rentski, is there any sign of Miss van Dam?' While he was speaking, Friedemann signalled to the group to assemble at the foot of the steps before making their way slowly upstairs.

'Haven't had a chance yet. I'm too busy dodging waitresses,' Dana replied softly.

They could hear the squeaking of her shoes and the clinking and clattering of crockery and cutlery.

Spanger looked down at himself and his black military gear. 'Well, if we *have* ended up in 1944, the way we're dressed they'll think we're some elite SS division.'

Viktor nodded. 'We can't go up in these clothes. We need some sort of camouflage.'

'Ms Rentski,' the professor radioed. 'Do you think you'll be able to blag us some serving attire? We're worried we might be shot on sight.'

'I'll have a look around.' They could hear Dana moving

forwards. 'I'm in a relatively large building complex – it's taken some serious damage and looks as if it's been hastily repaired with what they could find. Haven't found a room with any clothes in yet.' There was a clatter. 'Okay, found a wardrobe. There are some coats and hats in here which should be enough for us to move around outdoors. We can sort the rest out later.'

'Good. Bring it all down to us.' Friedemann started putting his armour back on.

After a few minutes, Dana returned to them, laden with coats and hats. She had chosen bulky items, the better to conceal their own clothing and gun holsters. Coco picked out the most expensive-looking coat and grabbed a stylish hat that made her look like a film star. They left their climbing harnesses in the cellar, hidden behind the huge wine barrels.

'It's a group of about a hundred or so men in uniform, and some four hundred civilians,' Dana explained. 'They're Americans and Brits – and all different ranks. But I thought it was the Russians in charge here after the liberation?'

Friedemann slapped his forehead with the palm of his hand. 'You're right! Thanks for jolting my memory. The Americans liberated Leipzig and then they handed it over to the Red Army in the spring of 1945.'

'Then we're still in the middle of the war?' Spanger put some sausages in his coat pocket. There was no way he'd be returning to the present day without extra provisions. 'Does anyone happen to know when Leipzig was bombed? I don't fancy being out in the open when it all kicks off.'

Viktor vaguely remembered his history lessons. 'You mentioned American troops – but what are the Brits doing here?'

'We can sit around here in this cellar trying to puzzle it all out, or we can go out and get a clearer picture of things.' Dana's mid-length blonde hair disappeared beneath a fashionable hat. Her G36 was concealed beneath the heavy winter coat and she had stashed her pistol in one of the pockets. 'I vote for the latter.'

'Have we got a plan for finding Miss van Dam?' Friedemann slipped on a cloth cap, which made his face look even gaunter. 'If you don't mind my asking, Madame Fendi?'

'Of course.' She laid two fingers on her temple. She had to make the others believe she had clairvoyant abilities. The pendulum had raised expectations and she did not want to disappoint them. 'I'm probing for her presence – the earring will help me to find her aura.' She was desperately hoping she would start to feel something soon.

Ingo bit his tongue to stop himself from commenting on her abilities, which did not go unnoticed by Viktor. 'You can do it,' he said, resorting instead to meaningless phrases.

Spanger was struggling with his new wardrobe. His corpulence was proving an obstacle in doing up the coat. 'Useless fucking thing,' he swore, squeezing his hat down onto his brown hair. 'I'm going to freeze my arse off.'

'I don't believe that. You've got pretty good insulation.' Friedemann gestured to Dana to move off. 'We need to find her quickly, before we lose touch with the real world.'

The door to the cellar suddenly opened.

A British soldier in a khaki uniform appeared on the threshold, his back to them, with a woman's arms draped around his neck. He was laughing, and clearly in the throes of a passionate encounter.

The group stood stock-still. It was too late to turn around and hide; any sound would attract the man's attention.

The laughter had turned into kissing noises.

'No, not down there,' said the woman. They couldn't see her from where they were. 'It stinks of sauerkraut.'

'Do you really care?' the dark-haired man asked. 'You didn't acquire your nickname by accident – you Germans love your sauerkraut,' he teased.

'And of course you're *all* called Tommy,' she retorted, laughing and pushing him gently away. 'It's true. I myself know four—'

Her playful push caused the surprised soldier to stumble backwards, losing his footing on the top step and tumbling down the stairs.

At that moment, the timer switched off the light and the cellar was plunged into darkness.

'Go,' Friedemann ordered quietly. 'Hide.'

No one would hear the sounds of the team scurrying around to conceal themselves over the frightened shouts of the woman and the cursing and thudding of the falling man. At last the woman found the switch and turned the light back on.

Spanger, however, was still stuck between the barrels.

The Englishman rose. The pips on his shoulder indicated he was a captain. 'Bloody hell,' he swore, clutching his bleeding nose while he dusted off the dirt from his khaki uniform with his other hand. 'That was a rather more energetic frolic than I'd intended.'

The woman hurried down the steps, her face a crimson picture of concern. She was blonde, her hair artfully arranged, and dressed in a white blouse and black skirt. She handed him her handkerchief. 'I'm so sorry, Tommy. I . . . I thought—' She dabbed the blood from his lips and chin. 'Oh dear, oh dear – I'll clean you up. And your uniform as well. Please forgive me – I didn't mean it.' Then she noticed Spanger, whose helpless efforts to squeeze himself into the tight space had betrayed his presence. Her swabbing motions faltered for an instant; she was clearly considering what to do.

'It was an accident, Elvi, I know.' Tommy kept still, allowing her to take care of him. 'Just be nice and gentle with it.'

Out of the gloom, Friedemann signalled silently to Elvi, pleading with her to not give them away.

The woman gave a barely perceptible nod, but when her dabbing slowed down, Tommy started looking around suspiciously.

'What on . . . ?' He took a step away from the woman and drew his pistol. 'Stop – don't move. Who are you and what are you doing here?' He pointed up the steps and ordered, 'Elvi, go back upstairs and fetch my sergeant. Tell him to bring a few men – and without making a scene about it.'

She nodded and hurried up the stairs without a word.

Tommy stood where he was and cast a quick glance around the cellar. 'Are you alone, man?'

Spanger stopped his foolhardy attempt at hiding. 'Yes I am.'

'What were you trying to do? Spy on us? Poison the wine?' asked Tommy warily. 'I'll have you hanged on the spot, if that's the case.'

'The Russians,' Spanger picked a lie at random. 'I'm in the pay of the Russians.' Now he just had to put on enough of a show to distract the Brit until the others intervened.

'The *Russians*?' The surprise in Tommy's voice was palpable.

'Yes, yes, the Russians.' Spanger pushed himself awkwardly out from between the barrels and raised his arms. As he did so his coat came apart, revealing his black military uniform and sub-machine gun.

'Russians, my foot! You're with the SS!' shouted Tommy. 'Filthy Nazi – get down! Face-down on the ground! *Immediately*.' He removed Spanger's semi-automatic. 'What was your assignment? Are you with the *Wehrwolf* department? Are there any more of you in the building to ambush us?'

'No, no, wait – I've come from the future!' Spanger raised his arms further in the air, making his Kevlar vest obvious. 'I'm from the future – you ought to know the Allies are definitely going to win the war,' he gibbered. His head was a jumble of confused thoughts. Where were the others hiding? 'Right – ask me something about the course of the war – something do to with Hitler – because I know . . . I know he's going to shoot himself in Berlin. In a bunker when the—'

'What sort of nonsense is this?' Tommy glanced quickly

back up the stairs. There was no sign of Elvi, his sergeant or his men arriving to provide reinforcement and that made him nervous. 'Your loathsome *Führer* is long dead. Stop your futile resistance and face up to reality like a man. This sort of behaviour won't get you anywhere: you know we've won the war.'

From their various hiding places, the group exchanged astonished glances.

'What shall we do?' said Dana quietly over the radio. 'Should we overwhelm the English guy before his mates arrive? Otherwise there's no chance of us getting out alive.'

'There aren't any windows in the other room – we'll be hiding in a dungeon unless the door lets us back out,' Ingo added.

'Right. So let's overpower him and then we can make our escape.'

Friedemann looked at Viktor and Dana. 'I'll divert him; you two grab him.'

'But ... that's dangerous,' interjected Coco.

'We're wearing Kevlar vests – they'll be more than enough for their old pistols.' Friedemann raised his arms and stepped out from where he was hiding. 'Sir, please don't shoot.'

Tommy swore and pointed his Webley at the professor. 'I knew there was more than one of you bastard Nazis down here!'

'No, we've just been forced to make a few preparations,' said Friedemann, walking slowly towards the captain.

At the same time, Dana and Viktor stormed out of the shadows of the barrels, their G36s aimed at the captain.

'Put the gun down,' Dana ordered. 'We just need to get out of the cellar.'

'Oh look.' Tommy ignored her and kept his gun fixed on Friedemann. 'A rat-infested hole. Looks like I was right. You really have poisoned the beer and wine.'

'No – as I said, we're from the future,' Spanger began.

'Shut up,' barked Friedemann. 'Sir, please. Put the pistol away. We just want to—'

'How do you think this will end for you? I could never allow any of you *Wehrwolf* bastards to simply up and leave,' Tommy interrupted. 'I am an officer in His Majesty King George VI's Armed Forces and it is my duty to stop you. This place will be overrun by my men the moment a single shot is fired. Your plan will not succeed. Your cover has been blown, so let's not make it any worse, shall we? Cooperate with the British Army and there's a very good chance you won't hang for this.'

'How many times do I have to tell you? We're from the future—' Spanger jerked his arms back down. 'And—'

Thinking the sudden movement was an attempt to reach for his rifle, Tommy fired at the professor before swinging the barrel to face Spanger.

'No!' Half a second later, Dana had squeezed her own trigger and shot the captain in the right arm.

Tommy cried out and dropped his pistol, but his moaning and the echoes of the two shots had been swallowed up by the vault and drowned out by the roaring of the music above, hiding any sound of the altercation.

Friedemann staggered for a moment, then collapsed in a heap.

Dana pocketed the captain's pistol and secured the staircase. 'Can't see anyone else,' she reported.

Viktor checked their injured opponent, then walked over to Friedemann. 'Professor? Are you okay?' He assumed the vest had stopped the projectile and it was the impact that had knocked the rangy man off his feet – until he reached the professor and saw his shattered glasses and punctured eyeball. The bullet had entered the skull through his right eye socket without touching the surrounding bone. 'Head shot,' he called back to the group.

Coco lifted her hand to her mouth, suppressing a scream, and turned away. She could not bring herself to look at the dead man.

Ingo moved to her side and hugged her tightly. 'Shit. What are we going to do?'

Viktor paused briefly to consider, then dragged the professor's body between two of the barrels. He bent down to remove the mysterious notebook from his pocket, assuming it contained important information about the doors, for why else had Friedemann been leafing through it so often? The records, whatever they were, might certainly be of use. 'We'll leave the professor here.'

He walked back to stand in front of the captain, who was glaring angrily around him. Tie him up; bring him with them; knock him out; kill him – none of these seemed like good options to Viktor. Whatever he did would lead to even more trouble and attention.

So he tried a different approach. 'We're not Nazis, sir – and we haven't poisoned the wine. You're perfectly free to continue celebrating the New Year, as far as I'm concerned.'

Tommy laughed through gritted teeth. 'Do you really believe your little band of—'

'Go upstairs, make up some story to explain your injury – tell everyone it was just a misunderstanding.' Viktor pointed at Friedemann's corpse. 'Leave him here. We'll take care of it later.'

The captain's expression was beyond confused. 'Take care of it? Who the devil are you people?'

'We're part of a special task force – it's top secret stuff, I'm afraid. I will just tell you it's a Jewish task force.' Viktor was doing a good job of mimicking Brad Pitt's tones. 'We're hunting down Nazis – we've got a list of the worst culprits. It's justice for our people, do you understand?'

Dana immediately recognised the film Viktor was quoting from. She gave Tommy a tap on the side of his chin with the barrel of her gun. 'Sir, you will do as you're told. Otherwise we won't be able to guarantee your people's safety. You would be foolish to stand in our way.'

'Quickly – otherwise our mission will come to nothing.' Ingo pushed a pale Coco forwards.

'Oh boy.' Spanger shuffled past the dead man, knowing he was partially to blame for the mishap. 'This is so fucked up.'

They climbed the stairs, one behind the other.

'I . . . I'm truly sorry.' Tommy looked at them as they walked away. 'But how could I possibly have known?'

Spanger put a finger to his lips. 'Don't tell a soul,' he instructed the captain.

They crept into the corridor and navigated their way through the hurrying waiters to the exit.

As they passed the great hall they saw the rhythm-and-blues band, who were taking a break. In their place, a chorus of voices had struck up a second rendition of 'Davon geht die Welt nicht unter'. 'One day it will be colourful again; One day it will be sky-blue again,' they sang. It looked like the German guests were partial to lyrically uplifting material in the interim.

Viktor knew the song had been written as a rallying cry when the Nazi soldiers were in dire need of hope. Now it was apparently giving the survivors fresh confidence. Just as they were opening the door, another song from the same film, also performed by Zarah Leander, was starting up, and the entire hall was singing along, 'Ich weiβ, es wird einmal ein Wunder geschehen.'

'We need a miracle as well,' Ingo whispered to Coco. 'You won't be able to find his daughter.'

'Because you don't think I'm a medium.' She smiled in an attempt to hide her insecurity. 'What if you're wrong, though? Will you start issuing me with even more certificates?'

Dana stayed close to Viktor. 'Good work, convincing the captain we were the Inglourious Basterds. Do you think he'll cover for us?'

'I don't know – but what else could we have done? Shot him and his girlfriend too?'

'No, you did the right thing. As you said, we're not Nazis.' Dana opened the door and had a quick look outside. 'Snow. Perfect for us.' She held the exit open and waved the rest of the team through. 'Where now, then?'

'Let's find a quiet alleyway and give Madame Fendi a chance to probe for Anna-Lena in peace.'

Viktor looked around – and was momentarily shocked at all the destruction. The bombing raids had certainly done their job around the Katharinenstraße. Dozens of houses had been hit; in some places only ruins and rubble were left.

Nevertheless, there were plenty of windows with lights burning within. Leipzig had obviously not been completely destroyed, despite the devastation around them. That could have been one of the miracles mentioned in the song that was haunting their steps through the ruined streets.

Suddenly the singing stopped and the sound of whistles could be heard.

Regardless of whether the alarm had sounded because of them, the five of them ran off. They could not afford more losses under any circumstances.

Frankfurt, Lerchesberg

'Professor?' Walter van Dam stared at the black screens. He had lost all contact with the group. There were no audio or video signals; the display was stubbornly showing the unhelpful message *No Signal*.

He reached for a bottle of strong rum on his desk and was about to start pouring, but after a moment's hesitation stopped himself. There were two potential causes for the signal failure: either the technology had failed, or someone had brought it about intentionally.

Van Dam tried to contact his chauffeur again, but Matthias still did not answer. He reckoned that was even less of a coincidence.

Van Dam made a decision: he had sent fifteen people to rescue Anna-Lena and he had lost contact with all of them. No matter how dangerous it might be, he had to go down there himself. His daughter's life was at stake.

He stood up, switching on his mobile, and diverted the incoming signals from the cave to it, then left the study and headed towards the room where the rest of the team's equipment had been stored.

He picked up a G36 assault rifle, checked it out, then put it into a compact travel bag, along with five full magazines. Ignoring the discomfort, he strapped on a Kevlar vest and attached a pistol holder before throwing on his overcoat and hurrying off through the house.

'Ms Roth, if there are any calls, tell them I'm in a meeting,' he called out to his PA as he passed her in the hall.

'Of course, Mr van Dam.' She looked at him in amazement as he walked away, then called, 'When do you think you'll be back?'

'Very soon, I hope.' Van Dam descended into the garage and unlocked the dark green Lamborghini Urus, a present from a grateful business partner. He would never have bought such a car himself, but now the time had come to test the 4x4's four-litre twin turbo engine promising 650 horsepower and a top speed of 190 miles an hour.

As soon as the gate had opened wide enough to pass, van Dam was thundering through, struggling a little to control the over-powered 4x4. His frantic braking and over-steering was making the car lurch around, and warning lights started coming on all over the dashboard.

But he ignored them. This choice was the correct one: Walter van Dam was prioritising speed above all else.

CHAPTER V

Leipzig, 31 December 1944

Ingo, Coco, Spanger, Viktor and Dana took shelter from the blizzard in the remains of a covered walkway lined with heaps of rubble.

The house it had belonged to had collapsed for the most part, but the clean-up and repair work had already begun. Leipzig was clearly not a city that dithered. The war was over and life went on.

Auerbachs Keller was not far away, according to the make-shift sign. Passers-by occasionally hurried past their hiding place, holding hats and umbrellas out in front of them as meagre protection from the driving snow and the biting wind.

Gusts of wind carried fragments of conversations, the people scurrying past them discussing the Red Army in full retreat while the Allies, under US control, rushed from victory to victory, even though they were taking heavy losses. Despite having been presented with an ultimatum, Japan had not yet given up and the emperor was refusing to sign the surrender declaration. As long as the Allies were busy keeping the Communists at bay, they had no time to wage war in Asia and the Pacific.

Viktor and Dana were standing in strategic positions against the walls, securing the area.

'Any sign of Anna-Lena, Madame?' Viktor asked Coco. There was no doubt the British would be sending their military police onto the streets to look for the alleged SS *Wehrwolf* unit, if they hadn't already. His story about a Jewish squadron hunting down Nazis to kill would not work in real life; no way would professional saboteurs and assassins be allowed to roam freely throughout the city, especially not on New Year's Eve.

Ingo and Spanger walked over to the medium, who was sitting down on the remains of a chair. Her eyes were fixed on the pendulum, while the index and middle fingers of her left hand pressed against her temple and the same hand holding the diamond earring. 'I'm still looking,' she replied. She was trying as hard as she could, furiously concentrating her mind on Anna-Lena van Dam.

Ingo fought the urge to comment, but then, astonished, he noticed a slight oscillation in the pendant, before the cylindrical weight slowly began to move diagonally to the left.

At the same time, Coco's expression went blank and her eyes glazed over as if she were dead. A scene emerged in her mind's eye. 'I can see Anna-Lena,' she announced in a vacant monotone. 'She's sitting in an office. Simple décor. Four – no, five men are questioning her. Englishmen. And one American.'

Ingo and Spanger exchanged shocked glances.

The pendulum corrected its path slightly, apparently giving a clearer indication of where they needed to go.

'From their conversation they believe she is a spy,' Coco continued, describing what was playing out before her as if through a veil. 'Anna-Lena's belongings are spread out on the table in front of her. She is being interrogated by a British soldier. His name is Attington.' Her breathing became faster. 'Danger! I can sense great danger from the man lurking in the shadows.'

'What man in the shadows?' Spanger nibbled his fingernails with excitement, although they were a poor replacement for the sausages that had fallen out of his pocket during their escape.

Outlines of men appeared through the snow from across the square. They were wearing German military coats, armbands and shakos emblazoned with a badge.

'Police,' Dana warned softly, making herself even smaller behind the pillar. 'Two men.'

'The man in the shadows,' Coco carried on, 'he's ... the American. He's not saying anything; he looks deep in thought. He doesn't believe her – he doesn't believe what the British are saying about her either.'

'Shhh.' Ingo touched Coco on the shoulder. 'Try to stay calm, otherwise they'll hear us.'

But Coco carried on, 'He has other ideas. His eyes, they—' She let out a scream. 'I can see death in them! *Death!*'

The policemen were making their way through the snow towards the walkway, their batons in one hand and their drawn pistols in the other. As they came closer, the team could see *Deutsche Polizei* was written on their armbands.

'Who's there?' the one on the right called out, as his companion put a whistle between his lips in anticipation of having to call for back-up at any moment. 'Come out and show yourselves.'

Spanger looked thoughtfully at the policemen.

It was his responsibility to atone for his actions in the cellar. The professor's death was his fault, so this time it was up to him to step into the line of fire. It had always been his deepest desire to be a hero – and to be recognised as one at that. It was what he had been fighting for his entire life.

And now he finally had the opportunity to prove his worth.

'I'll handle this,' he announced, stepping out of his hiding place with his hands in the air. 'Cover me.'

He called out to the policemen, 'Excuse me, officers. I was just relieving myself. I'm on my way to a dance.'

'Urinating in public,' stated the larger of the two men.

'These are just ruins – in fact, *ruin* and *urine* are nearly an anagram, if you squint hard enough,' Spanger intoned in a clumsy attempt at jocularity. He caught some snowflakes and made a show of pretending to wash his hands with them. 'Ooh, that's pretty uncomfortable. You'd have a hard time lighting a firework in this.'

'I thought I could hear a woman screaming,' said the man on the left, swapping his baton for a torch. 'Well? Are you in mourning, or are you all in black underneath that coat for a reason?'

'Screaming? No, that was just me. Cold hands on my cock.' Spanger shook his fingers theatrically at pointed at his clothes. 'Yes, my mother's just died. Yesterday. The war finally got the better of her. May I offer you a coffee? It can't be fun being on duty on New Year's Eve.' He pointed at the sign for *Auerbachs Keller*. 'Or maybe a mulled wine?'

The policeman with the torch trudged through the snow. 'Maybe later. First I'll have a quick look around, young man. Not that I think you've killed anyone, mind.' His tone was light-hearted; he appeared to be the good cop in this routine.

'And your papers, sir,' insisted his colleague dutifully. 'For all we know you could be a shill of the British Protection Division, here to keep tabs on us.'

'What if I told you I was a Russian spy?' Spanger grinned. 'Just for the sake of argument, mind. What would you do *then*?' He was hoping his questions would keep them distracted for as long as possible.

'You really are a peculiar chap, aren't you?' The sergeant held out his hand holding the baton and tapped him on the chest. 'Your ID, sir.'

'Вы знаете, где находится библиотека?' Spanger replied, still grinning. He had to lure them away somehow. 'You see? I'm Russian.' Laughing, he pointed to the sign and started walking towards *Auerbachs Keller*. 'Come on, catch me if you can. Last one there buys the first round of mulled wine. We need it in this cold.' He sloped off lazily into the snowdrifts, like a bear.

'You'll pay for this, pal.' The policemen followed him, cursing.

'I'll be along soon.' The second policeman shone his torch into the walkway. 'Just to make sure.'

The concealed group managed to avoid the beam of

light as it slid inquisitively over the walls, cutting through the shadows in an attempt to discover the source of the screaming. Viktor held his breath as the beam paused no more than six inches away from Coco. He lifted his hand holding the G36 and gently aimed it at the man.

Suddenly a snowball flew through the air and struck the policeman in the face.

'Right, I've had enough of this!' Puffing loudly, he wiped the icy white flakes off his face.

'If that'd been a Molotov cocktail, you'd be burned to a crisp by now!' echoed Spanger's voice. 'See if you can catch me! I'm a Russian saboteur and assassin.'

The two uniformed men promptly set about capturing the self-confessed rebel.

'Right, let's get out of here.' Viktor pointed down the street. As impressed as he was that Spanger had done something to allow them to escape, he considered his actions a little over-the-top. The police in 1944 were certainly not going to be as sporting as they might have been in the present. Throwing a snowball might easily be considered an assault. 'Where now, Madame Fendi?'

With Ingo's assistance she got to her feet, her eyes clear again. She had no idea how she had just performed such a feat. It was as if her gift had suddenly awakened. Because of stress? Panic? She had seen Anna-Lena, the officers and the room right in front of her eyes, like a projection on the walls of the ruins.

The pendulum was pointing straight ahead, giving them a clear sign of where they needed to go to find the missing woman.

'This way.' Coco moved to the front of the group as they cautiously made their way along the walkway and away from the police officers. Ingo, Dana and Viktor surrounded her like a retinue of bodyguards shielding her from the dense snow falling all around them.

Viktor was concerned about whether they would be able to find Spanger again. 'We shouldn't have split up,' he said to Dana.

'Because of Spanger? He'll be fine. He'll just hang out with the cops for a bit and then wait for us down in the cellar with a pocketful of sausages,' she replied. 'I trust him not to leave without us if we're not back in time.'

Ingo nodded in agreement.

Still following the pendulum, they trudged through the snow, climbing over debris and rubble and navigating the ruined buildings. They did not have to stop once. Coco had complete trust in the little weight tugging on its chain.

After a while, an enormous building resembling a castle loomed in front of them – a rather surreal sight, given its relative structural integrity. Despite its impressive size – and its tower – it looked like it had been spared by the bombs, with the exception of some scratches, a few random bullet holes and some scuffing on the stone façade.

'She's in there,' said Coco. 'That's where Anna-Lena is.'

'This is the new town hall,' Viktor realised. He remembered it had been modelled on a castle that had previously stood on this very spot.

'Decent location.' Dana regarded the devastation around them. There was far too little cover on the approach to the building: only a handful of rubble heaps, and not much in the way of hiding places.

Ingo drew their attention to the guards on patrol. 'How will we get in?'

'It won't be easy. Our little incident in the cellar must have raised some alarms. I'm sure of it.' Dana counted the guards. 'Ten of them on this side alone.' She looked up at the sky. 'If we're lucky it'll start snowing more heavily. Then we'll be able to sneak up on them.'

'I have to ask.' Ingo looked at her and Viktor closely. 'You both move around with your weapons with such ease. Have you had some sort of military training?'

'Only from action films and video games,' Viktor said dismissively.

'Gun club,' added Dana casually.

All four of them knew they were lying but no one challenged them. They could not afford to start a conflict among the team.

Ingo, regretting having asked the question, resigned himself to a simple, 'Okay then.'

'Now, the most important thing: can you use the pendulum to find out *precisely* where Miss van Dam is?' Viktor looked up at the large building, which had several windows lit up. 'Otherwise we'll be running around from room to room for days.'

'Of course.' She threw Ingo a triumphant look. Her successful probing attempt had been a personal victory over doubt – both hers and theirs. How she had suddenly succeeded was still a total mystery to her. She put it down to the force field on the door she had passed through. 'Piece of cake.'

Viktor was listening out for any sign of Spanger, but the road was empty; the last of the revellers must have arrived at their destinations, since wandering around on a night such as this would be foolhardy. 'Let's get a bit closer,' he commanded. 'Ms Rentski and I will be the vanguard.' He linked arms with her and positioned the G36 in such a way that no one would be able to see it at first glance; she did the same with him. 'We need to make it look as if we're just heading home.'

'Sounds good.' Ingo rubbed the snowflakes off his nickel-rimmed glasses. 'How will we know if the coast is clear?'

Viktor considered the matter briefly. 'We'll sing "Davon geht die Welt nicht unter" – everyone's singing that now, so it'll be inconspicuous.'

'And what if something goes wrong?'

'"Ich wollt', ich wär' ein Huhn",' Dana suggested.

The two of them hurried forward, approaching the new town hall through the swirling curtain of whiteness. The two hundred yards of terrain lying between them and the main entrance could be traversed quite easily without being spotted by guards, thanks to the piles of rubble lying around.

Two large floodlights were standing to attention at the entrance of the building in case the small number of street-lamps proved to be insufficient to illuminate the darkness.

'We'll talk later about why we're so good at what we're doing,' Dana whispered to him. 'Until then, let's just say it's an advantage that we each have military expertise.'

Viktor had known for a while that he had encountered Dana before – in Darfur, on a mission in his previous life, before he had started to earn a living as a climber – the mission that had got him thrown out of his old job. 'Agreed.'

'What do you think our best option is? Infiltrate the shafts along the side, go through the cellar or distract them by making a racket?'

He looked at the rough façade. 'We could try—'

Three powerful lights suddenly shone directly upon them; swift footsteps approached. 'Stop,' came an order in German, a man with a strong accent. 'Your papers, please.'

Viktor and Dana found themselves surrounded by a group of five men in British Army uniforms, holding pistols in their hands and wearing the red caps and armbands of the Military Police. They wore stern expressions and their guns were aimed squarely at the two of them.

'What's the matter, sir?' Viktor pretended to pat himself down. 'It's New Year's Eve.'

'Yes, that's right. But there are some dangerous Russian saboteurs on the loose in Leipzig. The report has just come in,' said one of the officers, whose accent identified him as a Scotsman. A thick red-blond moustache took centre stage upon his face, flecked with snow on each tip. 'Now, your papers please.'

Dana felt tense. At a moment's notice she could draw the G36 from the folds of her coat but, unlike the two policemen outside the walkway earlier, their opponents were on high alert and had their own weapons at the ready. Their chances of coming out of such a confrontation alive were slim at best. '*Ich wollt', ich wär' ein Huhn*,' she sang lustily, giggling. 'Chickens don't need ID.'

Viktor gave a slow shrug. 'Oh dear. Looks like I've left my things at home.'

The Scot took a step back, his expression behind his long moustache opaque. 'Well, well. I'm afraid I'm going to have to put you under arrest for now until we can—'

There was suddenly a loud bang as some squibs and firecrackers exploded nearby. Glittering sparks flew into the air, flanked by the spray of two fiery fountains as a group of children ran away, laughing.

The guards by the town hall responded with laughter, shouting back at them that they had started too early.

Interspersed with the bangs were several shots, ringing out like the crack of a whip but barely noticed amid the fireworks. One of the military policemen was shot in the head, while two others clutched their chest and collapsed.

Dana and Viktor dropped to the ground.

The fourth man twisted around, pointing his pistol haphazardly in an attempt to locate the shooter, but was immediately struck in the forehead by a bullet; blood was sprayed in all directions.

The last soldier fired, but the bullets roared harmlessly over Dana and Viktor before he too was killed by the invisible gunman with a clean shot through the ear. Blood spurted out of his mouth and nose.

'That can't have been Doctor Theobald.' Dana crept behind a wall to take cover.

Viktor rolled through the snow and came to rest behind

a fallen façade. 'Well, whoever it is, I'd say they're on our side – for now, at least.'

'Long live freedom! Long live Joseph Stalin!' cried a woman's voice. 'Come on, Comrades! We can't stay here.' A silhouette with a long rifle appeared at the upper window of a partially destroyed house. 'The Brits and the Yanks are already on their way to arrest you lot – you're lucky we spotted you.'

Dana and Viktor exchanged glances. Spanger's little game with the police appeared to have bought them their freedom.

'Okay, we're coming,' Viktor called out. They crept hastily from their hiding places and signalled to Ingo and Coco to follow them. They stayed as close as they could to the sniper, who leaped out of the window and pointed them in the right direction.

Snow fell on the five corpses in the field of rubble, covering them up so quickly that they soon blended in seamlessly with the surrounding debris.

Leipzig, 31 December 1944

Anna-Lena sat at a desk in a beige skirt and white blouse that she had been given to replace her green dress, which was so tattered it was indecent, at least according to the prison guard who handed over the change of clothes. Even for a Russian spy like her.

They had tied her red hair up into a ponytail, but had been amazed at her nose piercing, so they'd allowed her to leave it in. A lamp was shining in Anna-Lena's face, meaning she could not see what was going on behind it. They were talking quietly in English.

She knew there were five of them, four of whom in British uniforms spoke in the clipped tones of the British Isles, while the fifth, dressed in plain clothes, spoke with an American accent that was slightly distorted through the sound of his chewing gum, as if to confirm a national cliché.

Her handbag had been placed on the desk in front of her, arranged neatly alongside the rest of her belongings, including her mobile. Someone had given her a cup of coffee.

Anna-Lena grabbed the cup and took a sip; hot, strong and very sweet, the invigorating drink was a welcome intervention. She closed her eyes and breathed deeply in and out.

Although her situation was far from ideal, it was a relief to have escaped from the chamber with the forest and howling and relentless full moon. Not long after her unsuccessful attempt to open the bunker door, Anna-Lena had found a second one set in stone and had whacked it repeatedly with a branch until the flickering began to start up.

Without hesitating, she had rushed through and ended up in a cellar. In 1944. On New Year's Eve.

But the timeline did not fit the narrative she had been taught at school: Stauffenberg's assassination attempt on Hitler had been a success, Germany had capitulated and the Americans had placed Europe under their protection, with the British in charge of administration. There was still an enemy – Joseph Stalin – and the war was still being waged on several fronts.

The crackling of burning tobacco intermingled with cigarette smoke wafted over her. The officers had finished their hushed conversation and had evidently reached a decision.

'Miss, this is your last chance to answer our questions properly,' began one of the Englishmen. 'I am Lieutenant Attington. Your name, please.'

'Anna-Lena van Dam.'

'How old are you?'

'Twenty, born on the fifth of December in Frankfurt.' She gestured to the ID card in front of her. 'As it says on there. And what is your name, sir?'

'This ID is a work of fantasy. Whatever made you think of such a thing?' replied the officer. 'A Federal Republic of Germany . . .'

'Not in 1944. You're right about that.' Anna-Lena smiled into the light.

'Let's ignore that for now,' said the lieutenant. 'You were picked up by the military police when you tried to leave the cellar of nineteen Katharinenstraße. You were found in possession of this handbag with these items inside. Is that correct?'

'Yes, sir.'

'The handbag says "Made in Russia".'

'That's right: it's a brand called Fjodor and it's not exactly cheap. They're based in St Petersburg.'

A hand appeared in the light and pointed in turn at Anna-Lena's belongings.

'Lipstick, wallet, fake money that's as bad as your ID card – and similarly, a driving licence. A pen, some sweets, make-up and – his finger tapped her smartphone – this. An item we've been unable to identify.'

'Nothing special,' Anna-Lena said quickly. 'Just a paper-weight.'

'Really? I think not,' replied Lt Attington with a snort. 'With these little connection points? It rather looks as if it runs off electricity. Please demonstrate what it does.'

'I'm afraid I can't.'

'And why not?'

'The lith— the battery. It's dead.'

'There's no battery small enough to fit into a thing like this.' He slammed his palm hard down on the table. 'Miss van Dam, whatever it is you're up to, I have to tell you, it won't fly. We're not a bunch of fools here. My colleagues and I are of the opinion that you're a Russian spy, sent by Stalin to sow confusion among us.'

'More like a saboteur,' added an unknown voice.

Anna-Lena took a sip of her coffee before saying earnestly, 'I promise you I'm not.' She was desperately trying to think of something to tell them that would get her released, or at least, give her the opportunity to get back to the cellar. Although Germany had already been defeated in this universe, it looked like the Communists and the Allies were still locked in conflict. She had no desire to stay in this decade for any longer than she had to – even if revisiting the room with the full moon and howling wolves was her only means of returning to the present era. She really wanted to meet the man in the pin-striped suit on her way back and slam her club into his smirking face. He had ruined everything.

But first she had to escape from her current situation, one way or another.

'What exactly are you accusing me of, Lieutenant Attington?' Anna asked, going on the counter-attack.

'You have no valid papers, Miss van Dam, so we need to keep you here until we can find a way to confirm your true identity,' he replied, blowing smoke in her face through the light. 'Since Frankfurt's been more or less destroyed, I can't imagine we'll receive any official documentation from the authorities there in a hurry.'

'She's also going to need to explain what this *paperweight* really is,' said another man from behind the lamp.

'Miss van Dam, you're proving to be rather an enigma,' said Lt Attington. 'So let's try again, shall we? What exactly were you doing in that cellar?'

It was time for some new tactics. Without hesitating, Anna-Lena began to cry, wailing impressively in front of the astonished men, then hiccoughing out, 'All right, I admit it. I've been lying to you. My friends and I took something at a New Year's Eve party,' she told them, sniffing, 'but whatever it was, it was too strong for me. We got completely lost and the next thing I knew, I was waking up in this cellar – I must have been completely delusional.' She pointed at her property. 'The money, the ID and the driving licence are just pretend, of course – I like making that sort of thing when I'm bored. I'm a writer, you know. In my spare time.'

'Miss van Dam—'

'My name's not really van Dam – that's made up, like my ID,' said Anna-Lena with all the conviction she could muster. 'My name is Hermine Müller and I live with my relatives in Gohlis. At the palace,' she lied, pointing her nose at the ceiling. She had only been to Leipzig once before and her memories of it were rather faint. 'We've been bombed out of our flat in Brühl, sir.' She wiped the tears from her cheeks and looked pleadingly into the lamp. 'Please, sir, I can show you where I live. My parents will testify to everything I've said!'

The officer's finger pointed back at the smartphone. 'Perhaps we're getting a little closer to the truth, but that still doesn't explain what this is here.'

'I found it.'

'Found it?'

'On my way here, sir. When I was running through the ruins.' Anna-Lena shrugged. 'I suppose it could be part of a bomb. How should I know? Anyway, it's not mine. But I liked the way it reflected the light.'

There was a knock at the door and it opened a fraction. Anna-Lena could hear another quiet conversation taking place, but she was none the wiser as to what was being said.

'Well, it's goodbye for now, Miss Müller – although I'm afraid you'll have to spend the night here,' the lieutenant informed her. 'We've still got one or two questions about your story, but it's nearly midnight and frankly, I don't want to be cooped up in this place when the new year strikes. One of my men will take you to a comfortable cell where you can have a good old think about your drug use. And tomorrow I'll accompany you to your home.

I'm rather curious as to what might be waiting there for us. Goodnight.'

The four men went out through the door; she could hear the sounds of cigarettes being lit again, then Lt Attington turned back and asked, 'Captain Wallace, care to join us?'

'No, thank you. I'll just go back to my billet and sleep in the new year,' replied a sonorous voice. 'Gentlemen, I wish you a lovely rest of your evening.'

As the footsteps receded from the interrogation room, she heard, 'As you wish, Captain. If you wouldn't mind escorting young Miss Müller to her cell in that case . . . ?'

Thanks to the blinding light in her eyes, Anna-Lena could hardly see a thing, but the American was still in the room with her, and she knew that he had been waiting for this moment.

The lampshade was turned to face downwards, revealing a man in his mid-thirties wearing a dark brown suit with a waistcoat and tie. His dark hair was carefully arranged and his face was clean-shaven. 'My name is Captain James Wallace,' he said by way of introduction, all the while still chewing his gum. 'I'm on General Eisenhower's staff. As a . . . consultant.'

'I'm not a Russian spy,' Anna-Lena repeated, sighing. 'Look, I don't know how else I can explain this to you. I can't even speak Russian.' She pointed at her bag. 'The logo and IDs – they were all made by me.'

'Miss van Dam—'

'Müller. Hermine Müller, sir.'

Captain Wallace gave her a knowing smile as his chewing perceptibly slowed. 'Unlike my British friends, I believe the first version of your story is true.' He removed a packet of chewing gum from his pocket and offered her a stick. Anna-Lena declined. 'I don't know whether you are in fact from the future, but I believe you are withholding things. Secrets.' He leant forwards slightly. 'Nazi secrets.' He winked, as if trying to flirt in the most pathetic way.

'Um . . .' came Anna-Lena's weak reply. She had been taken completely by surprise. 'And that means I can't be a Russian spy?'

'I know you're not.' Wallace picked up the smartphone. 'We know your *Führer* had the best minds in the country working to come up with inventions in all areas: weapons, aircraft, small things for everyday life. A lot of those people are now working for us. And there are some we haven't yet found.' He turned the device over in his hands and examined it all over. 'I believe, Miss van Dam, that either you or one of your parents is one of those scientists. You look a little young for ground-breaking inventions. Or am I mistaken?'

Anna-Lena laughed in disbelief, thinking of ridiculous films like *Iron Sky* and *Sky Sharks* with their insane Nazi conspiracy theories. 'Is this one of those things like . . . the secret Nazi base on the Moon? Or those flying saucers with the engine from a V2?' She laughed. 'Oh, and not forgetting the base on the South Pole where Hitler's doubles are living—'

Wallace raised his eyebrows. 'You see? You know about these plans – our foreign intelligence services are still working on a lot of this stuff.' He sat down in the chair opposite her. 'Come on, Miss van Dam. Where are your parents?

I'd truly like to talk to them.' He put the smartphone down on the table. 'Whatever it was that brought you to us, I'm willing to bet that this here is very, very valuable to the people from the future.'

The direction of the conversation was making Anna-Lena feel rather uneasy. Wallace's way of thinking was different from the British officer's; what's more, he outranked the lieutenant. Should the American captain come to the conclusion that she really did have access to advanced technical expertise, things could become uncomfortable for her very quickly indeed. It was one thing to be a spy, but being in possession of unknown modern technology? That would provide a far greater incentive for someone to try to force information out of her.

Anna-Lena looked into her empty coffee cup. 'I told you, I don't know where—'

As quick as a flash, Wallace lunged forward and gripped her by the throat. He pulled her brutally towards him, choking her. 'That wasn't a request, Miss van Dam. It was an order. So we understand each other a little better.' Without releasing his fingers from her throat, he lifted up the smartphone and held it in front of her eyes, which had started to bulge slightly out of their sockets. 'This thing is state-of-the-art. And I want to know who built it and what it can do,' he said coldly. 'Do you think I've been waiting around all this time just to take you down to the cell?'

Gasping for air, Anna-Lena feebly shook her head.

'Those snooty Limeys – they're only good for keeping the European states under control for America, thinking they've still got an empire while we lay our asses on the line against Stalin and the Japs,' he said venomously. 'But *we're* the new world superpower now, Miss van Dam. Hitler has passed the baton on to Uncle Sam and *we're* running with it. People cheer us for getting rid of the evil Nazis and driving out the Commies – repelling the enemy and bringing freedom to the world. They won't mind us running things in return.' He laughed and pushed her away from him. 'But we need innovations – like whatever this here is.'

Anna-Lena clutched her bruised neck, wheezing and coughing.

'I've just made a decision.' Wallace smiled ruthlessly, still chewing. 'You will accompany me back to the States, to our headquarters. For "further investigation", we'll call it. General Eisenhower needs to see this. We can't have your friends turning up here and rescuing you by force – no way can I leave someone who knows about the lunar bases, flying machines and a fortress at the North Pole in the hands of the Brits in Leipzig, Miss van Dam.'

Anna-Lena remained silent. She knew she was in serious trouble now.

Near Frankfurt

Walter van Dam drove the Lamborghini along the bumpy drive to the villa. The fact that he was able to do so at break-neck speed was all thanks to the engineers who had designed the Urus to perfection. The 650-HP engine roared, sending dirt and gravel flying from the tyres and peppering the wheel arches.

Van Dam did not even think about slowing down.

He could see an abandoned BMW in front of the house; it had no business whatsoever being there. The Rolls and Mercedes people carrier were there as well. Matthias should have been on his way back to him a long time ago, with the woman who was identical to Anna-Lena in all ways apart from eye colour in tow.

When he got close enough, he could see the BMW had a hire-car number plate; that, and the presence of the three cars, was making him highly suspicious.

There was still no signal from the cave; no calls had come through to his phone. He no idea of anything that was going on deep underground.

Van Dam brought the 4x4 to a screeching halt, not showing any restraint or care whatsoever. This was his land and there were no neighbours nearby or within earshot, so he didn't bother to conceal anything when he opened his bag and took out the G36; he'd make it clear to the uninvited visitor that he was not welcome here. He had neither the patience nor the nerve for kindness today.

He got out and stood still, listening carefully. All was quiet apart from the singing of the birds and the rustling of leaves on the trees.

Van Dam slowly walked over towards the house next to his family's old factory, which had been abandoned years ago. He had spent the early years of his life in this house but he could hardly remember anything about it now.

He peered inside the BMW. The key had been removed but the doors were unlocked. A mini laptop was sitting on the passenger seat, with the charging lead plugged into the car. The display was lit up and showed a series of photographs of some faces that were very familiar to van Dam.

Troneg, Rentski, Theobald, Fendi, Spanger and Friedemann had all been photographed. The visitor had certainly not come to this house by accident.

He looked around once more, then opened the door and picked up the laptop, intending to leaf through the files. What information did the driver of the BMW have about his team?

But the device required a password or fingerprint to gain access, so Van Dam stuffed the little laptop underneath his Kevlar vest. He would have more than a few questions for this visitor when he found him. Then it occurred to him that there might be more than one of them – the car had space for five people, after all. That would mean he'd be significantly outnumbered.

He was not particularly well-versed in handling weapons, but he trusted himself to at least point the G36 in the right direction. That might prove to be enough of a deterrent. Step by step, van Dam approached the house, holding his rifle in one hand. He was disconcerted by how peaceful everything seemed. There was no sign of either his chauffeur or the unknown man.

The Rolls-Royce and the people carrier were sitting there as if abandoned.

In action movies or horror films, people would always call out something like, 'Hello?' or, 'Is anyone there?' in these sorts of situations, but van Dam had always considered that to be pointless. Nevertheless, he caught himself thinking of doing precisely that as he considered shouting out Matthias' name in an attempt to penetrate the silence.

He carefully climbed the steps to the verandah, which had traces of bloodstains upon the wooden surface. Droplets large and small were scattered around unevenly, as if someone had tried to stop a severely bleeding wound.

He looked around. There was a hand print on the doorframe; the position of the fingers suggested that the injured party had entered the house.

Van Dam took a deep breath, raised the G36 and gently pushed open the door.

CHAPTER VI

Leipzig, 31 December 1944

Spanger peered out from his cover at the entrance to the restaurant on the Katharinenstraße, whose cellar hosted the door back to the present. He would not let it out of his sight for one minute, so as not to miss the others' arrival with the younger van Dam.

Unfortunately, Spanger had absolutely no idea where the quartet had got to. He had secretly expected them to be waiting for him in the ruins of the walkway, but instead, they had disappeared from their hiding place altogether. At first Spanger had thought Ingo, Coco, Viktor and Dana had left him behind on purpose as he was the least capable – the person responsible for the tragedy in the cellar. Then he reminded himself that they'd had no alternative. He had given them the opportunity to escape while he was busy playing cat-and-mouse with the policemen and they had used it to go and track down Anna-Lena.

Spanger blew hard on his cold fingers; apart from that he was pleasantly warm, thanks to his Kevlar vest and all the running he had been doing. He had managed to ditch the policemen in the snow relatively easily after luring them away from the rest of the group. Their rescue mission had to succeed, otherwise Friedemann's death would have been for nothing.

The Brit had shot him in the head – right in the head! You arrived in the Forties with bullet-proof gear on, then that happens . . .

Spanger gradually began to feel the cold in his toes, so hopped from one foot to the other, all the while massaging his fingers. It was probably a stupid idea to wait outside.

He looked through the sprinkling snow at the gate to the complex, which consisted of two adjacent courtyards. He had played his part in the rescue by providing that distraction; now, sooner or later, his team would turn up at the inn with the young woman in tow and he would be able to join them while everyone else was celebrating the new year. Waiting here also had the appealing side-effect that he could go back down into the vault at any time and use the door to escape, should things become at all hairy. He had no desire to end up in the same condition as the professor. These were clearly dangerous times – although at least there didn't seem to be any danger of being caught up in a bombing raid.

Time passed. The cold became biting, as if it were trying to force him out of hiding.

Spanger was now blowing incessantly onto his increasingly blue hands; he was freezing over despite his winter coat and Kevlar vest. It was several degrees below zero and the combination of standing still and the sweaty clothes he was wearing produced a rather undesirable effect. He began to shiver uncontrollably, his body doing everything it could to stay warm.

Through the window he could see the shadows of men and women dancing with each other to the booming sound of the rhythm-and-blues band. He could hear laughter and clapping through the gaps in the windows, which had been left slightly open to allow the hot air to escape; it turned instantly into a white haze upon contact with the icy conditions outside. There was a strong smell of food and cigarettes.

'Shit,' Spanger muttered, stuffing his hands into his pockets, not that this had much of an effect. Even his teeth were chattering now. His thoughts came full circle and he found himself ashamed at having contemplated returning to the present day without the others.

Spanger had always wanted to be a hero – a bodyguard. That had been his goal. But an incident involving a trainee at work had stripped him of everything, or as good as everything. The longer Spanger stood in the cold with time to think, the more it angered him that people viewed him as a failure, and that anger was piling up inside him. Quiet moments were poison for the psyche, especially for the psyche of someone who had had to contend with humiliation, failure and constant underachievement throughout his life.

The group's attitude towards him appeared to be no different, as Spanger had clearly noticed from the outset. The professor's disrespectful remarks and Rentski having to tell him how to handle the G36, not to mention being looked at with such condescension by Viktor, with his obnoxious athleticism. And then he had gone and lost his rifle at the first opportunity like the rank amateur he was.

Spanger sighed.

They didn't trust him.

No one trusted him with anything.

It was precisely that reason that had made him forge his references as a bodyguard, fabricate his education and take on his first job with Walter van Dam: to rescue a young woman in distress. What a way to start his new life!

But heroism had been thin on the ground so far. Instead of being involved in the act of liberation, all he had managed to do was bring about the demise of their leader, and now here he was, standing alone on a freezing cold night, staring at an inn and waiting for something to happen.

Spanger was suddenly seized by ambition.

He might have lost the group, but there was still something he could do: reconnaissance. He could prepare the way for a hasty retreat, allowing them to escape through the door smoothly, away from this strange version of post-war Germany where nothing was what they had been taught. That aside, this course of action would be warmer and more comfortable.

Spanger blew on his hands once again and departed from his look-out post.

Circling the inn, which had by some miracle been spared the destruction around the Katharinenstraße and Brühl, he spotted two military policemen behind the door, which meant there was no chance of entering through the front door.

Instead, he found himself passing between neatly

stacked cairns and rubble on his way to the back of the estate. A wall was barring his way, however, and he was not a natural climber.

'Shit,' he muttered, looking around until he noticed some rat prints leading towards some loose stones, which he moved to one side to reveal a small trapdoor. The prints showed the rats clearly preferred using a hole in the wall.

He cleared away enough of the rubble to allow him to open one of the wings of the hatch. He could no longer feel his icy fingers, but he kept himself going with the thought of being back in the warm cellar, with its hoard of delicious sausages, beer and wine. He would certainly treat himself to a little something – a bit of everything. Not too much though.

He propped the hatch open with a piece of wood to stop it from hitting him in the back or slamming down on his fingers before squeezing himself down the narrow shaft, already panting with exertion. He supposed this had originally been intended for coal deliveries.

Spanger landed back in the dark vault, just as he had hoped. The guards hadn't counted on this. He had tricked them all.

The cellar smelled of meat, fermenting sauerkraut and sausage, which made his stomach jump for joy. After such a long time outdoors, it felt incredibly warm, even though it was probably no more than five or six degrees. In the light of his torch, Spanger checked out the place, walking past the barrels to the rack where the sausages were hanging to dry. He hungrily helped himself to a few, then turned back towards the door that had brought them to the past.

In the beam's illumination he could see it had once been painted blue, and the scratched dark wood beneath it was adorned with various carvings. A lion's mouth held the rusted ring which had had to be hit very hard indeed to build up a force field.

'This is insane,' Spanger whispered through a mouthful of sausage, walking over to the door. 'How are you able to carry us through time and space, eh?'

He stuffed the rest into his mouth and placed his free hand on the chilly wood. The ring was so badly corroded that it looked as if it might crumble under the impact of a particularly forceful blow. Perhaps the passage could only be used once more.

Spanger examined the edges, the hinges and the rim of the mysterious door. For some reasons he had the impression that the door hadn't always been located in the cellar. Maybe someone had found it elsewhere and installed it here as a way of keeping the rooms separate from one another.

Spanger tore himself away from it, remembering he had to return to ground level and keep an eye on the main entrance: if the group returned with van Dam's daughter, he would have to show them his secret way in. Otherwise they might find themselves in a pitched battle with the military police lying in wait.

'I'll just warm up for a bit longer,' he mumbled, still chewing.

It crossed his mind to use the door to go back and ask van Dam to send more men, in case of emergency – but what would happen if the rusty knocker disintegrated and made it impossible for the others to return?

No, he could not risk that. He was a hero. At last. He patted the door with his hand. 'See you soon. Then you'll bring us back through time.'

Clack!

The light in the cellar suddenly flared on.

Spanger almost choked with the shock. He dropped the sausages he'd been gripping, raised his sub-machine gun and tried to hide among the barrels. His eyes fixed on the staircase, expecting to see the intruder. Was it a patrol?

He was astonished when a man wearing a thick trench coat with a black hat perched on his head emerged from behind a wine barrel.

'Don't even think about it. We've been watching you the entire time,' said the man quietly, pushing his hands into his coat pockets. He clearly had no reason to be afraid: on his whistle, a dozen armed men rose from their hiding places. 'No doubt you're with the remarkable woman we captured earlier on in this cellar. You're with the SS.'

The man – Spanger thought he sounded American – removed one hand from his pocket and tossed him one of the badges that Ingo had stuffed back into the wine barrel's hidden compartment. 'All this nonsense about a Jewish taskforce is nothing but a bare-faced lie. Bold, but ultimately implausible. We've found your badges. Tell me what your mission is.'

Spanger thought about Friedemann with a bullet in his eye and slowly lowered his weapon. 'I'm not a Nazi.'

The man smiled with irritation. 'Do you know how many people say that to me at first? And how often they change their minds once I'm finished with them?' He tapped his hat. 'Captain Wallace, US Forces, Europe.'

'Carsten Spanger. Bodyguard.' He cleared his throat, wishing he didn't have bits of meat stuck in his teeth. 'What woman?'

'Anna-Lena van Dam, of course. I know her family is involved in some sort of scientific research and development. We've already recruited most of your best minds and taken control of their inventions.' He took his other hand out of his pocket, revealing a smartphone. 'But this is something altogether different.'

Spanger laughed at the sight of it. 'Oh boy.'

'You *know* what this is?'

'Of course. It's a telephone.' He pointed at it. 'It's like a radio, but more . . . more modern.'

Wallace's lips tightened. 'Very funny, Herr Spanger. Or would you prefer me to use your military rank?'

'I haven't got one. Like I said, I'm not in the SS.'

'And like *I* said, I don't believe you. You're all in black and you're wearing' – Wallace pointed at his vest – 'some kinda armour. And you're carrying an unidentified submachine gun. If you want my opinion, I'd say you're from the same division as Miss van Dam. And you're here to get her back.'

'And that's enough for you to think I'm some prick from the SS?'

Wallace signalled to his men, who immediately started moving in on Spanger. 'Please don't resist.'

Spanger didn't know Captain Wallace was already imagining his second big catch of the evening as another big step towards promotion. He thought about the shooting. 'I won't.' He allowed them to remove his coat, gun and vest, followed by the pistol, knife and torch. He had no idea how he could turn this situation to his advantage. There were thirteen of them, all soldiers. *Someone like me doesn't stand a chance.*

Wallace looked at the weapons and equipment. 'I don't know any of this – model or make,' he said. 'We've found their climbing harnesses as well. Very strange material. Oh, and your dead companion.'

Spanger considered rushing over to the door and using the knocker to escape – that would earn him some extra time to think up a new strategy. But what if the iron ring were to fall apart? Could he simply leave the others in this world? No: he absolutely refused to do that. That was not how heroes acted; instead, they asked questions like, 'What do you intend to do with Miss van Dam?'

'Take her back to the States for questioning and for closer examination of this device that you're trying to convince me is a telephone. Which it most certainly is not.' Captain Wallace studied Spanger; he looked a little unsure about what to do with his unexpected prisoner. 'I'll make a deal with you: tell me what you know about the Nazi fortresses at the North Pole and on the Moon – and what about these flying saucers? Where are their production sites? Tell me everything, and I'll make sure you lead a comfortable life in the States along with the other Nazi collaborators.'

Spanger laughed instinctively at this treasure trove of crap conspiracy theories. 'Did you get that from Miss van Dam?'

Wallace nodded. 'We've had our suspicions for a while. Everything's been very vague until now, but thanks to this young lady . . . and now you.' He had little patience with this man. He was visibly indecisive and uncertain. 'Where's the rest of your unit?'

Spanger chewed slowly on the piece of sausage in his mouth, trying to look as innocent as possible. He stole a glance at the door – at the knocker – and weighed up his options. Not that he had many: he did not stand a chance against thirteen heavily armoured men.

'Why do you keep looking at that?' The captain walked over to the door and fiddled with the creaking ring, lifting it up, then letting it fall. He did not share his prisoner's fascination. 'What's so special about it?'

'I collect doors.'

'Do you really?' Captain Wallace put his hands back in his pockets. 'So you'd be rather upset if something were to happen to it, wouldn't you?'

Spanger shrugged. 'Do what you want. There are plenty of doors in the world.'

'How about I start here? With your door?' He reached for the knocker and let it fall against the plate. A few specks of rust crackled and fell off, landing softly in the trodden-down sand. 'Would that bother you, SS man?'

Spanger kept a close eye on whether a force field had been created, but there was no flickering or whirring to be heard. 'I like the pattern. And the lion's head. That's it.'

The American made no secret of the fact that he did not believe Spanger. 'You're stuck in a hopeless situation and you're most concerned with admiring a door,' he summarised. 'You're full of shit, you know. What's so great about this door?'

'Well . . .'

'Why don't we speed things along a little?' The captain put his hand back on the ring and gestured to his men to move Spanger closer.

Two men grabbed him, twisted his arms behind his back, so tightly that the slightest of movements would have been enough to break a finger, and pushed him forwards. As quick as a flash, Wallace grabbed Spanger's mid-length brown hair and slammed his head against the door – which made it emit a dull rumble. Then he pressed Spanger's ear to the wood. 'If I don't get some answers out of you soon, SS man' – he brought the iron knocker down hard, producing a deafening roar in Spanger's ear – 'I'll keep on doing this until you're deaf in your right ear. Then I'll start on the other one, you understand?'

Spanger cared less about his hearing than the ring. If it broke, they'd be stuck here – all of them. He had to find a lie that would match Anna-Lena's story. He hastily ran through the plot of *Iron Sky* in his head: Nazis, the Moon, flying saucers . . . 'Wait, I—'

'Sir,' shouted a soldier coming down the stairs, snow-flakes falling from his coat, 'sir, message from a British patrol.' He saluted Captain Wallace. 'Four out of five dead; one survivor. They stopped a group of civilians because they were wearing black trousers and boots underneath their coats. Then a Communist opened fire on the patrol – a sharpshooter, sir, using a Tokarev SVT-40. We found the shells. The Communists all fled the scene.'

Captain Wallace pulled Spanger back by his hair and looked coldly into his eyes. 'Communists masquerading as Nazis? Or Nazis working with Stalin?' He slammed Spanger's forehead against the door again, this time opening a wound in his temple. 'Which one is it?'

Spanger immediately abandoned his previous plan in light of this new information. If the group had fallen into the hands of Communists, they would not wait for long. They were out of reach and certainly wouldn't be back here any time soon – and he needed support right now. Walter van Dam had to give him some more people, preferably a team of mercenaries – a team consisting solely of Chuck Norris clones. He wouldn't get anywhere with the American – that ship had sailed.

That meant his only option was to escape back to the twenty-first century.

Spanger tore his right arm loose, grabbed the rusty ring with his hand and slammed it down with all his might.

There was a loud crash. The buzzing sound emanating from the door was reminiscent of electrical energy. Blue lightning bolts flashed off the striking plate and shot off through the vault. Some struck the vaulted ceiling, causing stones and chunks of plaster to fall free, while others hit Captain Wallace's men, throwing them several yards backwards.

Spanger broke free. This was his opportunity! He gave the captain a swift kick in the balls and put his hand on the knocker. 'Arsehole,' he shouted.

The exit was slightly ajar. There was screaming all around him and the sound of shots being fired.

Spanger now had a glimmer of hope. He would be back soon, heroically, with firepower and—

The first bullet hit him in the leg, sending him to his knees, but before Spanger could push himself forwards to escape to his own era, he was hit in the chest by a shotgun blast and thrown to one side.

He hit the frame and slid to the floor as the entrance closed in front of his eyes. Through a veil of blood he saw the door slam shut; the crackling dissipated. The force field had collapsed – along with any hope of escaping from this nightmarish world.

The moisture rising in Spanger's throat made him cough, spraying the last of the blue lightning with red droplets. A metallic taste spread throughout his mouth. 'Don't leave me here to die,' he moaned.

Captain Wallace's boot sent him sprawling onto his back. The captain looked down at him triumphantly, holding a pistol in his right hand. 'Why not? You're of no use to me.' He tapped the frame with his free hand. He was certain of his promotion now. 'But this thing here is unique. Thanks for showing it to me, SS man. I'll have it shipped to the States along with the girl, for our experts to examine. Maybe it's got something to do with your secret bases at the North Pole and on the Moon?'

Spanger's lungs were filling up with blood; he was slowly suffocating. 'You Nazi,' he managed to squeeze out in frustration. Strangely enough, he could still taste a hint of that excellent sausage on his tongue, which at least gave him one final moment of happiness. He would never forget its aroma.

'Did you just say *Sieg Heil*? Fuck your *Sieg Heils*, SS man.' Captain Wallace pulled the trigger. 'Or whatever you are.'

Leipzig, 31 December 1944

'They're not ours!' Theo Schwimmer, a stocky man in his mid-fifties, peered down at the quartet sitting in front of him, tied to a bench. 'You didn't even blindfold them! What on earth made you think it was a good idea to bring them here, Greta?' He tugged at Viktor's field jacket, then Coco's shirt and finally at Dana's trousers. 'You see that? Black clothes – all of them. And they've all got the same strange weapons. I've never seen any comrade from the east using them before.' He gave a snort. 'This was supposed to be a nice, quiet New Year's Eve to lure the Brits and Yanks into a false sense of security.'

The dark-haired sniper stared grumpily at the wall. Her displeasure at being criticised in this way by her superior was evident. 'How was I supposed to know? The police were talking about hunting a down a Russian – they said there'd be more of them.' Like Theo, she had simple civilian clothes underneath her coat, including a skirt, to make her appear even more harmless. At least as long as no one could see her Tokarev SVT-40. 'They could well have been some of Comrade Stalin's saboteurs who were on the run!'

Viktor understood that Greta had taken them to a safe house for Communist sympathisers: Germans who had fought alongside the Red Army.

'You thought it'd be a good idea to shoot a British patrol

to save the lives of a bunch of strangers?' Theo shook his head reproachfully. 'We agreed we'd hold back for the time being, to prepare for something bigger. And now we've got the Tommies and the Yanks swarming around outside, leaving no stone unturned. Do you understand?' He pointed at the prisoners. 'All for some SS *Wehrwolf* Nazi troop!' He drew his revolver angrily. 'And now I've got to get rid of you all, since you've seen our hiding place.'

'Stop,' shouted Dana, 'please – we're nothing of the sort. If you'd just—'

Theo struck her with a blow, leaving a cut on her lower jaw. 'Don't you dare speak to me, you Nazi pigs. You gave the Americans an excuse to cross the pond. You and your . . . ugh, *damn it!*' Glaring at Greta, he shoved the gun into her hand. 'You do it – you messed it all up, so now you can shoot your way out of trouble. They're your prisoners.' He opened the door.

Bits of a soft conversation could be heard outside: 'I need a coffee. Then you'll have to find a way to get the bodies outside and dump them somewhere obvious. That's the only way to get the police off our backs.'

Then Theo slammed the door to the hut.

Greta came back in, rolled her eyes and sat down on the stool opposite the four of them. She looked relatively harmless if you ignored the Tokarev. 'Bit of a shitter, eh?' She held the revolver casually in one hand, while she removed a cigarette from the case on the table with her other. She lit it with a petrol lighter. 'First I save the wrong people and now I've got to dish out head shots all round.' She raised the gun. 'Nasty work.'

'Would you please listen to us for a moment?' Viktor began. 'We're not part of any group that's at war with Germany.'

'Are you having me on? The war with Germany's *over*. Uncle Sam and his island-dwelling lapdogs are fighting against Mother Russia now,' Greta replied, taking a long draw. 'Do you really think I won't shoot you just because you're a cretin?'

'We simply happened to be in the area,' Viktor tried again.

'With rifles no one's ever seen before. 5.56 millimetre. Who uses such a thing?' Greta pointed at the door. 'Even Theo doesn't know where they're from. He said he'd never seen anything like them before – neither the make, nor the design. And that's saying something. He's fought on every front.' She sucked once more on the cigarette, causing the tobacco to crackle briefly. 'You won't even count towards my killing stats. Pathetic. For real.'

Coco stared at the sniper. Mind control: that's what she required – but she needed more time. Maybe it would work in the same way as it did when she was trying to find Anna-Lena? 'What if we could prove we're working towards a higher purpose – serving higher powers?' she started.

'Isn't that what all Nazis say? For the Master Race and the *Führer*?'

'No, you really have got it all wrong. We're looking for a young woman. She's gone missing and we've been sent to find her and bring her home,' Ingo added.

Dana spat out blood. 'That arsehole almost broke my jaw.' She could clearly feel teeth missing from her mouth.

'Is that supposed to be your *higher purpose*?' Greta laughed out loud. 'How sweet. Dying for a cause and for your convictions – now *that's* a higher purpose. And there's no such thing as a higher power.' She weighed the revolver in her hand. 'This bit's never easy. When you're used to looking at your target through a scope, executing someone up close is ... different.' She drew back the hammer with a click. 'Anyone want one last cigarette? Afraid I can't offer you anything to eat. And we need the champagne for ourselves. It's new year.' She looked at her watch. 'And you've picked a good time for it. It'll still be 1944 when you die. Everything will be better in the new year.'

Coco could feel her powers rising and her gaze went blank. She suddenly found herself able to access the sniper's thoughts. Softly, she began to speak. 'Your name is Greta Weiβ. You trained as a sniper with the Red Army. Your father is called Wilhelm: he was an *Obersturmbannführer* who died at Stalingrad.

Greta's mouth fell agape. 'Where did you—?'

'You've had two miscarriages – one two years ago and one last year. Jürgen, your lover, would have been the father to both,' Coco continued in her trance-like state, flicking at will through Greta's most intimate memories. 'You didn't want to marry him, not until ...' She stopped. 'No, they weren't miscarriages. That's what you told him, but in fact you aborted them. Because you wanted to fight – first against the Nazis and now against the Americans.'

Greta leapt to her feet. 'Where did you get all this from, you fucking witch?' she shouted, suddenly terrified. 'You can't possibly know all this!'

'Higher powers,' Viktor reminded her with a smile, swearing never to doubt Coco's abilities again. The medium was proving to be their ace in the hole. 'There's a very specific purpose for this young lady we're looking for.'

'There's no such thing.' Greta's breathing quickened and she looked back and forth between the four of them. 'Is this a joke?'

'Your dog's name was Bruno; he died in the first bombing raid. Your mother reported you dead to stop anyone going after her if you'd been caught,' Coco pressed on. 'And your two children – they would have been girls.' Her pupils lost their glaze and she withdrew from the foreign mind. 'What more do I have to tell you before you start believing us, Greta?'

'You became part of our mission the moment you saved us from the Brits. You and your friends,' Ingo continued quickly. 'You've got to help us.' He did not have the faintest idea how Coco had been able to read Greta's secrets. He remembered all the failed experiments she had done before; something had clearly changed, but what that could be . . . ?

The sharpshooter looked confused, but still not convinced. 'I don't understand.'

'Let's just say we're from another world – a world similar to yours,' replied Coco cheerfully, 'and where we're from, the fate of this young woman is of great importance.'

'That's why we need to know as much as possible about your world,' Ingo said. 'So we can work out where best to begin.' They finally had the opportunity to shed some light on the historical darkness they found themselves in.

'You won't regret it.' Viktor nodded encouragingly. 'Trust us – at least a little.'

Greta gently eased off the hammer. 'This is inexplicable. It's a bit like . . . mysticism or some shit – all that rubbish the Nazis were into, like Himmler with his magic circle in that castle.'

'That's got nothing to do with us.' Coco smiled. She knew she had won. 'The Nazis never succeeded in their mad pursuit for cosmic secrets. We, on the other hand . . .' She proffered her bound hands. 'Would you be so kind?'

Greta placed the revolver to one side and took a knife out of her boot to sever the prisoners' cords. 'I'm not the one who gets to decide your fate. That's a job for Theo and the committee.'

'We'll convince him, just as we did you, my dear Miss Weiß.' Coco's smile did not falter. 'And by the way, your secrets are safe with me.'

Dana rubbed her wrists to stimulate the circulation, then touched the bleeding wound on her lower jaw. 'This is going to need stitches. Your comrade hit me pretty hard.'

Ingo pulled a handkerchief from his coat and pressed it against the gaping cut. 'Here you go.'

'I'll go and get someone.' Greta started to move towards the door.

But Viktor held her back. 'Before we prove to your colleagues that we're more than just an irritant, please could you tell us what happened? Why is the war already over?'

'The short version,' Dana growled.

'Okay then,' Greta said hesitantly. 'So the Allies landed in France this last summer and Nazi Germany capitulated almost immediately after Colonel Claus von Stauffenberg assassinated the Führer. Then the Americans rolled through Europe – for freedom, as they put it.' Her voice was laced with contempt.

Viktor, Dana, Ingo and Coco looked on with perplexity, thinking more or less the same thing: a parallel universe in which the Stauffenberg plot had been successful?

When Greta lit another cigarette, they noticed her fingers trembling. She continued, 'They came over, reorganised the war and liberated the country from the Nazis, just so they could install themselves and their island lapdogs in a ready-made nest.' She inhaled deeply. 'Those deluded morons: Europe doesn't understand that it's fallen under the control of Roosevelt, Eisenhower and his war dogs. The Yanks ordered the Allied troops to march east, then they were split up to fight a new war with Russia – which meant the countries involved didn't have enough soldiers left to protect themselves. So Roosevelt's henchmen graciously occupied those territories, leaving the Tommies sitting safely behind the lines. So the British Empire has a new colony now – and Europe is in a worse state than India.'

The quartet exchanged meaningful looks once more.

Greta puffed harder on her cigarette. 'They turned Stalin into a figure of evil. First they supported him against Hitler, but now they want to destroy him so they can take over Russia's territories. Once the Soviets and the Japanese fall, it'll all be over. Roosevelt *needs* success; he needs European riches to stop the States from falling into poverty. All this talk about the New Deal? It's a sham. Truth is, the USA is broke – it's on the brink of collapse. There's suffering *everywhere*. The war saved the President's bacon.' Greta looked at each of them meaningfully in turn. 'Communism is the only way for people to coexist. Everyone's equal. Everyone's worth the same. Capitalism is hell. And that's what the Yanks and the Tommies are trying to inflict upon us. But it looks like we're the only ones who can see what's going on.'

'You're guerrilla fighters?' Dana clarified. 'What's your end goal?'

'Freedom for Germany,' came her immediate reply, and it was full of conviction.

'Communism, you mean,' replied Viktor. Would it achieve anything to tell her the idea had failed in their world? He decided against it. There was a chance Greta might be persuaded, but Theo and the others . . . ? Not in the brief window of time they had available.

'First we need to be rid of control by the Brits, the lapdogs of the Americans. And then the German people need to decide what *they* want.' The sniper pointed to her rifle, leaning up against the wall. 'We've already got rid of the Nazis and now we'll get rid of the hypocrites who want nothing more than to bleed us dry, just like Hitler and all his hot air – all that rubbish about the Aryan race.' Greta laughed bitterly. 'Aryans with obesity and clubfoot, if you ask me. And Himmler was the least Aryan person imaginable.

'What happened to the Nazi grandees after Hitler's death?' Dana asked.

'Dead. Convicted and executed. Along with all the leaders of the Nazi administration.' Greta pocketed the revolver and picked up her rifle. An idea had struck her – a brilliant idea, concerning the struggle against their oppressors. 'I'll go and get Theo. He has to see that you're special. And he can help us.'

'Help,' echoed Coco.

'You, Madame, using your gift, will reveal the Yanks' and the Tommies' intentions to us.' Greta winked at them. 'That'll make Theo very happy. And you'll have the Leipzig Secret Red Regiment at your back.' She left the hut. 'I'll bring our doctor over as well,' she called through the wooden door. Her steps receded.

'Right.' Dana leaned forwards, pressing the cloth tightly against her wound. She picked up the lighter, plucked a cigarette from the case, put it between her lips and lit it. 'Don't get me wrong. It looks like the Nazis are dead and gone, so that's all well and good.' She inhaled deeply. 'But it doesn't look as if things have actually got any better.'

Ingo took Coco's hands in his. 'You have to convince this Theo: convince him to help us – before this Secret Red Regiment starts to think you might be an excellent permanent addition to their urban guerrilla war outfit.' He maintained eye contact with her. 'It's a game – like on stage.'

As Coco nodded, the worst stage fright she had ever felt washed over her, a combination of an urge to throw up and excitement – and a sudden desire to knock back a few stiff drinks. Ingo could say what he liked, but this was no stage show and nor was this the standard confidence trick he was used to seeing from her. This was something far, far greater than that. It was nothing less than a minor miracle – and it came with the knowledge that death was lurking just around the corner. And Coco still had no idea why her clairvoyant abilities had suddenly started working to such a degree.

Somehow this world had given Coco powers that she had previously needed to fake on stage. Concentration, eye contact and a thought were enough here for her to feel things she had never before imagined – but what if this new ability disappeared as quickly as it had arrived, here one second, gone the next? What if she were to become a fraud and an imposter once more – the same person who had used sex to convince Ingo to forge certificates?

The door swung open.

Theo crashed into the little room, followed by Greta Weiß with her rifle hanging loosely over her shoulder. 'Right, so these stories I've been told sound like a load of rubbish to me,' he began. 'If they're not true' – he held his hand out and Greta gave him back his revolver – 'your lives will be over in a matter of seconds.' He looked at Coco invitingly and pulled back the hammer. 'Impress me. Or you'll die. Right here in 1944.'

Coco was no longer suffering from stage fright. She was now in mortal terror.

Near Frankfurt

Walter van Dam stepped carefully into his family's enormous abandoned house, remembering the stories he had heard from his mother, his grandparents and his daughter.

For all these years he had had no interested in hearing or reading any tales about the estate – because he had always been afraid that there might be some truth to them. He had dismissed it all as nonsense, of course, forbidding anyone from speaking about the rumours in his presence. Of course he had noticed Anna-Lena secretly reading the old records. He should have destroyed those documents – just like he should have destroyed this house.

Van Dam kept the barrel of the G36 pointing forwards. He was afraid that he might accidentally unleash the entire magazine if he was attacked. In truth, his knowledge of firearms was rudimentary at best, merely a smattering of information gleaned from events business associates had invited him to. Shotguns, muzzle-loaders, clay-pigeon shooting and the like, they were just hobbies for eccentric gentlemen. The most he'd done was when he'd been in the United States, when he had been dragged to a shooting range, where for a whole hour his colleagues had had him fire off all manner of weapons. He was certainly no professional – and he had no intention of becoming one either.

The blood smears on the floor were less obvious, but a pair of smooth soles had left impressions in the dust. These were accompanied by a second pair with a clear outline; they had come from the right-hand side, meaning the person must have entered through a window.

Where are Matthias and the fake Anna-Lena?

It was rather dark inside. Van Dam switched on the rifle's tactical light before venturing further into the vast estate. He waved the beam of light around, prioritising his ability to see over the desire to make himself a less obvious target. A few items of furniture were covered with sheets, with dust glittering on top.

He swung the light around again and this time the glow was cast over his chauffeur, whose upper body was half-slumped over a chest of drawers draped with a blood-soaked white sheet; his cap was lying carelessly next to him on the dirty floor. The sudden onset of light elicited no response from Matthias.

Van Dam spotted the fatal gash gaping on the right-hand side of his neck. The knife responsible was nowhere to be seen, which meant it must still be in the possession of the killer, lying in wait for him somewhere in the dark.

The false Anna-Lena's body was resting alongside the chest of drawers, dressed in her badly torn dark green evening gown. Her neck had also been slashed; the blood looked like paint that had dripped down from her red locks.

Van Dam struggled to fight off feelings of nausea as he approached the dead bodies. He needed to be certain that this was not his daughter, but just a copy – a mirage.

He knelt beside the corpse, reached out gently and opened the murdered woman's right eyelid. The pupil was white, blind and soulless. The other eye was the same. He straightened up with relief. Whoever or whatever this had been, it was not Anna-Lena – not *his* Anna-Lena.

A rumble sounded from the staircase leading upstairs, followed by hurried footsteps scuttling across the first-floor landing.

Surely this was a trick to lure him up the stairs. His arrival in the growling Urus would certainly not have gone unnoticed.

But that knowledge was of no use to him. If he wanted to apprehend the murderer, he had to go upstairs.

Van Dam switched off the lamp, trying to recall what he knew about the house and the factory. Had there not been a second way up – a wrought-iron spiral staircase linking the library's three floors?

Van Dam turned right and entered a deserted hallway. There was a musty smell, probably due to the old wallpaper: the damp had caused the printed paper to come loose, and wide strips were hanging down everywhere. The red fabric covering next to it was torn and motheaten, showing the bare plastered walls behind it. Van Dam hurried through the twilight and finally arrived at the entrance to his grandfather's library.

To his surprise, the shelves were still crammed with a wide variety of works of all sizes, with loose papers everywhere, some complete amid tattered remnants probably picked apart by the local rodent population to be used as nests. Maps hung down like banners, tattered and decayed in places. The elaborate glass dome had somehow withstood time and the elements, although moss and algae were growing over it, obscuring the light.

On his left was the spiral staircase that led up to the higher levels, which were surrounded by a gallery-like peripheral track with ladders attached that provided access to the highest shelves.

Van Dam was amazed. He had believed the books had all been sold off or given away – instead, here they were, many piled on top of pallets as if they'd been left to ripen.

He climbed the black iron stairs, each step producing a

metallic clang that sounded even louder against the background of the engulfing silence.

When he reached the first floor, he crossed over to the gallery and began to circle around to the exit, planning to creep up on the unknown killer from behind – but then he noticed some books on the ground, surrounded by fresh smooth-soled footprints: the murderer's footwear. The shelf had been smashed and the wooden partition broken.

While he was considering what might have been hidden behind it, he was suddenly struck by a full-frontal blow to the shoulder coming out of the darkness, quickly followed by a sharp stabbing pain.

Van Dam cried out in agony, staring at the blade, the knife handle and the hand holding it.

CHAPTER VII

Leipzig, 1 January 1945

Coco waited with Viktor, Ingo and Dana outside the door, on the other side of which the Leipzig Secret Red Regiment committee were deciding what to do with the quartet. They were in the southern part of the city, in Connewitz, where the bombs had blown enormous holes in the roads throughout the entire district. The house where the council was meeting served as mass accommodation for the homeless; it had become a safe haven for the Communists.

They were all in local clothing now, which was far less conspicuous than their own high-tech black gear. They were guarded by four partisan fighters dressed in normal street clothes, all of whom were smoking like chimneys, armed with Luger pistols in under-arm holsters recovered from the *Wehrmacht*. No one was really paying attention to the prisoners, since it would be suicide for anyone to take to the streets now the Brits and the Yanks were hunting them.

'Happy New Year,' said Ingo, raising an imaginary champagne flute. This was certainly the most unusual New Year's Eve he had spent so far, but he thought a sense of occasion might do them all some good. 'Good performance back there, Coco.' He touched her on the shoulder. 'You really impressed Theo.'

'May this year be better than the last,' Dana replied drily. She now had a thin line of stiches across her chin. The doctor had taken good care of her.

'It will be.' Coco adjusted her blouse.

'If you say it will,' said Ingo, relieved, 'then it will.'

Coco was starting to feel rather afraid of herself. She had been able to tell the Communist leader things from his past that no one other than he had known – until now.

She had started with how he had broken his leg after jumping from a tree into a small lake and had almost drowned; he'd been saved by a Sinto traveller whom the Nazis had later thrown into a concentration camp. This revelation had convinced the Communist that he was dealing with a real medium here, but after another fifteen minutes of scarily accurate reporting on his life, Theo Schwimmer was utterly speechless. Speechless, fascinated and shaken to his core, since she had elicited so many memories from within him – good, and bad.

It was with this firm impression in mind that while the rest of the city was celebrating the new year, he had convened the council of the Leipzig Secret Red Regiment. While a few fireworks were being set off and illuminating the night sky, six men and four women were busy discussing how best to deal with Coco, Ingo, Viktor and Dana.

'I still don't understand,' Ingo whispered to Coco.

'Neither do I. But these things happen,' she replied perfunctorily.

'What are we going to do if they decide to execute us anyway?' Dana folded her arms. She felt unusually feminine and fragile in a blouse and skirt. The clothes had changed her in a way she was not at all comfortable with. 'You and I both know what our skills are. Maybe we'll need to use them soon.'

Viktor knew she was referring to Darfur. They had each been there, albeit on opposing sides. 'We can decide that as and when – but I certainly won't wait too long again.' He nodded, to show he was willing to consider using force, should it be necessary for their escape. 'Let's see what this Red Regiment has in mind for us first.'

'So we're agreed: our real story stays between us,' Ingo said. 'We won't tell them anything until they agree to our demands, right?'

'Yes,' said Coco firmly with a fixed gaze. 'Only once we know where Spanger and Anna-Lena have got to will we make a deal with them.'

Viktor gestured to the door, which was being opened. 'The council must have reached a decision.'

Their guards escorted them into the little room, which was now drowning in cigarette and pipe smoke.

The council members, all sporting red armbands with hammer-and-sickle insignia, were standing around with relief and curiosity etched on their faces; empty beer and wine bottles littered the wobbly table, alongside a few dirty glasses.

Theo Schwimmer approached them with his arms outstretched and handed them each a glass of something smelling faintly of alcohol. Vodka. '*Na zdorovie!* Good news,' he whispered to them. 'You're *not* going to be executed. And we've received new information about your friends.'

The quartet sipped anxiously, waiting.

'As for you, *tovarishch*,' said Theo solemnly, pushing a perplexed Coco forwards, '*you* will be the key to our victory against the oppressors. Down with British and American colonialism! Freedom for Germany; freedom for Europe! Long live Stalin!'

'Long live Stalin!' came a chorus of voices.

'We've discussed the matter,' said Theo to the four of them. 'We will help you; you will help us.' He laid a hand on Coco's shoulder. 'You, Madame Fendi, will allow us to see into the future, foreseeing the actions of the Tommies and the Yanks, meaning we can strike where they're at their weakest.'

'Sabotage, assassinations, ambushes,' said one of the council women. She was wearing tweed trousers and a white shirt under a matching tweed jacket. Her light brown hair was cut short. 'Supply lines, high-ranking army officers, secret bases and entrances,' she added, shaking hands with each of them in turn. 'My name is Sonja Smetana – Political Commissioner. We've recognised the possibilities we might have with your aid, relieving the pressure on the Red Army behind the lines of our new colonial rulers. That will give Comrade Stalin the chance for a glorious victory.' Before Coco could stop her, she gave her a kiss on each cheek. 'You're a true blessing, my dear.'

Coco, wanting nothing more than to down her vodka in one, was prevented only by Ingo's gentle movement.

'We're looking for our friends,' Viktor reminded those

present. 'You can be sure of our help once we've got them back, Comrade.'

'No, not *once*. There'll be a certain degree of concurrence to our actions,' replied the commissioner with a smile. 'You'll understand what I mean soon enough.'

Theo beckoned to Greta, who was just entering the room, her sniper rifle slung over one shoulder like a rucksack. 'She's made a few observations.'

Greta also received a glass of vodka, which she drained in one go. 'She's gone,' she reported. 'Anna-Lena van Dam. She's been taken off, along with her friends' bodies. First she was interrogated by Lieutenant Attington – he's Intelligence. My informants told me an American, a captain by the name of Wallace, was particularly interested in Miss van Dam – and that it had something to do with the cellar at the tavern.' She looked regretfully at their concerned faces. 'I was lying in wait nearby when a lorry pulled up. I saw Wallace leaving the building. Shortly afterwards, two body bags were brought upstairs, and a Tommy was taken away in a third.'

'That means they got Spanger.' Ingo exhaled loudly. Another loss. Their team was being decimated. 'Fuck it.'

'What was he doing in the cellar?' Dana looked at Viktor. 'Are you thinking what I'm thinking?'

'I guess so.' He supposed Spanger had tried to escape – without them. 'He might have been waiting for us there – to cover our retreat,' he said, trying to put a more honourable gloss on the whole situation.

'Who's this Wallace?' Ingo asked.

'Officially he's on the staff of General Eisenhower,

the military governor. He handles counter-espionage and everything relating to that,' Smetana explained. 'He's also responsible for tracking down people with specialist knowledge about the Nazis. The Americans have seized almost all of Germany's brightest inventors and researchers from lots of different fields, promising them impunity from punishment for their Nazi past.'

Greta took another glass of vodka. 'Wallace was also watching his Tommy lackeys load an old door into the lorry. Massive it was, frame and everything. Then they all scarpered.'

The political commissioner frowned. 'A *door*?'

Now the quartet understood Wallace's interest in Anna-Lena. The American had somehow discovered that it was a portal – or at the very least, something with a mystery behind it. And because he must have worked out their weapons and equipment weren't from this era, he was holding young Miss van Dam to interrogate her.

'Then you must know where they've taken our friend?' Ingo took another glass of vodka as well. He could scarcely hide his dismay. How could they possibly return to the present without the door? 'You'll help us to get them out, won't you?'

'What do your spies say, Commissar Smetana? You've got friends everywhere,' said Theo, turning to face the commissioner. 'And in very high places, I suspect.'

She clasped her hands together. 'Before I answer that, I'd like to know why Wallace was moving a door out of a vault.' She looked at the sniper. 'I assume you made enquiries?'

'Of course, Comrade Commissioner,' replied Greta, 'but no one in the inn had any explanation for it.'

Smetana smiled at the quartet. 'And you? Any ideas?'

'No,' Coco lied. The last thing they needed was to spark off a race to find the door; they needed that passage to return to their own time and that would be quite out of the question if the Red Regiment got wind of what it could do. 'I suspect our friend made something up on the spot to set Wallace on a false trail.'

They guessed the matter was far from settled in the eyes of the commissioner, but she left it for the time being. 'If Attington and his intelligence cronies are interested in particular prisoners, they're normally taken to a secret location,' she explained. 'So far we haven't been able to figure out where this might be, but we suspect it's most likely to be a Nazi facility taken over by the Tommies.' She looked at Greta and Theo with a sudden mixture of anger and regret. 'We've got a lot of friends imprisoned there. So we'll free Miss van Dam and at the same time save some decent Communists from execution, imprisonment or life in a labour camp.'

Viktor was not at all happy with how the situation was developing. Wallace, Smetana, the door, Anna-Lena – they were all connected. He was sad about losing Spanger, but in a battle there would always be casualties. But he had not, however, expected to find himself in such a situation, or having to switch into this mode. 'So that's where our friend is?'

'I imagine,' said Greta, 'Wallace will take the young lady with him. I've heard rumours that he's recruiting people for a special unit in the States to investigate paranormal phenomena, just like the Nazis did. And the Red Army.' She winked at Smetana. 'Is that not the case?'

'If Anna-Lena van Dam's been taken across the pond, we won't be able to do anything about it,' Dana pointed out. Then she added softly, 'And we'll never be able to return home.'

'I agree,' said Viktor. 'Wallace won't waste any time in turning this precious discovery into one of his assets.'

'Anything to give the States an advantage in their war against Russia and Japan,' Dana concluded.

'Exactly – that's it! Now it's just a question of where to find your friend,' Theo added eagerly. 'We need to track down where that base is.'

Smetana turned to Coco. 'Can you find it? You're a medium; Comrade Schwimmer was mightily impressed with your gift.' Smetana looked around to see the rest of the council nodding in encouragement. 'I can get us some soldiers to help with the operation. This is about our people as much as yours.'

Coco stiffened. She'd have to hope once again that her new abilities would not abandon her – but she did already have an idea of how to track down the hidden base. 'I need a map of Europe.' She took out her pendulum. 'I can find this place.'

The Communists found the map she had asked for at lightning speed; the bottles and glasses were cleared from the table and the large piece of paper was rolled out over the surface.

Dana stood next to Viktor. 'We could always try grabbing

the commissioner and exerting a little more pressure,' she whispered to him. 'The Communists are completely under the spell of our medium here.'

Coco pressed two fingers against her temple and swung the pendulum over the map.

Ingo put his hand on her back to show he was with her. He found it a little depressing to not be able to contribute very much to their mission. His gauges were back in the cave, and in any case, there probably wasn't a huge amount he could have done with them.

'No,' replied Viktor after a few seconds. He watched Coco's blank expression moving back and forth across the table. The engraved cylindrical golden pendulum was tugging on its chain and guiding her hand. 'We've still got the upper hand.'

'What will we do if they ask Madame Fendi to make a list afterwards? A list of important sites?' Dana looked over at the guards by the entrance, who were completely distracted by the performance. 'You heard them: they're after information for sabotage, attacks and assassinations.' Their medium was going to be in high demand, for the Communists were determined to use her to bring about victory for Stalin.

Viktor picked up another glass of vodka. 'I don't know what our next move is,' he admitted. 'I think we might just have to improvise.'

Dana's feeling of unease remained, but there was little she could do by herself.

Coco conjured an image of Anna-Lena in her mind, concentrating intensely and with all her strength, just as she had done the first time she tried to make contact with her. The pendulum pulled on the chain, giving her new directions; she followed its movements and her intuition – and then there came a long pulse.

'There!' shouted Coco. She looked around for a pen and quickly marked a spot on the map. 'That's where the base is.' She took a deep breath, her face a picture of exhausted radiance. She was delighted to have passed her test and hugged Ingo with relief.

He held her close, whispering, 'Very well done.'

Everyone huddled around the faint pencil mark drawn on the paper, which was in the middle of an idyllic green area in what looked like East Prussia.

'But . . .' Ingo looked uncertainly at Coco, then back at the map. 'There's nothing there. Nothing there at all. Are you—?'

'No, your girlfriend's right. Her clairvoyant powers haven't lied. There's something there,' Smetana interrupted, stony-faced. She shut her eyes. 'And it'll be impossible to get there.'

She opened her eyes, her jaw clenched, and looked at the quartet. 'I'm sorry. We can't help you.'

Near Rastenburg, East Prussia, 4 January 1945

Anna-Lena sat in the comfortable quarters she had been taken to after a short flight and a long drive. There was running water, expensive furniture and even a small bar in a large cabinet. A picture of Adolf Hitler on the wall was host to several small holes, and three darts were lying directly underneath it. Someone had clearly been having fun with the *Führer*.

The sound of vehicle engines and occasional scraps of conversations from patrolling guards could be heard through the locked and barred windows. She had heard the roar of large propellers at a great height on several occasions, suggesting Allied bombers were passing over the area, probably heading east to the front with a view to raining hell upon the Russian positions.

Anna-Lena got up from her chair, looked through the window pane and watched the nocturnal activity of the base. The idea of staying in this reality filled her with terror, but how could she possibly escape? Was there even still a route back to the twenty-first century?

Escaping imprisonment by herself seemed impossible: too many soldiers, too many lights and beady eyes watching her; they'd discover her the moment she set foot outside her quarters. And even if she were to get away, she would be stuck in the middle of nowhere. The journey had started across open countryside, then they'd travelled through a forest until they arrived at a military facility that had been built by the Nazis. The British and Americans were using it as a base now; Captain Wallace had appropriated it to coordinate their offensives against Stalin's Red Army.

What had once been known as the *Wolf's Lair* was now renamed *Fort India*, with the buildings all named after Anglo-Indian provinces and their capitals. It was, Anna-Lena suspected, getting equally notorious in the hands of the new colonial rulers.

Britain was making no secret of its intent to administer Europe on behalf of the United States. The Empire was back, full of verve and colonial condescension – only this time as an appendage to the greater power.

Anna-Lena's attention was directed to a heavily guarded truck.

In the glow of the headlights, she could see a group of British soldiers were carefully loading a door onto it – the very door from the cellar in the Katharinenstraße. They had not removed a worn old door and driven it miles through the countryside to a heavily guarded military base simply for a lark. Wallace must suspect that he'd found something special.

How do they know what it does? Excitement and hope flooded through Anna-Lena. She put her hands on the windowsill and watched the action unfolding. If she could make it to the door, hit the knocker and activate the force field, escape would be possible.

The workers laid the door onto a mattress and put another on top to give it extra padding, then they lashed the two covers together to stop the door from being damaged.

'They're taking it away,' muttered Anna-Lena to herself. 'Captain Wallace is going to fly us both to America.'

There was a knock at the door and two soldiers in British uniforms entered. They asked Anna-Lena to accompany them, adding, 'Quickly now, Miss.'

'Certainly. Of course.' Anna-Lena feigned being intimidated, hoping to lull them into complacency so she'd be able to snatch any chance of escape so she could reach the door before the truck drove off. One strike of the knocker and she would be back, able to carry on with her investigations, find the man in the pin-striped suit who had tried to trap her in that hellish world of sirens and howling wolves – and punish him.

As they strode quickly through the building, she asked, 'Where are you taking me?' Her voice was whiny.

'To Captain Wallace,' replied one of the soldiers, taking her arm to guide her. 'And some more of your ilk.'

Anna-Lena's ears pricked up. *What's that supposed to mean?* she wondered, but she gave no reply.

She glanced out the window at the lorry. They were still loading it, as the door was not the only object being prepared for a long journey. It reminded her of Indiana Jones and how the Ark of the Covenant had been stored by the Americans in a large warehouse – and had disappeared for ever.

She was still furious with herself for telling them all that nonsense about the Arctic bunker, the headquarters on the Moon and flying saucers. She had completely underestimated their interest in all that – and now they thought she was a sort of super-Nazi.

They arrived at a meeting room where Captain Wallace, a handful of British and US officers and a man and a woman in grey overalls were sitting around a large table covered with maps and sketches, outlines and exploded diagrams of various pieces of equipment. Many of the papers bore the swastika.

'Ah, Miss van Dam.' Captain Wallace, now dressed in a plain grey three-piece suit and tie, pointed to an empty chair. 'Come on in.' He gestured towards the two civilians.

'This is Dr Wilhelm Theissen, and this is Professor Eugenia Zulke. They worked at the research facilities in the Robinson Complex and at Breitenheide. They've very kindly lent us these beautiful plans.'

Anna-Lena could not tell precisely what the drawings were, but from the inscriptions and sketches she guessed it might be some kind of engine.

'Good evening,' she said politely, playing up her uncertainty.

'This is the young lady,' Captain Wallace announced to the group, 'who told me all about a few secret Nazi projects – a bunker in the Arctic, planes in the shape of discs, and plans to set up a base on the Moon, apparently.' He pointed to the plans. 'These are improved drive units for jet aeroplanes and V3 missiles that were never put into use.' He looked at the Nazi scientists. 'Doctor, Professor, we need your advice. With these drives, would the regime have been able to reach the Moon?'

The two Germans shook their heads in unison.

'And I have to add,' said Professor Zulke, 'that that's the biggest load of rubbish I've ever heard.' She looked at Anna-Lena through her round nickel glasses and laughed indignantly. '*Tsk*. I've never seen this young lady at any of our research institutions before.'

'It might have been a secret SS project,' interjected an officer. 'Himmler had a bit of a thing for these sorts of matters. The *Führer* as well.' He thumped the solid concrete wall. 'Just think about *this* monster of a base, for a start. The *Wolf's Lair*. As soon as we track down the documents from Organisation Todt, we'll perhaps know a little more.'

'Rubbish,' snarled Doctor Theissen, whose right cheek bore a large scar. 'How was anyone supposed to live up there? On the dark side, to stop them from being discovered? Utter nonsense. We haven't got the technology. Just ask Wernher von Braun and his specialists – they'll confirm it.' He also gave Anna-Lena a condescending look. 'I've never seen this girl before in my life. Plus, she looks barely eighteen, so what could she possibly offer? She certainly doesn't look like a genius, with that little ring in her nose. What's that even supposed to be? Are we all Hottentots now?'

The men laughed softly. Captain Wallace wore a pained expression.

'Well.' One of the American officers rose to speak. 'Just as I thought, you've found yourself a little imposter, Captain. She can stay in Germany and take her punishment here, I reckon.'

Bugger. Anna-Lena was desperate to find out where the door was – her only way out. She feverishly racked her brains for everything she knew about the movies' conspiracy theories, knowing she couldn't afford this to turn into a technical battle with the scientists, as she would stand no chance there. But it was crucial for her to at least remain interesting.

'I should add we picked up two of her people as well,' said Captain Wallace, turning around. His hand reached for a suitcase, which he then placed on the table. He opened it and showed them the confiscated weapons: a P99 and a Heckler & Koch MP5.

My people? Anna-Lena had no idea who Wallace was

talking about, but those weapons looked far too modern for 1945.

'See these? They were made in Germany – but I've never seen these models before and neither have any of the prisoners we've interrogated.' He pointed to Anna-Lena. 'Your people were captured in a cellar in Leipzig – with this thing here.' He pulled out the Kevlar vest and threw it at Theissen, who caught it reflexively. While it was still in motion, the captain drew his pistol and fired twice at the perplexed scientist.

The vest caught the bullets, though the impact threw the screaming Theissen onto his back. The officers began shouting loudly, while Anna-Lena put her hands over her ears.

Captain Wallace removed the Kevlar vest from the whimpering scientist. 'See? Not a damn scratch.' He showed them the vest containing the compressed projectiles. 'What kind of material is this? It's not a flak jacket, nor is it Russian plate armour.' He turned it over, examining it curiously. 'Come on, boffins! *What is it*?'

Doctor Theissen touched his chest, trying to find any wounds. The professor was still shaking from the shock.

This was Anna-Lena's chance. 'It's Kevlar, made from carbon fibre. My father helped to develop it.' She looked at the prisoners in their overalls. 'In a secret location. The same place where the sub-machine gun was made. And the portals. He was part of a special unit, but he was shot by the SS to stop him from passing on his expertise.'

'What *portals*?' The British officer looked at his American allies. 'What portals is she talking about? We do seem to be underestimating her rather.'

'It's not important,' said Captain Wallace, trying to play down the door's significance for him. 'The weapons and the – the *Kev-lar* – they're proof that there was a unit capable of making these sorts of things. Things that you' – he looked at the scientists – 'apparently know nothing about. That's our evidence, gentlemen.'

Anna-Lena decided to play around with a few conspiracy theories from her own era. She tried not to grin at the thought that she might be the one to plant the seeds of such myths. 'New *Berchtesgaden* One and Two.'

They all looked at her expectantly.

'That's what the projects were called,' Anna-Lena continued, trying to remember the details from a programme she had once watched about Nazi conspiracy theories. 'Bunkers – in the Arctic and Antarctic where U-boats or long-range bombers could retreat to.' She looked around at the officers. 'That's all I'm willing to say – for now. If you want to know more, I've got a few demands of my own first.' She tried to catch the captain's eye. 'About the portal I used to enter the cellar: you have no idea how to operate it or how dangerous it is.'

'Good Lord,' cried a British officer who looked well over sixty; he stroked his well-kept pencil moustache, 'this is all most curious.' He looked around at his men, then at the Americans. 'Well? What are our spies saying? Seen anything anywhere where we've given Adolf's boys a damn good hiding outside their Thousand-Year Reich?'

The soldier standing next to him – his aide-de-camp, maybe – cleared his throat. 'General, in advance of this meeting I took it upon myself to do a little research. It matches what this miraculous young lady is telling us.' He reached into his pocket, pulled out a map and unfolded it. 'In fact, the Germans did launch an expedition to Antarctica, in the winter of 1938–39, on the MS *Schwabenland*.' He passed the documents around. 'She was a catapult ship, equipped with two Dornier flying boats. Our spies believed the Germans wanted to secure access to whaling territory, sir, because we had the Atlantic locked down by that point.

'Whaling?' Captain Wallace guffawed. 'Holy shit, you thought Adolf was looking for some Aryan whales or something?'

'Moby Dick – the white whale!' shouted another, laughing. 'How could we possibly have overlooked that?'

The group roared with mirth, except for the aide-de-camp, who murmured quietly, 'Whale fat and blubber, sir. The Germans need it just as much as we do, for nitroglycerine.'

The general wiped the tears from his eyes, picked up a magnifying glass and looked at one of the photos from the folder. His expression suddenly turned serious. 'Gentlemen! Gentlemen, look at this,' he thundered, silencing the room immediately. 'This spot over here.'

Anna-Lena leaned forwards. The picture showed the expedition party, with a swastika flag planted in the ground.

'The words *New Swabia* can be seen over the part of coast nearest to Queen Maud Land,' explained the aide-de-camp, taking another sheet out. 'And then there's this. This appeared on 31 December, but the message got lost among all the New Year celebrations. The intelligence officer concerned has already been reprimanded, sir.'

Anna-Lena read the message and had to force herself not to burst out laughing. It was all she could manage to remain calm and not give the secret away.

In December 1944, two German submarines – U-530 and U-977 – docked at the Argentine port of Mar de la Plata. The orders to arrest the men on board had already been issued, but no one had given any thought to the route taken by the submarines. The captains were thought to be fugitives, trying to escape captivity as far away from Europe as possible – but that was all about to change thanks to Anna-Lena's story.

'Mar de la Plata. The submarines could have dropped off cargo or passengers in Queen Maud Land before being discovered,' said the general. 'Bigsby, what the blazes—? How can we only be finding all this out now?' He threw the folder down onto the table. 'I'm sending a unit out immediately to investigate this ice hole. If there are any frost Nazis out there, I want them destroyed.'

'Rightly so, General Blacksmith, sir,' Captain Wallace agreed. 'The last thing we need is for Nazis to turn up at the poles after we've already unleashed our nuclear arsenal on Russia and Japan.'

The uniformed officers banged on the table, making it rattle dully.

Anna-Lena could not erase the images of Hiroshima and Nagasaki from her mind's eye: two cities utterly devastated, razed to the ground. Thousands dead, burned alive by radiation, children born with deformed features and a lifetime of suffering for the descendants of those affected.

And Wallace had spoken about an arsenal . . .

How many bombs were the Allies going to drop? The scale of the destruction would be enormous. If the Russians and Japanese did not surrender, they would be obliterated.

Moscow?

St Petersburg?

Tokyo?

How many cities would perish in atomic fire, burning to a crisp for the sake of their squalid idea of peace? Anna-Lena began to feel very queasy.

'Very good, gentlemen,' said Captain Wallace, addressing the staff. 'Then within the next few days I'll be leaving our beautiful Fort India, along with my cargo, my prisoners and our miraculous Miss van Dam. Your information's vital – indispensable for the outcome of the war.' He put the guns back in the suitcase and threw the vest over his shoulder like a saddle-bag. 'I'll keep you updated, gentlemen.'

'You have our blessing, Captain,' said General Blacksmith. 'Oh yes, and what about these . . . portals?' He regarded Anna-Lena suspiciously. 'What was all that about, young lady?'

'My apologies,' the captain interjected with a dismissive smile. 'That's a matter for *my* secret services.' He turned to the guards at the door. 'Take Miss van Dam back to her room. I have to finalise my preparations.'

To stop them from making any further enquiries, he waited until Anna-Lena had stepped out into the hall, flanked by the same two British soldiers, then followed her.

This part of Anna-Lena's plan was working just as she'd intended. 'When are we leaving?' she asked.

'Soon,' said Wallace with a nod. 'Either from Breitenheide or the Robinson Complex, depending on which aircraft are available. Everything that's got a propeller is currently hauling bombs over to Russia. My friends in Washington are really looking forward to meeting you. Sleep well. I'll send someone to pick you up.' He disappeared down a side corridor.

On her way back to her quarters, Anna-Lena looked through the windows at the truck, which was now being painted over with new military insignia by two American soldiers. When they had finished, they dismissed the British troops standing guard, to be replaced by three American soldiers who climbed into the cabin. The engine started and the lorry rumbled its way down the road to a big building like a hall.

As she watched, the doors opened to reveal numerous crates that were evidently also meant to be removed.

'Just like in *Indiana Jones*.' Anna-Lena's plan to steal away secretly to the door and escape through it before she could be shipped off to the States had just become significantly harder.

Near Frankfurt

Walter van Dam was spectacularly relieved that he had put on the Kevlar vest, which had stopped the knife from fully entering his body. The tip was buried about half an inch deep into his shoulder.

His attacker was too late in noticing this; he ripped out the blade and stretched his hand in an attempt to cut van Dam's throat and finish the job; his other hand was pushing down the barrel of van Dam's G36.

He did the only thing he could think of: he dropped the assault rifle and drew his pistol – he couldn't pull the trigger, for it still had its safety on, but he managed to block the path of the descending blade.

The knife broke with a buzzing snap, the force of the impact driving the muzzle into van Dam's face. The taste of blood spread through his mouth immediately and he could barely make out his attacker through the stars in his eyes.

A few inches of metal protruded from the knife's handle, which his opponent tried to use to launch another assault. 'I'll open you up, old man,' he threatened. 'You won't stop us. Your grandfather would be turning in his grave if he knew what you were doing – how unworthy you are of the family name.'

Van Dam turned the muzzle in his assailant's direction, released the safety and fired off a series of bullets in quick succession.

The shots rang out as the powerful recoil caused the barrel to swing wildly upwards. The fourth bullet hit its target, passing right through his assailant's hand, followed immediately by the fifth. Blown-off fingers flew through the air, splattering blood everywhere, and the plastic handle of the knife burst into splinters flying in all directions, piercing both men's skin.

With a scream, the attacker backed off, but he was

reaching for the nearby G36 with his uninjured left hand. 'You're done for now!'

Van Dam carried on firing, despatching the rest of the magazine wildly into the man's body.

Bleeding and panting, his merciless adversary fell onto the weathered floorboards and began to vomit blood. Red liquid streamed out from four different wounds, staining the wood and the surrounding books and pages. After what felt like an eternity, his agony ceased and he lay dead, his left leg twitching a macabre farewell.

Van Dam slumped against the railing. Wheezing, he stared at the dead man and the pool of blood he was sitting in. The knife left him in no doubt: he had found his chauffeur's murderer and had come within a hair's breadth of becoming his third victim. Without warning, van Dam found himself vomiting wildly. As he threw up, he turned away from the gruesome scene before him.

When he had recovered, he spat to clear his mouth, then hauled himself into a kneeling position in an attempt to compose himself. He had to get to the bottom of these mysterious attacks.

The dead man had a shoulder bag, full to the brim with items he had ransacked from the villa. Van Dam picked it up and opened it.

Loose sheets of paper, torn pages and a notebook fell out. He saw some handwritten lines and recognised his grandfather's script. The thief-cum-murderer had obviously taken these for a reason.

Van Dam skimmed the contents, but the more he read

and understood what the notes were about, the less he wanted to believe it all. It was primarily concerned with a group of conspirators who ruled the world; with portals located all over the earth through which initiates could pass to spin their webs of intrigue; with events in the past that these people had set in motion to maintain their influence in the present – wars, disasters, assassinations, calamities and deaths.

And his grandfather had been part of it.

That's why his grandmother and his parents had wanted nothing to do with the mansion and the factory – they had known about all of this; they had wanted to keep their distance.

Van Dam stuffed the pages back into the bag, and as he did so, a drawing caught his attention: a sketch of a door, marked with numerous annotations in small, barely legible handwriting.

He switched on his torch to see it better.

The door's knocker and the base plate were apparently made from a specific material, referred to here as a *Particula*. The scribbled notes suggested that these were fragments from an unknown comet, and if they were to strike each other, a force field would be generated that would allow the users to travel enormous distances in a fraction of a second.

Van Dam turned the page with growing horror.

The notes were for the most part blurred and illegible, but they were enough to give him an idea as to the scope of the disaster that might occur.

... abandon the headquarters within the next three months, even if it might be seen as unexpected.

My calculations are unequivocal: the Particulae are losing their stability.

These so-called 'accidents' are no such thing. Several portals have already disintegrated in the past because the fragments have become worn out, creating an enormous exothermic reaction.

The more you use the doors, the faster the Particulae will become unstable. More and more agents will die if they go through the old portals. So I strongly advise against using them any more. Nothing we had originally set out to achieve is valid now. We've only succeeded in creating temporal shifts and arbitrary realities.

Based on this knowledge, I have changed our manufacturing techniques. There is a next-generation door in the workshop, equipped with protection against Particulae. I'm working on the assumption that

Van Dam stood up. The dead man's blood had seeped into his trousers in several places, causing the fabric to stick unpleasantly to his legs.

His eyes fell upon the fingers he had shot off. He quickly removed the mini laptop from underneath his Kevlar vest. The computer had remained unscathed so he picked up the detached index finger and pressed it against the scanner.

The display lit up, revealing photographs of his second team. He swiped through them, reading the information that appeared over each member's name when he clicked on their pictures. A quick read-through revealed that they had been keeping secrets from him. All of them.

He lowered the laptop and considered his options.

He was now free to go down into the cellar, although he'd have next to no chance of success if he followed in the footsteps of his latest team, all of whom had lied to him. But the mere thought of the darkness and the narrow corridors and chambers sent his pulse rate and breathing into overdrive.

Or he could march into the burnt-down workshop to see what this supposed next-generation door was all about. Perhaps he could use it to save Anna-Lena, like a sort of back entrance or secret passage, rather than fighting his way through a series of long underground tunnels.

Or maybe that hope is simply cowardice, thought Walter van Dam, as rain tumbled from the dark cloud above the property, hammering down loudly onto the library's glass roof.

CHAPTER VIII

Near Rastenburg, East Prussia, 8 January 1945

The dart flew through the air and hit the middle of Adolf Hitler's right bollock.

Anna-Lena grinned and marked down 1000 points. Looking at the other holes in the photograph, it appeared she was the first guest to have achieved such a feat.

There came a knock at the door and it swung open. 'Miss van Dam, would you please gather your belongings and come with us?' demanded the British soldier.

'If you were a true gentlemen you'd carry my bag for me.' Anna-Lena had not intended the rebuke seriously, but smiled at the sudden uncertainty in the man's face. 'It's fine. I haven't got much with me.' She hurriedly packed up the last of the clothes and toiletries that she had been given. 'Where are we off to?'

'To the United States of America, Miss.'

'Well, yes, I gathered as much.' She closed the suitcase and snapped the clasps into place. 'I meant more where are we going *from*?'

'That's for Captain Wallace to know.' He tipped his cap

apologetically. 'But I've heard,' he continued in a low voice, 'we're going to Rominten. In the Robinson Complex.'

'Will it be a long journey?'

The soldier shook his head and went to pick up her suitcase, which she refused. 'It'll be relatively quick, I reckon.' He indicated she should lead the way. A second guard was waiting in the corridor and the three of them walked quickly through the house and out into the open.

This was the first time Anna-Lena had seen Fort India and the former *Wolf's Lair* – at least, those parts which were above-ground. She counted more than forty buildings; the soldier who'd spoken earlier volunteered the information that there were at least a thousand people working in the different buildings, which were split into a number of restricted zones.

To her surprise, the runway on the private airfield was empty – but there was a railway station, where a train was waiting for them instead. Billowing smoke, black and white, rose from the funnels as the engine snorted and hissed out its excess steam. There were eight carriages attached to the locomotive, with armoured vehicles equipped with flak and light gun battery at either end. A machine-gun turret stood imposingly on a platform in front of the train.

Anna-Lena read the signs mounted on the barbed wire fences, warning about a minefield. This was where the Nazis had waged war from; now the Allies were using it against Russia. Radio and telephone wires ran from here to every location on the front, as well as to the larger German cities.

It looked like she was not the only one being taken to Rominten. The loading of prisoners was in full swing, with men and women dressed in civilian clothes settling into their comfortable cabins. The contrast between this and the horrific transport conditions to the Nazi concentration camp could not have been more pronounced. At least the victors had not copied this particular piece of barbarism.

'Who are they?' Anna-Lena asked her British escort.

'Important people like you, Miss van Dam,' replied the soldier vaguely.

'Scientists?'

'That too. I'm afraid I'm not allowed to tell you anything, but I'm sure you'll get to know one another on the train,' he said, lowering his voice and adding, 'There are some high-ranking Communists and Soviet spies from a few different European countries, Red sympathisers and a handful of former Nazi bigwigs from whom we're trying to get information. Defectors like you.' He lowered his voice even further. 'Be careful, Miss.'

'What do you mean?'

'Well, the Reds hate us as much the Nazis – there have already been some fights and even a few deaths on previous journeys. So stay on your guard.' He sounded genuinely concerned.

Anna-Lena nodded.

The lorry with its newly pained lettering drove out of the hangar and deposited its crates into the penultimate carriage behind the gun turret. There was a long wide box marked *Top Secret*, which Anna-Lena supposed contained the door.

Anna-Lena's plan was clear: to find a way into that carriage while they were travelling, then use the portal. If that didn't work, she would have one final opportunity on the aeroplane, after which, once she arrived in the States, all hope would be lost. Her ominous allusions to ice bunkers, flying saucers and bases on the moon would fall apart like wet tissue paper under scrutiny by experts, and in one stroke she would become an imposter, with no value to them at all.

Captain Wallace stood in front of the train, holding a list several pages' long and directing the boarding prisoners to their respective carriages. 'Ah, Miss van Dam,' he greeted her coldly. 'My second most valuable piece of cargo, if you'll pardon the expression.'

'I haven't really got a choice, Captain.' She pointed at the train. 'It looks rather comfortable.'

'It used to belong to your *Führer*, or one of the other Nazi higher-ups. I'm sure you'll feel honoured to travel in it,' he said. 'The flight over to the United States will be much more Spartan: we'll be crammed inside the belly of a long-range bomber. There was nothing better available.' He pointed to the runway. 'This is a bit too short, sadly – otherwise we wouldn't be having to charge around the country like this.' He looked down at his list. 'Carriage three, compartment three. Have a safe journey.' At his signal she was moved on, but she was still in earshot when he added, 'And don't even think about trying to escape on the way.'

'Why, because you'll capture me again?' she teased as she walked away.

'No. Because you'll be shot on sight. We can't afford for your knowledge to fall into anyone else's hands,' came his serious reply. 'I hope you understand, Miss van Dam.'

Anna-Lena most certainly did not understand, but it still remained to be seen how they would react if she tried to break into the freight carriage.

A few minutes later she found herself in a compartment with two men and a woman in civilian clothes sitting silently. There were books, newspapers and magazines piled on one seat, with bottles of lemonade, glass tumblers, biscuits and sandwiches laid out on the table. The woman and one of the men were smoking, enveloping the cabin in a haze of tobacco.

'Have a good journey, then,' said her guard in farewell, shoving her suitcase through the door and towards the other passengers' luggage.

'Thank you. For everything.' Anna-Lena smiled at him as she sat and folded her hands in her lap. Through the window she watched Wallace sorting out the last of the prisoners. Then he gave a signal to the driver and hurried towards the locomotive.

A piercing whistle rang out and the train set off with a jerk. Glasses and bottles jiggled around in their holders and the tower of sandwiches collapsed. Fort India was already gliding past them and before she knew it they were passing through a dense forest that swallowed up all light, making reading impossible.

One of the smokers stood up and lit the four lamps with his lighter. The compartment immediately became brighter. 'Major Karl Tandroff,' he said by way of introduction.

'Division of skulls, runes and futurism. And who do I have the pleasure of accompanying on this most exclusive trip?'

'Hertha Grünmann,' replied the female smoker. 'Typist with the Witch Project.'

'Anna-Lena van Dam, weapons and development,' she lied.

'*You're* van Dam? The one with the base, UFOs and ice bunkers?' The second man laughed loudly. 'I must be going mad. They've put me in with all the loonies.' Then he cleared his throat in an attempt to regain his composure. 'Captain Hermann Obermüller, SS Vril Division.'

Tandroff and Grünmann instantly broke into fits of laughter, much to Anna-Lena's bafflement. *Vril?* She thought it best not to ask. It was bad enough that every man and his dog already knew about her and her fantastical stories.

'What a stroke of luck! For a moment I was worried I'd be put in with a bunch of Nazis with sticks up their arses', said the major, flopping down onto his seat and sinking slightly into the upholstery. 'This should prove far more fun.'

'I'll drink to that.' Obermüller reached under his seat and pulled out a bottle of wine. 'I bet this was the stuff Goering used to get nice and drunk on before his morphine hits.' He poured the alcohol into the glasses. 'Chapeau, Miss van Dam. You've played the Yanks for fools.'

Anna-Lena blinked, feigning ignorance. 'By which you mean . . . ?'

'Oh leave off. We all know it's bollocks,' said Tandroff, clinking his glass with each of them in turn. 'A toast – to the Americans bankrolling us while we send them on a wild goose chase.'

She took a small sip. The wine was not bad at all. 'Why were you all laughing?'

The trio exchanged glances.

'I understand,' said Obermüller. 'You're afraid we'll be overheard.' He and Tandroff began did a quick sweep of the compartment. 'Good thinking, Miss van Dam.'

That had not been her intention, but Anna-Lena nodded nevertheless. 'And any one of you could be a spy,' she added.

'No, nothing like that. The Yanks don't bother – not during transit anyway,' Tandroff replied in a relaxed voice. 'I know none of your stuff exists – stations, bunkers, flying saucers. My brother was on the staff until Stauffenberg's bomb did for him. I'd have heard about it if it were true.'

'Good story, though – well done. The Americans lap up that sort of thing. They believe the Nazis had a sort of technical omnipotence.' Obermüller pretended to give a slow clap, then pointed at himself. 'Alongside all that occult shit.'

'It's going to be a long journey. Might as well tell our stories to keep up our spirits.' Grünmann laughed. 'Well, I was a typist with the Witch Project.' She pulled a secretive face. 'What powers was Himmler trying to release with his witchcraft? What spells was he trying to cast in Wewelsburg to win the war with black magic? Who was part of his witch battalion, putting curses on the enemy from the front lines?' She took a long draw on her cigarette and held it elegantly in the air. 'Of course I told Wallace I had information for him.'

'Witchcraft.' Anna-Lena had no idea what she was talking about. 'Sorry, help me out here? I don't get out much.'

'Oh, sure – you wouldn't have known. The project was top secret.' The woman smiled. 'Himmler actually sent people to investigate witch hunts. We visited dozens of libraries – we must have trawled through hundreds of archives, let me tell you.'

'To . . . find their ancestors and set up a battalion?' said Anna-Lena in disbelief, suddenly finding herself thinking about *Hellboy*.

Grünmann laughed brightly. 'No, no, that's all made up. It's just the story I told the Yanks so they'd take me to the States. Then I can live out the rest of my days there in peace. That's our – what did Wallace call it? – *deal*.' She lit another cigarette. 'To get that deal, I've been feeding them all these sensational stories – and they *actually* believe me! They want the same things for themselves, you see.'

Anna-Lena was beginning to understood that her fellow travellers had done precisely the same thing as she had: there were no such things as a department of skulls, runes and futurism, nor an SS Vril Division. 'I see,' she said.

'I told them,' Tandroff piped up in a sonorous voice, 'that I'd been one of Erik Jan Hanussen's students before the Berlin SA did for him in '33.' He adopted a dramatic pose. 'Hanussen confided his knowledge in me, teaching me occultism and mesmerism, even showing me how to predict the future.' He slumped back into his seat. 'I warned the *Führer* about Stauffenberg, but he didn't want to hear it. Then one day – boom!'

Anna-Lena vaguely recalled the fortune-teller, a charlatan who had earned a great deal of attention with his prediction of the Reichstag fire and his apparent knowledge about the perpetrators – combined with a hefty prison sentence. She had seen a film about him, starring Klaus Maria Brandauer.

Tandroff laughed, blowing cigarette smoke from his mouth, and drank some more wine. 'And then these signs – the black sun . . . at Wewelsburg . . .'

'Oh? What did you do?' Obermüller leaned forwards eagerly.

'Well, Major?' Hertha Grünmann took a sandwich. 'I hope you didn't tell them anything about witches? As that's my metier, if you please.'

'The Yanks seriously believe Wewelsburg is some sort of centre for the occult – just with a snazzy façade.' Tandroff burst out laughing and slapped his thigh. 'And that's all come from Wiligut, that stupid Austrian who escaped from the sanatorium and started bragging about how he was the last survivor of Atlantis. Himmler only went and made him his personal magician!' Tears streamed down his cheek. 'All a load of nonsense dreamed up by some lunatic whispering insanity into dear Heinrich's ear.' He drew the black sun on the window with his finger. 'And now, behold! Do you know where this symbol comes from?'

'Something Germanic?' Grünmann guessed.

'A sun circle made of swastikas?' ventured Obermüller.

Anna-Lena could not stop grinning at the thought that

the whole myth about the Nazis being devotees of the occult was turning out to be entirely made up – a total farce, from the imagination of a madman. Just like her own flying saucers and lunar bases. 'A child's drawing?' she said.

'Bingo!' Tandroff pointed at her enthusiastically. 'Right you are, Miss van Dam. A child's drawing!' His laughter became a cheerful roar. 'And you're also right, Captain Obermüller. An SS officer's son was bored one day and just started scribbling swastikas on top of one another. And that junkie drunkard Wiligut found it and thought he could turn it into something mystical. Oh, he put on a great show all right, but it had bugger all to do with magic.'

They were all laughing now, as much because of the major's infectious laughter as the story itself.

'Everything – *everything* – that Himmler heard from his little Rasputin was just as made up as the stories we've been telling the Americans.' Tandroff wiped his tear-stained face. 'Children, children, I can't go on.'

'And we all wondered why Germany lost the war.'

Obermüller had the bottle in his hand once more, swirling the contents around. 'My turn now. Vril. The SS Vril Division. We killed people using the invisible power of the primal cosmic force *Vril*, which—'

Tandroff let out another screeching laugh, accidentally spitting a mouthful of wine across the compartment. 'Fuck no! You really managed to get the Yanks to believe all that *Vril* bollocks?'

'This coming from Hanussen's student,' replied the captain. This time it was Grünmann's turn to snort wine.

'*Vril?*' Anna-Lena asked helplessly. She had completely

lost track of the conversation. 'Forgive me, I know almost nothing about these sorts of esoteric things.'

'Ah, such innocence. Wait a sec, I've got something for you.' The captain stood up and produced a bundle of letters from his suitcase. 'Correspondence with an author called Ley. Willy Ley. Used to write science fiction. He emigrated to the States nearly ten years ago because Goebbels banned reports about rocket technology, rocket cars or rocket aeroplanes, even if they were in works of fiction, so Ley couldn't write about any of that stuff any more. But he wrote about a circle called the *Society of Truth*, which is supposed to be based in Berlin.' He sat down. 'Read this – maybe you'll be able to use some of it for your flying saucers.'

'Thanks very much – good idea.' Anna-Lena scanned the notes about the secret power *Vril*, created by a writer called Edward Bulwer-Lytton for his novel *The Coming Race*. This 'Society of Truth' in Berlin believed Bulwer-Lytton had been using his satirical book as a way of spreading *actual* knowledge and truth about this force.

It might have enabled the British, who kept all this as a state secret, to expand their colonial empire, wrote Ley. *The Romans certainly possessed it, enclosed in small, metal balls called* lares *that provided protection for their homes.*

Anna-Lena returned the papers, still grinning. 'I have to admit your stories are all excellent.'

'You're still queen of the liars, though,' replied Tandroff. 'Ice bunkers? Lunar bases *and* flying saucers? Insanity!' The trio applauded her again.

She stood up and bowed gracefully. All that laughing had done a wonderful job of alleviating the stress she had been under for days – but now was the time to put the first phase of her plan into operation. 'The queen needs to excuse herself,' she announced solemnly. 'Back in a bit.'

She pushed open the compartment door and moved into the narrow corridor, which was dimly lit by a few small lights. It was much cooler, if not much cleaner out here, with the steam scenting the air rather than all that cigarette smoke. She couldn't see any guards as the train rattled through the twilight towards its destination.

She began to walk off slowly; she really did need the lavatory, but finding the carriage with all the crates was a far greater priority. And even if she were to find the Ark of the Covenant there, this mission was all about the door.

Near Rastenburg, East Prussia, 8 January 1945

'This'll work,' Greta reassured the quartet, who were sitting with her and Theo in the back of the lorry. 'We've got George with us – I promise you, no one does a better imitation of a Tommy officer than him.'

'Because he used to be one,' said Theo. 'But now he understands that Communism is the only way to stop the world from sinking into inequality.'

Viktor considered discretion to be the better part of valour at this point. History would show that Stalin and his cronies were no better than Capitalists when it came to self-enrichment. Not to mention the cult of personality he had created around himself.

Greta, like the other guerrilla troops, was wearing the

same thickly lined grey uniform that Viktor, Ingo, Dana and Theo now had on, stolen from the German auxiliary divisions that the British were using to keep the peace on German soil. There were plenty of unemployed *Wehrmacht* soldiers who had refused to return to the Eastern Front to die fighting Stalin, so the British found other jobs for them, such as ferrying prisoners back and forth. In their case, it was Coco who was pretending to be the prisoner.

It was thanks to Viktor's tireless urging that they were now sitting on the hard pallets, rumbling their way through the cold evening. The last few days had been a haze of preparation and uncertainty. After their meeting with Political Commissioner Smetana, a long discussion had broken out between Viktor and the rest of the council members about the feasibility of taking Fort India by force. A full-frontal attack would lead to large losses, even taking the element of surprise into account, but he had finally managed to come up with an alternative – although this was no less controversial. In the end, the more daring of the Communists, emboldened by the fact that they had a medium on their side now, won out over the procrastinators.

Their small team was to contain the initial shock troops, while the political commissioner was hanging back with a larger unit, to be deployed as soon as she received the signal.

Ingo handed a chocolate bar to Coco, which she gratefully accepted. He knew she always needed something sweet before performing on stage. 'This all seems a little too easy for my liking,' he said quietly. His concerns had not abated simply because the others were all in agreement.

'It is usually the simplest plans that work,' replied Dana. 'Why shouldn't it? We pretend we've got a clairvoyant here for Wallace to add to his collection, we hand her over – and we find out where Anna-Lena van Dam is.' She took a bar of chocolate as well, feeling her own blood-sugar levels were beginning to fall. 'We sabotage their defensive positions and give the signal for the combined soldiers and partisans to overrun Fort India. The Allies will suddenly be weakened in their fight against the Red Army – they might even have to negotiate terms. And we can be out of here for ever.'

'Once,' Theo added, 'Madame Fendi has told us about a few more Allied plans – not before.'

'I will. Once the fort's been taken,' said Coco firmly. She bit into her chocolate, savouring the creamy sweetness. She was not considering going along with the exchange for one moment: as soon as they had Anna-Lena and the door, the four of them had secretly agreed to abscond immediately. It was not their responsibility to interfere with the course of history. Bad enough they had already lost two members of their team.

The lorry slowed down and finally came to a halt; the engine idled.

'What's going on?' Greta called out towards the front. 'Problems?'

'No, just a level crossing,' replied the driver. 'We'll be off again in a minute.'

The taste of chocolate in Coco's mouth suddenly took

on a bitter note, stabbing her temples as if in warning. Her gift was trying to tell her something.

'Wait a second.' She furrowed her brow and removed the pendulum from her pocket. 'I can feel something.' She probed the aether, her eyes closed.

The metal vibrated slightly on its chain, then pointed east in the direction of Fort India.

The pounding and rattling of the train rolled past. A whistle sounded to herald the presence of the locomotive and the road beneath the lorry began to shake violently. The carriages looked extremely heavy, and they appeared to be travelling at great speed.

'Armoured train,' shouted the driver over the racket. 'With two gun turrets. Don't see that very often. Must be something important.'

Coco stared at her pendulum, which was turning as if synchronised with the train – then it pointed in the opposite direction to the fort. 'Anna-Lena's on there,' she announced excitedly. 'We've got to go after that train!'

Ingo put his hand on her back. At the moment his job was merely to provide comfort and support. He hoped it would be of some help to her.

'Well, that's fucked our plan up royally,' said Dana. 'And it was such a beauty as well.'

'Sounds like it's improvisation time.' Viktor looked at Greta. Giving up was out of the question. Anna-Lena was their goal and the door was their way out. 'Let's follow the train – we'll need a map to find out where it's next due to cross over a road.'

Theo muttered, 'It won't stop for the likes of us.' But he

dug out a map and shone his torch on it. 'An armoured train like that would make short work of our truck. Or they'll just shoot us to pieces a mile off.'

The lorry accelerated, following a route that would keep them as close as possible to the railway tracks. The passengers bounced around on the hard benches; every bump sent them unceremoniously into the air and every corner either pushed them into a heap together or flung them apart.

'Where do the tracks lead?' Viktor called out, trying to collect the scattered cargo.

'To the Robinson Complex,' said Theo, after examining the map for a long time. 'Used to be a Nazi research facility for V2 rockets and aviation. A bit like the one at Breitenheide.'

'So they've got their own runways – bigger than the one at Fort India,' Viktor said, comprehending the urgency of their situation. A plane could take off from there and fly straight to the USA.

'We need to find out where the train's due to start slowing down so we can jump up onto it,' Dana suggested. 'Just after a corner, perhaps, where the driver will have to take it a bit easier anyway.'

'The turrets are usually teeming with guards,' warned Greta. 'If they spot us anywhere near the tracks, they'll sound the alarm immediately – or shoot us on sight.'

'Not necessarily,' remarked Theo. 'They won't be expecting a confrontation. Sometimes they leave their guns unmanned. It might work.'

'We must be getting pretty desperate if we're now

considering jumping onto a moving train.' Ingo studied the map. He doubted he was the right man for the job. He did not even know how fast a steam locomotive could go – sixty miles per hour? Ninety? Far too fast for his liking in any case.

The lorry skidded around the next bend, the driver shifting through the gears, doing everything he could to get them there safely as well as speedily.

Viktor pointed at a spot on the map where the tracks appeared to curve tightly. 'There – that's our best bet, I'd say. It goes under a bridge, so we can abseil down.'

'How far off is it?' Dana looked at Greta. 'Is it doable?'

'It's pretty winding.' The sniper banged on the front wall. 'Armin, get a move on. We've got ten minutes to get to a bridge twelve miles from here.'

'You've got to be joking,' replied the driver, then he added, 'Better hold on tight then. This'll hurt you more than me or the truck.'

The engine roared and the heavy vehicle immediately began to sway all over the place, wobbling round even the slightest curve. The wheels squeaked over the surface of the road, causing small stones to fly loose – but they were making good progress.

'If we're lucky,' Coco whispered to Viktor, 'the door'll be on the train as well. Wallace had it dismantled. He's going to take it to the States with him – for further investigation.'

'We'll have a look as soon as we're inside,' he replied just as quietly, not wanting to draw the Communists' attention to the portal. 'That would be the perfect situation.'

'What if they catch us?' Ingo looked around. He was

really dreading the idea of jumping. 'We can hardly just admit we sneaked on in secret, can we?'

Viktor grinned. 'On the contrary!' He thumped his fist against the badge on his uniform. 'That's exactly what we'll say.'

'Another easy plan, eh?' Dana rolled her eyes. This would almost certainly escalate into a shoot-out, for which she was not even remotely well enough equipped. The Kevlar vest provided a deceptive sense of security – but it had not done very much for Friedemann. Ricochets always hit where you're least protected.

Greta laughed. 'It's so mad it might just work.' She pointed to Coco. 'After all, we've got a Top Secret prisoner with us – who no one was allowed to know about before departure.'

'Surely Wallace should have known?' Theo interjected doubtfully.

'No, Wallace is an American. But we' – Greta pointed to the driver's cabin – 'have our fake Tommy with us. If we can get him to provide an explanation, I reckon they'll buy it. He's only got to say that she's to be put on a flight to the States as well, as a present from King George to the President. And with one eye firmly on his career, Wallace will swallow it whole.'

'So we get on and look through each carriage,' Viktor concluded. *And hope our cover lasts long enough to prevent us from being shot.*

'They've got some high-ranking comrades on board as well – we'll free them and outnumber the handful of guards they've got in no time,' Greta said confidently.

'Then once we've seized the train we can go back to Fort India – or any other camp, for that matter. It'll be our Trojan horse. We'll ride from victory to victory.'

Coco looked at the pendulum, which was still pointing towards the train where Anna-Lena most likely was. She kept doubts about the plan to herself. They needed every ounce of confidence possible.

'Then once we've taken over the train we can . . .' She was a hair's breadth from saying *leave through the portal*, so desperate was she for the door to be on one of the wagons. 'We can support Stalin's battle for freedom in Europe,' she finished.

The lorry took the next corner so fast that they were all thrown in a heap together – then it screeched to a stop. 'The bridge,' called Armin, the driver. 'We're here.'

They hurriedly jumped out into the cool evening air and found themselves on a structure that was built about thirty feet above the railway line. It was dark now, with only the stars illuminating the conspirators.

The rumbling of the train could be heard in the distance, and plumes of smoke were rising majestically; the grey-white ribbon painted onto the night sky could be seen for miles around. Their target was racing towards them.

The driver was looking for some wire in his toolbox; a coil of rope was already lying next to the rear tyre. 'This is all we've got,' he said apologetically. 'I didn't know there was going to be abseiling.' He dug out some carabiners from the box. 'Will this be enough?'

'Oh my word,' groaned Ingo. Nightmare scenarios were swarming through his mind's eye. 'I'll fall like a stone.'

Dana handed out the carabiners. 'I'll quickly show you what to do. Tie the knot, attach it, then we're off.'

Viktor was very familiar with the types of knot that could be made with a simple rope to create a reasonably suitable safety-catch; he and Dana explained each step to the team as they started tying.

Ingo was riddled with fear and Coco did not look much happier. They stood next to each other, holding hands – being honest with each other, if only for these few precious seconds.

Greta and Theo walked over to the railing with George and two other fake German auxiliary troops to find the best position from which to descend. The ends of the rope were quickly fastened.

'The train's nearly here!' shouted the driver, who was standing on the roof of the lorry and looking through a pair of binoculars. 'Get ready.'

The group shook hands one by one, then headed over to the ledge.

'I'll go first, with Viktor across from me on the second rope,' Dana announced. She was immeasurably calm, as she had been on every other operation. This was her metier: death, destruction and adrenalin. 'Then Greta and Theo, followed by Ingo and Coco, and finally the rest of you.' She pushed the coiled ropes forward until they were almost hanging off the edge. 'Our goal's not the final armoured car, but the passenger carriage in front of it.'

'The cannons are unarmed,' the driver called out. 'No lights behind the gun hatches and no one on look-out.'

As expected, Wallace and his men did not appear to be anticipating an attack.

Viktor could feel the sweat on his palms. He had learned how to climb and abseil, but these conditions were unique. He admired Dana's detachment. Then it struck him. *Darfur.* Had it not been for the sandstorm, she would almost certainly have killed him.

The train passed under the bridge. The metallic rattling and clanking of wheels, gears and suspension swelled to create a loud mechanical concerto. Plumes of white and black smoke shot up in front of them, enclosing them within its tendrils.

'Now!' Dana pushed the coil of rope down and immediately jumped through the haze of smoke from the train's smokestack and began to slide down the rope.

Like an overzealous spider, she fell towards the carriages that were whizzing past her. She had intentionally left a reasonable amount of slack on the rope to allow herself to descend rapidly. When she reached the end she snapped the fastener into place, which brought her to a sudden stop; then she released herself from the carabiner.

The impact on the roof of the third carriage was hard, which was in no way helped by the train's acceleration unwittingly doing its best to throw her backwards and off the edge. With great difficulty she managed to stay on her feet and looked over her shoulder to see how the rest of the group was faring.

Her team had already landed. Greta and Theo had made it, as well as Viktor, Coco, George and two other Communists dressed in German uniforms.

Only Ingo was still dangling from the rope, blocking the route for the final two men above him. He was fiddling with his knot and fastener like a madman. 'It's jammed,' he cried out desperately as the carriage roofs flew past a couple of feet beneath his dangling legs.

Dana could see the rearmost armoured car approaching. Its steel superstructures, gun turrets and four flak cannons protruded ominously above the wagons. 'Cut the rope!' she shouted. 'The rope—'

The final carriage rushed forwards and clattered into the dangling man. The barrel of one of the forward-facing flak cannons sliced through Ingo's back; the muzzle emerged from his chest, along with a torrent of blood.

The rope tautened. The force of the unstoppable train was so great that the muzzle tore through the parapsychologist and split him in half. Blood and intestines splashed down onto the armoured car before the gun became entangled with the rope and snapped off. The body parts and the two screaming men behind Ingo disappeared in the darkness.

Coco threw up violently; even Dana was struggling to fight the nausea rising up in her. She had seen many dreadful things in her life, but nothing like this.

'Shit.' Viktor swallowed against the tightness in his throat. Gusts of wind tore at his body, tugging him this way and that, while the cold served to drive away the shock. He was on a mission – he had to keep his cool. First he helped the pallid, shaking medium to her feet, then shooed Dana into action. 'We need to get to the last carriage!' he called out into the din.

The headwind was forcing them to lean forwards,

wrestling to keep their balance. The group somehow arrived at the roof of the final cabin without the spotlights on the flak cannons lighting up. They had not been discovered yet.

The skylight above an empty compartment was quickly taken out and they slipped inside one by one. The whistling of the wind abated instantly, producing a relative silence that felt almost surreal to their ears.

'We're in the luggage carriage,' Dana announced after a quick look around. 'Nobody here.'

Sobbing, Coco collapsed onto a crate and held her head in her hands. She would never be able to erase the horrific demise of her former lover – skewered by a cannon, ripped apart – from her memory. 'He's dead,' she stammered. 'Ingo's *dead*.'

Greta, Theo and the remaining Communists were also ashen-faced; they had lost two of their own as well.

Dana decided to follow Viktor's lead: *keep calm and carry on*. She put her hand on Coco's shoulder. 'Come on. I know it's hard to keep going, but we have no choice – otherwise this'll all be in vain.'

'Secure the entrance, Greta,' Viktor ordered, as he started inspecting the shelves and aisles. Eventually he came upon a large, curiously long, wide, thin crate, marked *Top Secret*. Could this really be the door?

He walked over to Coco and inclined his head in what he hoped would be a comforting gesture. 'You were right: I've found the portal. This is our way out,' he whispered. 'Now we just have to find Miss van Dam and disappear.'

'Why can't we go now?' Coco replied tearfully. She could

not stand being here any longer in this fever-dream of a world. She raised her eyes and looked back and forth between Viktor and Dana. 'This isn't what we agreed. My contract with Walter van Dam is void.' She braced herself against a wooden partition. The door was only a handful of steps away – her own world, far safer than this nightmare that was devouring people one-by-one.

'Can we get a move on?' Greta asked impatiently. 'If someone spots all that blood and mess on the armoured car, the entire mission will be ruined.'

'Schwimmer won't let us leave now,' Dana shouted across to the other two. 'They want to get their people back first. And they'll need us – just like Anna-Lena needs us.'

Coco sniffed, wiping away her tears. She knew that their plan depended on her, that Ingo would have wanted them to find the missing girl. That it was her duty to bring a daughter back to her father. She would do it: not for the money, which would provide no balm to soothe her pain, but for Ingo. 'There'll be hell to pay if this Anna-Lena isn't worth saving!'

'She most certainly is.' Viktor smiled at her, knowing the Communists would go ballistic if Coco were to go on strike. 'Once we're back, she'll make the world a brighter place. Our world – where we belong.' It felt a bit grubby using this tactic to convince Coco to carry on.

'Good. Let's be off then.' Dana moved forwards and looked at George. *Back to the plan. Back to death, destruction and adrenalin.* 'Let's bring our little clairvoyant to Captain Wallace and be rid of this train.'

Suddenly a torch lit up from a row of shelves,

accompanied by a clicking sound that suggested someone had just cocked a pistol.

'Stop!' came a harsh voice. 'Who are you? What are you doing here?'

Anna-Lena hurried along the aisle, desperately trying to reach the door that would provide her with safe passage out of this world.

But her attempt to reach the luggage area came to a sudden stop at the transition between her carriage and the next one along. She was stopped by two American guards and informed that she was allowed to move freely within her own carriage, but nowhere else.

Anna-Lena thanked them kindly, in an attempt to once again appear harmless. She stood no chance against armed men. Compared to the pleasant Englishman who had accompanied her to the train, these two appeared to be officious and alert.

Anna-Lena entered the lavatory and considered her next move.

Could she climb out the window and onto the roof, maybe inch her way along on the outside of the train?

She discarded the idea, considering it far too bold and dangerous.

She wandered back down the aisle, throwing glances into the occupied compartments. She was not particularly interested in who else was party to her nocturnal journey – all she wanted was a way to buy some time so she could come up with a way of sneaking into the luggage carriage.

The other compartments were considerably calmer than

her own. Most of the passengers were sleeping, reading or playing cards. Occasionally someone had drawn the curtains to block out any curious eyes.

Behind a glass door sat several men and women, dressed in civilian clothing that bore no distinguishing features. Some of the men had bandages on: soldiers with souvenirs from the battlefields on which they had fought, be they for Germany or Russia. It was now immaterial to them.

'. . . said it's too early.' Anna-Lena could hear Captain Wallace's voice in the next compartment along. She could not see anything through the divider but the door had been left ever so slightly ajar. 'The President and his staff are of the same opinion. We have to wait. British Intelligence have to find a way to influence German public opinion in our favour. Then the last of Adolf's *Wehrmacht* troops will join us voluntarily on the Eastern Front to unleash hell on the Ruskies.'

'I agree with the captain,' replied a woman with a British accent. 'If all the deaths can be blamed on the Communists and their sympathisers, there'll be nothing left to stand in the way of our offensive and our claim on Germany. We'll be overrun by volunteers desperate to fight on our side.'

The captain laughed wickedly. 'The Krauts will come to love us – even after we've defeated them.'

'*Liberated*,' another man interjected. 'The word you want is *liberated*. From old Adolf. Which gives us the right to whatever spoils we want in Germany – and the rest of Europe. This couldn't have worked out any better. A toast to Roosevelt's foresight!'

The man laughed darkly as they clinked glasses, followed by a moment of silence as they each took a sip.

The British woman continued, 'Well, gentlemen. Your smug sense of heroism can hang. You actually owe the defeat of the Nazis to another Nazi.'

'You mean Stauffenberg?' Captain Wallace snorted. 'That was a stroke of luck for real. Without the *Führer*, boom, the Krauts threw in the towel.'

'Because the generals knew they couldn't win. It was both smart and strategically sensible. No point in throwing away more lives and resources,' said another. 'That shows clear tactical thinking. Which had a useful side effect for us – more cities and industrial centres to put to use.'

The mysterious group laughed once more.

Anna-Lena wished she had her phone on her so she could record the conversation. There were so many details to recall, and genuine cruelty. The Americans and British were making sinister plans, but to what end? World domination? Anna-Lena reminded herself this this was not her world, not her reality.

'Speaking of which, when are the nuclear strikes due to happen? I'd prepared everything in Rominten. We've managed to convert the *Aggregat* missiles,' came a different man's voice, cutting through the martial cheerfulness. 'Do you know anything about that, Captain?'

'That's for Washington to decide. And I've got someone on the train,' he replied, 'who's quite the expert in aircraft and technology and could give us an advantage when it comes to transporting nuclear weapons. So we'd have to postpone the attack for two reasons. But it's not my decision. I'm just the guy bringing her back.'

'General Norton, we've been dying to know: how did you and your industrious little helpers manage to convert the V2?' enquired the British lady. 'And how did you even come up with the idea?'

'Don't call it a V2 – that was the language of Nazi propaganda. I prefer *Aggregat 4*,' said the general. 'Converting it was hardly rocket science, if you'll pardon the pun. Our spies had known for a while that the *Luftwaffe* headquarters were in Rominten, at least since the Nazis turned on Stalin. Goering had an air raid shelter built there for him and his staff, under the code name *Robinson Complex*. It was built up over time, first with barracks and buildings, then a runway and finally' – the general paused dramatically – 'a research facility for the *Aggregat 4* rocket engines. Or so we thought.'

He laughed softly, like someone who had just bluffed his way to a winning poker hand. 'To our surprise, when we took over the site we discovered new models for rockets in the hangars, all loaded onto launchers but completely inoperative. Rather a stroke of luck.'

'New?' The British woman seemed surprised.

'I really don't know if I'm supposed to . . . oh sod it.'

Anna-Lena heard the clink of glass and guessed he had put his drink down.

'Higher performance – the old missile could carry a ton of explosives two hundred miles in less than five minutes. But the new piece of kit we found, which combined *Aggregat 9* and *Aggregat 10*, could travel five thousand miles. *Five thousand!*'

The rattling of the train could be heard over the stunned silence that followed this revelation.

'Then . . . it could have flown to America,' said the Brit. 'Good Lord!'

'That's why the Nazis called it the America Rocket,' Norton added. 'Good job someone did for Adolf. But we can now send these vicious little bastards against Stalin and the Emperor of Japan – with a one-ton nuclear bomb on board.'

Anna-Lena suddenly felt less sure about her plan to disappear through the door as quickly as possible. The idea of knowing about an impending mass-murder of millions of people and not doing anything about it sent shivers down her spine.

'Heavens!' The British woman clinked her glass with the others. 'We've certainly picked the right allies. How many of them are there?'

'Enough to do some serious re-landscaping on a few Russian and Japanese cities. Stalin and the Tennō will have to surrender after that,' the general replied. 'Not a single one of our bombers will have to take off. Isn't that wonderful? These things are so damn fast – several times the speed of sound. Nothing can catch them.'

'Well I never! Let's raise a toast to Stauffenberg in that case,' exclaimed the British woman exuberantly. 'The Nazis would have bombed us off the map.'

The sound of glasses clinking rang out again – alcohol was clearly helping to keep their spirits high.

So, Anna-Lena thought, the train was taking her and the other prisoners to Rominten, where the *Aggregat 9* and *10* missiles were located, loaded and ready to fire. Was there a way to prevent their deployment without setting off the atomic bombs? The Americans had no idea about the powers of these bombs, no matter what tests had been carried out. But once you'd seen the pictures of the aftermath at Hiroshima, you could never forget them.

The task at hand seemed enormous. Anna-Lena told herself again that this was not her world and all she had to do was go back through the door and return to her own reality. No one would ever know about the fate of the people in this world or dimension, or whatever it was.

But was that better?

The conversation in the compartment had turned to the state of the war, the situation with Russia and Japan and how the USA wanted to subsume these stubborn states, with Britain administering them, and then take over the Middle Kingdom. China would fall, sandwiched between the newly made vassal states of Japan and Russia, now with the Stars and Stripes and radioactive dust flying proudly overhead.

It was not a future that Anna-Lena could wish on her worst enemy.

She looked down towards the end of the corridor, where the two guards were standing. Could she risk starting an uprising on the train, or would there be one last opportunity in Rominten to use the portal?

But her heart had already made up its mind a while ago.

CHAPTER IX

Near Frankfurt

Walter van Dam stood on the threshold and stared into the darkness stretching out in front of him, dead and silent, like a void representing the infinite nature of the universe.

He held on tightly to the door jamb with one hand and grasped the steel cable in the other. All that mattered was that his daughter needed help – that someone needed to find her and bring her back to safety.

He had sent out two teams, but they had both gone quiet.

He was Anna-Lena's father; he should have gone himself – it should have been him, carving his way through the darkness, searching for his own flesh and blood with every weapon on earth.

Van Dam swallowed hard. Fear could not overcome his concern for his daughter, but it could freeze him solid. It paralysed his will, destroying every intention he had to follow the groups he had sent down before him.

The blackness, the prospect of narrow passages and chambers and the idea of breathing stagnant air while enclosed by walls of rock all around him made him panic.

Ever since entering the cellar, his heart had been going a mile a minute. He could still go back: he could slip quietly back up the stairs and he'd be outside again.

But his whole world would change once he crossed over into the darkness.

Walter van Dam had learned that there was no feeling stronger than fear, no matter how irrational. Intermingled with his debilitating terror of the dark were pangs of shame. Shame at his having let Anna-Lena down.

Tears rolled down his ageing cheeks, moistening his stubble and beard, trickling underneath his collar. He had been peerless in business, achieving every target he had ever set for himself.

But down here he was a failure.

'Anna-Lena,' he cried out into the void. 'Hold on, Anna-Lena. I'll find a way!' He squeezed his eyes shut, forbidding himself from crying.

Then he took a step back onto the cellar floor. His brown eyes focused on the door to the entrance of this kingdom he had known nothing about – hadn't *wanted* to know anything about.

He ran his right hand over the carved wood and touched the door knocker. What if his panic came from some suppressed memory in the villa? He had lived here for a while, after all – before the sudden move. So what had happened here before?

The wood felt warm to the touch, far too warm for the cool temperature down in the cellar. He examined the door more closely in the glow of his lamp, moving it back and forth on its hinges, illuminating the knocker, the mouth, the ring, the contact plate, the carvings and the dust secreted within the inlay, which someone had tried to wipe off in various places.

The beam of light flickered over the wall, revealing a small recess in the rock, one he reckoned would fit the door handle seamlessly.

He took a few steps back and increased the size of his torch beam. Only from a distance did the stone frame become visible, into which the wooden door could be neatly slotted when moved to the left.

'A double door,' he whispered, moving closer to give the rock face a closer inspection. But apart from the recess for the handle – which he now realised had been made in such a way that it could be pushed down when it was closed – there was nothing there.

The force field mentioned in the records would probably only begin to build up once the other one had collapsed – which was impeding the steel cable.

Or was there nothing there at all?

Van Dam had reached the end of his knowledge. He needed more information about the portals. He needed to do some research – lots of research.

The notes his grandfather had made, and which Anna-Lena had devoured, were stored at his house in Lerchesberg. But before returning home to study them, he wanted to be absolutely certain that there was nothing left in the old library that might be of use.

Van Dam trudged back up the cellar stairs and made his way through the villa.

The darkness had given the corridors, rooms and halls

a macabre quality. His footsteps and breathing echoed around him, as if he were accompanied by an army of apparitions who were keeping a close eye on what the latest visitor to their abode was doing. The rain continued to fall heavily, the patter swelling to a crescendo formed of a thousand wings. It sounded as if giant birds were encircling the property, waiting for him to depart.

Van Dam looked at the panes of glass above him, admiring the water racing over the surface and making the outside world appear blurry, as if he were extremely short-sighted. The twilight was absorbing the last strains of light.

He put down the bag containing all the records.

He would keep looking for what was described in the notes for as long as there was still enough light to see.

Van Dam stripped down to his underpants and shoes before stepping outside and leaving the shelter of the porch canopy – he didn't have a change of clothes with him; this was the only way to ensure he'd have something dry to put on when he returned from the remains of the workshop.

He pounded his way across the damp ground and climbed up into the remains of the sawmill-cum-joinery. The rain slapped down hard onto his bare skin; it felt strange to be standing outside, utterly defenceless against the elements. Anyone who might happen to see him in his current state would almost certainly think he had lost his marbles.

A few burned-out walls were still standing defiantly, with only some rusting metal supports protruding from the rubble to keep them company. The rest was a mangle of collapsed walls and weathered wood, of which some was rotten and the rest splintered and as fragile as parchment, falling apart like a cheap suit as soon as he stepped on it.

He picked his way past the remains of corroded machines and enormous saw blades to begin his search, heading towards the area that had once been the central hub of the production site. The building bordered the rampant forest that had now fully encroached into the property, as if Nature wished to seek revenge for the routine dismantling of trees on this site.

Dark green firs loomed overhead, swaying back and forth in the wind and whispering to van Dam, who pushed the rainwater out of his eyes and looked around. Old tools could be seen sticking out from the scattered stones and planks. They were rusted and blunt; they would surely break if anyone tried to use them again.

He was freezing cold now, and desperate to dry off, but he could not bring himself to return to the villa and the library without having found at least one clue about this special door. Shivering and with his teeth chattering, he rummaged at random through the rubble, scraping his fingers on rough edges and cursing the cold that had overtaken all other senses.

But after an hour of frantic searching he still had nothing to show for his efforts – not even the merest hint of what might previously have been a frame or a door. The fire that had raged on that fateful night had done a thorough job, ably assisted by decades of weather.

Hopefully I'll find more in the library, he thought, looking at the fir trees as they bowed before him, whispering. He stopped, then, putting his hands over his eyes to shield them from the driving rain, he slowly walked forwards, directing the beam of his torch at the uppermost branches.

The light revealed a door frame concealed deep within the fir tree, covered in moss and lichen, with the door held in place by the branches underneath. The tree had evidently dragged the whole construction up with it as it grew.

Van Dam ran to his car to find his tow ropes, tied them together and began to climb the fir tree to secure the door with the rope and liberate it from its natural bracket. The tree resisted stubbornly, though, giving him several deep scratches as if trying to defend the door from his advances.

Van Dam was in good shape for his age, but all this scrambling around among the branches of a conifer in the wind and rain was pushing him to the limit.

He finally managed to haul the door down to the ground and drag it back to the house, every sinew in his body burning with the effort. With one final heave he deposited it on the front porch, no longer feeling the cold after such strenuous exertion.

Then Van Dam switched on the headlights of his Mercedes to better examine his discovery. He gently scraped off the moss and lichen to reveal its true colour: a light, almost white wood, very old and slightly warped, yet with a beautiful, angular simplicity to it. Several black-and platinum-coloured bands were carved across it; they made it look very much like Art Deco.

He was filled with renewed confidence, in spite of his

now uncontrollable shivering. The door made by his grandfather was in his possession and hopefully he could use the records to work out what to do with it. Perhaps he could reach Anna-Lena directly without having to descend into the darkness?

He dragged the door inside and shoved it underneath one of the dust sheets for safekeeping before heading back outside and getting into the people carrier. He switched on the heater and bathed in the warmth quickly spreading throughout the vehicle's interior.

He waited impatiently for the tremors to subside, then sprinted back into the property and got dressed. He hurried over to the library, lit the large fireplace with some of the old papers scattered on the floor and smashed up a chair to use as the main source of fuel. At first it was difficult to get the smoke to pass through the chimney as it had not been cleaned in years, but the blockage began to clear as some of the leaves and fallen branches shifted under the influence of the heat.

As the rain continued to pound on the glass dome and a low rumble in the distance heralded a thunderstorm, van Dam searched row after row of shelves. He tapped the floor and walls, even smashing a couple of them open, and reached into cavities in the plasterboard that he thought might contain more secret information.

After he had finished rummaging through the first floor in vain, he climbed the wrought-iron spiral staircase and continued his search on the second floor. This was where he had disturbed the intruder, so perhaps there was something to be found up here.

Time passed. Despite his body temperature increasing to a more acceptable level as he worked, he was still in considerable discomfort from the scratches and abrasions he had sustained. His stomach growled impatiently with hunger. He had not considered bringing any food with him and this was already coming back to haunt him as his rapidly declining blood-sugar levels were causing him to lose concentration. But should he leave the villa and drive around looking for something to eat? Or order pizza and potentially arouse the delivery driver's curiosity? No.

Then he remembered there was a small fridge in the Mercedes, which the estimable Ms Roth kept stocked with drinks and snacks for long journeys. And he could bring the door he had found back to the library with him for closer examination.

After half an hour he returned to the library, invigorated and with the door in tow. The flames in the fireplace had started to dwindle.

With a few violent kicks he smashed another chair and started to feed the fire with the broken legs. Despite the food, fatigue was spreading through his body. He knelt down in front of the fire and held out his fingers, watching the flickering tongues of flame performing their hypnotic dance, crackling over their latest wooden offering, soon to turn it to ashes. *Have a short break, gather my strength and—*

'I believe the information you're looking for is up here,' came a sudden voice from the third floor, as if delivering a sermon from the pulpit.

Van Dam jumped. He scrambled to his feet and craned his neck back to look up at the dome overhead.

In the faint glow of the scattered light appeared the figure of a man on the overhang, wearing a chauffeur's uniform with a peaked cap. The stranger was holding a sheaf of papers in his left hand, to which he was now gesturing. 'I came across this in a hidden drawer. You'd never have found it. You're too hasty and destructive by half. Why is that, may I ask?'

Van Dam drew his pistol, regretting the G36 was too far away. 'Who are you?' He aimed the gun at this unwanted visitor. Could he be one of the conspirators he had read about?

'Wait there. I'll come down. Then we can have a proper chat.' The figure leaped onto the railing and jumped straight down, feet first.

Near Rominten, East Prussia, 8 January 1945

'I said, *who are you?*' repeated the voice as a bright beam of light shone into their shocked faces. The British lieutenant's uniform and the insignia of the German Auxiliary Brigade had given the security guard a moment of doubt after he had bundled them into the baggage carriage. His accent revealed him to be an American.

Viktor put a hand over his eyes to shield them from the blinding light. 'Special Forces. Now put that light down.' He pointed at George. 'This is Lieutenant Darling.' The distraction should be enough for them to eliminate the guard.

'Forgive me, sir. How did you get into my carriage, Lieutenant?' The man lowered his torch. 'Captain Wallace and General Norton haven't said anything – and I still need to see your ID . . .'

'Sure, of course you do. Rule Britannia!' George drew his silenced Browning and shot the surprised guard twice in the chest. 'Britons never will be slaves.'

The American soldier groaned and collapsed to the floor between the shelves.

Dana had moved silently alongside the enemy, ready to intervene. She quickly removed the dead man's keyring from his pocket, which had dozens of keys on it. 'We can break into every carriage with these, all the way up to the front,' she said with relief.

'Not bad,' said Theo. 'One occupant down. We'll keep doing this until we find your Anna-Lena. Might end up being pretty easy.'

'Don't be so sure.' Viktor walked over to the long box that he suspected contained the door from the basement. He gave Dana a brief nod and picked up a crowbar lying on the floor, then opened the container with a crack. 'We're better off working under the assumption that it's going to be far from straightforward.'

The mattress on top was quickly removed with Dana's help, revealing the arched door. The rusted metal ring appeared to be breaking down rapidly.

'Do you think it'll even cope with another hit?' Dana asked, now doubtful. In some areas there were only a few millimetres of material left. The ring had definitely suffered since the last time they had seen it. She assumed this was as a result of Spanger's failed attempted to return to their reality.

'We'll just have to risk it – there's no other choice.' Viktor propped the door up between the shelves. The fact that Wallace had placed a GI in the luggage compartment for protection might mean he was trying to keep the British away from the portal. 'Now we just need to get Anna-Lena.'

'What's going on?' Greta looked at the door with irritation. 'What are you doing with *that*?'

'I've been looking for a certain valuable painting for ages now and I thought this was it. But it's not,' said Viktor, tapping the frame and smiling encouragingly at Dana and Coco. Even if the brittle handle disintegrated after it had been used, the force field should still appear, allowing them to pass through. They wouldn't be stranded here. 'Come on, Comrades. Let's find that missing girl.'

Theo signalled to George and they assumed their formation. It looked as if the medium's hands had been tied up, but this was an illusion. She could slip out of the bonds at any time. The charade could now begin.

Dana unlocked the door to the corridor and pushed it open. 'Let's go.'

The team moved from the luggage compartment into the armoured train's first cabin, striding past the astonished American guards with such a high degree of military-style matter-of-factness that nobody thought to stop them or ask what they were doing.

'Special mission from Captain Wallace, men. As you

were,' said George as he passed by. The lieutenant's pips on his uniform and the badges on the coats of the auxiliary troops, combined with the fact that they had a handcuffed prisoner in tow, painted a coherent picture.

They marched past the compartments, ignoring the stares of the civilians, and finally arrived at the other end of the carriage. At this point, two of the resistance fighters pretended to have forgotten something in the luggage compartment. They turned on their heels and swiftly slit the throats of the unsuspecting guards, before shoving their bodies into the luggage rack. One by one by they opened the compartment doors to tell the passengers to remain quiet.

Meanwhile, George was pushing his way down the aisle towards the next carriage. There were two soldiers stationed just behind it, who were now hurrying into the carriage with a look on their face that suggested they had been caught doing something they shouldn't.

'Where can I find Captain Wallace?' barked George, pointing at Coco. 'We're on a special mission.'

'Sir, Captain Wallace is in the second carriage from the front,' replied the soldier on the right obediently, raising his hand in a salute. 'Together with the officers.'

'What officers? No one said anything about any officers,' snapped George, mimicking the arrogant tones reminiscent of the British Army. 'That should be a secret, shouldn't it? Some ally you are.'

'Sir, you'll have to ask Captain Wallace. The US Secretary of State and the Secretary of War are on board – travelling incognito. But I recognised them,' the soldier gabbled.

'I think they're trying to get an idea of the situation in Rominten, sir.'

'And what situation would that be, man?' George shouted, now standing so close to him that the tips of their noses were almost touching. 'Damn it all to hell! Do I have to shake you by the ankles to get a sensible word out of you?'

'That's all I know, sir!'

'Then I'll just have to ask Captain Wallace myself.' George pointed at Coco. 'And before you start acting up, we've captured a medium – a verified clairvoyant and fortune-teller. I've heard Captain Wallace will be able to put her to good use.' He gave the prisoner a shove, to which Coco responded with a look of indignation. 'You can show off some of your tricks to the officers and their staff.'

'No staff, sir – only the ministers and their bodyguards. Incognito, sir, if you recall,' reminded the guard. 'It'll be rather a small performance, sir.'

'Indeed. And our performance finishes *here*.' George drew his knife and stabbed the soldier, while Theo dealt with the other. They had succeeded in taking over the first carriage.

Dana was doing everything she could to keep her hands clean. This was not her fight, so she preferred to leave the killing to the people living in this particular timeline.

Coco had closed her eyes and was leaning against the wall. She couldn't stand to see any more death. 'This is cruel,' she whispered, unable to erase the memory of Ingo's demise from her mind.

'Listen up,' shouted Theo over the heads of the passengers crowding around outside the compartments, before briefly introducing himself. 'We're taking over the train. In secret. The US Secretary of State and Secretary of War are on board. We're going to take them prisoner and submit our demands to the President of the United States.'

A few small cheers could be heard, though not everyone joined in. Some had clearly been hoping to use the journey as a way of escaping.

The weapons belonging to the four dead guards were distributed among the passengers who appeared the most physically capable.

'Anyone who doesn't want to help us can get off as soon as the train comes to a stop,' Greta added. 'We're not forcing anyone to make history today. But I'll be sure to memorise the faces of any cowards very carefully indeed.'

'Plus she's a sniper,' remarked George.

There was some uneasy laughter.

Viktor, Dana and Coco looked down at the stabbed guards as they were being dragged into a nearby compartment to keep them out of the way of their growing army. The medium was particularly troubled by the sight of it all. Fear and a grave feeling of uncertainty was starting to overwhelm her, which was poisonous for her newly discovered gifts.

'This is war,' said Viktor softly. 'It's just what happens.'

'It is.' Dana pulled out her G36. 'But it's not ours. We just have to find the girl and head straight for the door.'

'It's all so horrible,' said Coco. Her fear was increasing

more and more while the smell of blood and piss invaded her senses. 'I . . . I can't go on. I' – she looked imploringly back and forth between Viktor and Dana – 'I'll wait here. You need to come back this way anyway. To the door. Through this carriage.'

'We need you to find Anna-Lena. And we can't just leave you here without anyone to protect you – especially not with these people. It could all go to shit in a heartbeat,' replied Dana.

'Anna-Lena's on this train, which means there's a limited number of places where she might be.' Coco threw her shackles onto the floor and leaned back against the wall. 'I can't look at any more murders. I've had enough.'

Greta eyed the medium coldly. 'I disagree.' She picked up the rope. 'We need you to play your part.'

'You need to fuck right off!' Coco hid her hands demonstratively behind her back. 'Find someone else to act as your medium.'

Suddenly the door to the next carriage swung open, revealing another American soldier standing in the interstice, alongside a red-haired young woman in civilian clothes and wearing a nasal piercing that looked utterly incongruous with the 1940s.

'Miss van Dam!' Dana took a step forwards, squeezing past the resistance fighters. 'You're Anna-Lena van Dam – your father sent us.'

'My father?' Anna-Lena looked at the two of them. 'How did you—?'

'Stop! All of you!' The GI had no idea what to do with this new information, but it was prohibited for any of the men and women in the compartments to be milling around unaccompanied in the aisles. 'What the hell's going on here?' He put a hand on the grip of his pistol and disengaged the safety with his thumb. 'Sir?' He looked at George, whom he had identified as the ranking officer. 'How did you . . . ?'

'Secret mission. For Captain Wallace,' George snapped, grabbing him by the shoulder. 'Quickly now, with me.' He dragged the man, who had been taken completely by surprise, into the first carriage – and right into Theo's blade, which pierced the GI through the ribs. He collapsed to the floor without a sound. His weapons were immediately distributed among the insurgents.

The scene made Coco think of a shiver of sharks, greedily devouring their prey. Her disgust continued to grow and it took every ounce of her self-restraint to stop herself from fleeing.

'Please come with us, Miss van Dam,' said Dana.

Viktor reached out to grab Anna-Lena and dragged her unceremoniously into the first empty compartment. She tried to pull away, but Dana pushed her inside.

'Hey, what are you doing?' Theo tried to follow them. 'We've got to—'

'We'll be right back,' Viktor called back.

Coco pushed her way through the throng to join them. She barred the door behind her, pulling the curtains shut to prevent any prying eyes.

'How do you know who I am?' Anna-Lena tore herself away and eyed the three of them suspiciously. She was astonished to find she suddenly had some allies here. 'And what's all this shit about my father? He wasn't alive at this time. And certainly not in this world.'

'I'm sorry we had to drag you into the compartment. But we haven't got much time. We reached this universe in the same way as you.' Viktor quickly introduced himself, Dana and Coco. 'The door – in the basement of that tavern in Leipzig. On the Katharinenstraße.'

Anna-Lena noticed their modern weapons, then thought about the Kevlar vest, Wallace's gun-case and the fact that he had said something about picking up 'her people' in the basement. What they were saying sounded entirely plausible. 'He . . . sent you after me?' She raised an eyebrow. 'Then you're a second team – and you've made it much further than the first.'

'Yes.' Dana kept a close eye on the compartment door. The Communists were rather impatient and were insisting that the train be captured as quickly as possible. With the train hurtling through the night at a perceptibly high speed, Rominten was rapidly approaching. 'Do you know what happened to the first team?'

'Dead – wiped out by something I couldn't see. But I managed to escape – through a second door – and found myself in this dimension,' said Anna-Lena briefly, brushing the red curls off her face. She did not want to rekindle the memories of those sirens and howling wolves. 'What did my father tell you about the doors?'

'Nothing,' Viktor replied. 'We just stumbled through, like you did.'

'But *you* know something.' Coco clasped her hands together and sank back. Her panic was gradually subsiding while she rested in the compartment, allowing her time to catch her breath and contemplate their imminent return. It was within her grasp now. But without Ingo. She pointed in the direction of the luggage carriage. 'And I don't want to stay here any longer than I have to. There's been too much death.'

Anna-Lena looked at the trio's weary faces. 'I understand. There were more of you at the start of your mission.' Her lips narrowed. 'I'm sorry. I didn't mean to cause all of this.'

'We knew it'd be dangerous before we started,' said Dana reassuringly.

'I didn't,' retorted Coco in a hollow voice, with her eyes now closed. She was in no frame of mind for being indulgent or understanding. All she could think about was Ingo's wretched, ill-deserved death. The way his body had been torn apart. 'We've lost three people. None of us knew we'd be descending into the pits of hell.' Without opening her eyes, she let the pendulum dangle from its chain. It was pointing directly at the young redhead. 'We were only supposed to be looking for you. No one said anything about shoot-outs, interdimensional portals or . . . death. Or whatever shit we've found ourselves in now.'

An uncomfortable silence fell upon the compartment.

The discussions of the released prisoners could be heard outside in the corridor, intermingled with the pounding and rattling of the train creating a loud, monotonous background drone.

Coco sighed and opened her eyes. There was nothing she could do to change what had happened. 'Okay, let's just go back to the luggage car and get out of here.' She stood up.

Viktor and Dana rose as well, checking their G36s in preparation for a fight against the Communists.

'I'll tell Schwimmer we need to check something in Miss van Dam's luggage,' said Viktor. 'If he and his comrades try to stop us because they want to keep our medium, we'll show them what the G36 can do.'

Dana slid the curtains slightly to one side and peered out into the passage. 'He's outside the door with Greta. Looks like they think something's up.' She pointed to the window. 'Reckon that'd be a better option?'

'I don't care,' said Coco softly. 'I'll climb around the outside of the train or across the roof if I have to. All I'm interested in is getting away from here.'

'No.' Anna-Lena had remained seated.

'No?' Coco's face froze. How dare she? 'Did you just say *no*?' The redhead nodded and began to stammer an explanation, but the medium grabbed her by her hair and yanked her to her feet. 'I don't care if you've found the love of your life here – or whatever reason you might have for staying in this world,' she barked, 'but we're leaving now. *Now!*'

'Easy now,' said Dana, pulling the two women apart and holding them at arm's length from each other.

'Why do you want to stay?' Viktor asked.

'Because something awful's going to happen and I have to stop it. I heard the Americans: they're planning to drop atomic bombs on cities in Russia and Japan, using converted German rocket technology,' said Anna-Lena, touching the spot where Coco had torn out a few strands of hair. 'The rockets are being stored in Rominten and they're ready for use. They've got a range of 5000 miles or more and they can carry bombs that weigh a ton each. I don't know how powerful these nuclear strikes will be, but with the numbers they're talking about . . . it'll be hundreds of times worse than Hiroshima and Nagasaki! Millions of deaths! Fallout and radiation that'll last a lifetime!'

'You say you *heard* this? Well whoop-di-fucking do,' Coco shouted angrily. She could not contemplate throwing herself head-first into another nonsensical project that would only lead to more death.

'*Heard*, as in I *overheard* them – Wallace and a few of the generals were discussing it in their compartment,' Anna-Lena clarified. She avoided making eye contact with Coco so as not to rile her up any further.

'The two American ministers,' added Viktor. 'That explains what they're doing here. They're looking at the rockets and attack plans – for Roosevelt.'

'I don't give a shit!' shouted Coco. Tears of anger were flooding her cheeks. 'Let them all bomb themselves into oblivion. We don't belong here – and no one in our world will ever find out about this universe. It's none of our business.'

'I know this is a different dimension,' Anna-Lena responded firmly, 'but they're still people. Living beings. A whole world will perish if the Americans follow through with this insane plan.' She looked at Viktor and Dana, trying to win them over to her side. She knew she wouldn't be able to stop Coco from using the door. 'The US President wants to have everything and everyone under his control. Wallace and his people said

Hitler sowed the seeds for them and now they're simply reaping the harvest.'

'Miss van Dam,' Viktor began, in an attempt to talk her out of the impossible task she was about to undertake. Even if they were able to take over Rominten with the Communists, Theo would commandeer the bombs and send them straight to Stalin. And there was no doubt that he'd promptly use those same bombs immediately on the United States. There was nothing to be done here – all they could do was postpone the inevitable.

'I won't just stand by while humanity is annihilated,' said Anna-Lena resolutely. 'The door brought me here for a reason.' She looked around. 'You as well.'

'Us?' Coco gave a bitter laugh. 'If there *is* a reason, it's for us to die. Trying to save *you*.'

Viktor thought long and hard, remembering the images of Hiroshima and Nagasaki. These would be multiplied ten-fold if Roosevelt were allowed to put his plan into action: waves of fire, radiation, heat and endless suffering. He just had one question. 'Miss van Dam, how are *we* supposed to stop these missiles from being fired?'

'The train.' Anna-Lena thumped the cushion. 'It's got two gun turrets, if I recall correctly. We can use it to bring the base under our control and . . .' She paused. This was as far as she had considered.

'Then what?' Coco folded her arms over her chest. She should have been in the luggage carriage long ago, rather than listening to a load of nonsense that amounted to nothing but suicide. 'Then we'll have a bunch of warheads, ask the US President very politely not to use them and he'll simply come to his senses?'

'Well, you're the clairvoyant here,' remarked Dana. *Death, destruction and adrenalin.* Anna-Lena's plan sounded right up her street. 'You of all people should know what to do, right?'

'Are you really saying you're in favour of this madness?' Coco was losing her temper again. 'You seriously want to try to save this world from a nuclear war? This world's got nothing to do with us!'

'I just want to stop these atomic bombs from being dropped. After that the war will take its own course.' Dana had made up her mind. One day she'd use her skills to do the right thing. Without any clients.

'There's one more thing.' Anna-Lena fiddled with the sleeves of her blouse. 'Wallace said the British secret service was planning a series of attacks in Germany – potentially across the whole of Europe: enormous attacks with hundreds of deaths – and they're going to blame it on the Communists.'

'To stir up hatred of Russia, meaning the Europeans will advocate nuclear strikes against Stalin and there won't be any real resistance.' Viktor knew all about those sorts of tactics. 'It's called "a false flag" – it's disgusting.'

'Spot on.' Anna-Lena looked at Coco pleadingly. 'I can't force you to do anything, of course. But we've got an opportunity on this train to prevent an enormous amount of suffering and misery. It could well be that we bring about an end to the war and start an uprising against these American so-called *liberators*.'

'There'd be so much bloodshed,' said Dana. 'The US war machine against a weakened Europe – and the British . . .'

'The British people will rise up against their government and their allies when they hear about America's criminal plans,' Anna-Lena continued. 'It's worse than any of the Nazi war crimes. Nuclear bombs – on dozens of cities! And unprovoked attacks on civilians.'

Viktor was beginning to feel overwhelmed. His gut instinct was to go along with Anna-Lena, but the prospect of their success was beyond slim. None of his previous assignments had been as desperate as this: no reconnaissance; no air support; no supplies; no back-up teams; but facing a countless number of well-trained opponents. What had started off as a rescue mission had transformed into an interdimensional journey where they had a chance to dramatically influence the course of history in this world. His mind was racing, but no bright ideas were forthcoming.

Dana also remained silent. She had made her decision, but what would she do if Viktor decided not to join them? Just go on her own with Anna-Lena and the Communists, who would never give up the bombs? Absolutely not.

Coco stared out of the window, gazing into the darkness. 'This isn't our fight,' she repeated, suffocated with anger and helplessness. 'I want to go home! Can none of you understand?'

'I want to go home too,' said Anna-Lena kindly. 'As soon as we've stopped this nuclear attack. As I said, I can't make any of you help me. But it would be useful – extremely so. For this world.'

'I'm in, said Viktor, breaking the spell.

'Me too,' added Dana, relieved. She took Anna-Lena by the hand. 'Madame Fendi will make up her own mind. But you have to promise us something. We're just going to take over the base and secure the bombs. Any negotiations with heads of state and all that are to be left for Schwimmer and his people. None of the rest is of any concern to us.'

'Thank you!' cried Anna-Lena with relief. She could see Coco's face in the reflection of the window and tried to catch her eye. 'What about you, Madame Fendi?'

'I can't fight and nor do I want to.' Coco would have liked nothing more than to throw herself to the floor and scream like a toddler. Or use her powers to infiltrate their minds and manipulate them into returning. She hated being put under pressure like this. She hated this world. She hated everything at this moment. But the Communists were waiting outside the door and they weren't about to let her leave. She wasn't just in a predicament: she was in a trap.

'You'd be of great help to us. You can use your powers to find out how much the ministers, Captain Wallace and the generals all know. Perhaps you could even defuse or deactivate the bombs. That way they won't be able to do any harm.' Viktor put a hand on her back. 'No one's going to make you use a gun. But you're still important to us.'

Coco turned around. How could she possibly negate uranium? It all sounded so ridiculous.

In her mind's eye she could see Ingo, perforated and torn apart by the flak barrel; she thought about the professor being shot and Spanger's corpse being dragged away in a body bag. The three men had forfeited their lives without any idea about where this mission would lead them.

'I want to go home,' Coco repeated in a whisper. 'I don't want to die. This isn't my world.'

CHAPTER X

Near Frankfurt

The stranger landed on his feet, and Walter van Dam noticed he didn't bother bending his knees to cushion the impact. He stood upright without moving a muscle, like a statue that had just fallen from the third floor.

In the light of the fire, van Dam could see a face with the curved eyebrows of a woman and an angular chin with a long beard, white with black streaks. Snowy white hair tumbled over his head, giving the androgynous creature in Matthias' bloodstained uniform a strangely majestic appearance. There was no doubt at all that this splendid being with pupils glowing silvery pearlescent was not human.

Van Dam had absolutely no idea what he was dealing with. He refrained from firing his pistol, not least because he seriously doubted bullets would have any effect on this being.

'This is what you were you looking for, isn't it?' The stranger held out the bundle of papers. 'Take it.'

Van Dam reached for the folder. 'Thank you.'

The being raised his head, white beard rustling over

the bloody jacket, and looked around. The rain was still crashing down onto the domed library roof, but the light from the fireplace illuminated the room with a soft, yellowy shimmer. There came a flash of lightning and a peal of thunder, then the storm paused temporarily.

'This is a nice house. I should have come earlier.'

Van Dam did not take his eyes off the visitor. Responding in kind to the disarming tone, he said, 'Forgive me for not being able to offer you anything. This villa's stood empty for a long time now.'

The creature nodded, almost incidentally. 'Did you know the person whose clothes I'm wearing?'

'My chauffer. Matthias.'

'A chauffeur is a . . . ?' The stranger seemed to cast his mind around for the word's meaning. 'I didn't kill him, by the way. Nor the woman. Someone had already murdered her. But you must have already noticed that.'

'A chauffeur is a driver.'

'Ah. A pilot.'

'More or less. A pilot for cars.' Van Dam put the gun away and opened the folder. He probably wouldn't stand a chance anyway if the stranger decided to attack him. Evidently one of the monsters from the cellar had found its way to the surface – a very human monster with good manners but little knowledge of the outside world. His curiosity got the better of him. 'Your name?'

'What about it?'

'You haven't told me what it is.'

'Ah, right! What is it about humans and their desire to give *everything* a name? It's as if they think it grants power. Like a . . . spell.' He put his hands in his pockets and looked at van Dam. The creature's white hair, stance and bloodstained suit made him look like a character from a Tarantino film. 'I'm not very good at making things up. What name would you like me to have?'

Van Dam was reminded of the fairy-tale Rumpelstiltskin. Was this all just a joke? 'What is this?'

'A game. People like games.' He smiled, revealing two rows of gleaming white teeth, between which hung something that looked suspiciously like raw meat.

Van Dam suddenly suspected that Matthias hadn't simply left the stranger his clothes. 'Hopkins,' he said.

'Good. Suits me. Hopkins it is then.'

'Why are you wearing my chauffeur's clothes?'

'Appearing before you naked seemed a little . . . immodest. I don't like how linen feels and the woman's clothes didn't fit me.'

'Right. Okay then. My name's—'

Walter van Dam, came Hopkins' voice in his head. His lips weren't moving, though his silver eyes flashed impishly. *I know. I've been interested in you for a while now. Your past in particular. There's nothing I love more than investigating why people turn out the way they do.*

Amazement suddenly turned into unease. Van Dam decided to affect a business-like manner, although he suspected Hopkins would be able to read his mind. 'Where do you come from? And what do you want?'

'Where do I come from? Well let's just say for the time being that I come from the cellar – from where your daughter currently is.'

Van Dam forgot his fear for a moment. 'Have you seen Anna-Lena?'

'Briefly. She was having a whale of a time wandering through the passages.' Hopkins sat down on one of the chairs that were still intact and gazed into the flames. A handful of strands from his beard had soaked up some of the blood, adding another hue to his palette and giving him the appearance of a god of war.'

'Why didn't you rescue her?'

'Because that's not my job. Or wasn't. At least not till recently.' Hopkins put his elbows on the armrests, making him look even grander. 'You know, I was such an idiot for trusting Ritter!'

'Ritter being ... ?' Van Dam was trying desperately to keep up and remember as much information as possible. Even the smallest hint might help him to save his daughter. Perhaps he could enlist Hopkins' help? It was worth a try.

'Ritter's a nasty little prick.'

'No, I meant who does he work for?' said van Dam.

Hopkins laughed quietly. 'You're not very receptive to my jokes, you know. I've had to wait such a long time to try them out on someone.'

'My daughter's stuck in that labyrinth – that's why I'm not as keen on games and jokes as you appear to be,' he replied.

Hopkins' eyes changed from silver to light blue. 'Let's start again, van Dam. To help you to understand why I didn't just bring your daughter back up, or the two teams you sent down.'

He nodded. What else was there to do?

'Even though humans for the most part don't have any access to advanced technology, they're a resourceful species.' With his little finger, Hopkins pointed at the wooden door that van Dam had retrieved from the fir tree and dragged into the property before removing some of the dirt caked on during its years of abandonment. 'A small group of people created some portals that were designed to allow them to travel quickly from A to B.'

'How do they work?'

'*Particulae* – that's what they call the splinters and fragments they use, mainly in the door-knockers,' Hopkins explained. 'They're pieces of rock from a comet which have unusual physical and chemical properties; they have been collected and hoarded by people who wanted to find a use for them. If you hit them hard enough, the energy produces a reaction – and if you've got a frame, a force field will build up within it. Then once you step through you'll find yourself at your destination.'

'Sounds rather sophisticated.'

'It became so over time, yes. In the past no one really knew what they were trying to do and the journeys used to go wrong an awful lot.' Hopkins looked at the fire with fascination. 'I'd forgotten how warm it is. And how beautiful it looks.'

Van Dam also found an unbroken chair and sat down, silently congratulating himself for not having turned them all into firewood immediately. 'And where do you come in?'

'Ritter belongs to an organisation which knows the secrets of these doors. They've been passing on the knowledge for centuries, using it to their advantage.' Hopkins smiled.

'It is, in effect, a global conspiracy. Everything people have ever said about the Americans, Russians, Jews, Freemasons or Illuminati is actually . . . *them*.'

'And you're one of them?'

'No – oh no,' replied Hopkins quickly. 'No, I . . . was captured. By Ritter.' He picked up a broken chair leg and tossed it into the fireplace. Sparks crackled and danced up through the chimney. 'The headquarters where your daughter disappeared was abandoned a long time ago, because the *Particulae* stopped doing what they were supposed to. The journeys through the doors began to turn into disasters.' He pointed at himself. 'Ritter refused to follow the instructions not to continue using the doors, deciding instead to keep looking for artefacts, creatures and knowledge that he could put to use in this world. That's when he found and kidnapped me.'

This revelation rendered van Dam speechless for a few seconds. An inhabitant of another world, sphere, dimension or reality? He really did have to find out more. 'Where . . . from where did he kidnap you?'

'Far away. That's all you need to know. I don't want to worry you too much, Mr van Dam.' Hopkins sighed. 'I served him faithfully because he promised me he'd take me back. I believed him at first. But then he tricked me and disappeared. And before that, he tried his best to kill me.' He slapped his thighs with both hands. 'Our agreement is void now. So I escaped from the cave. Let's see what this world's got in store for me.' He got to his feet and looked up at the glass dome, onto which the water was still drumming. An inaudible flash of lightning blazed high above them, illuminating them briefly in its glow. 'Exposure to your sun will probably kill me, though. Might be tricky.'

'What do you intend to do?'

'Find the new headquarters and grab Ritter for myself,' Hopkins replied. 'I've got a few clues to work from. Then I'll ask the Organisation to take me home – otherwise they'll find themselves with a new enemy who'll do everything in his power to destroy them.'

Van Dam leant forward. This all sounded rather good to him. It looked as if he might have found a new ally. Now was the time for the suggestion that he had been turning over in his mind. 'You know your way through the labyrinth?'

'Like the back of my hand.'

'What would you say to going back down and finding my daughter?' he suggested. 'You'd be better than any team I could send down.'

'I knew you were going to ask me that.' Hopkins laughed loudly. 'No, thanks.'

Van Dam's despair turned into courage; he stood up and walked over to the white door he had found. 'But what if I could take you back to your world, dimension or whatever it is? Not this evening or tomorrow – I'd need time for research and experimentation. You'd need to stay put and not expose yourself to the sun, but you could make yourself comfortable in my house while I – we – sift through all these documents and decipher the mysteries of the door.' He spread his arms wide. 'You can read minds, so you'll know I'm being deadly serious. Sincere. No trickery or hidden motives.'

Hopkins contemplated him for a moment and ran his fingers through his white beard, which van Dam realised was now free from any blood, as if it had been absorbed or drunk by the hair. 'Not the worst option in the world.'

'And far less dangerous than running around, looking for a new headquarters.'

'At least on the other side of the maze.' Hopkins looked at van Dam. 'I've been conned before by a human. What's to say it won't happen again?' He tapped the side of his head. 'You're a businessman, Mr van Dam. You'd be able to trick me if you're clever about it.'

'I give you my word.'

'What's that supposed to mean?'

'A promise that I'm putting my reputation on the line. It's ... an oath attesting to my integrity.'

'That's not enough.' Hopkins' eyes suddenly gleamed red. 'What about *your life*? That sounds far safer to me than an oath. Or your word.'

He'd give anything to get his daughter back. And Hopkins was his last chance, his way out, the ace up his sleeve. 'And if I agree, you'll go down and look for Anna-Lena?'

Hopkins gave no reply. He stood up and crossed over to the white door. He placed it upright, opening it slightly to allow it to stand up by itself, then walked around it with his hands behind his back. 'What's to stop me from killing you, taking the papers and trying to decode everything myself?'

'Nothing at all,' replied van Dam calmly. 'But I'll do it faster than you. Most of the records are written in my family's old mercantile language. We knew how to encrypt information long before the invention of the internet.' He gestured at the glass dome. 'And in the meantime, the sun might destroy you. Or you'll die of starvation and thirst.'

'Who said I needed to eat and drink?'

Van Dam tapped his teeth with his index finger. 'I can see you've still got some leftovers. Did you eat my chauffeur?'

'I admit I did. He was delicious, if I may say so. You must have kept him in excellent condition. And the woman—'

'I didn't *keep* him – he was my employee! And my friend.'

'My apologies. Then you took excellent care of him. Better?' Hopkins patted the door's warped frame. 'It doesn't close properly any more. That'll be a problem when the force field starts to build up.'

'I can have it fixed.'

Hopkins laughed. 'That's precisely what I'd say if I were in your position. To get me to start looking for your daughter.' He looked into the flames once more. 'But maybe I should go back down again. I left in a bit of a hurry. It'd be nice to find the old headquarters before the *Particulae* disintegrate – to find some clues about Ritter's little journeys.' Hopkins was thinking aloud, van Dam thought.

Hopkins looked at the businessman. 'We should close the door as well – the one in your cellar. And the steel cable needs to be cut. I'm not the only creature who could find its way to you.'

The idea made van Dam shudder; his scalp tingled. 'Only once we've found my daughter,' he forced himself to say. *The monsters in the cellar. The rope. An unpleasant combination.*

'Of course.' Hopkins adjusted his suit and examined the

blood drying on it. 'I like your plan, Mr van Dam. And it'd be shame if the villa were destroyed.'

'Why would it be?' He suddenly recalled the word *disintegrate* being used.

'Because the *Particulae* are breaking up and the reaction is incredibly violent. If the doors open, the plasma and pressure waves will break through, destroying the property completely. The whole area will subside massively.'

'But . . . how is the door going to help?'

Hopkins massaged his hands, as if to loosen stiff muscles. 'It's not just a door – it's a passage. If it's closed, the building will be saved.' He strolled towards the exit. 'Very well. We have a deal. I'll go and find your daughter.'

'And I'll start working on the records,' said van Dam gratefully. It looked as if he had sent down a third team to look for Anna-Lena. A one-man army. Hopkins certainly appeared to be the most promising candidate so far. 'Don't hurt the people I've hired. You can work together.'

'I'll think about it.' Hopkins had already half-disappeared into the shadows, but his white beard and bright hair were still visible. 'You're laying your life on the line. Don't think I won't remember that.' With one final step he was one with the darkness. 'It's your decision whether or not I end up finding out what you taste like.'

Van Dam bent down and threw some more wood into the flames.

Near Rominten, East Prussia, 8 January 1945

Coco walked past Viktor, Anna-Lena and Dana and unblocked the compartment door. There was nothing more to be said. 'I wish you all the best of luck.' No one could force her to remain part of this commando unit, whose actions she considered utterly senseless. Why risk her life for an alien world, for a nightmare that had already brutally ended three people's lives? *Ingo's* life. She could never have imagined his death would have affected her so much. She also resented Anna-Lena who, after all the hardships they had endured, now wanted to play the heroine rather than accompanying them back home. 'Hopefully see you on the other side. In our world. I'll let your father know what's going on.' She opened the sliding door and headed out into the corridor.

Theo and Greta were waiting on the other side. 'Where do you think you're going?' he asked.

'To the baggage car.' Coco tried to push past him. She concentrated hard, knowing she needed to use her powers. 'I'm no longer required.'

Theo gripped her arm tightly. 'Forgive me, but have you foreseen anything that's going to end the war in the next ten seconds?'

'No, but—'

'Then you're not going anywhere.' Theo looked her straight in the eye. 'Go on. Try to read my mind. You won't find anything in there other than my intention to take over this base and negotiate with the States. If I suddenly give an order that contradicts that, Greta will know you've manipulated my thoughts. And she'll shoot you on sight.'

The sniper looked at her indifferently. 'I wouldn't enjoy it, but we've got a job to do. As do you, Madame. Whether you like it or not.'

'But . . .' Coco looked at the trio in the compartment, desperate for help. Strictly speaking, she had abandoned Dana, Viktor and Anna-Lena. They didn't owe her anything now. She was on her own: all alone against the Communists.

'We have an agreement – with them,' Theo reminded her. 'We'll help you to save your friend and you'll tell us anything that might be useful for the war. As far as I'm aware you've done nothing of the sort yet.'

Coco released herself from his grasp and stumbled back into the compartment, followed closely by the resistance fighters. Her eyes blazed with helpless rage. Viktor had promised her she could escape – that's what they had agreed.

'I have some important information. Something not involving clairvoyance.' Anna-Lena rose and stood in front of the medium to protect her. The situation urgently required de-escalation. 'You're in charge, right?'

'Yes.' Theo sat down in the first seat, with Greta positioned blocking the door. No one would be able to escape from the compartment. 'What have you got for us, Miss van Dam?'

Viktor and Dana were following the exchange with interest. Coco sat down and folded her hands in her lap.

'I know what they've got in Rominten – what the US troops are up to and who's on this train,' said Anna-Lena, who then proceeded to describe what she knew about the missiles, the nuclear bombs, the false flag attacks in Germany and Europe and the two American ministers who were travelling incognito to the base to report back to the President. 'I assume that'll be crucial to the war, won't it?'

Theo and Greta put their heads together, conferring in whispers. Their muted conversation sounded heated and excited. This information would expose their enemies' evil intentions once and for all.

'Can I go now?' Coco enquired hopefully. Anna-Lena surely must have given them enough. The door was calling for her. 'I need to get something out of the luggage compartment. Urgently.'

'No,' said Theo, 'you're not going anywhere on your own. Under no circumstances will I allow you to abscond. You still haven't predicted anything for us. Or do you fancy making amends now?'

Coco slumped down into the upholstery. She didn't even know what the fighters wanted to hear.

Viktor could see that she was completely finished. He touched her on the shoulder. 'We'll find a way out for you,' he whispered to Coco. 'It'll be all right.'

'I'll also need you to be there when we're questioning the general and the ministers. You'll know when they're lying.' Theo sat up straight. 'We'll take over the base and load the missiles onto the trains. Then we'll announce the Americans' plans to the world.'

Greta leaned against the door. 'The train's got a long-distance radio, which we can use to make contact with our people and have them join us. Smetana and her team are still nearby,' she explained. 'We'll interrogate the military staff and the ministers, send photos of the bombs to every major newspaper in the world, as well as every intelligence agency, along with the confessions from Wallace and the two ministers. The people of Europe will rise up against the USA and the UK.'

'We thought we were rid of a monster when Hitler died,' Theo added angrily. 'But sacrificing dozens of cities in nuclear fire is . . . it's . . . I can't even put it into words.'

'But we'll have to get the train under our control first. Before the crew send a radio message to Rominten.' Viktor lifted the G36. 'We're on it.'

'Well, I'm not,' said Coco defiantly. 'You can come and get me if you need anything.' She crossed her legs ostentatiously to show she was just going to sit and wait there. She was not prepared to look at another dead body. She *hated* this world.

Theo pulled a pair of handcuffs out of his pocket and secured Coco to the armrest of her seat. 'That won't be necessary.'

Coco gave Viktor and Dana an unmistakeable look. From that moment on she would always consider them traitors for not helping her.

The group assumed the same formation as before, still led by George. One of the prisoners they had freed was now going to play Coco's role as the alleged medium. With Theo, Greta, Dana and Viktor at the head of the group, the surprise attack on the next carriage began.

The guards were deceived by the appearance of their British defector for long enough to allow the team to eliminate them without having to fire a shot. Greta and Theo's knives cut the cords of more lives, while Viktor and Dana had their G36s at the ready to secure the aisle further down the train.

After a few minutes the second carriage was under their control. Their small band of liberated prisoners had grown with the addition of a handful of new volunteers. Those who chose to wait in their compartments were locked in.

They were about to repeat the trick in the third carriage when George opened the door to reveal six American soldiers unexpectedly standing in the short passageway linking the two carriages. They were holding roll-ups between their fingers, which they were about to light. Their badges and uniforms with white armbands identified them as members of the Military Police. The loud rattle of the train's iron wheels could be heard through the side windows that they had opened to allow their smoke to escape through.

The six Americans stared at the group.

Dana knew immediately that they had no chance of subduing all six of them with knives alone, so half-raised her G36 in preparation while she was still concealed behind the backs of the others. 'Nothing else will work,' she whispered to Viktor.

'Agreed.' He readied his own assault rifle, feeling the adrenalin begin to course through his veins in anticipation of a gun battle.

'*Attention*,' George called out in an attempt to exploit the soldiers' natural reflexes when they're in the presence of an officer. 'Report please, Sergeant. What are you and your men doing, hanging around here? Has Captain Wallace not expressly prohibited smoking on the train?'

'You can suck my dick, Tommy,' one of them replied.

'Where's this little island monkey come from then? It's got to be MI. The rest are all German auxiliaries,' said a second. 'But there were none on board when we left Fort India, were there?'

George lost his nerve the moment he realised their masquerade had failed. He stabbed at the foremost military policeman with his knife, in an attack that was far too easy to predict.

The enemy dodged the blade, but it lodged in the shoulder of his colleague standing directly behind him. His cry of agony rang out loudly through the passage and into the carriage itself.

'Get down!' Dana ordered, raising her G36. She still didn't have a clear shot.

Viktor sprang up alongside her. 'I'll do it.' His extra height meant there was no one blocking him. He unleashed a rapid volley.

Three of the military policemen were struck in the head and neck, with the bullets fortunately not penetrating the galvanised wall behind them. They crumpled to the floor without a sound, their white helmets rolling over the carpeted floor.

Greta also fired off a round from her pistol, but missed. She was far more experienced with a sniper rifle than at close quarters.

The remaining military policemen disbanded in an attempt to escape and raise the alarm. If they succeeded, the attempt to capture Rominten by train would be scuppered.

'Stop them!' Theo dived forwards, stabbing at his opponents with his combat knife, and another American sank to the floor, screaming.

The two remaining enemies fired their pistols, retreating into the long corridor separating the compartments and desperately trying to find cover behind a tea trolley. Loud screams rang out; any vestige of secrecy had well and truly vanished. Bullets shattered wooden panels, while splinters and dust flew through the air, making aiming almost impossible.

'Get behind me,' Dana shouted to Viktor. She followed the soldiers with her G36 at the ready and peered around the trolley, where she could see the two military policemen as well as a handful of guards who had now entered the fray. Dana unleashed a few volleys, swinging the muzzle from one enemy to the next after each salvo. Her movements were routine and safe, practised hundreds of times over countless operations. She was never likely to miss at this distance. One by one, they fell to the floor and stopped moving. 'Targets down.' She pushed her excitement to one side, keeping her breathing calm and controlled. The real test was yet to come.

Viktor jumped to her side and knelt down. Dana's aim had been spot on, as if she were simply performing an exercise at a rifle range. 'There are hostiles in the compartments. No prisoners,' he whispered to Dana. His heart was pounding, sweat running down underneath his Kevlar vest. He couldn't help but admire how calm Dana was. 'That's going to be tough.'

'I know. We need them alive.'

'Let's get to work then.' Theo pushed forward with his armed squadron behind him and caught up with them. Using a power lead that he had torn out of the control panel, he created a voltage jump on the thin wires belonging to the train's telephone system, putting them out of action. 'You go first. Right at the front. Secure the radio room, otherwise our success will be short-lived. I'll bet losing two ministers is a price the President will be willing to pay. There must be absolutely no chance of Rominten receiving advanced warning. Go, now!'

Viktor and Dana marched on in military fashion, in action on the same side for the very first time.

Coco sat in the compartment, handcuffed to the armrest and listening to the noises outside. It was quiet in the corridor now that the small army had made its way to the front of the train.

She'd heard brief skirmishes turn into sustained fire-fights as the Communists encountered their first real resistance. Every bang and every whir that accompanied a bullet missing its target and whizzing down the aisle or thudding into a compartment wall made her wince.

This world made Coco nauseous; she hated the dimension that had taken Ingo's life. She had a huge amount to thank him for and still felt guilty about how she had behaved towards him before. She really liked him; he was a dear friend, one she'd wanted to remain a presence in her life – whose absence would leave a vast hole.

How many times had she wanted to apologise to him – but

now Ingo was lying in two halves, discarded on a railway line, torn apart and discarded like slaughtered cattle. And all because he had been hired to drag a youngster out of a cave. And to look for ghosts. She would never forget his child-like enthusiasm when his devices displayed their first set of results. Nor would she ever forget the image of his death.

Coco could feel the anger and despair growing inside her. She was being held prisoner, compelled to serve the Communists as their resident fortune-teller – as Stalin's oracle . . . as a tactical scout who was better than any spy. And then there was the small matter of those horrific rockets with atomic bombs loaded onto them. Coco didn't care one jot what happened in this world. She wanted to be rid of it. Alone. The fates of Dana, Viktor and Anna-Lena were no longer of any significance to her.

An older, grey-haired lady scurried into the compartment, crouching down to avoid any ricochets and shielding her head with her hand as if high-velocity metal could be stopped by flesh and bone. Her clothes looked as if they had once been expensive but had deteriorated in captivity. She was definitely one of the arrested Nazi scientists.

She flung herself into the seat next to Coco and looked at her chained-up hand. 'Are you the clairvoyant?' she asked breathlessly.

Coco sighed quietly. Even in this world people wanted her to perform a private séance. 'No.'

'Yes you are! I overheard you earlier!' The woman intertwined her fingers in Coco's. You have to tell me what's going to happen to me. Please.'

'Why do I *have* to?' Coco would have liked nothing more than to kick her away. What was she playing at?

'Because I'm scared.'

'Aren't we all?'

The woman let go of her hand and rummaged through her pockets. A few gold coins appeared and she added her ring to the small pile in her hand. 'Here! Take it. And now—'

'I'm under no obligation to do anything for you,' Coco snapped. 'And if I were free, I wouldn't be sitting on this train. I'd have got out of here a long time ago.'

'Free?' She looked at the handcuffs. 'Oh. Yes, I understand. I'm not on this train by choice either, you know.' She removed a needle from her handbag. 'This'll open the lock. It's not too tricky.' She gave Coco a penetrating look. 'But first you have to tell me my future. And you can keep all this as well.' She placed the money and jewellery into the medium's pocket.

Coco considered her improved offer. What did she have to lose? 'Agreed.' She took the stranger's hand and gazed at her face, concentrating on the darkness of her pupils.

Her powers announced themselves by a weak tension in her temples and above the bridge of her nose. Coco's world suddenly turned blurry. She entered the woman's thoughts, whose name she now knew was Alexandra. Alexandra von Münster.

She was the wife of a scientist and doctor who was also on the train. Hubert. Hubert Erich von Münster, who had been one of Mengele's students, renowned for his particularly grizzly experiments. The Americans were interested in him because of his research into pain, which they were hoping to use for their own interrogation methods.

'What can you see, Madame Fendi?' echoed the strange voice through the haze.

'I . . .' The images in Alexandra's head rendered her speechless.

The woman had been her husband's assistant. She had passed him instruments, made notes, taken photographs and films of his horrific experiments. She had never touched the children, men and women herself, but her memories contained feelings of overwhelming joy at their suffering.

Coco could feel nausea rising in her stomach, her mouth developing a sour taste.

'One moment. I'm trying to see a little more,' she said, seething, wishing more than anything that she could punch the woman there and then.

She began to probe, trying to look into the future. As this was the first time she had tried this, she had no idea whether the results would be in any way reliable.

Coco saw the train, saw the guards firing from all angles, saw the bodies of British and American soldiers collapsing to the ground, saw buildings ablaze and a violent explosion, followed by the vision of a burning aircraft hull on an airstrip that had turned into an inferno.

Coco looked for Alexandra amid the chaos and found her. She was standing at the edge of the runway, pushing a burning body back into the flames before running away from the battle and escaping through a gap in the fence to disappear into the surrounding forest. Apparently this sadistic criminal was going to avoid the doom about to befall Rominten.

'I've got you,' said Coco flatly. 'You're ... you're going to die – today.'

'No,' Alexandra gasped. 'Is there anything I can do? Can you see anything?'

'Yes. If there's a battle at the base later on and you want to run away, don't. It'll cost you your life – death awaits you in the forest,' she warned. 'Stay in the hangar and hide. If you do that, you'll live a long life.'

'Thank you! Thank you so much. I'll include you in my prayers.' Alexandra shook Coco's hand vigorously. 'Oh, and you'll forgive me for not keeping my word.' She put the needle back in her bag without opening the lock, then walked over to the exit. 'If it were to come out that I'd helped you to escape, the Communists would kill me. Me *and* my husband. And I can't risk that. Apologies.' She turned and scurried out as quickly as she had entered.

Just as Coco had suspected. She felt no remorse for sending Alexandra von Münster to her death. She deserved it for all the atrocities she had been party to.

Her insight into Alexandra's future had shown her something else: the Communists were going to fail in their attempt to steal the missiles. Judging by the detonations and fireballs in the vision, the base was condemned to destruction.

And that would make no difference to Coco whatsoever, were it not for the fact that she was still stuck on this cursed train to Rominten.

She shook the armrest to test its strength, causing the

panel at the back to squeak softly. Coco increased the force until the metal rail tore out of the panel on the wall, leaving a hole in the thin partition.

Then Coco managed to pull the end of the handcuffs off the armrest, though the other part was still attached to her wrist. She was willing to put up with the pain if it meant she could make her way to the baggage compartment and disappear for good.

She rose quickly and scampered out into the aisle. The shooting had moved further away from her current position, towards the locomotive. The Communists were fighting their way through the compartments, eliminating anyone who stood in their way.

Coco hurried in the opposite direction as fast as she could.

Viktor could barely hear the fighting taking place behind him between Theo's men and the guards. He and Dana were already a long way ahead of the Communists. The guards had been surprised by their rapid advance, as if they were two horse riders galloping through a camp at full tilt. 'Nearly there,' he murmured.

They sprinted through the final carriage before the armoured car. They had eliminated several opponents with their precise shooting, sweeping through the passage too quickly for any coherent resistance to be organised. They wanted to make as much ground as possible. It was up to the Communists to sweep through and clean up after them.

Two thirds of the carriage they were rushing through contained conventional compartments, but the rear of it was partitioned off by a steel wall and secured by a bulk-head that made it difficult for unauthorised individuals to access it; it bore two locks like those on a safe.

Radio operators were sitting on the other side, apparently entirely unaware of what was happening on the train.

That's how it should stay, otherwise when they arrived at the base in Rominten the train would probably be shot to smithereens, or the railway tracks would simply be blown up.

Dana couldn't help but notice how well she and Viktor worked together as a team, almost as if they had always been part of the same unit with dozens of battles under their belts. 'Three more up there.' The Americans hurried out of a compartment, trying to reach the heavy steel bulkhead: as the telephone line had been destroyed, they had to try to warn the operators in person.

Viktor checked how many bullets he had left; he was alarmingly low. 'Ten rounds left and one magazine.'

'I've got twenty-one and a magazine,' said Dana, drawing her P99. 'Then just this thing.'

She was saving the G36 ammunition for the attack on the base, where the fighting would take place at long range. Dana had no chance of finding any modern cartridges here; guns from this era didn't use 5.56-calibre rounds. In this period almost everyone – friend and foe alike – used 7.62-millimetre rounds, meaning you could just pick up and use your enemy's ammunition. But that wouldn't work on their rifles.

'We'll need one of them alive to unlock the door.' Viktor was running behind her and was about to swap weapons when a shadow dived out of the window of the compartment they were passing.

Screaming with rage, the GI crashed into him, slashing wildly with a long knife – but his attack missed and the blade became embedded in the wall behind them.

Viktor was knocked off his feet; his opponent landed on top of him and immediately put him in a lever hold to immobilise him. 'Keep going!' he shouted to Dana. 'Stop them.'

'I'm on it.' Dana lunged towards the three remaining soldiers, who were fiddling with the bulkhead, hastily opening the latches.

One of them turned and raised his gun. Dana's bullet drove into his throat, staining the steel door behind him with red speckles. He collapsed silently.

The second soldier turned immediately, his sub-machine gun at the ready. He squeezed the trigger.

Dana saw the muzzle flash in front of the barrel. There came a loud rattle and countless tiny fists pummelled against her torso. The pain of the impact on her Kevlar vest drove the air out of her lungs, testing her circulation to its limits.

As the burst of fire was moving upwards as the weapon recoiled, Dana fell back, before the bullets buzzing around her could reach her neck or head.

She landed face-up in the corridor, less than two yards away from the two Americans, barely able to draw breath. She desperately fought against the all-too familiar phenomena of pain and shock, which were severely impeding her breathing.

'Okay, the bitch is dead,' said the soldier over his shoulder. 'You go in and get the operator to warn Rominten and ask what we should do. No idea if any of the officers or ministers are still alive. I'll go and help Jeff take down that other prick.'

'Fine.'

Through the dancing circles of fire, Dana pointed her pistol at the GI as he was walking past her. 'Whoops.' She pulled the trigger twice, putting one bullet in the man's chest and one in his head.

The final GI had released the locks and stormed into the radio room beyond, rather than turning around to shoot Dana. In a panic, he decided to prioritise sending out the emergency alarm over eradicating the imminent threat.

Dana scrambled to her feet and looked around for Viktor. He was still grappling with Jeff but had visibly gained the upper hand. She would have loved to help him but the radio message could be sent off at any moment, so she followed the American.

'Stop – or you're dead!' Dana shouted as she stormed into the cabin, where two uniformed women in headphones were operating a series of buttons on switchboards the size of cabinets. The control lights were still flashing red, meaning the radio hadn't made contact yet.

'Contact Rominten. Code: Hornet,' the GI ordered, turning to Dana. He now remembered his weapon, yanking it waist-high with both hands. 'You dirty fucking Communists!'

But before he could fire, Dana executed a perfect head shot with her P99, killing him immediately.

The enemy soldier fell backwards into one of the radio operators, who cried out and reflexively tried to catch him. The shotgun landed in her hands.

She looked up, then at Dana. In the blink of an eye her thoughts could be seen etched over her face – whether she dared to shoot. Fear that she might die. Determination not to hand over radio communications to the enemy. *Delay. Weigh up all the options.*

'Don't,' Dana said quietly, aiming the barrel of her gun at the radio operator. 'Don't do it.'

The woman didn't move, still clutching her newly acquired weapon.

The second operator's hand suddenly darted across the control panel to flick the call switch.

Dana shot her in the shoulder.

Screaming, the women recoiled and fell off her chair.

The muffled crack of a shotgun cartridge, which unleashed its load at Dana at a distance of barely two yards, roared deafeningly in her ears and made her dizzy all of a sudden. She had lost her sense of hearing.

The impact of the hundreds of tiny projectiles on the Kevlar vest sent Dana staggering backwards. Her foot became caught on a cable on the floor and, in her dazed state, she could no longer support her own weight. She crashed into the steel bulkhead, her head slamming into the frame. Her world began to spin ever faster and she could only see in double vision.

'Stop!' Dana shot at the enemy half blindly. 'I don't want to have to kill you!'

The bullets thudded into the dead GI, who was lying

with most of his body covering the radio operator like a shield.

'Not before I kill you, you red bitch!' The woman raised the shotgun muzzle a little higher.

Dana corrected her aim and squeezed the P99's trigger.

The operator cried out and clutched her chest. Her trigger finger twitched.

A second shot roared out, tearing off half of Dana's face and neck. Pieces of flesh, tufts of hair and a torrent of blood flew out in all directions.

The transmission lights were still flashing red when Viktor burst in, as a white as a sheet.

CHAPTER XI

Near Frankfurt

Walter van Dam sat cross-legged on a stack of cushions in front of the fireplace, working his way through all the files, documents and various notes scattered around the door he had discovered in the fir tree. Decoding his family's old language was a relatively straightforward task, as he often used it for his own memos.

The supply of snacks and drinks around him had come from the Mercedes. He had also smashed up several more items of furniture and thrown them into the flames to ensure a steady supply of heat and light. The rain had not relented at all; the constant drumming on the domed roof was accompanied by a gurgling and bubbling in the downpipes.

Van Dam had used a tattered old sheet to clean the worst of the dirt off the door and now he could see that despite the weathering it had endured, there were still hints of the former beauty it must have boasted shortly after completion. Every now and again he rose from his austere throne to compare the signs and symbols described in the documents with the markings engraved on the door.

It creaked occasionally as the drying wood reacted to the warmth, apparently desperate to return to its previous shape.

'What have you found?' came Hopkins' voice all of a sudden.

Van Dam jumped and turned around. The fact that the creature was still wearing Matthias' uniform, covered with blood and dirt, served only to increase his discomfort around the being who had dined so enthusiastically on his unfortunate former employee and his counterfeit daughter.

'You're back!' he exclaimed, disappointed and concerned to see that neither Anna-Lena nor anyone from the search party had returned with him.

'I know where your daughter is.' Hopkins drew closer and stood next to the door. 'But there's nothing I can do for her.'

'What? Why can't you—?'

'She's alive, Mr van Dam. But she's in a very difficult situation with the second team.'

'At least she's not on her own any more,' he replied, a little relieved. 'What sort of situation do you mean?'

Hopkins touched the inlays in the wood, stroking the fine detail with his fingertips as if trying to memorise or read them. His white beard and hair shimmered in the light of the glowing hearth. 'Your daughter's in a place where I can't easily reach her. Either she and the team will make it out on their own or they'll die in there.'

Van Dam refused to accept this possibility. 'You must be able to do something!'

'I really can't – because of the lock. It can only be opened from the inside.' Hopkins gestured at the files. 'Are you making any progress?'

Van Dam handed the pages he had translated to the strange being. He was the only one who appeared to be able to enter and leave the labyrinth at will without succumbing to its strange effects. How could he persuade Hopkins to come up with a solution? 'We had an agreement that you'd rescue my Anna-Lena.'

'Your daughter and the team will have a better chance of surviving if we let them get on with it. They've got everything they need to escape. As soon as they leave the chamber, I'll find them and bring them back upstairs.'

'How can you know all this when they're so far away?'

'I can feel it.' Hopkins scanned the translated lines, repeatedly looking at the door and symbols. His lips moved silently as he started once again tapping certain areas with his fingertips. 'But there's something that's giving me more cause for concern.'

That was precisely what van Dam didn't want to hear. 'What's that?'

'The *Particulae*: they've become even more volatile. The intensive use of the doors by your daughter and the people looking for her has accelerated the stones' self-destruction. They're heating up.'

'And will eventually explode.' Van Dam had turned pale. Not only was Anna-Lena stuck in a world they couldn't enter, but the basement was becoming a far more dangerous place with every passing second. 'How long have we got?'

'Not long at all. Maybe a couple of hours before the chain reaction starts. And remember what I said about the tunnel system and the villa – the door's open.'

But he couldn't close it, not while his daughter was still down there. He directed his gaze at the flames. 'You said something about her being in a chamber?'

'More like in a new world.'

'Will that world go under as well if everything starts blowing up?'

'She'll be stuck either way, as there won't be an exit.'

'And there's nothing we can do other than wait.'

'It's out of our hands.' Hopkins crouched down to inspect the slight damage caused by the fir tree branches. The door itself was unharmed.

Van Dam feverishly considered his options – and to what extent he could believe what the stranger had told him. He had no reason to suspect Hopkins of lying; what would he have to gain from Anna-Lena's death? There appeared to be no solution whatsoever. 'It's all so frustrating,' he admitted.

'It is. And I really am sorry I can't do any more to help.' Hopkins rose and handed back the translations. 'Thank you. This has helped me a lot. I understand now what this portal can do.'

Van Dam tried to distract himself from the prospect of impending doom. He needed to find a way to save Anna-Lena and Hopkins might still have some useful information. 'I've found some notes about a project by the name of Arkus.'

'Oh?' Hopkins grinned. The last remnants stuck between his teeth had gone. 'Anything in particular?'

'You know about it?'

'I heard someone discussing it once, a long time ago. It piqued my interest, even back then.'

'Just a sec. I've got it here.' Van Dam rifled through the sheets of paper piled up around his upholstered throne in search of the right document. 'A group of people are looking for the *Particulae* scattered all over the earth,' he said as he was looking, trying to recall more details. 'I couldn't work out whether this was the same group of conspirators or some sort of splinter faction.' He found the note and picked it up. 'Here – here it is. It's about building some sort of arch, as large as possible. A gate or portal of some kind.'

Hopkins stroked his long, white beard contemplatively. 'How is it different from the doors? Just the shape?'

'No. This Arkus will be made up entirely of *Particulae*.'

'Is there anything there about its dimensions?'

'The Arkus should be big enough for a human. It's an arch, built on a platform,' Van Dam read aloud, showing the sketch to Hopkins.

'They'd have to connect an insane number of fragments.' He tapped a small inconspicuous splinter embedded in the white door. It was metallic grey, and barely the size of half a stamp. 'See that? Can you imagine how many of these you'd need?'

'A lot.' Van Dam turned the page and scanned the lines. 'It says here you should check the impact sites of meteorites as well as plundering them from the doors. There's some great higher purpose, apparently.'

Hopkins circled the door, removing any remaining dirt. 'What sort of purpose?'

'Our friends at Arkus don't say.' Van Dam handed him the paper. 'We can only speculate. Accessing a foreign world, finding God, space travel . . .'

'Transforming people into something else,' Hopkins added speculatively. 'Eternal youth. Heroic powers to rival the gods.'

Van Dam tossed another log into the fire, then looked up at the glass dome. The rain had stopped during their conversation; the storm had passed on. The sky was gradually turning pink as the sun announced its imminent arrival. 'A few hours, you said?'

'Yes.' Hopkins noticed the dawn as well. 'I think I'm going to have to come up with something pretty special here.'

'Because of the destruction—'

'Because of the sun. And yes, also because the *Particulae* in the doors are disintegrating. I know I won't be able to persuade you to cut the rope, but . . .'

Hopkins' voice tailed off.

'Can you hear that?' he asked after a few seconds.

'What?' Van Dam listened carefully. Soft footsteps could be heard approaching through the library. 'Intruders!' he murmured.

'Armed intruders. I can hear their weapons clinking.' Hopkins turned to face the front door as it swung open.

'Good morning,' said the man in the pin-striped suit as he stepped deliberately into the high-ceilinged room, as if he were on a sightseeing tour of the property. 'Lovely to see you here, even though you do look a little worse for wear.' Ten armed men followed him inside, wearing

Kevlar vests and armed with assault rifles. They spread themselves out in a circle around van Dam and Hopkins with their guns trained on them. Faint green laser sights were just about visible in the twilight. 'My name is Ritter and I've got a few questions for you, gentlemen.'

Near Rominten, East Prussia, 9 January 1945

'Do you confess that the US government was planning to use Nazi A9 and A10 missiles to launch nuclear bombs at Russia and Japan?' Political Commissioner Sonja Smetana stood next to the camera that was filming the interrogation, alternating her questions between the American Secretary of State, Edward Reilly Stettinius Jr, and Secretary of War, Henry Lewis Stimson, who were sitting on stools in the radio room. Smetana had put on a red armband bearing a hammer and sickle with her Russian uniform, leaving no doubt about her allegiances.

The microphones were all on, allowing the confessions to travel through the aether to resistance groups all over Europe, as well as handed over to broadcasters and newspapers, and the film would be copied and distributed as widely as possible.

Viktor and Anna-Lena skulked in the background while Theo and Greta stood in the corridor, accompanied by a few of the Communists, who were smoking and listening intently to everything being said.

'We've got a medium with us who can read your every thought. So there's no point denying it.' Smetana smiled.

'And we won't even have to torture you to find out the truth. There'll be no pain required for this confession at all.'

Coco was sitting alongside the ministers on a stool, with her index and middle fingers pressed against her right temple. She was playing the role of the insightful medium, leaping from one mind to the next depending on who was being addressed. 'Stimson's thinking about the cities. Leningrad. Moscow. Stalingrad. Tokyo, Kyoto . . . no, he's crossed that out. Instead it's Nagasaki, Hiroshima, some holy island,' she told them. 'He doesn't know what it's called.'

Coco's attempt at pushing through to the portal had been thwarted once more. Several of the men and women she passed on her way to the baggage compartment had stopped her with questions about what was happening at the front of the train, which had been just long enough for Viktor to catch up with her.

Coco had never seen the man so upset. Dana's death had rocked him to his very core, putting him in a state of such evident emotional turmoil that she didn't dare to object when he brought her back to interrogate their high-ranking prisoners. He asked her to help him this one last time, after which he swore he would do everything he could to ensure Theo and Smetana left her alone and she would be allowed to leave.

So Coco would at last have her opportunity, and very soon.

'Yes. Yes, I admit it,' said Stimson, 'but not to cause more suffering – just to bring Stalin and the Tennō to their knees. To liberate the people from tyrants trampling on their human rights. To give people their freedom back.'

Smetana laughed uproariously. 'I suppose you're right – death is a form of freedom, you disgusting capitalist pig. There's nowhere in the world more cynical than the United States. Concealing the deaths of millions of people under the guise of liberation? It's a miracle you haven't killed yourself with the shame of it all! You're a pitiful human being – just like your president.'

Viktor was watching the interrogation but his thoughts were with Dana. He hadn't been quick enough to help to secure her position – to advance together as a team. .

He looked down at his hands.

He had washed them thoroughly, three times, but he could still see some dried blood underneath his fingernails. *Dana's blood.* There was nothing more he could do for her.

The train was between stations, allowing Smetana's main unit of Communists to be radioed over so they could climb aboard. They planned to attack Rominten with fresh troops and replenished weapons.

The prisoners had been freed and those who chose not to take part in the upcoming mission had been forced to disembark. The Nazis among them had been shot.

Smetana was thorough and efficient. She had already extracted a confession from Wallace about the planned false flag attacks; he had assumed responsibility for the bombings and the release of poison gas in Germany, both of which had initially been intended to be blamed on the Communists and Stalinist sympathisers.

Viktor was impressed by the idea of broadcasting what

the British and Americans were saying over the radio and capturing it all on camera. That way there would always be a record of it: millions of people around the world would see and hear the confessions.

'You presume to lecture me about freedom? Don't make me laugh! Stalin's no better than Hitler,' Stimson replied with contempt. 'Everyone knows what they do to their political opponents – and anyone who stands in their way.'

Smetana stopped the camera and turned off the radio.

'Aha, not so keen to stay on the record now, we are?' said Stettinius. 'You know perfectly well that Stalin's got his own concentration camps for opponents and dissenters. He cleans up the party and makes himself the sole ruler, just like Hitler or Mussolini or Franco.'

Smetana drew her pistol from its holster.

'What are you going to do now?' said Stimson mockingly. 'Kill me? As Secretary of War I'm far too valuable for you to—'

The political commissioner shot him in the chest. The bang made Anna-Lena and Coco flinch.

Stimson choked out a gasp and put his hand over the hole in his shirt, through which blood was now oozing, coating his fingers. After a final wheezing breath, his eyes glazed over and his body went limp.

'Comrade Smetana! What are you doing?' Theo pushed his way through to her.

'None of you are valuable.' Smetana waved the pistol at Stettinius, who raised his hands in defence, pleading for his life as smoke drifted ominously out of the barrel of the pistol. 'They've served their purpose.' Without a moment's hesitation, she turned to the Secretary of State and executed him on the spot.

The bodies fell against each other, slid off their chairs and landed on the metal floor of the radio room.

Theo pointed accusingly at the two murdered men. 'Do you know what we could have negotiated with these two alive?'

'Roosevelt doesn't negotiate. Neither would I in his position. He's far more likely to appoint two new ministers and turn these pigs into martyrs.' Smetana secured and holstered her pistol. 'No, Comrade Schwimmer, these two have served their purpose and it was an absolute pleasure to be the one to execute them. Their confessions have been recorded and can now be distributed all over the world. The US government's been exposed for what it really is.' She called some of her people over and ordered the ministers' bodies to be dumped off the train. 'Leave them for the crows and foxes. They're no use to us any more.'

The ice-cold manner of the political commissioner made Viktor uneasy. He had come across dozens of people like her on missions in his former life. The next massacre would be the one she was about to instigate at the base.

Coco slowly removed her fingers from her temple. 'They haven't got any more thoughts to read now.'

The lifeless ministers were dragged outside. The dead men flopped over the edge in the light of the lamps, coming to rest beside the tracks with their limbs twisted in an unnatural pose.

Smetana looked around. 'Good. Start the train again. We'll let Rominten know we're coming for them.' She summoned Theo and Greta over to her. 'The plan remains unchanged.'

The plan was to use the armoured cars against the defences of the Robinson Complex. After one or two salvoes the shocked and overwhelmed Americans would in all likelihood surrender there and then.

'What are we going to do with our loot?' Viktor asked. Rominten was well known; it would be vulnerable to an aerial assault. 'It'll need to be taken somewhere safe.'

'I've already thought of that.' Smetana turned to face Viktor. 'We'll load the nuclear warheads onto the two trains that are still there, plus this one here. We'll hide the wagons in tunnels so the British and Yankee aerial surveillance systems won't be able to detect them. Then our people will disseminate Wallace and the minsters' confessions to the public.'

'What's that going to achieve?' Anna-Lena severely distrusted this approach. She had imagined preventing the use of nuclear weapons would have required a different tack. But she had never met Smetana before.

'I'll tell you, Miss van Dam: we're going to make people all over Europe rise up in rebellion against the United States and that wretched British Empire.' Smetana smiled thoughtfully. 'I'm counting on the Scots and Irish to support us; we've already sent negotiators to their underground nationalist organisations to take charge of the resistance. The king will be truly amazed at how fast his palace burns.'

The train started moving again, the carriages squeaking forward. Through the small side window, Viktor could see the lights shining out of each of the slots in the armoured car at the front. The Communists had already prepared the guns and flak they were going to use to storm the base.

'As our most experienced fighter, I've got a very special role for you. You're going to be in the vanguard.' Smetana walked over to Viktor. 'I'm sorry about your friend's death, as well as all the other losses. They were fighting for a just cause, though.'

'I don't care about politics. Innocent people don't deserve to die in a nuclear attack.'

'If we were to conduct our affairs according to guilt or innocence, Mr Troneg, we'd have to exterminate the whole of humanity.' Smetana put her hands behind her back. She was enjoying her role as an aspiring heroine, bringing about victory for Stalin and instigating an uprising in Europe. 'No one's completely innocent.'

Viktor donned Dana's G36 and distributed the magazines between his pockets. 'Let's just start by saving cities from annihilation.'

'My sentiments exactly.' Smetana pointed at the sniper. 'You'll go with Greta's second team. Your two friends are better off staying on the train. I don't expect it'll take us long to overrun the base.'

'Yes, I'd much rather stay here,' agreed Coco. On the train and near the luggage compartment. With the door and her opportunity for escape. The impending battle would be just the distraction she needed. Anna-Lena was welcome to accompany her as well, if she wished.

'Please follow me, Madame Fendi. I've got one or two more questions for Captain Wallace and I need you to tell me if he's lying or not.' Smetana beckoned her invitingly.

'Then I'll have you and Miss van Dam taken to the luggage area. That's where you'll be safest.'

'Fine by me.' Coco didn't dare to show her joy. The best-case scenario would now be for her and Anna-Lena to be long gone from the train and this universe at the time of the attack.

'You know what I'm going to do. I'll bring you with me,' she whispered to Viktor. 'As soon as I've got an opportunity.'

'Okay.' He put his hand on the G36. 'I'll finish this.'

Coco nodded and followed Smetana, flanked by two guards. 'Don't be afraid,' she said to Anna-Lena as she walked past. 'It'll all be over soon.'

They passed through several carriages, finally arriving at the compartment where Wallace was sitting, guarded by four people. The political commissioner entered first, with Coco behind her. Anna-Lena had to wait in the aisle with the two men.

The door was shut with the curtains closed. There was a guard in front of the exit and one next to the window, with another sitting next to the captain. At Smetana's direction, the final guard cleared a space for Coco, then departed.

'Ah, got it. You've brought reinforcements.' Captain Wallace looked at Coco. His face bore the marks of the beating he had received during his first interrogation. He was missing two fingernails; the wounds were still fresh. 'Are we playing a game of good Com, bad Com now?'

'This is Madame Fendi,' said Smetana. 'She's an extremely gifted woman who can read your mind – or at least tell me whether or not you're lying, Captain.'

'Aha.' He made an inviting gesture, though his broad grin betrayed the fact that he did not believe a word of what Smetana had told him. 'Let's get started then. I'll put you through your paces.'

Coco once again put her two fingers against her right temple. 'It won't hurt,' she promised. 'You won't even notice I'm in your head.'

'Have you ever been to Rominten?' Smetana began.

'No.'

'Lie,' said Coco. Reading the American's mind was child's play. Since he didn't believe in her abilities, he was making no attempt to stop her from intruding.

'Will we need a special password once we arrive at Rominten?'

'Fuck you!'

'Yes,' said Coco. 'It's *The Beautiful Destruction of an Artificial Sun.*'

The captain visibly lost his temper. 'Shit, it's actually working!' When he tried to lean forwards, the guard next to him pulled him back into position.

Smetana instructed the guard to go to the locomotive and tell everyone the password. 'How many people are stationed there? More than usual because of the ministers?'

'Find the answers for yourselves,' came his snappy reply.

'Four hundred extra men have been drafted in, along with some more tanks and anti-aircraft turrets; they'll make Rominten look well defended,' said Coco as she read the prisoner's mind. 'They're not expecting an attack.'

'Go to hell, witch!' barked the American as the guard next to him struggled to hold him back.

'This is much better than pulling out nails or giving you drugs.' Smetana laughed cheerfully. 'It seems it's impossible to hide the truth from you, Madame Fendi.'

'What do you want with the missiles?'

Wallace glared at the political commissioner. 'When the President learns they're in the hands of a bunch of red bandits, he'll send his long-range bombers. Imagine what this patch of land will look like once the nuclear bombs have detonated!'

'A bit like the Russian and Japanese cities you and your President are so desperate to destroy. But neither of those things will happen,' replied Smetana confidently.

Coco tried a little test. She probed the commissioner's thoughts, just out of curiosity, to see what she really thought about Wallace and the war.

She immediately felt queasy: Smetana wanted to force Coco to work for them by taking Viktor and Anna-Lena prisoner. She wanted to turn Coco into a spy and use her during interrogations to find out secret information and win the war for the Reds. Stalin would rule the world within a year, thanks to superior information. *Coco's* superior information.

'I asked you what our captain thinks about the duty roster?' repeated Smetana impatiently. She turned her head towards the silent clairvoyant. 'How many men are on patrol and how many are stationed by the guns?'

Coco had evidently missed the first question. 'I'm tired, Comrade Smetana,' she said, requesting a break. 'Give me an hour.'

'Are you mad? There's a battle on our doorstep! We

need this information. The train's going to pull in at any moment.'

Coco dived back into the political commissioner's mind, searching for her true intentions regarding the future of the missiles.

And she found it: Smetana was lying – and about the worst thing imaginable. She was planning to send three or four warheads to Fort India by train and detonate them, destroying the headquarters and blaming it on the Americans: another false flag that would contaminate a vast area of land. The rest of their plunder, including the A9 and A10 missiles, were to be taken to Russia on the two remaining trains. To Stalin. To be fired from ships, wiping out major American cities.

Coco noticed that everyone in the compartment was staring at her. 'I'm sorry but I really am exhausted,' she said, finally breaking her speechlessness. 'I'm in no state to be of any use to you.'

'You've been in my head.' Smetana's expression was fixed. 'You've acquired knowledge you're not entitled to.'

Captain Wallace laughed out loud. 'And you thought this lady was better than any torture or drug.'

Coco rose, trembling. *The luggage compartment.* All she had to do was go back down the aisle and use the knocker. Then she'd be gone, together with Anna-Lena. 'Please, let me rest for a bit. There are two mattresses in the luggage compartment that I could—'

'No.'

'I . . . won't tell anyone what you're up to,' Coco stammered. 'Please, I just need some rest.'

'I know what you want,' said Captain Wallace. 'You want to go through the blue door.'

Smetana looked back and forth between Coco and the captain. She didn't understand what he was talking about. 'What blue door?' Her features suddenly became brighter. 'The one your people removed from that basement?'

'It's a portal,' explained the American, 'a passage to some secret Nazi facility at the North Pole. Or wherever. Somewhere better than this shitty train, at least.' He winked at her. 'Take me with you – get us out of this compartment and I promise I'll deliver you safely to the luggage compartment with my gun.'

'There's nothing there! She's going to stay and serve the Socialist Revolution.' Smetana grabbed Coco's arm. 'Stalin needs you. The Red Army needs you. With you we'll—'

'You want to carry out the same massacre the President had planned!' shouted Coco in a panic, backing up towards the door, where she bumped into the guard. Wallace was dangerously close to the truth: he had revealed the secret of the not-so-harmless old door and now the political commissioner would keep it under lock and key. That meant only one thing: Coco was trapped. For good.

'Do you have the power to influence our guards' minds?' Wallace's body tensed. 'Come on – make them shoot each other!'

Smetana yanked her own pistol from its holster and aimed the barrel at Coco's head. 'Don't you dare.'

'Do it!' shouted the captain, who promptly received a blow in his face from the guard's elbow, causing him to fall back against the backrest. 'Do it, Madame. If you don't, Smetana won't hesitate to get rid of you.'

The political commissioner nodded to the guard by the door, who immediately put his arm around Coco's throat from behind. 'If I notice any of my people behaving differently, I'll have your neck broken immediately.'

'I know you can do it!' cried Wallace, clutching his bleeding nose. In an attempt to provide a distraction, he hurled the blood at his guard, then threw himself upon him. 'Come on! I'll give you—'

Smetana's hand jerked to the side, her finger squeezing the trigger several times.

The bullets slammed into the captain, who was struck several times on his upper body and collapsed, pulling the guard he was intertwined with down to the floor with him.

The compartment door flew open and a gust of wind blew the curtains up. They billowed around Coco like a pair of soft wings, rendering her temporarily blind.

'What's going on?' came Anna-Lena's concerned voice.

Coco tried to warn her but the man's arm was still around her throat and he had started to squeeze.

The political commissioner fired again, this time into the middle of the scuffle taking place within the heavy material.

Once—

The bullet hit Coco in the chest. The Kevlar absorbed the projectile but the intense pain in her torso forced her to her knees. Her guard stumbled forwards, surprised by the sudden weight.

'No, I . . . I don't want to die in this shitty world . . . !'
she managed to gasp.

Twice—

As she slid to the floor, Coco fell into the path of the
second bullet, which pierced the soldier's arm – and her
neck. She tried to scream, but no sound emerged. She could
taste blood in her mouth and feel air through the hole in
her throat. The man released his grip on her with a scream
and went staggering sideways into the aisle.

Coco fell to all fours, coughing wetly. Her surroundings
grew darker as Smetana towered over her like a slender
black rock. She could hear Anna-Lena crying out from
behind her.

Three times—

Anna-Lena fell silent.

Coco's arms gave way. She was already losing consciousness the moment she hit the floor, but in her confusion,
she read Smetana's thoughts.

*Good shot. That fucking bitch almost . . . Oh, I've killed the little
one as well. No matter. Might be better that way. Who knows what
she might . . .*

With her next breath, Coco died on the compartment
floor.

As did Anna-Lena.

'Miss van Dam and Madame Fendi are in the luggage
compartment, Mr Troneg, resting. Nothing will happen to
them, I assure you. I've taken care of the matter personally.' Political Commissioner Smetana nodded at him with

a friendly smile. 'Before you start, I'd like to thank you for all yours efforts. They've been exemplary.'

'Well, we have to thwart Roosevelt's insane plan.' Viktor checked his G36 one final time as the train rolled into the base at Rominten.

There was nothing on the outside to suggest there were Communist fighters stationed in the carriages. The turrets remained facing forwards, trying to look harmless.

'Thanks to you, we're in possession of some crucial information. The world will hear of it and rise up against the Americans and their British lapdogs. The people will come to understand that the US President is nothing more than Hitler in a more expensive suit.' Smetana signalled to her troops. 'Thank you, Mr Troneg. On behalf of the world.'

The train's brakes began to bite, slowing the train down with a shriek.

The brightly lit military base appeared outside the window. The American and British soldiers had all lined up beneath the Stars and Stripes to welcome the arrival of the US Secretaries of State and War. Tanks stood opposite one another, with their guns slightly raised, as if to form a martial trellis.

Viktor recognised an A9 missile that had been mounted on an A10 and driven out of one of the six brick hangars to be presented to the dignitaries. It reminded him of the missiles the Soviets and Americans would later send to space and the moon – which was not at all surprising: the Allies had been known to use Nazi technology for their own purposes in his world too.

The way it stretched into the sky, painted black and white, with the Stars and Stripes gleaming in the light of four anti-aircraft beacons, was truly impressive. It even had the nuclear warhead mounted upon it, as revealed by the radioactive warning on the missile's yellow tip.

Anxiety was burning a hole in his stomach. 'No one is to fire at the missile,' he said to Smetana. 'If the warhead ignites for any reason whatsoever, we'll turn to ashes in an instant.'

The political commissioner quickly relayed these instructions to the crew in the armoured car.

'All units,' she radioed through a portable device to the carriages that had been added when the reinforcements boarded. 'We'll let our larger calibre weapons do the heavy lifting. If there's still any resistance, we'll handle the rest personally.'

The squealing of the brakes grew louder as the locked wheels slid over the rails. Then the train came gradually to a halt.

The band playing as part of the reception committee for the honoured guests could be heard as the driving noises ebbed away. It sounded like *Yankee Doodle*, a song which had originally been used by the British to taunt the Americans during the Revolutionary War, before the Colonialists had reworked it with so much pride that it ended having precisely the opposite effect from the one intended.

How appropriate, thought Viktor, *a song to unite two nations who were preparing to turn Europe, and perhaps even the entire world, into their colony.*

The train's gun turrets turned in unison, aligning the long barrels.

Viktor noticed the dismay suddenly appearing on the faces of those waiting. The band continued to play. It was still possible that some of the crew at the base might have considered the movement by the armoured turrets as a gesture of respect.

Smetana looked at her watch. 'Get ready,' she said over the radio. 'Open fire in three, two, one – *now*!'

After a brief delay, the cannons on the train sprang into life. A lightning machine went into operation, dealing out flames, smoke and destruction to the world on the other side of Viktor's window. Machine-guns, grenade-launchers and field cannon brought death in a variety of ways upon the unsuspecting troops.

The earth shattered into a damp haze of brown and red. Torn flesh intermingled with mud, fountains of dirt and spurting blood and tissue, forming a gruesome mass.

In the midst of the carnage, the field cannons roared, punching holes in the tanks; two of them were struck by ammunition right in the sweet spot and blew apart in a series of spectacular detonations that almost shattered the windows of the armoured car. Meanwhile, the flak sawed the watchtowers into tiny pieces, causing broken glass, wood shavings and human body parts to rain down onto the ground.

Viktor had never experienced anything like this before in his life as a soldier. His special forces unit operated differently. Death was part of the job, either for their unit or for their enemies. Bullet holes, broken limbs, cuts, wounds inflicted by grenades or mines were all familiar sights. But the chaos inflicted by the constant fire of these machine-guns and anti-tank weapons was nothing short of a slaughter – a massacre almost beyond human comprehension.

He suppressed the urge to vomit, refusing to allow himself to feel pity for these people. They were working for a criminal regime who had wanted to rain A9 and A10 missiles and nuclear weapons down upon unsuspecting cities. None of them deserved to be spared, and yet he would have preferred there to be a ceasefire to at least give them the opportunity to surrender.

The smoke from the grenades and guns combined with the wandering mass of dust to form a reddish-brown veil that stuck to the glass and blocked his view. The flashes on both sides continued, along with the crashing and pounding. The train was shaking under the forces acting upon it from the armoured cars.

'Listen up,' Smetana shouted through the infernal staccato. She was still looking at her watch. 'Shelling ends in three, two, one – *now*!'

The deadly storm suddenly stopped. Only the clouds and smoke drifted around, graciously covering the sight of the slaughter outside.

'Windows down,' the woman ordered. 'Listen carefully and be prepared to sit down.'

The windows opened with a clack.

A copper-smelling mist of dirt squeezed its way into the carriage's interior, with a conglomerated stench of vomit and ruptured intestines and burnt skin, broken earth and hot metal seeping inside.

Viktor could hear gagging coming from the ranks of the Communists, but his entire concentration was instead focused on *sound*.

It was deathly silent. Apart from that and the soft crackling of the flames ignited within the destroyed tanks, nothing else could be heard. No one was calling for help; there was no shouting or crying whatsoever. Nor had a single shot been fired at the train.

'Out!' Smetana ordered, letting half a dozen of her people leave before she disembarked from the carriage herself. 'Lock the whole area down. Round up any survivors and take them captive.'

Viktor also hurried outside, his head bowed as he looked through the sight of his loaded G36. He was the only one moving through the acrid smoke in that way. It was clear that training from 1944 was significantly different from modern methods.

His boots strode through torn earth and puddles of blood, soft flesh and bone fragments and all manner of tattered . . . *things*. It reeked as if an abattoir had exploded.

Viktor had tried to suppress it for as long as possible, but now he had no choice but to lower his rifle and throw up. He had often wondered what conditions were like in Verdun and other warzones. Now he knew.

The wind was blowing the smoke away and through the haze, Viktor could now see the faint fires burning inside the tanks, accompanied by the absurd sight of the A9 and A10 missiles towering over them, still illuminated by the anti-aircraft lights, as if it had been they who had brought annihilation upon them like an angry mechanical god.

On either side of him he could make out the members of the Secret Red Regiment trudging through the devastation in search of survivors. But there were none.

'Where are you, Troneg? You should stay with Greta,' Smetana called out. I need you up at the front.'

Viktor raised the G36. 'Coming,' he shouted back, his gaze directed at the missile. It hadn't been hit by any bullets. The shell was intact, with no punctures or chipped paint. 'Have you found anyone?'

'All dead,' came the voice through the smoke. 'No resistance. All the other divisions have reported the same. The first of our men are already at Bunker One.'

Viktor was about to reply when he sensed that the missile was tilting. Slowly. Forwards and directly at him, like a magnet being drawn towards him. To punish him for the massacre at the base.

He stopped and stared upwards. 'Smetana? Can you see this?' Viktor could hear the first shouts of alarm from the other insurgents. 'The missile. It's swaying, isn't it?'

'Oh, no!' she gasped in horror. 'What ... *how?*'

Viktor was not wrong. Missiles 9 and 10, equipped with a nuclear warhead weighing one ton and with the potential for obliterating everything within a radius of several dozen miles, was falling to the floor. No one in the area stood a chance of surviving a nuclear denotation of this kind. Not even in a tank.

But if he could make it back to the luggage compartment and the door ...

Viktor turned and sprinted back through the gradually

dissipating smoke towards the train, discarding everything that might slow him down.

There came a loud crash behind him as the missile hit the ground, followed by an explosion that detonated the fuel. The heat and brightness was now chasing Viktor.

Panting, he arrived at his goal. The side of the luggage car was open; he jumped inside and hurried past the shelves towards the battered, blue-painted door, which had been unpacked and was lying harmlessly between the boxes and crates, just as he had left it.

'Anna-Lena? Madame?' he called out. After receiving no reply, Viktor assumed they had already left through the door, as per Coco's intentions.

Viktor looked back over his shoulder at the burning missile. The warhead was shedding its yellow warning paint, which was burning with bright, unhealthy-looking flames. On the inside the temperature would be rising all the time and would sooner or later detonate the explosive charges, initiating an atomic reaction.

He placed a hand on the rusty door knocker.

'Wherever you're escaping to,' Smetana's voice rang out behind him, 'you're going to take me with me – or else you'll end up like your friends.'

Viktor stood stock still. 'What have you done to them?'

'Have a guess.' Smetana jumped into the carriage, clutching a pistol in her right hand. 'What do you have to do to travel through this portal?'

'How do you know that's what it is?'

'Wallace said something to that effect.' She gave the door a kick. 'Well?'

'No.' Viktor was now in no doubt that the political commissioner had killed Coco and Anna-Lena. This had all been for nothing: the job; the attempt at securing the bombs; even his escape attempt – because that would allow an unscrupulous murderer to escape as well. 'I'm not so sure about that.'

'Then make yourself sure and be quick about it.' Smetana aimed the barrel at his head. 'I can't imagine you particularly want to save my life.'

'Correct.' Viktor removed his hand from the ring. 'And if you shoot me, you won't achieve anything except for killing me before the explosion does.'

Smetana licked up her lips and squinted at the missile, whose warhead was now roasting amid the blaze surrounding it. 'I'll take my chances then.' She suddenly grabbed the ring and slammed it down with considerable force.

There was a loud crash and the door began to shimmer as the force field built up. At the same time, the rusted iron crumbled. The portal could not be opened again.

'I knew it!' Smetana shot Viktor twice and opened the door. The bullets brushed his left thigh and slammed into his right knee; he collapsed, screaming in agony. 'Follow me if you can.' Laughing, she took a step into the glow on the other side.

A dark rumbling could be heard outside. Something had exploded, potentially another fuel tank.

Or the atomic reaction was about to start.

Then Viktor did something Smetana was not expecting: he remained on the ground, drew his pistol and shot the political commissioner in the back, legs and anything else he could hit from where he was lying. He emptied the entire magazine.

She fell back into the luggage compartment, gasping for air. 'You ... you're ...' Then her chest, riddled with bullets, sagged and did not rise again.

Viktor hauled himself up onto a couple of pieces of luggage and jumped forwards on his wounded leg; his right knee was now entirely useless. Adrenalin dulled the pain somewhat, spurring him on for one final effort. The door stood open before him, promising him an escape route back to his own time.

Where someone could take care of him.

Where he wasn't about to burn to death in a nuclear inferno.

Where he had to deliver the tragic news of a man's daughter dying in an attempt to save an alien world from annihilation.

A blinding flash erupted at the top of the missile, following by an unimaginably hot blast of air.

A litany of thoughts passed through Viktor's mind simultaneously.

What the landscape would look like once the explosion had detonated the remaining warheads.

How deep the crater would be.

How stable the earth's crust really was – and whether it would crack open.

How strong the subsequent earthquake would be and what the range of the devastation would be.

And whether the explosion had ended this war, meaning at least the losses would not be entirely for nothing.

The wind lifted him up, swept him through the force field and slammed the door behind him.

CHAPTER XII

Near Frankfurt

The man in the pin-striped suit who had introduced himself as Ritter looked like a lawyer with a striking penchant for Italian fashion – or an old-fashioned model. His armed companions with their combat gear and balaclavas were certainly not in keeping with his appearance.

'This is private property.' Walter van Dam felt ridiculous the moment the words had left his mouth. How could saying that prevent the stranger from roaming through the villa, or even simply shooting him on sight?

But Ritter was only interested in Hopkins. 'You've killed our assassin, the clone and the chauffeur?'

'No.' Hopkins pointed to van Dam. 'He's the one who killed your man and he—'

Ritter raised his hand. 'Fine. I was just curious.' He nodded in the direction of van Dam. 'I'm here on behalf of my friends to make up for something that's been neglected over the last few years.' He rubbed his fingers over the dusty mantelpiece. 'A good clean-up job.'

'You're including me in that.' Hopkins leaned casually

against the white door. In his torn, bloody suit he looked like the anti-Ritter.

'You've broken your promise.'

'So have you.'

'I've been busy trying to come up with a solution.' Ritter pulled an E-cigarette from his pocket and began to puff on it. White smoke seeped out of his mouth and nose, giving off the distinctive sweet scent of plums. 'And you were supposed to kill anyone who found a way into the passages. It was your responsibility to protect the old headquarters.'

'A place that's about to disintegrate and crumble to dust. You knew perfectly well I would have died down there.' Hopkins gestured to van Dam, who was observing the conversation in silence. 'Actually, it's thanks to him and his team that I'm more or less free now.'

'More or less free?' Ritter gave a piercing laugh that echoed back off the glass dome. 'You'll burn to a crisp the moment you step into sunlight.'

'I've got a door – a new, completely unused one, not like the ones down there.' Hopkins touched some of the symbols carved into the white surface. 'I don't know precisely where I come from, but anything's better than living a life of a forgotten shadow.'

'I'm afraid I can't allow that. As you might have noticed.' Ritter took another puff. 'Sorry for dragging you into our little family tiff,' he said to van Dam. 'This is all rather uncomfortable for me. Do you know, I found him—'

'You tricked me and kidnapped me,' Hopkins interrupted, 'and left me alone in the dark. You exploited me for your own purposes.'

'More like, "discovered him, brought him to Earth and had grand plans for him",' Ritter continued. 'But matters became more complicated than I'd expected. My friends didn't see the trove of possibilities I see in him. Or rather, *saw*.'

Van Dam didn't dare to move for fear that the gunmen would consider it an attack.

Ritter gestured around the library with his E-cigarette. 'I'll take as much as I can get my hands on. Your documents as well, Mr van Dam. We'd classified you as harmless, but we'd overlooked your little Anna-Lena. Curiosity brought her far too close to her ancestors – and our past, our old headquarters.' The next time he exhaled, his head disappeared among the white smoke for a couple of seconds. 'That's all been taken care of now, though. I can already see the headlines: *Entrepreneur and Daughter Die in Cursed Family Villa*.'

Van Dam knew he wouldn't stand a chance against the ten men with sub-machine guns. His Kevlar vest wouldn't protect him from a head shot and he had no idea how well the material would last against sustained fire. He was not the man for this sort of work.

A violent gust of wind blew unexpectedly through the library, scattering the loose papers around the upholstery throne upwards towards the glass dome.

Van Dam couldn't see what was going on through the wall of spinning papers. He could hear the rustling and thudding of heavy bodies falling to the ground one by one, as well the clatter of discarded weapons.

'You need to leave the villa,' he heard Hopkins' voice in

the background. 'It won't be long before the *Particulae* disintegrate. You can at least save yourself. Have a good life.'

There came a metallic thud, as if someone were banging on a bell, while the air suddenly felt full of electrical charge. The flying leaves were surrounded by blue St Elmo's fire that was drifting towards van Dam.

He covered his ears; the crash was too loud to bear. For a brief moment he thought he could feel his feet lifting gently off the floor. Gravity appeared to be failing, before the effect ended as suddenly as it had started.

The notes landed with a light crackle, covering eleven bodies lying on the floor with puddles of blood surrounding each of them. The papers were immediately soaked in the red liquid.

Van Dam gasped in shock and horror. His enemies' throats had been torn out, almost shredded. It was a mystery how Hopkins had managed that; he suspected he'd never solve that mystery.

The door stood in front of him, now, pure white and adorned with elegant ornaments, as if by magic, completely clean: as beautiful as it had been on its very first day. There was a small amount of heat radiating from it, causing the wood to crackle a little more loudly than before.

Van Dam knew precisely what that meant: Hopkins had passed through the door to escape both the sunrise and the imminent demise of the estate.

He, on the other hand, would succumb to his fate as soon as the *Particulae* in the labyrinth had disintegrated, bringing destruction upon him through the open door in the cellar. His final thoughts would be with Anna-Lena. This was far better than continuing to live without her, racked with guilt about her death.

There came a loud hissing sound, interspersed with crackling and rustling, as if to signal that a large amount of energy had been released. A flashing streak of reddish-white lightning bounced off the walls and rumbled inexorably down the hall towards the library, leaving scorch marks in its wake. The energy was coming from the basement, seeking its way up like a messenger desperate to announce a grave disaster.

The bundle of rays hissed and struck the white door frame – but did not go out. Instead, the *Particulae* in the wood flared with a dark whirring sound, searing themselves deep into the material as the decorations caught fire and blazed with flamelets the size of fingers.

The bright whining of the ball of energy shooting from the depths below up to the surface was already increasing, attracted by the radiance of the white door. A force field appeared with a loud popping sound and the door opened.

Van Dam took a step backwards and closed his eyes.

Viktor regained consciousness face-down in the mud, with the taste of dust and metal in his mouth. Heavy rain was pelting down upon him. This was followed by a feeling of intense cold through his body. Viktor was shivering uncontrollably from the shock, combined with his body's efforts to retain its core temperature.

The pain in his right knee suddenly flared up – a cruel reminder of how close his escape from death had been.

He gasped and groaned as he raised his head and looked around in amazement.

The skyline of an enormous city revealed itself to him, with clusters of skyscrapers dotted all along the horizon. The tallest of them towered more than a quarter of a mile into the cloudy grey midday sky. It was obvious the door on the train hadn't brought him back to his own world. Or in any case not back to the year in which he had left.

From his elevated position he could see the city's foothills, with what looked from here like suburbs and industrial centres, above which helicopter-like vehicles of various sizes flitted back and forth, sometimes lined up like strings of pearls, sometimes in clouds resembling flocks of birds or swarms of insects. The small rotors of the vehicles hummed and whirred softly, reminding him of drone technology. Through the curtain of rain, banks of lasers were projecting colourful images over the roofs and down into the urban canyons. He could not see whatever it was that was being advertised.

Viktor wiped the water from his eyes and gritted his teeth in agony.

There were raised streets and closed-off tubes leading in all directions throughout this unknown metropolis. The wilful door that had spat Viktor out in this place was embedded within one of the titanic struts supporting a flyover.

Viktor had never seen a city like this before.

There was a rubbish tip no more than ten yards away down the hill, piled high with scrap metal and plastic.

Drones bearing blinking lights purred their way above it, hauling tubs the size of cars filled with miscellaneous small parts through the air, skilfully dodging the cranes hoisting steel containers.

Viktor looked up again and this time he almost recognised the skyline. 'This is ... Frankfurt!' he murmured aloud.

He had ended up in the future – or perhaps an alternate future, a little like the one he had just left – the sole survivor.

But he could not stay here.

He had to go back to tell van Dam what had happened. He was utterly overwhelmed by the deaths of the rest of the team. Six people had died for a just cause, yet they had still failed. At least one of the bombs must surely have detonated.

And what then?

First, I must get back. He hastily bound the bleeding wound on his knee with his belt and after looking around, spotted a metal rod on the ground he could use as a crutch.

With a choked cry, Viktor stood up and hopped towards the entrance by the pillar, which was protected by a partially destroyed chain-link gate. From what he could see in front of him, it looked as if the blast from the explosion had flung him through the door like a cork from a bottle of champagne.

He hobbled inside the hollow pillar; a brutalist array of grey concrete walls, covered with colourful graffiti and artfully decorated with assorted rubbish including empty crisp packets and piles of leaves in the corner. Rust-brown water dripped from the ceiling, while subdued sunlight drifted through the entrance gap.

Viktor could see the words *Staff Only* written on the door through which he had just been hurled. The force field was still shimmering.

He looked at it contemplatively. If he stepped through, would he end up back in the middle of a nuclear explosion? Or the cave he had originally departed from?

There was a burning smell coming from the door frame, which he could now see was smouldering and had slightly swollen. A few dark scorch marks had begun to appear, as if something were heating up underneath the paint.

He was afraid the portal might be damaged and there would be no way out of this world, but there was still hope, however, that he could go back in time to tell van Dam what had happened. The man had a right to know what had become of his daughter.

But what if he ended up in the middle of a nuclear fireball?

He was rapidly running out of time. What was more, his injuries needed to be attended to, as he was feeling faint again.

Viktor hopped quickly through the shimmering door.

Moonlight fell through a set of closed wooden shutters, barely illuminating the furnishings in the room: a simple wooden table; a handful of chairs; a bed with someone sleeping in it and another person lying on the floor in front of it; a number of what looked like mediaeval travelling coffers; a large, ornate wardrobe and a bowl filled with water lying on a sideboard. There were two spears and two shields leaning against the wall, though in the murky light he couldn't make out the coats of arms painted on the shields.

Viktor glanced over his shoulder to see that he had not come out of a door, but rather from a suspended frame belonging to a large painting. The force field's minor oscillations could still be discerned through the canvas, which was also giving an occasional soft crackle.

He had landed neither in his own time, nor in 1945 – but where, then?

Assuming this wasn't some concocted scene and he had in fact arrived in the Middle Ages, his situation was looking even bleaker. There wouldn't be any doctors here to tend to his wounds, let alone the impending inflammation that was bound to accompany them.

The smell of fire coming from the frame was increasing. *Not a good sign.*

Viktor needed to be certain. Perhaps he *was* in the twenty-first century, but somewhere rather more primitive?

He limped across the creaking floorboards towards a glassless window, in front of which was mounted a frame covered with what felt like some sort of treated animal hide to protect against the elements.

He pulled it aside and looked outside.

The room stood several feet above the ground. Hundreds of half-timbered houses with rickety roofs spread out before him. He was in a town with a decidedly mediaeval appearance; on one side, he could see a relatively modest castle or fortress.

Flags and banners flew in the gentle wind, wafting a

distinctive scent of flowers through the air, and beyond the wall and ditch enclosing the town, corn was standing tall in the surrounding fields, which made him think it must be early summer. Most of the windows in the houses were dark and he could hear none of the noises common to modern life. He caught sight of what he guessed was a night watchman prowling through the narrow alleyways, clutching a lantern in one hand and a spear in the other.

Viktor could only guess what century this was. *Wrong place again.* He looked back at the frame, where the force field had been trapped.

He wouldn't be able to walk back and forth through it endlessly. His relatively healthy leg was trembling more than the rest of his body under the strain, while his heart was racing with adrenalin and exertion, just as it used to on combat missions. It was like before – only this time he felt as if he might collapse with weakness at any moment.

Smoke was rising from the frame now and the crackling sound was still coming from the wood. It was only a matter of minutes before the first flames would start to appear and once the frame caught fire, the energy field would disappear – and that meant he'd be stuck in this period – in this universe – for ever.

He limped back, panting slightly and leaning on his metal stick. It was a miracle that the people sleeping in the room hadn't woken up and confronted him yet.

After what felt like an hour, he was finally through.

It felt different this time. The pain was intense, as if tiny pieces were being cut out of his body by a pair of burning pliers. His chest was being compressed; his heart began to pound ever faster.

Viktor stumbled into a dark room and fell with a scream over several bodies lying on the floor. Single beams of torchlight criss-crossed through the darkness, as if trying to form barriers of light. Bones cracked beneath him.

When his eyes had become accustomed to the gloom, he realised the bodies had been lying there for different lengths of time. The most recent wore modern military clothing, complete with helmets, climbing harnesses and weapons – just as he had worn a long time ago. The men and woman sprawled in pools of blood had been killed by deep gouges in their bodies. Viktor had found the missing first team.

Or do they belong to a previously unknown enemy?

'Who are you?' came a loud voice, the glow of a torch swinging into his face.

'Stop – don't shoot!' Viktor held out his trembling fingers. 'Walter van Dam sent us.' He didn't care whose care he fell into, as long as he could get some medical attention. The low-quality air, moist with blood, was making breathing difficult. His senses began to fade. 'Walter van . . .'

The world around him turned to black.

'Hey – hey, get up!'

Viktor kept his eyes closed, trying not to reveal to the stranger that he was awake. *I've been asleep – but for how long?* He could no longer feel any pain or thirst. His mind was racing at full speed to try to work out what had happened.

'Come on. I know you can hear me. Your eyelids are twitching.'

Viktor gave up the pretence. He sat up on the floor of the chamber, moving so his back was resting against the rock. The lights were now shining on the walls, providing some indirect light. A needle with a tube and IV bag attached to it was protruding from a vein in his left arm. Both the glancing shot on his thigh and the nastier wound on his knee had been seen to.

'Thank you,' he said to the young blond man sitting in front of him, holding a French FAMAS G2. Aside from his military clothing, he was wearing gloves, worn-out knee and elbow pads and two long, antique daggers hung on his belt.

'No problem.' He shook his hand. 'Alexander. The last member of Team Solution.'

'Viktor. The last member of . . . our team,' he stuttered. 'Were we both in the same scenario? 1944? Germany: the missiles?'

Alexander shook his head. 'No – but you were talking in your sleep. You mentioned Wallace, Smetana – some Americans who were taking over Europe . . .'

'Atomic bombs dropped on Russia and Japan.' Viktor pressed his temple. 'It . . . it was real.' He looked at the scattered skeletons among the fresh corpses; their clothing was now barely discernible.

'These are the remains of the people who died in this disgusting place before us. I reckon they must have killed each other.' Alexander's speech was calm, in spite of the circumstances. 'Your colleagues have also died then?'

'Yes.' Viktor was finding it difficult to understand everything that was going on. He had passed through the door, the only one left. 'Anna-Lena van Dam is dead as well.'

'Well, that's that then,' replied Alexander pragmatically. 'We'd better get out of here. There's nothing left to do but survive.' He stood up. 'I've given you a couple of pain-killers – the IV was to improve your general condition. Fluids, salts, the usual.' He held out his hand. Only now was the large amount of blood on his glove visible. 'We've got to help each other out.'

Viktor suddenly realised that the daggers on Alexander's belt had blades that looked like they would match the wounds on each of his team members. But he remained calm – after all, the mercenary had had the opportunity to tear him to pieces like a slab of mutton while he slept, if that had been his intention.

'Thanks again.' He pulled himself to his feet and examined the door frame of the only exit available. He alerted Alexander's attention to the smoke now rising in a steady plume from it. 'I don't know what it means, but our first priority has to be to get out of here. We can discuss everything else once we're back on the surface.' He was curious to find out the reason behind the slaughter. He didn't want to place his trust in his rescuer, but he stood no chance of escaping from the caves and passages alone.

'I'm with you all the way.' Alexander hung a FAMAS around Viktor's neck, then took a Beretta and a magazine from one of the dead men and handed them to him as well. Then he walked over to the door and opened it. In the light of his torch they could make out the hall way behind it. It looked as if they were back where they had started. 'But the creature's still out there.'

'What creature?' Viktor checked his FAMAS over, then the pistol, before putting it into its holster. Then he removed the needle from his skin and pressed down on the puncture wound. Whatever the soldier had given him was working wonders. Even though he couldn't put very much weight on his knee, it didn't hurt otherwise. He climbed into a discarded climbing harness as quickly as he could manage.

'It's got four legs and looks like a cross between an apex predator and a lizard. It can camouflage itself and moves like lightning,' he explained. 'I've managed to escape from him a few times, but he accounted for a few of our group.'

'Best stay clear of that then.' Viktor raised his FAMAS and they departed from the chamber.

All the doors were smoking and had black scorch marks on them now; pieces of stone were chipping off and flames were erupting out of the wooden sections.

'It's because of those little splinters,' explained Alexander as they were walking. 'The *Particulae*. They're producing an enormous amount of energy because they're disintegrating – just like when they make the force fields.'

'How do you know all this?'

We found an old headquarters of some sort, with a load of partially destroyed records left behind. But even that couldn't save us. This place turns you mad.'

'Then let's get out of here.' Viktor secured every crossroad they passed through. For now, at least, the enemy they hoped never see to was nowhere to be found.

The two men had to rely on their memories to find their way back. Alexander's persistent attempts to contact van Dam and bring him up to speed were in vain: the radio was unable to reach the businessman in his warm, cosy office.

'Right, we'll soon be back at the plateau,' said Viktor, and in the twitching, dancing glow of their tactical lights, they hurried towards the small natural platform. The rusted steel cable – their only path to freedom – was precisely where they had left it, though the notches someone had made trying to destroy it were clearly visible.

'Was the naked man with the bolt cutters also from Team Solution?' Viktor asked.

'Yes. He lost his marbles after we found ourselves in a jungle with a load of sirens and all sorts going off.' Alexander clicked their climbing harnesses into place while Viktor secured the area with his FAMAS. 'And then the others went mad – they all claimed they were hearing voices and before long they'd all turned on one another.'

'And you didn't hear anything?' Viktor looked at the mercenary's bloody gloves.

'I did – but I just ignored everything. Fought my own mind.' Alexander gave him a shove, causing him to fall into the belt and hang on the rope. 'Come on. Before that creature turns up.'

They began to make their way back towards the open door that would lead them back to the cellar. Viktor would never have been able to haul himself along the rope without the assistance of all the painkillers and stimulants he had been given, not after everything he had undergone in the 1944 world.

Before long they were several yards away from the edge of the outcrop, no longer within range of a predator's jump. Or at least, not any normal predator.

'Good. Almost there.' Viktor shone his light towards the plateau with relief.

In the cone of light there suddenly appeared a large creature with an outline that looked almost blurry in the bright light. Its body was a cross between a wolf and a crocodile, just as Alexander had described, with scales and fur that somehow complemented each other perfectly.

'Fuck!' Viktor raised the FAMAS. 'What's it doing?'

In the blink of an eye, the beast was right next to the rope and biting down hard on the corroded metal at precisely the point where the notch was. Then it shook the cable, making it rock and sway wildly back and forth.

'No!' Alexander, twisted around the rusty cable, but was unable to pull out his assault rifle. Viktor tried not to get in the way, but all the shaking was making it impossible.

The creature's enormous jaws opened for a second bite, the light revealing rows of very sharp teeth. Viktor feared the monster's strength would be more than enough to tear through the damaged cable.

A sudden flash of lightning hissed through the long passageway, bouncing off the walls and picking up momentum each time it did so. The energy rushed into the centre of the beast and it burst open, sending a warm spurt of flesh and intestines flying towards Alexander and Viktor.

The shimmering ball of lightning crackled, charging the air. It smelled of excrement and blood, ozone and electricity and hot stone.

'Watch out!' shouted Viktor through the angry hissing sound that sounded like a thousand electrical substations.

The pair ducked their heads as the bundle of energy hurtled towards them like a runaway comet, a tail behind it appearing to be feeding the ball of electricity so it stayed both strong and bright.

Alexander gave a piercing cry.

An almighty eruption of sparks followed, sending them exploding in all directions. A tingling sensation flowed through the vibrating cable and into Viktor's fingertips.

The lightning surged past them, forming an oscillating, jagged line above the cable that led right up to the door and into the villa. It illuminated the entire cellar, illuminating the way out and making it look tangible.

Alexander hung limply in his belt for a few seconds, then opened his eyes and screamed as if he had only just realised that the lightning had struck him directly. Smoke rose from the right side of his torso. 'Shit.'

'Are you—?'

The mercenary pulled a shard from the pocket of his armoured vest; it was glowing and giving off small sparks. 'I only wanted a fucking souvenir,' he growled, dropping it into the bottomless chasm.

'Quickly!' Viktor ordered with relief. 'Wherever that's coming from, it's no friend of ours.' He grabbed the steel rope and pulled himself forwards, with Alexander close behind.

'I assume the doors are disintegrating. The energy doesn't seem to be bundled together any more, so it can't create a force field.'

'Whatever.' Viktor's muscles were trembling under the strain. 'I just want to get out.'

The two survivors combined their strength to haul themselves along the cable to the door and into the cellar. The glittering beam hovered above them all the way with a warning crackle, chasing them up the stairs before disappearing once they were in the villa.

They hurried to the front door as quickly as they could, then paused beneath the roof of the verandah.

The air smelled fresh; it must have been raining, for droplets could still be seen on the roofs of the six cars parked outside. The sun was slowly rising over the top of the forest, giving the sky a distinctive pink hue.

'Beautiful, isn't it?' whispered Viktor, taking a deep breath and leaning against a pillar. Never before had he felt so glad to be alive. So much had happened in the worlds he had inhabited over the last few hours, and each had left their mark on him.

The peace and beauty of the nature before him released the tension. Viktor placed a hand over his eyes and began to cry silently, trembling uncontrollably as warm tears streamed down his face. 'That was some of the worst shit I've ever seen,' he admitted. Visions of his lost companions swam in his mind's eye: Coco. Dana. Friedemann. Ingo. Spanger. And not least, Anna-Lena.

Alexander grimaced in confusion. The fleet of cars was enormous. 'Are those your two vans?' He pointed at the two abandoned Mercedes people carriers.

Viktor sighed, wiping away his tears. 'No. And the BMW wasn't here when we arrived. Nor the Lambo.' Judging by the number plate, it looked as if it might have come from his client's garage.

'Did van Dam leave his office to look for his daughter himself?'

'Maybe he hired another team when he stopped getting a response from us?' Viktor took his phone out of his pocket and switched it on. He picked up reception immediately and the clock revealed it had only been a few hours since they had left, despite having been in the other world for days. Now wasn't the time to start wondering about that, so instead he looked through the window, trying to find the blazing cluster of energy – where was it flowing to? What was there inside that was attracting it? There was smoke rising from a chimney in one of the wings, and the glowing light was dancing behind the windows next to it.

'What do you reckon's over there?' he asked.

Alexander had spotted the smoke. 'Someone started a fire – maybe van Dam?'

'Or maybe whoever was in those vans and the BMW.' Viktor had a suspicion that their assignment was not yet over, even though they had returned to the surface. Too much was amiss. 'Let's have a look around. If van Dam's in danger, we've got to help him.' He dialled his client's number, but there was no answer. They hadn't been able to bring his daughter back. Looking for him was the least they could do.

Alexander nodded and, to be on the safe side, gave Viktor a cocktail of painkillers and stimulants from his backpack. Then he grabbed hold of Viktor and offered his shoulder to bear some of his weight. 'Let's finish this.'

They advanced slowly, their assault rifles at the ready.

The bundle of lightning led them to a three-storey library. It had clearly found its destination, for it was slamming into a new door; the inlays were glowing and spraying in all directions, almost as if there were liquid gold flowing inside it. The portal stood open: a force field had built up.

Ten bodies dressed in military clothing with balaclavas on their heads and automatic weapons lying alongside them were lying on the ground, together with a man in a pin-striped suit who had had his throat slashed.

'I know the man in the suit,' said Alexander. 'He and his people were hunting us. Now we know who was in those white vans.'

They suddenly caught sight of Walter van Dam, waiting in front of the door, with his eyes firmly shut to protect himself from the glare. He was about to step through the wall of energy.

'Mr Van Dam,' Viktor called out urgently, '*don't!*'

Van Dam opened his eyes and he turned to face them. 'You're back!' He hurried towards them, simultaneously overjoyed and bewildered. 'Where's my daughter? Is she outside? By the car?' He looked back and forth between the two men. 'Where are the others? Are they still down there? If so, they've got to come back up immediately and leave with us – this whole place is about to be destroyed.'

'We're the only ones who've come up. From either team. And if you've sent a third ...' Viktor could see in his employer's eyes that he'd never go with them if he learned about his daughter's death at that moment. 'Anna-Lena's outside,' he lied. 'We'll have time to talk later.'

'Oh my God! That's . . .' Van Dam's voice trailed off, then he became business-like again. He gestured at the papers scattered around him and ordered, 'Quick, grab all these. And—'

A bright beam of light blazed through the hall leading to the library. A malodorous, hot wind blew into the room and doused the flames in the fireplace.

'Too late! The *Particulae* are breaking up!' Van Dam stuffed a handful of papers underneath his armoured vest, helped Alexander to support Viktor and pushed him towards the windows. 'Get out!' Without another word, they jumped out and ran over to the car, the two men almost carrying Viktor.

But the blazing light had reached the cavernous library – and it was followed shortly thereafter by a silent explosion that melted the rock underneath the villa.

The energy released in their wake destroying the mansion hallway by hallway was felt by the people living in the region as an earthquake – one that shook the area to pieces, causing large portions of the forest to subside.

The three survivors were already seated in the black Mercedes people carrier, with Alexander behind the wheel.

'Where . . . where's my daughter?' asked van Dam, who was now attempting to get out of the car. 'Anna-Lena?' he called out, 'where are you? We've got to—'

Viktor struck his employer on the head with the grip of his pistol; he slumped into the seat, unconscious. 'Let's go.'

Alexander pressed the accelerator. They hurtled along the road at top speed, disappearing as far as possible away from the annihilation taking place behind them.

CHAPTER XIII

Near Frankfurt

Walter van Dam had regained consciousness before their high-speed van reached the foothills of Frankfurt. He quickly realised that his daughter was not there – that Viktor had lied to him to save his life.

He gazed out of the window, his face as white as a sheet, a fist pressed against his lips. A tear rand down his ageing skin.

'Has anyone noticed the explosion yet?' Alexander wondered aloud. They could feel the tremors on the road under the wheels of the people carrier, and the lightning blast had lit up the dawn breathtakingly.

A headline appeared on the screens embedded in the backs of the seats, with a report about an earthquake of unknown magnitude in Germany. Alexander turned up the volume.

'. . . we've received eyewitness accounts of an earthquake, followed by a detonation. A house – an old mansion that has stood empty for years – has been razed to the ground,' said a reporter. 'Helicopter images are showing where the surface has collapsed, as well as the subsidence of the surrounding forest, which is now on fire as well.

'My God,' groaned Viktor.

'Rather spectacular, in its own way,' Alexander remarked.

'Before we discuss anything else,' van Dam announced in a grave voice, 'I'd like to know what happened down there. How my daughter died.' He looked at Viktor accusingly. 'And why you still felt the need to save my life, Mr von Troneg.'

Viktor had been afraid of this moment, but he told the grieving father everything, about the expedition, about how they'd worked together – and how Anna-Lena had refused to leave so that she could prevent the atomic bombs from detonating and destroying that world.

As a mild act of consolation, Viktor remained silent about the fact that at least one of the bombs had exploded. It would serve no purpose for van Dam to learn his daughter's death had been entirely in vain.

'She gave her life to save millions,' he concluded, taking a deep breath. The sight of van Dam looking at him with tearful, red eyes, did nothing to assuage his inner turmoil. 'They all did.'

Van Dam nodded and looked back out of the window. 'And my daughter said the man in the suit had stopped her from returning to the surface?'

'Yes – and she said something about a new headquarters.'

Silence fell upon the Mercedes. Alexander gave no report about what had happened to Team Solution, nor where he had acquired those two ancient daggers.

Van Dam finally cleared his throat. 'The *Particulae* – the

little stone splinters that are responsible for the force fields,' he began, pulling the hastily gathered pages out from beneath his Kevlar vest. 'I came across this creature from another dimension who'd been kidnapped by the organisation the man in the suit worked for.' He briefly summarised his encounter with Hopkins. 'I think this Ritter – the leader – and his gang of conspirators wanted to prevent us – or anyone else – from ever entering the labyrinth again to see what else is down there. Ritter called his operation a clean-up job.'

Viktor examined the old documents about the doors that had come from the van Dam family's secret library. 'What do you want to do with all this?' He pulled out Friedemann's notebook, which he had never let go of. 'I think this might have something to do with it too. It looks as if there could be some more clues in here about everything.'

'The conspirators' old headquarters has been destroyed in any case.' Alexander glanced back over his shoulder at the drawings Viktor was studying.

'It had been abandoned anyway, if I understood Ritter and Hopkins correctly.' Van Dam stared out of the window again. He had made up his mind. 'I'll get to the bottom of it, and think about how best to undo the damage my grandfather caused. My family's got an obligation, after all – and I've got one to Anna-Lena. She gave her life for a good cause, so how can I possibly carry on as before?' If he had supported her, believed her, encouraged her research and gone along with her, none of this would have happened. And his daughter would still be here.

Viktor looked at him in astonishment. 'Surely you're not planning to—?'

'Yes. That's *precisely* what I'm planning to do. My family had something to do with the doors and the strangers who sent my child to her death. This organisation has to be brought down and its global interests stopped.' He took Friedemann's notebook. Dejection had given way to determination. Van Dam now had a new life's work: to honour Anna-Lena's memory. 'This and the records I managed to save are the tools that'll help me.'

'I'm in,' said Viktor without hesitation.

'Me too. Those pigs deserve nothing less than total eradication.' Alexander's voice was thick with emotion.

'Gentleman, it's an honour to form an alliance with you.' Van Dam shook hands with them both. 'And I'd like to thank you in particular, Mr von Troneg, for saving my life. I'll put it to better use from now on.'

Viktor wanted to reply but the pain in his knee flared up again. The drugs were wearing off. 'You don't happen to have a very discreet doctor at home, do you?'

'It's all taken care of. As promised.'

The Mercedes drove into the gated grounds in Lerchesberg; within a few minutes the van Dam family's city home loomed in front of them.

Just as they were about to arrive, the businessman's phone rang.

He answered the call. 'Walter van Dam. Who is this?' He frowned and turned on the car's speakerphone. 'Would you please repeat that? I'm on speakerphone.'

A woman could be heard laughing on the other side.

'Of course, Mr van Dam. You don't know me, but your daughter and those little rescue teams you sent down got to know us a bit – our organisation. I'm Mr Ritter's superior, if you will.'

The group exchanged sharp looks. They had expected to encounter resistance and pique the conspirators' interest at some point, but it came as a nasty surprise to discover that the other side had got in touch so quickly.

'This conversation is a one-time affair and is happening only as a result of your bravery. You need to know just how easy it will be for us to kill you – and in a matter of minutes,' the woman continued. 'You've done some truly remarkable work; that's why we've granted you your life. Think of yourself as a bomb with an enormous radius. Should you mention what you've been through to anyone, it'll go off and result in your death, as well as those of your friends and your friends' friends.' The woman exhaled loudly. 'If you carry out any more research, you'll be blown up. If we ever see you anywhere near those special doors, you'll be blown up.'

'This is an *outrage*,' whispered van Dam with barely suppressed anger.

Alexander steered the vehicle up the drive, stopped it and switched off the engine. They were all listening, spellbound.

'This is the *truth*. And you know we don't make empty threats, Mr van Dam,' the woman corrected him harshly. 'You're being watched, gentlemen. Do anything along the lines of what I've just told you and you'll be ruined. You have to understand, you see: from this day on you'll responsible for the deaths of everyone you care about, or anyone you've ever come into contact with – or even looked at.' She cleared her throat, now sounding strangely satisfied. 'At some point today we'll send over a messenger to collect all your documents: the notebook, as well as everything the van Dam family possesses about the doors. 'I wish you all a pleasant life. Use it wisely.'

Click.

Van Dam sat motionless and expressionless in the passenger seat, then glanced down at the papers and the notebook he was still holding. The look on the men's faces told him they were thinking the same thing. The Organisation would wipe out everyone around them. Just because they could. Because they had the means to do so. 'Can we really be responsible for that?'

Viktor coughed to stifle his groaning; the pain in his knee was becoming more intense with every passing second. 'Should we be discussing this inside? After a shower, some refreshment and a bit of rest?' He pointed apologetically to his injury.

'Everything I've just heard is one more reason why we need to wipe out these cunts once and for all.' Alexander opened the driver's door. He didn't appreciate being threatened. It aroused the rebel in him. 'But I've got to make a call first.'

'Who are you calling?' Viktor asked curiously.

'My dad. He and I go out for supper together after each of my assignments. And I need to tell him to be careful.' He got out of the car and walked around to help Viktor.

Van Dam and Alexander held Viktor between them and

together they dragged themselves across the drive and up to the house.

'Make yourselves at home,' said van Dam cheerfully. 'The bathrooms and my guestrooms are at your disposal. The doctor will see to you in a moment, Mr von Troneg.'

Viktor smiled gratefully.

'And first, I have a sad duty to undertake. My lawyer needs to draft letters to the families of our five heroes.' Van Dam took a deep breath. 'Officially, they'll have died in the accident at the villa – tragic victims of the earthquake.'

Viktor's thoughts turned to Dana. He would never have the chance to talk to her about Darfur. Had she seen an unusual door in the ruins?

Van Dam looked at his watch. 'Shall we all meet back in my office once everyone's in a reasonable condition? Four hours enough?'

Viktor and Alexander agreed.

They entered Walter van Dam's office a few hours later, closely followed by Ms Roth, who brought in provisions for them all.

Their short break had brought them no respite at all. Viktor's injuries had been treated and he would be taken to hospital after the meeting. The doctor told him he'd be given a new kneecap and have his ligaments reattached, followed by rehabilitation, just like a professional footballer would. Van Dam would be covering all the costs.

The medical team had also attended Alexander, but there was nothing wrong with him aside from a few bruises and grazes.

'Before we begin, perhaps with a few new ideas regarding

our current situation, I'd like to inform you that we've been conned by fraudster. Or rather, I have.' Van Dam turned the monitor around, revealing a gaunt face that looked a little like Rüdiger Friedemann. 'This is the *real* professor. He'd been misled by a fake email.'

Viktor stared at the image. '*Bugger.* I knew something was amiss when he couldn't get into his climbing harness.'

'The professor rang me when no one came to pick him up from the airport. Our imposter had joined you to gain access to the caves,' said van Dam, pointing to the notebook. 'I gather he'd stolen it from someone. The owner wrote their name in the book – someone called Nicola. So these doors appear to have presented us with yet another riddle to solve.'

Viktor helped himself to some food. 'Who was the fake Friedemann then? How come he knew so much?'

'We'll find out soon enough,' said Alexander contemplatively. 'Among other things. I don't like being threatened.'

'Likewise.' Viktor cleared his throat. They belonged to a very small group of people capable of doing something about these global conspirators; like van Dam, he still considered it his duty not to let the fate of humanity fall into the hands of an avaricious secret society. The unknown woman's threats over the phone had reinforced their determination.

Van Dam had his dander up now. 'We really must delay them somehow . . .'

Alexander took a deep breath. 'Let's go, then!'

Van Dam gratefully shook hands with his new colleagues. 'Our alliance has cleared the first hurdle.' It helped to know he was not alone in this fight. It was going to be hard. But Ritter was dead and they'd make sure more followed until the circle was broken. He pointed to the array of documents he had already read. 'We know the doors are portals – passages that are easy to open if you know what you're doing. We need to find out as soon as possible how to get to their current headquarters. Then it's a question of frustrating their plans.'

'Nicola's notebook has also got a list of other doors that might help us to track down this headquarters.' Viktor grinned when he saw the others looking at him wide-eyed. 'I read it when I couldn't get to sleep.'

'I'll provide all the financial support we need.' Van Dam looked at the photo of his daughter on his desk, smiling at him out of the frame. 'And I'll take care of research – contacts and so forth. Hopefully, we can make up for what my grandfather once inflicted upon the world.'

Viktor opened the notebook. 'These are the doors we need to have a look at. They've been marked down separately by the author.' He positioned it in such a way that both van Dam and Alexander could see it as well. 'She's added their locations as well. We've just got to go there and have a look around.'

'Where do you want to start?' The mercenary leaned forward. 'They're all over the world.'

Van Dam touched his signet ring. 'Well, for now I'm going to translate the notes my grandfather wrote. He might have left some clues behind.'

'Oh.' Viktor marked the page he had had open with another piece of paper and flipped forward a few pages.

'There's something else written down here: the Arkus Project. It only appears to be tangentially linked to the doors – it looks like a completely different site. Bigger, it would seem. Do any of your contacts know how to read Old Iberian script?' He tapped one of the notes scribbled there. 'That's what the author calls it. There's a place where we can find out more. These records are extremely old . . . from the Iberian peninsula – what's now the Basque region.'

Van Dam quickly searched online to see how common the language was. 'Look at this. I didn't know Basque culture was unrelated to all other European cultures. It's linguistically completely isolated.'

'Another puzzle. But I promise' – Viktor placed his hand gently on top of the notebook, as if he could probe it with his fingers and mind like Coco – 'we'll get to the bottom of it. All of it. And we'll raze this damned Organisation to the ground. Just like their old headquarters.'

How badly Viktor wished the objects on the desk would start to vibrate and dance around, moving under the influence of an invisible force emanating from him.

But nothing happened.

ECHOES

Aachen, Spring 841

Aysun al Arabi had been pretending to be asleep when the second visitor emerged from the old frame and quietly began to look around. Instead of scurrying off or quietly rummaging through the boxes to steal a couple of daggers, like the first man had done, this particular stranger had simply stopped to look out the window for a while, before limping back through the frame. And disappearing. Like someone who had got the wrong door.

The old Moor sat up on his bed and stared at the empty wooden square that he had previously covered with a thin linen cloth to stop it from getting dirty. The cloth had slid down to the floor and the shimmering had stopped.

It wasn't the first time, nor would it be the last, that this strange kind of magic had occurred.

Aysun looked at his servant, who was asleep on the floor next to his bed and hadn't even stirred. As was so often the case.

He looked at the artefact he had brought with him on each of his journeys since the time it had accidentally come into his possession many years ago; he had known immediately that there was something special about it.

He was significantly older than was usual for the inhabitants of Aachen and the Empire. Empress Judith valued his opinions, which derived from both his prodigious study of scholarly texts and the sheer number of years he had lived. Aysun had stopped counting them; it no longer mattered. Every day that he woke up in the morning and was allowed to praise his god was a cause for celebration.

Sometimes there was no certainty he would wake up at all, as his past had been war-like – as war-like as the present.

Aysun had moved to Zaragoza with the empress many years ago; when the alliance she had formed split, she took Aysun's father hostage. He and his brother Matruh then allied with the Basques, freeing their father after annihilating the Frankish army at the Battle of Roncevaux Pass.

Later, after the murder of his father, Aysun had switched sides, conquering Zaragoza on behalf of the Emir of Cordoba, while also taking part in campaigns against the Basques and Cerdanya.

It was while he was in the Basque country that he had acquired the frame, along with encrypted records he was still trying to decode.

His servant was convinced that Aysun's advanced years were due to his refusal to die until the final sentence had been decrypted.

Aysun rose from his bed and walked over to the frame. It was no accident that he was here in Aachen.

Empress Judith had taken him in as a guest for good

reason. Around twenty years ago, Aysun had wanted to find out whether he could be a warrior as well as a scholar. He had therefore led an uprising in the Hispanic Marches against Bernard of Septimania, who was a young count at the time. Many Gothic noblemen and Moors who supported peace with the Frankish Empire had joined the insurrection, and Bernard had hated him ever since, as he had had to ask the empress for aid.

Aysun considered Bernard to be a weakling and a coward, a man whose primary interests were scheming and womanising. A person like that had no business being in the presence of Empress Judith.

After a few skirmishes, the uprising was quashed and Aysun had fallen into the hands of Judith's troops, who expressed their amazement at how an old Moor could have led a vigorous young nobleman on such a merry dance.

The empress had wanted to meet Aysun, and it had not been long before her curiosity turned into profound trust. The Moor had soon taken over from her own son as her senior advisor – for advice and support were urgently required: a rival empress by the name of Ermengarde was dreaming of a large Frankish empire under her leadership. Her husband Lothair was encouraging her schemes, meaning war was looking inevitable. The forthcoming battle would result in the deaths of thousands of men, as each ruler had a vast number of swords sworn to them.

Tactics. Cunning. Wisdom. These were the virtues that were in high demand and Aysun possessed all three.

The old man put his ossified fingers on the frame. The veins beneath his wrinkled, dark brown skin appeared as dark lines, while his knuckles protruded boldly from his fingers, which were adorned with loosely held rings.

'Why can't you send me a visitor who'll be of use in the battle?' Aysun asked the artefact softly. 'Not just these people who disappear straight away. Or thieves who only want to steal from me. Or some wretched creature I have to fight off.' He stroked the wood gently. 'Help me, just this once. Me and Empress Judith.'

As an unexpected response to his supplication, a bluish shimmer appeared within the frame.

Would you like to know what would have happened to our team of rescuers if you had opened the door marked with an exclamation mark or the door with an 'X'?

Pick up *DOORS X TWILIGHT* or *DOORS ! FIELD OF BLOOD* and discover a whole new adventure!

ABOUT THE AUTHOR

Markus Heitz studied history and German language and literature before writing his debut novel, *Schatten über Ulldart* (*Shadows over Ulldart*, the first in a series of epic fantasy novels), which won the Deutscher Phantastik Preis, Germany's premier literary award for fantasy. Since then he has frequently topped the bestseller charts, and his Number One-bestselling *Dwarves* and *Älfar* series have earned him his place among Germany's most successful fantasy authors. Markus has become a byword for intriguing combinations: as well as taking fantasy in different directions, he has mixed mystery, history, action and adventure, and always with at least a pinch of darkness. Millions of readers across the world have been entranced by the endless scope and breadth of his novels. Whether twisting fairy-tale characters or inventing living shadows, mysterious mirror images or terrifying creatures, he has it all – and much more besides.

DOORS is a work of new opportunities and endless possibilities, with each book following our team of adventurers as they choose a different door. Do you dare to cross the threshold and explore the unknown worlds beyond?

WHICH DOOR WILL YOU CHOOSE NEXT?

When his beloved only daughter goes missing, millionaire entrepreneur Walter van Dam calls in a team of experts – including free-climbers, a geologist, a parapsychologist, even a medium – to find her . . . for Anna-Lena has disappeared somewhere within a mysterious cave system under the old house the family abandoned years ago. But the rescuers are not the only people on her trail – and there are dangers in the underground labyrinth that no one could ever have foreseen.

In a gigantic cavern the team come across a number of strange doors, three of them marked with enigmatic symbols. Anna-Lena must be behind one of them – but time is running out and they need to choose, quickly. Anna-Lena is no longer the only person at risk.

Who could have imagined that the portal marked with ! would take the rescuers into a different time completely: it is now the early Middle Ages – and they are about to find themselves in the middle of a world-changing battle . . .

DOORS: THREE DOORS, THREE DIFFERENT ADVENTURES.
WHICH DOOR WILL YOU CHOOSE?

Available in paperback and eBook

Jo Fletcher
BOOKS

WHICH DOOR WILL YOU CHOOSE NEXT?

When his beloved only daughter goes missing, millionaire entrepreneur Walter van Dam calls in a team of experts – including free-climbers, a geologist, a parapsychologist, even a medium – to find her . . . for Anna-Lena has disappeared somewhere within a mysterious cave system under the old house the family abandoned years ago. But the rescuers are not the only people on her trail – and there are dangers in the underground labyrinth that no one could ever have foreseen.

In a gigantic cavern the team come across a number of strange doors, three of them marked with enigmatic symbols. Anna-Lena must be behind one of them – but time is running out and they need to choose, quickly. Anna-Lena is no longer the only person at risk.

The team knew their mission would be perilous – but how do you defeat your own demons? Trapped in their own nightmares, their only hope of escape is DOOR X, which leads to a threatening vision of the future . . .

DOORS: THREE DOORS, THREE DIFFERENT ADVENTURES.
WHICH DOOR WILL YOU CHOOSE?

Available in paperback and eBook

Jo Fletcher
BOOKS